bleak

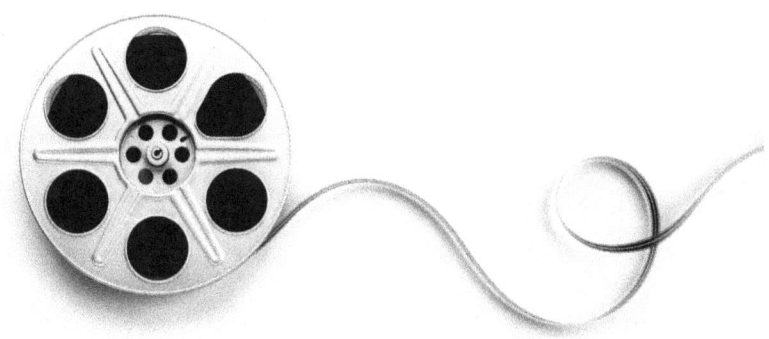

LYNN MESSINA

potatoworks press
greenwich village

ISBN-13: 978-0-9849018-2-1

www.lynnmessina.com
www.zombiedating.wordpress.com

For information on Potatoworks Reading guides,
please visit www.potatoworks.wordpress.com.

For everyone who's heard it all before.
And Charles Dickens.

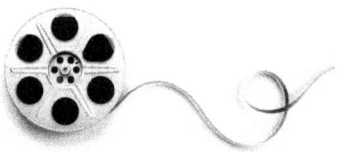

Day 774

MARLA HERTZBERG CALLS me into her office just as I'm turning on my computer at 8:51 in the morning, and I quickly unwrap my wool scarf and grab a note pad. The temperature in the office is somewhere below Arctic, but we're not allowed to shiver. The partners at Hertzberg, Wright, Silver and Penn interpret any effort to stay warm as ingratitude for their generous use of air-conditioning, especially from the paralegal staff; we are supposed to be more grateful than the junior associates. It's the same thing in the winter. They keep the thermostat in the mideighties, then frown whenever they see someone in short sleeves.

Hertzberg, Wright, Silver and Penn is an aggressively conservative firm. Casual Friday means a tie with a pattern on it.

Marla doesn't look up when I enter her office, which is fine because she never does. Three years ago, when she first joined the firm, I took her lack of interest in my presence as a personal rebuke. Whenever my mother is angry at me, she always says she can't bear to look at me, and, from the way she darts her eyes around the room, avoiding not only my face but my figure too, I believe it's true. There is genuine pain in her aversion.

With Marla it's different. She's simply too busy piling up billable hours for eye contact. Working three cases at one time is her special talent. Right now she's taking a meeting with Collier Enterprises, writing a memo to Judson Tobacco and giving me an assignment.

There's an element of overcompensation in her manic behavior. The only child of former attorney general Albert Hertzberg, she has much to prove to the world, namely that she's her father's worthy successor and that her meteoric rise at Handelman, Finch and Burleigh wasn't due to the fact that she was sleeping with Handelman and Finch (an impressive accomplishment, as both men are well into their eighties).

The speakerphone drones on about fiduciary responsibility as Marla pounds forcefully at her keyboard. She's hands-down the most emphatic typists I've ever seen. She presses each letter as if it's the final exclamation point in a twenty-thousand-word paragraph.

"The Roberts case," she says, gesturing with her chin to a file on her otherwise spotless desk. Marla doesn't just preach the religion of organization, she lives it. Everything is color-coded, labeled and returned to its rightful place within seconds of her putting it down. One of her three secretaries' sole job is filing. She's like Henry VIII having a servant devoted exclusively to fluffing his pillows.

I grab the folder, which is slight and contains an index of the other files relevant to the case. Before she can explain what she'd like me to do, she shifts a hand over to the phone and presses the mute button. The gesture is smooth and quick, like she's done it a million times before, and doesn't interrupt her typing.

"We found the promissory note during discovery," she says.

A melee erupts on the other side of the line as six, seven, maybe a dozen voices insist all at once that Christian Collier never issued a personal IOU to Danver Bobek. The disagreement continues for so long that Marla comes dangerously close to working on only two cases. Just when I think Roberts has been pushed completely to the back of her brain, she lifts a hand from the keyboard and writes "redaction" on a Post-it. The printer hums as the Judson memo rolls out.

Marla hands over the Post-it and dismisses me with an absent wave. As I leave the office, the senior Hertzberg brushes past me. Unlike his daughter, he has no idea I'm there. An old-school businessman, he focuses on one thing at a time, giving it his complete attention until the problem, case, issue—whatever—has been resolved. As a result, there's a quiet dignity about him, an air of serenity and stability. He's nothing like his daughter.

Returning to my cube, I drop the file onto my desk and put on my scarf. I consider taking out the fleece blanket but decide to try coffee first. Sometimes that keeps me for a good two hours. I wander to the kitchen, fill up a cup with weak corporate French roast and read the notices on the bulletin board. My hands warm, I head up to thirty-flour, where files are stored in a large meat locker of a room with bright florescent lights and hard wooden chairs.

The space is empty save for Josie, who is redacting another file. She nods absently when I enter but doesn't otherwise acknowledge me. Although we're friendly, I don't take offense. Redaction is like that. It's mind-numbingly boring work wherein you peruse thousands of pages of documents looking for privileged information to black out with a thick, sturdy marker. As if that weren't deadly enough, you have to keep a log of all your deletions. Once you start you don't want to stop because the thought of starting again is unbearable. You get into a groove and you go with it. Momentum is everything.

Although the storeroom's frequent blasts of sub-Arctic air keep you especially alert (when they're not giving you hypothermia), I take the file to my cube and plunk it solidly at my desk. In no rush to get to the Roberts redaction, I pull up Google, type in Moxie Bernard and click on the top ten news stories to see what damage she's done in the last twenty-four hours.

Some people have sports scores or stock quotes or the front page of the *New York Times* to distract them from work. I have the hottest teen star on the planet and a train wreck waiting to happen.

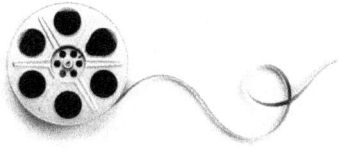

Day 795

MY HOLLYWOOD FILM agent calls during lunch to announce that Chancery Productions has finally settled on a date for the relaunch party celebrating my novel, *Jarndyce and Jarndyce*. I take another bite of tuna fish and wash it down with lemonade as Lester Dedlock tells me to mark down August 21. As this is the fourth time in five months he has spoken with such definitiveness, I'm reluctant to follow his advice. Still, I jot the date down on a Post-it. On previous occasions, the event was rescheduled because the preferred venue was booked, Lloyd Chancellor's father would be in Europe and Hake Hudson was opening a restaurant on the Sunset Strip and Moxie's boyfriend, Carlos Wenders, who stars with Hudson in the NBC Tuesday night hit sitcom, *Getting Nowhere,* would probably go to that instead, taking his überfamous girlfriend with him.

Who knows what they'll come up with this time.

Lester, however, thinks I'm being unduly pessimistic.

"It's set in stone. Chancery Productions sent out invitations two days ago. They couldn't change it now without a great deal of expense and embarrassment. Trust me."

Lester speaks quietly but forcefully, with the full weight of thirty years of successful power brokering. He knows how things work, and when he tells me to trust him, I do—implicitly. I didn't need to read Dominick Dunne's flattering *Vanity Fair* profile to know he is the last of the old Hollywood guard. During our first telephone conversation, he exuded the calm self-assurance of the establishment, asserting confidently that he could sell my novel to a producer. If film agenting had an aristocratic hierarchy, Lester Dedlock would be a baronet at the very least.

But reading the *Vanity Fair* piece didn't hurt, of course. It was certainly nice to have my first impression reaffirmed by the most respected pop culture magazine in the country.

Seven months later, it was reaffirmed again when Chancery Productions, helmed by the imperial Lloyd Chancellor, made an offer: ten thousand dollars to option the rights for eighteen months, then five hundred thousand to buy.

The money, although staggering to contemplate, was nothing compared with my excitement at the thought of my book being a movie. Instantly, I could see my name in ten-foot letters gliding across a darkened screen as I imagined my characters speaking the lines I actually wrote. In ten minutes I had the entire premiere planned: who I'd invite (everyone I ever met), where I'd have it (the Ziegfeld), what I'd serve at the after-party (beer and french fries).

The giddiness wore off sometime in the past 794 days as the deal dragged on. I thought it would all happen immediately, but Hollywood moves at a glacial pace. It took Lester and the lawyers from Arcadia studios nine months to settle the contract, a 142-page behemoth that plans for every contingency, however unlikely. The last two issues—how much I'll get for the sixth hour of a TV movie adaptation and how much I'll get for each episode of a half-hour sitcom spun off from the half-hour sitcom based on the movie—were both highly unlikely to happen, but I was happy to let Lester fight for the going rate. Even though *Jarndyce and Jarndyce* is never going to be a miniseries or spawn a spin-off, let alone two, I wanted parity, even for things that don't exist. At the heart of every negotiation, there are a few intangibles that mean more to the other person than they do to you, and those are the things you should care about the most.

A few months after I finally signed the contract, *Variety* announced Moxie Bernard's intention to star in the lawyer vehicle, a development so surprising I told the first six people who called to congratulate me that they were crazy. But it was true. Lloyd Chancellor had lined up Moxie to star as well as co-exec produce.

Suddenly my name was everywhere—in *Variety, Entertainment Weekly, People, Hollywood Reporter, Newsweek*. I couldn't believe my luck.

Since then the publicity has been almost constant and people talk about Moxie's involvement as if it were a done deal. Much to my regret, it's not. She is merely attached, a Hollywood dodge that means she might star in the film or she might not, depending on how she feels tomorrow or the next day or the day after that.

Still, all indications seem to be good. Lloyd Chancellor is a master of hype who can effortlessly create interest and fascination in a project that's barely in the planning stage. The party is a perfect example. He's throwing it to capitalize on the Moxie momentum, relaunching *J&J* in high Hollywood style. Even though there are thirty thousand copies of my book sitting in a warehouse in Jersey, he somehow convinced my publisher to reissue the novel with a younger, sexier cover announcing, "Soon to be a major motion picture." Gone is the Hershfeld-like pen-and-ink drawing, replaced by a neon starburst of greens, blues, pinks and yellows. The heroine, Ada Clare Jarndyce, is now bent provocatively over the desk of coworker and love interest. She has a sparkling smile and a pixie haircut that looks suspiciously like Moxie Bernard's. As if the connection weren't drawn clearly enough, there's a quote from Moxie six inches above my name: "Ricki Carstone's wit makes the law so funny, it should be illegal."

I'm sure she didn't come up with the blurb herself. No doubt her crackerjack team of handlers and assistants thought of it. But the result is the same. Moxie is in. She, along with Lloyd and the executives at Arcadia, isn't promoting my book because she likes me. They're not founding members of the Ricki Carstone Advancement Society. No, they see a worthwhile project that could bring them success and they want to help get it off the ground. I have nothing to do with it. Never once in all the discussion about dates for the event was my calendar consulted. It's a launch party for a book I wrote and yet my attendance was always incidental.

Rather than being insulted, I find this callousness comforting. Only something so much bigger than myself could make me feel so irrelevant. It's the one thing that cuts through my cynicism and makes me think, despite the incredibly long odds, that we might actually make a movie.

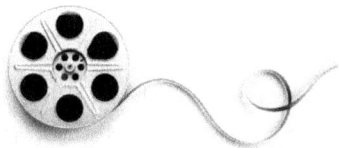

Day 796

THE STORY OF Moxie Bernard's secret pact with the queen of England breaks just as I'm being called into a meeting with a junior partner, and by the time I'm released forty minutes later, they are two dozen messages in my in-box telling me about it. In an e-mail wildly circulated among Moxie's friends, then leaked to the press, the planet's most famous teen outlines their plan to make movies expounding on the dangers of teen alcoholism. The arrangement is simple: Moxie will write the scripts; the queen will produce them.

The e-mail, almost touching in its absurdity (and lack of self-reflection), reveals not only Moxie's frail grasp on reality but also her feeble understanding of the English language. Her spelling is deplorable, her sentence structure imperceptible and her punctuation nonexistent. All her thoughts run together in one endless jumble like experimental modernist prose. The movies, if they ever were to exist, would quickly become psychedelic classics like Pink Floyd's *The Wall* and the Teletubbies.

Responding to a deluge of calls for comment, Buckingham Place issues a dignified statement asserting that the queen has never met Ms. Bernard but hopes she gets the help she so clearly needs.

The paparazzi, here and abroad, swarm over the story with their usual enthusiasm, and news programs gleefully speculate on the meaning of the megastar's latest public debacle. For months now, they've been following her increasingly erratic behavior with giddiness. Moxie caught with fake ID! Throws cell phone at bouncer! Film at eleven!

Every move she makes provokes a feeding frenzy, with the tabloid sharks only a few meters ahead of the mainstream press. Her drug problem is the best plotline on television, and grateful network execs refuse to miss a riveting second of it. Their pursuit is so single-minded and dogged, a confused young woman with large breasts and overnight success might be forgiven for thinking this is how an eighteen-year-old starlet is supposed to behave.

Still, there's a point where self-destruction ceases to be entertainment, and Moxie Bernard flirts with it daily. Sometimes, her exploits are so painful, I can't bear to watch.

And yet I can't make myself turn away.

The correspondents on shows like *Entertainment Tonight* and *Access Hollywood* hurt me the most. They always shake their head before throwing it back to Nancy in the studio, as if they're personally saddened by the latest development and not secretly delighted. Sometimes the anchor in the studio will ask the reporter follow-up questions before heading into the next segment—the life and miseries of Moxie Bernard reduced to banter.

As much noise as everyone makes, there isn't anybody who actually cares about Moxie herself. Her father is a deadbeat drunk who resurfaced six years ago when she hit it big with *The Nancy Drew Files* to exhort whatever he could from her. He's since been arrested twice for trying to break into her Malibu compound. Her mother is no better. A former Olympic skating hopeful and Ice Capade star, she's living her dreams of fortune and fame through her daughter. It's the same old story of unfulfilled stardom and exploitation made especially salacious by her party-girl reputation. Everything Moxie does, Lola Bernard does, too, including the cocaine. A recent E! Online report identifies her old skating coach as their hookup (an inspiring story of a washed-up has-been finding an unexpected second career).

With no one to help her but a seemingly incompetent publicist, Moxie digs herself deeper and deeper into the hole. In a follow-up e-mail to the *New York Post,* she provides actual dates for her meetings with Queen Elizabeth and gives the plot of their first feature.

As I read about the young gerl [sic] from small-town Montana who winds up in a Dumpster behind a strip club in Vegas, all I can think is, There's no way in hell Moxie is going to hold it together long enough to make my party, let alone my movie.

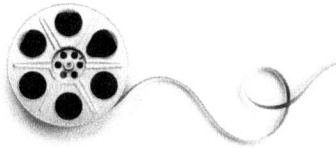

Day 798

ACCORDING TO THE Hertzberg, Wright, Silver and Penn employee handbook, requests for vacation time must be submitted electronically on RQ456 forms at least four weeks prior to the proposed date. Because the party has been rescheduled so many times, I wait seventy-two hours to make sure Lester doesn't call me back with yet another delay and fill out the RQ456 per policy.

It is instantly rejected. The program won't accept forms dated fewer than four weeks from the requested time.

I don't panic. HWSP is a large, inhumane company with lots of rules and regulations, but the people in the human resources department are very nice. At the bottom of the totem pole, below—impossibly—even legal secretaries, they are remarkably un-ground-down by the corporate heel on top of them. When my father had a triple bypass two years ago they arranged a four-week leave of absence with pay so I could go home and sit by his bedside. That I wound up doing all the mundane domestic tasks that my mother has spent the last thirty years unlearning—vacuuming, laundry, washing dishes, microwaving Smart Balance frozen dinners—was hardly their fault.

Henry, the HR associate who shepherded my sabbatical through the system, shakes his head when I present him with my problem.

"I'd like to help but requests for vacation time must be submitted at least four weeks prior to the proposed date," he says, quoting the employee handbook verbatim. His expression is sympathetic, but there's something vaguely passive aggressive in his automatonic repetition of company policy. Suddenly I get the feeling that he really wouldn't like to help. "There's nothing I can do."

I smile. Summers spent at the Hartford branch of Avis car rental taught me that nothing can be gained by taking your anger out on the person behind the desk. The meaner you get, the more entrenched they get. I can't tell you how many times I told customers that upgrades weren't available when shiny Town Cars were sitting thirty feet away in the parking lot. For the powerless, there are few things more satisfying than a power play.

"Are you sure about that?" I ask, leaning forward.

Henry nods. "It's out of my control. The system won't accept forms later than the four-week cutoff. It's automatic."

"But you're human resources," I say admiringly. "We all know that you guys secretly run the company. A decision doesn't get made by upper management that isn't first vetted and approved by you." I have no idea if this is true, but it sounds good. More than that, it sounds like something I'd like someone to say to me. "Can't we type in a code and override the system just this once? I wouldn't ask if it weren't very important."

He blushes but doesn't deny his importance in the corporate hierarchy. "I wish I, could but we don't have the ability. The program doesn't allow for any exceptions. All I can do when I want days off is fill out the form and hit send just like you do at your desk."

It's inconceivable to me that there isn't an override command. Every program has an escape clause, even missile launch programs. That's the whole point to computers: They're fluid little machines that respond to a tincture of numbers stroking.

But it's obvious to me that even if there is a code, Henry doesn't know it. He's only an associate. Knowledge is something that increases with salary.

"What about personal days?" I ask, changing tacks.

Henry shakes his head sadly. "I'm afraid you've used up all your personal days. There were two in January"—a long weekend to Vail with my sister—"one in April"—nobody should have to work on her birthday—"one in June"—an irregular pap smear that turned out to be nothing—"and one earlier this month"—damn it, I *knew* that stupid house share on Fire Island was going to fuck me—"so there's nothing until next year."

I sit quietly for a moment, considering my options. The only thing left is to call in sick. I tried to do it on the up-and-up and not take advantage but clearly the company doesn't want truth from its employees.

Sighing deeply, I thank Henry for his time.

"It won't work," he says as I stand up. Surprised, I look at him. I have no idea what he's talking about. "Calling in sick. It won't work. The computer records all requests for vacations, even the ones it doesn't accept, and will remind management that the day was asked for if the employee calls in sick."

I sink down into the chair again. "Seriously?"

"Oh, yes, it's a very smart program," he explains proudly, "and wonderfully efficient. It's a huge improvement over the old one. Do you remember when you had to fill out time sheets by hand? We'd spend all morning on Monday entering the information. Now it instantly pops up by three o'clock on Friday."

As Henry continues to list the many advantages of his evil little program, I stare at him, looking for horns. With his polite smile and perfectly parted hair and chirpy "have a nice day," he's the archetype of soulless corporate cog. I always knew Satan was a bureaucrat.

It's obvious to me now that Henry has the ability to override. With the flick of his wrist, he could not only grant me vacation days but make August 21st a national holiday. But he won't. He's a company man. The only reason he was so helpful in arranging my leave of absence is sabbaticals are in the handbook; compassion is not.

When he finishes his litany, Henry shakes his head again. He seems sympathetic, but I'm not fooled this time. "The only thing I can suggest is getting special dispensation from the managing partner."

His telephone rings, signaling the end of our conversation. It's meant to seem like a coincidence that a call came in just when he's done with me, but I recognize the forces of evil when they trill in my ear.

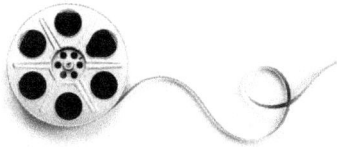

Day 799

I CUT GLENN a slice of apple pie while he runs his hand up and down Carrie's thigh. His fingers tread so high along her leg, they brush her crotch, then reverse direction and graze her knee. Carrie is wearing a pair of tan cords, which he rubs at with an almost desperate determination, as if he can make her pants disappear if he just presses hard enough.

Embarrassed, I concentrate on the knife as it slices through the warm graham cracker crust.

My sister continues to talk about the renovations for her new kitchen—the concrete countertop, the stainless-steel appliances, the dazzling red cabinets from Ikea—as if nothing is amiss. It's like she doesn't even notice his extremely inappropriate behavior. The longer she raves about the Walker Zanger backsplash in shades of silver and gray, the more I want to say, "Um, I'm right here. I can see you."

It's always been like this. Glenn has a pathological need to hold on to my sister. The first time we met, he ate sushi with his left hand so he wouldn't have to release hers. It was hilarious watching him trying to maneuver the chopsticks with uncoordinated fingers. He kept dropping pieces of dragon roll into the soy sauce, splattering the white tablecloth with pretty, abstract patterns.

Back then, I thought it was cute if a little insecure. I figured he'd get over it.

Eight months later, it's worse. His oily tentacles are in constant contact with her body, chaining her to his side so she can't draw a breath he doesn't share.

It's a problem for me. A mild annoyance has spiraled into intense dislike. I've stopped inviting Carrie out for dinner because Glenn always comes along with his octopus hands. I would have made up an excuse to get out of tonight but there was just no way. I always cook dinner for my sister on her birthday.

"I'm not so sure about the red," Glenn says. "It's really bright and shiny, which might look dated in a few years. I think we should go with something more classic like ashwood."

He uses the word *we* with a natural sense of entitlement like my sister's kitchen is his kitchen, like—even worse—my sister's apartment is his apartment. Carrie has spent her whole life saving to buy a place. The money our maternal grandparents left her has been sitting in the bank for fifteen years waiting for this moment. Thirty thousand dollars became sixty-two thousand became the down payment for a five-hundred-square-foot co-op on Fourteenth Street.

It has nothing to do with Glenn. He showed up just as she was signing the mortgage contract.

Over a pint of vanilla Häagen Dazs, Ruby looks at me. She's thinking the same thing. Unable to stand Glenn any more than I, she finds his tendency to explain Carrie to her—the way he sometimes says in response to one of her teasing comments, "Well, what Carrie meant to say was..." —intolerable. She's known my sister for twenty-five years, since the very first day of Miss Teddy's kindergarten, when they had to write their name in pastel-colored finger paints. He's known her for twenty-five seconds.

"Yeah, cause blond ashwood isn't already dated," Ruby says. "Hello, 1993."

"Red sounds great," Lionel says in the silence that follows. Carrie and Glenn are oblivious to it, but the room is filled with Ruby's crackling anger. She's about to snap. "I think it'll look fabulous with the polished concrete counters. What are you thinking about for the floor?"

"Slate," Carrie says.

Ruby's impatience, justified as it is, somehow gives me patience. I know Glenn is a decent guy. He has a job, cleans up after himself, calls my dad Mr. Carstone and buys Carrie thoughtful little gifts for no reason. For her birthday, he went down to the florist to pick out a bouquet, rather than have his assistant order flowers over the phone.

He makes my sister happy. That has to be worth something.

Feeling unusually fond of annoying old Glenn—some things are merely a case of mind over matter—I ask if he'd like more coffee. His cup has been empty for at least ten minutes.

"I'll get it," Carrie says, grabbing his mug. As she gets to her feet, Glenn squeezes her ass with both hands like he's testing the ripeness of a melon.

And just like that, my goodwill evaporates. I look at my watch and calculate how many minutes until I can get him out of my apartment.

Lionel reads my expression and asks how things are at Hertzberg. He's a former lawyer who dropped out and went to cooking school. He's now a line cook at one of Mario Battali's restaurants in the Village. He works even longer hours under more arduous conditions and is blissfully content. It's taken Ruby a while to get on board with the new career—she didn't sign on to genteel poverty in a Lower East Side tenement—but now she fully appreciates the difference between living with someone who's happy and living with someone who's not. Accepting the new status quo, she's started taking on freelance graphic design assignments to supplement her painting income.

"Work's all right," I say with little enthusiasm. It's hard to get excited about photocopying and redacting. "The same as always, except I'm locked in a mortal battle over vacation days with human resources. They've scheduled the *Jarndyce and Jarndyce* party and——"

"That's fantastic," Carrie calls from the kitchen. "I thought it'd never happen."

"Me neither. It's on the twenty-first and HR won't give me the days because it's not enough notice."

Ruby licks ice cream off her plastic spoon. "What are you going to do?"

"I have an appointment with the managing partner tomorrow. I'm sure he'll be reasonable. I mean, it's a party in Los Angeles for my book. It's not like I'm asking for the days so I can sit on a beach."

"Will Moxie be there?" Carrie asks, returning with two steaming mugs. She puts them on the table and sits down next to Glenn. He immediately starts caressing her shoulder.

I shrug. "There's a good chance. They kept changing the date to accommodate her schedule."

"You should drop Moxie," Glenn says. "I can think of at least ten other girls who would be better in the part. She's washed up. You should get Rooney Mara or Jennifer Lawrence. Why don't you?"

Although I've explained a million times to Glenn that I have nothing to do with the movie, he doesn't get it. He thinks my name on the book gives me complete creative control. Usually I take the time to correct him, but the image of his hands clutching my sister's cord-clad ass is fresh in my mind and I don't bother. "You're right, Glenn. I'll call Rooney's agent tomorrow. It's so good that you're here to think of these things. I mean, all those people in Hollywood and all they could come up with is washed-up Moxie Bernard."

He smiles uncertainly as he tries to decipher my tone. He might work with computers all day, but he interacts enough with people to recognize sarcasm.

"I like Moxie," Ruby says, perhaps just to be contrary. "She's a movie star, and they're supposed to be self-destructive. It's part of their glamour."

Carrie agrees with her. "Yeah, Jennifer Lawrence seems grounded. We want Marilyn Monroe."

"And Judy Garland," Ruby tosses back.

"And River Phoenix."

"And John Belushi."

They go back and forth, throwing out the names of dead celebrities like they're bingo numbers and creating their ideal *J&J* cast. Glenn watches, waiting for an opening to insert himself, but it never comes. Ruby glances at him out of the corner of her eye, smug and delighted by his inability to keep up. There's nothing like the bond formed over pastel-colored finger paints.

Before they leave, Carrie grabs a sponge to start cleaning, but I wrestle it from her grasp and push her out the door. The birthday girl never does dishes. Besides, there's not that much left aside from some plates and glasses. I'm an organized cook and always wash as I go.

Lionel and Ruby hang around for a few minutes to review the worst offenses of the evening. Mild-mannered Lionel, who always takes the high road, shudders as he recalls the crotch rubbing. "It's not normal. Casual touching is casual. That's heavy petting like in sex."

"Ha!" Ruby shouts triumphantly as she pokes her husband in the chest. Then she turns to me. "I keep telling him it's indecent, but he doesn't believe me."

Ruby I-told-you-so's all the way to the elevator, and even as I smile at her self-righteous delight, I resolve to be more accepting of Glenn in the future. Successful relationships are a rarity for the Carstone girls. We tend to attract emotionally stunted men on the rebound. My last short-lived misfire was with a recently divorced hedge fund manager who bought me plastic underwear and kept an eight-by-ten glossy of his high school girlfriend on his nightstand. Whenever we had sex, he'd turn the photo down so she couldn't see.

Compared with him, Glenn, even with his uncontrollable touching to bridge the unbearable distance between him and Carrie, which amounts to inches but must feel like miles when measured by his compulsion, is a paragon of sanity.

In life, every reaction has an equal and opposite reaction, and relationships are no different. Each positive creates a negative. Happiness itself produces a toxic byproduct like a paper-manufacturing plant or a nuclear reactor. Glenn's creepy caressing hands are the knives in the Little Mermaid's heels.

Love without the huge, gaping downside is just infatuation.

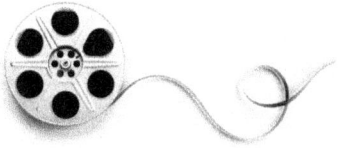

Day 800

IMPATIENT, I ARRIVE for my 11 A.M. with Carson Wright ten minutes early. I know he has nothing going on—the only items on the managing partner's schedule are his Monday morning manicure at Elizabeth Arden and his Thursday escargot with the partners at 21; in between nails and snails, he sits at his desk and reads the newspaper—but his secretary makes me wait until the clock chimes before she lets me in.

Wright founded the firm with Hertzberg in 1967 but was quickly shunted to the side as the latter became increasingly famous for high-profile clients. Hertzberg even argued before the Supreme Court in a civil rights case I learned about in a political science class in college. Carson Wright's name was never uttered at UConn.

With all the hours he's not practicing law, Carson has plenty of time to manage the firm and frequently sends out memos detailing new billing procedures. Each successive update contradicts the one before it, keeping the entire staff in a constant state of confusion.

Wright, with his straight, gaunt face and unruly white mane that tumbles over his Brooks Brothers collar, is the villain of my novel, the puppet master who makes everyone at Jarndyce & Associates jump to his bidding.

Uninterested in my problem, he passes me along to Victoria Penn, the youngest partner at fifty-one as well as the scariest. Famous for skewering Justice Scalia on points of Constitutional law at a Harvard luncheon, she has a withering command of Latin and a short fuse. With an ingrained sense of respect for her peers, she takes her temper out only on underlings—secretaries, junior associates, paralegals, mailroom staff, members of the cleaning crew and security guards—frequently issuing death threats whenever something doesn't go her way. Anyone unlucky enough to be within ten feet of her when she's angry stands in danger of losing his head to a machete. It's mostly an empty threat—unless you're in her office, where the aforementioned weapon is mounted on her wall as a souvenir from her trip to the Amazon.

Victoria Penn is also a villain in the book. Actually, they all are: Hertzberg, Wright, Silver and Penn. *Jarndyce and Jarndyce* is a black comedy.

Although her secretary tells me to go right in, I knock discretely at Penn's door. She's on the phone with a junior associate who's working on the London deal with her. Important documents arriving tonight need to be turned around by morning. Wendy assures her it won't be a problem.

Victoria rolls her eyes and notices me standing in the doorway. She waves me in. "Fuck it up, Gorman, and you're history. The police will never find the pieces," she says. She issues the threat because it's expected of her, but I can tell from the matter-of-fact tone that her heart's not in it. She appears tired. Her slate-gray eyes don't look as icy as usual. They seem more dead than cold, like a heroin addict's.

Realizing she has no idea who I am, even though she's offered to mutilate me on several occasions, I introduce myself. She nods abruptly.

This is hardly a warm welcome, but it's the best I'm going to get, so I launch into an explanation of why I'm there. I start with an apology for bothering her with such a minor matter.

"Then why are you?" she snaps.

With some effort, I ignore her impatient tone and continue with my explanation.

"Requests for vacation time must be submitted at least four weeks prior to the proposed date," she says. "It's in the employee handbook, which is issued to every employee at orientation. I'm sure if I call down to HR they'll confirm that you signed for it." She eyes the phone but doesn't pick it up.

"But," I point out in response, "the handbook also says that partners can make exceptions on a case-by-case basis." I don't know if this is true, but it sounds like something a law firm would put in writing.

Victoria doesn't belabor the point. Instead, she fixes me with her cold, vacant stare and asks why would she do that.

Throwing myself on her mercy, I explain about the book and the option and the once-in-a-lifetime party. I tell her Moxie Bernard is going to be there and the entire cast of *Getting Nowhere* and probably Bella Masters, the tobacco heiress with the best hipbones this side of an Ethiopian famine, who, according to Cindy Adams in the *Post,* wants to be in the picture with her new bestie. I stress how important this opportunity is for my career.

Every syllable I utter is another nail in my coffin. I can see it in her eyes, which, it turns out, are capable of emotion after all. Her contempt is almost palpable, and as I listen to myself rattle off the details of my exciting future, I can almost understand her scorn. I sound insufferably blessed.

But it's not just the party. It's the book itself and the hope it represents. I'm not supposed to have other coals in the fire. I'm a paralegal. My career is being Victoria Penn's slave.

"Even if I wanted to give you the day off, we simply can't spare you," she announces without an ounce of sincerity. Her tone implies she could spare me all over the place, just not for a dazzling party among Hollywood elite. If I told her it was for my cousin's bar mitzvah at the Friar Tuck Inn in Weehawken, she would have consented with a barely concealed smirk. "The last week of August is one of our busiest times and we're already short-handed as it is. Every employee will have to work extra hard to pick up the slack, myself included. Knowing this, I can't in all good conscience let you take off and make the burden heavier for everyone else. What kind of boss would I be?"

It's hard to smile without sneering, but I somehow manage to pull it off. "Of course. I understand," I say, realizing I'll have to suck it up and take days without pay. They're frowned upon because no employer wants an underling who values her life over her work, but there's no other solution. I'm *not* missing that party.

"And let me add before I finish with this topic forever," Victoria says as I stand up. "You *will* be here on the 21st. I don't care if your grandmother dies in a freak anvil accident or your appendix bursts on the F train or you're held hostage in a burning building by the ghost of Osama Bin Laden himself. The only acceptable excuse for your not being here is a death certificate, and you better make it good as I'll be checking the body myself. Got it?"

And just like that, I'm out of a job.

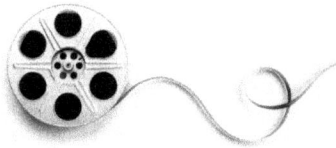

Day 801

ALTHOUGH THE PLAN is to sleep late, then read the paper over a steaming mocha latte at the café on the corner where all the dog owners hang out, I wake up at six A.M. and lie in bed, anxious and nervous about the future. I try assiduously to fall back asleep. When that fails, I get up, turn on my computer and open the new novel I started a year ago.

I might as well make myself useful.

But by noon I know it's a waste of time.

The problem is, I never intended to write a workplace comedy or any novel. *Jarndyce and Jarndyce* began life as a series of e-mails to friends and family relaying the efforts of Marla Hertzberg to penetrate the upper echelons of HWSP management. Disgusted with her presumption as well as her reputation, the old guard closed ranks, ignoring her many memos to implement change. Unintimidated by a bunch of institutional gray-hairs doddering on the brink of doddering, she confronted Wright, Silver and Penn wherever she found them, most usually within a few feet of my desk.

I typed the first argument—about adding a one-cent-per-page surcharge on all copies to compensate for machine wear and tear—verbatim as an outraged Wright, who considers photocopiers as well as computers and faxes to fall under the rubric of office supplies, not office equipment, chewed her out for discourteous parsimony. As a famous penny-pincher himself, his response was pure contrariness, and no doubt in his tight-fisted little heart he was angry at himself for not coming up with double amortization years ago.

The squabbling continued for months, and I recorded all of it, delighting in the overt pettiness of these supposedly mature and dignified lawyers. The battles were intense and the escalation swift and fierce, as was the peace negotiation. After two financial quarters of conflict, the senior partners brokered a deal with Marla, inviting her to lunch at 21 and putting her in charge of employee affairs. Still, it was only the end of open hostilities, not the war. Too old-fashioned to embrace a woman who rose through the ranks in such a disgraceful manner—sleeping your way to the top was a time-honored tradition but not with two eighty-year-old men who were raised like brothers by the kindly old man who adopted them after WWII—the partners made sure neither Marla nor the staff forgot her humble beginnings, making snide comments whenever possible. Their spite campaign worked. The specters of Handelman and Finch are a constant presence in the hallowed halls of Hertzberg, Wright, Silver and Penn, their white flaccid penises like halos over Marla's head.

Their revenge gave my e-mails a satisfying conclusion. I wrapped up my narrative and returned to giving the job my all, which, even at its best, is still only sixty percent of my attention.

Unbeknownst to me, my sister forward my e-mails to a friend at a literary agency, who thought they'd made a great novel if we could just punch up the through line. She thought more should be made of the Oedipal conflict between Marla and her great-statesman father. Never one to turn down a free lunch, I took the meeting, extremely doubtful that anything could be made out of a jumble of overheard conversations.

But Julie had a clear vision and worked with me until it was on the page. Taking her suggestion, I added a sexual undertone to Marla's relationship with her dad, making him strangely envious of her gray-haired lovers, and I stepped up her frugality until Ada Clare Jarndyce is Dickensian in her Scrooge McDuck greed. In the end, she's the only one remaining; even her father, John Jarndyce, is downsized in a final cost-cutting measure that replaces him with a cardboard cutout.

A year later, the trade paperback of *Jarndyce and Jarndyce* hit the bookshelves. It sold about thirty thousand copies, a number, I'm told, that's fairly decent for a first-time novelist.

The problem with having a moderately successful novel with movie aspirations is everyone wants a second one. Now that I'm not working long hours, people will expect things of me. I can no longer use my job as an excuse.

But my state of employment has nothing to do with my lack of productivity. I'm not a writer.

I'd tried to get a sequel out of the discontented grumblings of my coworkers. The ninety-dollar annual subscription fee to the company's coffee plan generated a lot of outrage among the rank and file but nothing ever came of it. Support staff is powerless to effect change; all they can do is complain. Sometimes their invectives rise to the level of poetry, sonnets of dissatisfaction fueled by diluted bagel-cart coffee that sets you back sixty-five cents. But grousing over deprivation isn't a novel. It's the mind-numbing routine of regular life.

And the world already has enough of that.

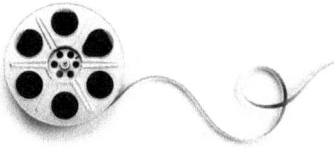

Day 805

I DON'T TELL my parents about my unemployment. They were raised by Depression-era survivors to prize comfort and stability over happiness and did their best to instill their children with a fear of insecurity. For years I took business classes at UConn Storrs, studying Managerial Statistics and Information Systems for Management. My future was set: After graduation, I would work at a brokerage house just like my dad. I'd wake up every morning in my white suburban house with blue-gray shutters, thick tan carpeting and impossibly green lawn and take the same train into Manhattan for forty years before retiring to Florida, where I would form a tight-knit community of other former commuters. Nothing seemed more glamorous to me than the regularity of the 7:51 out of Norwalk.

Real life could not live up to the fantasy. My ability with numbers fell well short of passing and my marketing ingenuity failed to impress any of my professors. After five semesters of barely getting by, I admitted defeat and switched to the College of Arts and Sciences. Much to my embarrassment, I excelled at English literature. Deeply ashamed, my parents could not bring themselves to ask about my classes, even when my analysis of Eliot's "The Four Quartets" won the prestigious Pershing Award for concision.

For several years, my name was noticeably absent from the Carstone Christmas newsletter.

Paralegaling was not instant redemption. It was too far removed from actual legaling—that is, the profession of lawyer—for my parents to embrace it. They saw the job as too dependent on the whims and wishes of an egotistical attorney who would blame those closest and least powerful for his own failings. Although this prediction has proven true, being a whipping girl has in no way impeded my ability to make a steady living. The paycheck arrives every Friday with Mussolini-like regularity. The money is decent, if not wonderful, and keeps me in the middle-middle-class luxury to which I'm accustomed.

I can even afford to take my parents out to dinner every once in a while.

Becoming a full-blown, full-time lawyer has always been the long-term goal. My parents' dreams for me are nothing compared to those I have for myself. I don't want to bow and scrape forever, to be overlooked and underestimated, to fetch and carry and sit by a photocopier as twenty copies of a thousand-page document spit out with pathological repetition.

The only thing holding me back is the LSAT. I've been studying for years. With my verbal skills, I've got the reading parts down pat and even the analytical. The logic questions remain a problem. I'm sure I can master the section if I just apply myself. But it's hard. I simply don't care who the coach of the Smalltown Bluebirds hockey team will put into the starting lineup if George only starts when Bart does and Dexter and Bart never start together and George starts when Marlene doesn't and three out of the four fastest are always chosen.

Seriously, what is that? It's not law. In my eight years at HWSP, we've never had a case involving the starting lineup of any team, let alone a third-rate hockey club from a small Midwestern town.

Now that I've got some time on my hands, I plan to devote myself fully to the LSATs. It's hard to come home after a long day and take out books. My brain is fried from too little thinking and sometimes it's all I can do to sit on the couch and watch old episodes of *Buffy*.

The only reason I was able to churn out a book at all was I did most of it at the office. If you type industriously enough, your boss will assume you're hard at work on a very important case. Stop the second she walks by and you'll have personal-e-mail guilt written all over you. Novels, like undercover work, are about believing in the part.

Although they've never said anything outright, I know my parents are disappointed by *Jarndyce and Jarndyce*. To them it represents a backslide into the miasma of liberal arts. Nobody ever paid the gas bill with clever ideas.

The movie is worse. Publishing is at least an industry they believe in. They've had books in their hands—*Seven Habits of Highly Effective People, How to Win Friends and Influence People*—even if they've only glanced at the contents (that is, the table of contents). But filmmaking is pure charlatanism, a series of undelivered promises made to people who should know better. The last movie they saw was 1974's *Towering Inferno*. They enjoyed it immensely, but narrative, the ongoing account of familiar and sometimes likeable characters, requires too much, holding your attention captive until it drops you cold. Now they stick to Bloomberg, which demands nothing more interesting than money, a resource they're happy to expend in the pursuit of comfort, the only intangible they understand.

When I tell them about the party, they look at me with such worry and concern that I feel like a bad daughter for even bringing it up. Far from giving the movie credibility, the proposed event undermines it completely. Only a project with shaky foundations would have to work so hard to seem legitimate. For reasons I don't understand, my parents seem convinced Hollywood will ruin me.

It's like buried deep in their minds is an ancestral memory of a ne'er-do-well Carstone holding out for the easy buck. They look at me and see him.

The only way to convince them I'll be all right is to show them. When the party's a complete success, when the media gushes over the affair, when Arcadia green-lights the film, when Moxie gives the performance of her life, when *J&J* wins an Oscar, when my book becomes a best-seller, when I have so much money I never have to work again, then they'll get on board.

Up until that moment, I'll leave them in the dark about my job. I hate the thought of worrying them further.

Plus, it saves me a lot of aggravation.

I call my sister and swear her to secrecy. She works for a Swiss reinsurance company doing actuarial tables and rarely has time to talk during business hours. Today, however, I convince her to take a long lunch and come to Barney's with me. I need an outfit for my Hollywood debut.

"This is crazy," she says as I hold up a white coat dress by Betsey Johnson. It has a round neckline, elbow sleeves and a large belt around the waist. It's very fashion forward but I'm not sure I can pull off the poufy shoulders. They look oddly like a sketch for a Frank Gehry building. I put it back on the rack to show Carrie that I haven't lost it completely.

She doesn't appreciate my effort. "Look, you can't spend"—she grabs the tag on a Narciso Rodriguez linen dress—"fifteen hundred dollars on an outfit when you just got laid off."

I shake my head and walk over to the next rack, where a bright blue Pucci hangs provocatively. With very little effort, I can see myself in the signature abstract print. I'd be a classic. "Not laid off, quit."

Carrie looks around stealthily. "Will you stop saying that? You can't collect unemployment if you keep saying that."

Collecting unemployment isn't a simple matter of he said–she said but my sister believes so strongly in the power of semantics that I let it go. She's too much of a Connecticut Carstone to understand impulsiveness. My job isn't my job anymore. Victoria Penn isn't going to let me have it back if I ask nicely, nor is she going to let my unemployment insurance papers slide across her desk.

As soon as I run my fingers over the Pucci, I know it'll never do. Jersey is too casual a material. I'm going to a hot L.A. party, not a clam bake. I eye a white A-line skirt with teal stripes down the front and alternating black and gray square accents. It's beautiful. I imagine it with the perfect top, something equally sleek and summery, perhaps silk in a complementing color.

Noting the interested look in my eye, Carrie grabs the skirt. "Absolutely not." She holds up the tag. "One thousand and ninety-five dollars and that's just for the skirt. You can't afford this."

Although I don't think eleven hundred dollars is necessarily too much to pay for a skirt to wear to such a major event, it is slightly on the high side when you consider the designer, Diane von Furstenberg, has a line for Gap Kids. I seek out the Dior section.

I pause briefly over an asymmetrical dress gathered at the waist, but the neckline is too plunging. Even with fabric tape, I'd worry obsessively about a wardrobe malfunction. Next I admire a bright abstract print. The neck is a respectable V, the skirt a flattering A. The material is lovely to the touch, a warm, silver silk.

"How about this?" I ask, consideringly. It's the first one I feel serious about. It's lovely, summery, by a high-end designer and on the edge of edgy. And at $1,095, it's practically a bargain—the same price as the DVF skirt but without the need for a top.

Carrie runs her hands over the hem. "I suppose you could wear it again."

I stare at her goggle-eyed. *Of course* I can wear it again! It's a Christian Dior, not a bridesmaid dress.

"Or," she says, lowering her voice as she follows me to a dressing room, "you can leave the tags on and return it after the party."

Her suggestion is so ridiculous, I don't even dignify it with an answer. It's obvious my sister knows nothing of Hollywood. She's doesn't read *People* or *Us* or even *In Style*. Embarrassing snafus like leaving the tag on a dress are exactly what the paparazzi are after. Humiliation is their raison d'être.

She continues to chastise me for my irresponsibility as I wiggle out of my jeans, and I wonder why I asked her to come at all. I should have known she'd spoil my fun. Family is always a wet sponge on a good time. When I was seven, she ruined by birthday party at the Houdini Factory in the mall by explaining how all the tricks were done. It's almost the same thing now. She's breaking the dress down to its components—silk, thread, dye—to take away its magic.

I tune her out as I pull the dress over my head. I don't think $1,095 is *that* much money. My credit card can take it. And if it couldn't, I'd pay it off in installments. Nothing is more important than this party.

Running my hands over the silk to smooth out the dress, I look at myself in the mirror. I don't know what I think. The length is right: just above the knees. The neck is good: not too revealing. The material flows nicely over my body, revealing a shape beneath without actually clinging. My arms look a little flabby but that's only to be expected with narrow shoulder straps.

Overall, it's hard to imagine the finished product. I'm wearing no makeup at all and my hair is a messy ponytail.

I pull the curtain aside and step out of the dressing room, goose bumps forming as the cold air-conditioning hits my skin. Carrie turns, breaks off her litany of other bad decisions I've made in my life and stares. She doesn't say anything for a long time; she just blinks and blinks. Then, in a voice so soft, I can barely hear her, she says, "Wow."

And that's when I remember why I brought her along.

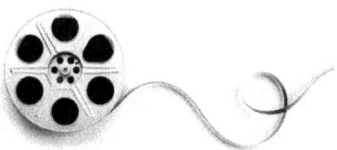

Day 807

THREE WEEKS AFTER the queen-e-mail incident, Moxie stops wearing panties. In photos taken at the Paris premiere of her new film, *Red Scarlet,* there it is: the milk-white luminescence of her freshly shaved labia. Helping her out of the limo—though, clearly, not well enough—is the swarthy Frenchman twice her age whom she's reputed to have dropped Carlos Wenders for. He's holding her hand and gazing down at her with a mix of lust and fondness, as if he wants to screw her brains out, then buy her an ice cream cone. There's an element of distasteful voyeurism about the look: as if he knows that you know that he knows Moxie's not wearing undies.

The suave Frenchman is absent from the photos taken the next day in front of her hotel, but her hoo-ha is fully present. *Vive la exhibitionism.*

The papers dutifully pixilate out the indecent parts, and to see the uncensored photos you have to go online. I don't recommend this. The image is horrifying; her vagina looks like some sad little undernourished animal in a third-world zoo, like a bald mouse or a decrepit old bat.

I glance once and click off immediately. Nobody is looking over my shoulder, but I still feel like a perv. It's hard to see the photo and not imagine a thousand middle-aged men getting a prurient thrill.

As soon as the pictures hit the Internet, Moxie's publicity machine goes to work proving they're fakes. Her new PR firm, Hornet Associates, releases the original shot of her at the premiere, which shows her demure white cotton undies firmly in place. Stalker.com obediently posts the photo with an apology to Moxie and her family. Twenty minutes later, the host amends the entry again, this time adding fresh evidence that the panties have been Photoshopped in—and very badly, too. Gleeful—he *knew* Moxie was a big ho—he refers readers to GalaFotos.com, the internationally respected company that took the photograph. There, visitors can see the real original shot.

Hundreds of other sites around the world do the same. Moxie's bare beaver is reproduced in forty-eight languages.

The next day, when the second batch of photos makes the rounds, Jessica Hornet tries a diversionary tactic, announcing on CNN Moxie's literacy initiative, a plan to set up reading programs in twenty of the poorest districts in the United States. It's a desperate and cynical ploy, but the mainstream press covers it with the usual enthusiasm. Oprah calls her an inspiration. The president invites her to the White House to join a blue ribbon panel on reading skills.

Two days later, when Moxie climbs out of a gondola and flashes all the pigeons in St. Mark's Square, hardly anyone notices.

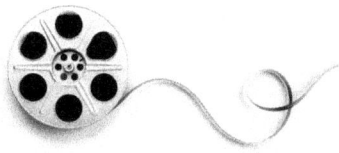

Day 819

DURING THE PLANE ride to Los Angeles, my editor, Elaine Smart, and I brainstorm topics of conversation just in case Moxie comes to the party. My list is short but thoughtful. 1) Ask about *Red Scarlet*. What was it like to bungee-jump across the Grand Canyon? Would she do her own stunts again? 2) Ask about singing career. Has she thought of recording an album with Yoko Ono? (Per an interview with Barbara Walters, Yoko is her favorite Beatle, followed by Stella McCartney and Ringo Star.) 3) Gush over catchy hit single "Waiting." Query lyrics. Does "Waiting is a large, ripe peach" mean that waiting is sweet or that the narrator is from Georgia? 4) Mention that I grew up in Norwalk too and that I too think Hunan Gourmet totally rocks. (If necessary, remind her of signed *American Grrl* poster in window of restaurant: "To Hunan Gourmet, the best around. You totally rock. Love ya, Moxie.") Ask which she likes better: their egg foo young or beef with broccoli.

With little more than twenty-four hours until the party, it's still not clear whether Moxie will be in attendance. Her status changes hourly. This morning she was definitely in but by noon she'd agreed to fly to New York to do a top ten list on Letterman. Four hours later, the appearance was in jeopardy, as Letterman refused to cut #2: Because underwear is for children and the elderly.

Lester Dedlock assures me this is quite normal. Nobody is anywhere in L.A. until they're somewhere and even then they're sometimes not there.

The whole guest list is like that. In the past two weeks, I've heard every name from Julia Roberts to Robbie Williams as a possible attendee. At one point, the entire cast from *Revenge* was coming, then only Emily VanCamp, then everyone but Emily VanCamp. Bill Clinton was even mentioned during one breathless conversation.

The only person, it seems, who has definitely rsvp'd is me.

With such a fluctuating guest list, it's impossible for me to come up with conversation for everyone. I gave it a really good shot at first but when Gwyneth Paltrow was removed for the third time, I realized it was a waste of energy. I'd just have to wing it.

This concept terrifies me. I find awkward silences devastating—the steady buzz of nothing, the hum of my rattled brain desperately trying to come up with a clever retort. Whole empires have crumbled in the space of time it takes me to think of a clever rejoinder to the simple question "How are you?"

To this baseline anxiety add professional photographers and celebrity snapshots and you have my worst nightmare. Every time I imagine Katrina, Sunset Press's publicist, introducing me around a shiver runs through me. "Excuse me, Gwyneth, this is Ricki Carstone, the author of the book. Do you mind if she stands stiffly beside you while these nice men take your photo? I promise it'll only take a second."

It is mortification wrapped in embarrassment topped with a shiny ribbon of humiliation.

Next to me, Elaine reads my list of Moxie topics but doesn't make her own. An L.A. native and child actor—she had a small part in the hit series *The Martin Family,* playing the fatally adorable Leila Martin after the fatally adorable Sheila Martin outgrew her fatal adorableness—she doesn't believe in celebrity. There are only varying degrees of obscurity—where you fall on the spectrum is simply a matter of timing.

She can afford to be philosophical. On the obscurity-o-meter, she falls somewhere below Keisha Knight Pulliam and above Jeremy Miller.

Unwilling to reminiscence about her industry background, Elaine always fobs me off by asking—snidely, I'd say—how the second book is coming. That shuts me up quickly enough.

Elaine hands me my notebook just as the plane starts to descend. She puts her chair in the upright position and opens her shutter. Below Los Angeles twinkles like lights on a Christmas tree. "What about Lloyd?" she asks.

A flight attendant with a garbage bag breezes by before I can toss my cup away, so I put it in the seat pocket. The plastic cracks. "What about him?"

"He'll be there. What will you talk about with him?"

Distracted by the ever-evolving roster of famous names, I've given no thought at all to my host and benefactor. Of course I need conversational topics for Lloyd Chancellor. He's the most important person I'll ever meet. The weight of his significance strikes me dumb. I don't have a single thought in my head.

Not a one.

Elaine sees my stricken look and laughs. "Good Lord, you're hopeless. To review, Lloyd Chancellor is the son of Duke Chancellor, the former head of Arcadia Studios, and Danielle Doyle, eighties rom-com star. He has made three movies—*A Fall from Great Heights, Presenting the Dissidents* and *Catcher and Rye*—the last of which is his only commercial success. He's in his mid-thirties, has never been married and is currently between breakups with supermodel Levienne Jordana. He has curly red hair, green eyes, a smattering of freckles, and the most collagen-stuffed lips of any man, woman or child in Hollywood."

"That's only a rumor," I point out, some of my panic fading as she runs through his vitals.

"His plastic surgeon confirmed it."

"His alleged plastic surgeon. They can't prove he's Patient X."

Elaine rolls her eyes. "Nobody has lips the size of porterhouse steaks without a little medical help."

While this is most likely true, it's hardly fodder for small talk. But that's all right. There's enough to say about Lloyd's three previous films to fill any number of awkward silences. *Catcher and Rye* was even a pretty decent screwball comedy. The banter didn't have quite the zingy rat-tat-tat of Hepburn and Tracy, but it was sharp and very funny in places.

By the time we land, I have nice things to say about all his movies, even the ones I didn't like. (*A Fall from Great Heights*: "Excellent theme song by Taylor Swift. So short and to the point." *Presenting the Dissidents*: "Blake Lively's dress in the final scene was stunning.")

We disembark and I follow Elaine through LAX. One airport is pretty much like any other, but I feel an uncontrollable sense of excitement being surrounded by these gates and those signs. There's something almost unbearably West Coast about the utilitarian building, as if the air itself is laced with palm tress and movie stars. When we get to baggage claim, our luggage is already waiting, and we breeze through the crowd to the arrivals hall, where a livery driver in a black cap and white gloves is holding a sign with my name.

And here we go.

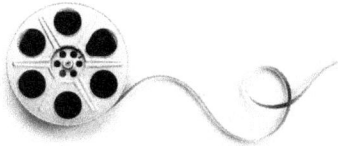

Day 820 (a.m.)

I HAVE SO many appointments scheduled for August 21st that I actually have to figure out how the calendar function on my phone works. This level of organization is unheard of. Usually the details are my life are comfortably contained on random scraps of paper.

Suddenly I feel important.

Lester Dedlock meets me in the lobby of my hotel and suggests we have breakfast poolside. Before I can respond, he's leading me toward the elevator and relaying the history of the Marmont Tower, an art deco grande dame from 1929. While we wait for the car to come, he ticks off a list of the famous people who have lived here—Errol Flynn, Claudette Colbert, John Wayne, Elizabeth Taylor, Marilyn Monroe, Howard Hughes.

I respond with an appropriate series of wows and no-kiddings, but I already know the information. After three weeks of cyberstalking, I'm intimately acquainted with the Marmont Tower. I can rattle off the dimensions and amenities of each room (junior suite: 550 square feet, Egyptian linen, Kiehl's products, Wi-Fi, flat-screen TV, iPod station, gourmet mini-bar, twenty-four-hour room service).

Lester selects a table at the far end of the pool, almost out of earshot of two squabbling children and their ineffective nanny. Within seconds, a waiter appears with menus. I order a latte and instantly regret it. I'm having breakfast poolside at the Marmont Tower with dazzling sunlight spilling over my shoulder. I should have something vibrant and decadent like a champagne cocktail or a Kir Royale.

Lester gets a cup of tea, Earl Grey, no sugar.

My film agent looks in person exactly as he does on the cover of *Vanity Fair,* save for an array of deep wrinkles around his severe black eyes. His face is long and angular, with a sturdy chin and patrician nose, and his thick white hair spills over the collar of his pristine white shirt.

He is ferocious looking, and when he stares down at me from his imposing six-plus feet height, I feel as if I'm having an audience with Zeus himself.

Except...those fierce white brows are far too neat to be natural. Sometime in the past week, they've been trimmed and plucked.

This small display of Hollywood vanity brings him solidly back down to earth.

The latte arrives in a delicate white cup, and I inhale it deeply, trying to calm the butterflies in my stomach. They've been there all morning, ever since I woke at six to see the sun rising over the Hollywood Hills, its golden fingers reaching through a panoply of pinks and orange.

After breakfast with Lester, I have lunch with the publicist to go over what I should expect at the party. Then a seaweed wrap, massage and mani-pedi at the spa. Hopefully that will calm my jitters before the woman from Frédéric Fekkai arrives to do my hair and makeup.

Yes, I'm maxing out my credit card for this party, but if I can't max it out for the Hollywood launch of my book, then when can I?

Lester recommends the eggs Benedict, but I can't imagine eating anything so heavy. I settle on an oat bran muffin and a bowl of fruit.

"I trust you're settling in all right?" Lester says as the waiter takes the menus. "Everything as you'd expect to find it? No unpleasant surprises? Good. Good. The Marmont is a reliable establishment. I always put my daughters up here when they're in town. The chairs in the lounge are particularly comfortable. Just the right amount of lumbar support. And of course there's the view."

Yes, the view. The entire city of Los Angeles stretches around us in every direction. I love the sleek compactness of Manhattan, but there's something primally appealing about the wide-open space of urban sprawl.

"It's beautiful out here," I say, soaking up the sun. It's warm in New York now, too, but it feels different, somehow more desperate.

"The event site is only a few blocks away," he says, as he points east. Or maybe west. "A little too far to walk, especially in the spindly heels pretty young women like to wear, but a short cab ride."

Although my heels are far too sturdy to be called spindly, I don't belabor the point. I'm far more interested in the venue—an ultra exclusive club whose members make up the crème de la crème of the Hollywood elite. "Have you been there?"

"Indeed, yes," he says with a slight nod. He leans back in his wicker chair, mindful of the insufficient lumbar support, and raises the cup to his lips. "It patterns itself on what used to be called a gentleman's club before that term took on lewd implications, but with its rented rooms and catering service, it's really more of a nouveau pastiche."

The description—a pejorative, to be sure, no matter how warmly it is said—almost makes me smile, and a few of the butterflies cease their fluttering. "Are you a member?" I ask. According to the *L.A. Times,* the membership process is arcane and selective. Hopefuls have to be recommended by a "proposer" and seconded by two "affirmers." Then their name "languishes in a book for a spell," collecting signatures, until there are roughly thirty-five. "But," warns the anonymous source, "the signatures have to be from people who can personally attest to whether or not the prospect is a 'good bloke.' " Blackballing is common, with no obligation to provide a reason.

Nevertheless, this is still L.A., so the unaffiliated mega famous like Bono can stroll in for a game of billiards whenever they want.

"For my sins, I am, yes. But it's a business arrangement, not a social one. I have to go where the deals are or suffer the consequences," he says, then smiles broadly, the wrinkles around his eyes deepening. "Obviously, it's no hardship to be surrounded by rich leather and excellent brandy. I think you'll find the rarified setting is perfectly suited to your novel. Lloyd Chancellor is an astute promoter."

The waiter delivers my muffin, which looks all healthful and worthy with its smattering of oats on top. He places a dainty bowl spilling with strawberries and melon next to it, while another server lays down a platter of beautifully garnished eggs benedict. Lester immediately dives in. I eye my muffin suspiciously, trying to figure out how much butter I need to make it palatable.

I pick up the knife and cut the muffin in half. "Have you done deals with him before?"

"No, I haven't. Not with Lloyd. I've done several deals with his father. He was a good man to work with, a straight-shooter, as they say, always able to see what the fuss is about. I can't abide people who don't even try to understand the other point of view in a negotiation. If nothing else, it's simply poor manners."

There are so many things I want to know about Lloyd Chancellor and every person who works in the office of Chancery Productions and all the Arcadia executives who are mentioned in the press release announcing Moxie's involvement that I don't know where to start.

I want to say, Tell me everything—every seemingly minor, tedious little detail that you wouldn't even mention to the lead detective in a murder investigation. *Everything.*

Instead, I ask him about his career as if I hadn't memorized every word of the *Vanity Fair* article.

The man who invented first-dollar gross easily launches into a detailed description of the shifting politics of the Ashley Famous mailroom as the agency merged with Creative Management Associates to become ICM. The moment was rife with opportunities, and he took advantage of every one.

"After all these years, the most important thing I've learned about the film industry and the most important thing I can tell you is don't expect anything," he says seriously after the waiter asks if he'd like more hot water. "Don't expect the movie to get made, don't expect Chancery to buy the rights to your book, don't expect them to renew the option, don't expect the party to go off. Don't expect anything to happen a moment before it does and you'll be amazed how delightful a business this is.

"Now, you are," he continues, "in a better position than most, and I'll admit that things seem to be toddling along smoothly, but this is Los Angeles. It's like a small African nation. It's a bunch of warlords in Hummers firing their machine guns into the air; the regime in charge changes daily. The only thing you can do is keep your head down and wait it out. Right now it all comes down to the script. Lloyd has the two most-coveted writers in town lined up. Let's let them finish the screenplay and then we'll see."

Lester has been talking about the "two most-coveted writers in town" for months as Lloyd negotiates their contract. Since they're so coveted, their fee far exceeds Chancery's small discretionary fund. The studio, therefore, has to step up with the money to pay them. Once it does, Arcadia will be officially on-board as the movie's fiscal sponsor. When that happens, I get a set-up bonus of twenty-five thousand dollars. I'm not relying on the money to cover rent or anything, but it's a nice chunk of change. A girl could easily pay off a few shiatsu massages.

"The thing I don't understand is how they can be coveted—"

"The most coveted," Lester inserts pointedly.

"—the *most*-coveted writers when their last screen credit was *The Good Times Movie* in 2002. That seems so…I don't know…uncoveted."

The waiter clears our plates and asks if we'd like anything else. Lester requests the check, which the waiter immediately produces. He puts it on the table, assures us there no rush, and returns to the staging area to the left of the entrance.

"Credits aren't necessarily an indicator of success," Lester explains. "Many writers make a wonderful living out here without a single one of their scripts getting produced. It's the way the business works. So trust me, Tipston and Field are the hottest writers in town right now. Lloyd would be very lucky to get them."

"When do you think that will happen?"

He shrugs as he signs the credit card receipt. "It could be tomorrow. It could be a year from now. There's no time frame for this. Every movie is different. Granted, *Jarndyce and Jarndyce* is in a better position than most, but there are no guarantees. Everything is up in the air. Remember, no expectations."

I nod. "Right, no expectations."

He smiles approvingly. "Good. I have another meeting to get to, so I've got to run. But I'll see you tonight. Have a restful day and don't hesitate to call if you need anything."

Lester Dedlock walks briskly past the unruly children, one of whom is crying hysterically now, and steps onto the elevator. I watch him go, leaning back in my chair as the nanny tries to comfort the wailing boy. Lester's advice is appreciated but entirely unnecessary. Even without his industry-insider lecture, I know what extremely long odds I'm facing: Only one in a hundred book optioned ever makes it to the big screen. I'm not so full of myself that I'd assume mine would be one of the lucky ones.

Still, whatever he says, I'm determined to enjoy the ride. Already I've gotten a new edition of my book, a gushing quote from the hottest teen star in the world and a party celebrating me in a swank Los Angeles club out of the experience. It's more than most writers get, and if a few more book sales and some special memories are all I take away, I'll be more than content.

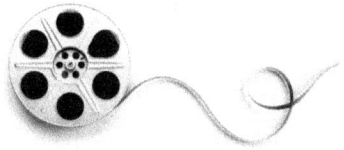

Day 820 (P.M.)

I DON'T KNOW how to stand. Keeping two feet on the ground while remaining upright—that I can do. But I can't *stand,* not like models and movie stars and debutantes whose entire life is lived in the bright lights of a camera flash, the shoulders-back, hips-forward, eyes-smoldering stance photographers beg for in the dark silence before the click.

All I can do is stand like a dead weight, like a fallen soufflé, my smile as wide and clumsy as a hyena's. A predator among gazelles, I wait frozen as paparazzi call my name over and over again—Ricki, Ricki, Ricki, Ricki—until it starts to sound like nonsense, gobbledygook, an onomatopoeic sound meant to convey gracelessness.

Over, amid and through the clumsiness and petrified jaw is giddy astonishment that I'm standing—wrongly, yes, but standing still—on the red carpet as men with rough voices take my picture. This is happening to me. I'm in Hollywood, California, in front of Boodle's, where Bono likes to play pool when he's in town, being photographed by every major wire service in the country.

I have no idea how long I've been here. Time stops under the blinding glare of a Klieg light. Moments exist side by side with each other, so that Katrina is introducing me as the author of *J&J* at the very same instant a statuesque blond wraps her arm around my shoulder and poses.

The world is a fucking strange place.

Reporters assembled behind a velvet rope ask me questions as I go down the line, Katrina at my elbow introducing me to everyone like the social chair at a country club cotillion. Each asks me the same question about Moxie so that by the time I get to the end, my sound bite is honed to a fine, sharp edge. Film is a collaborative medium, I say, and I'm delighted to pass the baton to the next participant. I gloss over the eleven years that separate Moxie

Bernard from Ada Clare Jarndyce. A tepid smile, a demure blush. What does a girl like me know about translating a novel to the big screen?

Katrina tells me I'm doing great as she escorts me through the somber halls of Boodle's to the Biddle's Lounge, a dark-wood-paneled room with a gilded bar, red banquettes and thrashing music. Beautiful people are gathered around tables, the bar, the DJ. Snifters with caramel-colored brandy sweep past my nose. Katrina leads me to an oak desk piled high with books and hands me a black marker.

As soon as I sit down, a line forms. Dozens of women rush forward to say how much they love my dress. I return the compliment whatever they're wearing. It isn't a lie. Everyone is gorgeous. Hair smooth, makeup perfect, bodies svelte and tanned limbs. I sign each book simply, with their name and mine, because I don't have time to write anything more. The line keeps growing. Person after person gushes how incredibly eager they are to read my book. Kitty Dunleavy, who played the youngest sibling in the short-lived hit drama about homeless children in Seattle, *The Home Brigade,* shoves her surprisingly large chest in my face (poor Stephanie with her cello lessons and her angst) and says she can't wait to read it. A fashion designer in a white silk scarf tells me he wants to discuss a project. The editor of *Gossip* magazine promises to do an item on me. The reporter from *Variety* who broke the story about Moxie starring in the film drags over a chair and asks how it feels.

Beyond real, I say. Absolutely beyond real.

Through it all, *Access Hollywood* keeps a camera focused on me.

Lester comes up just as I'm signing the last book. "You look like you're having fun," he says.

I'm not sure that's how you'd describe it.

Katrina pulls me to the side. "Lloyd's here."

I don't know what this means other than I have to leave the relative safety of my table and venture further into the room. I take a deep breath and follow her to the other side of the bar, where another backdrop for photos has been set up. Lloyd Chancellor stands imposingly before it in a beautifully tailored gray sharkskin suit, his overly thick lips pressed together in a sexy pout. On his right is the statuesque blond; on the left is a statuesque brunette. Everyone looks famous.

Katrina brings me to Lloyd's publicist and says, "This is Ricki Carstone, the author."

The woman nods and leads me to Lloyd. "The author," she says, positioning me between the producer and the beautiful blond.

Cameras snap as we stand there.

"Now with Lloyd and Ricki alone," the publicist says.

More cameras snap. It's so strange to stand there dumbly and not talk.

"Thank you for the party," I say, keeping my eyes forward.

Snap.

"Thank you for a wonderful book," he replies.

Snap.

"Thank you for your vision."

Snap. Snap.

"Thank you for your appreciation."

His publicist puts the brunette back in the picture.

After another minute, I'm released. Disconcerted, I head to the bar and order a Manhattan. It's strong and bitter and tastes like home. I have one quiet, calm moment before—to my utter amazement—Moxie arrives.

I know the second she enters the building. Her presence has a texture, knotty and rough, and everyone feels it. Even with the music thrashing, a hush falls over the room. Her megawatt smile shining brightly, she floats across the floor in a long, slinky red dress. With her hair pulled back in a simple twist, she looks like old-fashioned Hollywood glamour, a very proper starlet who wears panties wherever she goes.

Every step she takes is record by cameras.

After a starstruck minute people return to their conversations, but they keep one eye on her. Every single person in the lounge knows where Moxie is the entire time.

I finish my drink and get another.

Katrina finds me by the bar and introduces me to Kevin Sands, the representative from Maire Haircare, which, along with Sunset Press and Sky Lab Vodka, underwrote the party. I've never had to schmooze a sponsor before but it comes easily. I gush about the fabulous party and how great Maire products are. I've never actually used any, but it doesn't feel like lying. Graciousness is about making the other person feel comfortable. How you do that doesn't matter.

Lloyd's publicist taps me on the shoulder. "They want one with you, Lloyd and Moxie."

Holy shit.

Neither Lloyd nor Moxie acknowledges my presence as I join them in front of the backdrop. I stand first next to Lloyd, then between him and Moxie, then on the other side of the superstar. Photographers call our names and say, Look here, look here. I try to follow Moxie and Lloyd, so I can be in the same pictures as them, but I don't know if I succeed. I remember my prom stills, with all four of us looking in different directions.

Lloyd moves to the side out of the shot, and now it's just Moxie and me. I smile woodenly and try to remember what I mapped out. I have conversation prepared. I'm ready for this moment.

But I'm not. In my head we have a one-on-one chat in a quiet room like regular people. I didn't calculate hot lights, loud music, busy publicists, distracting photographers, enthralled spectators. Or her vapidity. Up close, she's nothing but gorgeous smile.

"I'm Ricki Carstone," I say softly.

She looks at me but there's no recognition.

"I wrote the book."

Still nothing.

"*Jarndyce and Jarndyce.*"

She blinks.

It's very possible she has no clue why she's here.

I glance around the room and suddenly it seems very possible that nobody has a clue why they're here. This launch is just another reason for them to dress up in their glad rags and take pictures against a backdrop. It has nothing to do with me. I'm simply the excuse Lloyd needs to get Maire to underwrite this lavish affair.

Even that, I realize, as lightbulbs flicker, is giving myself too much credit. This party is happening around me, not to me. My presence is the happy result of scheduling, not planning. The book's the excuse. No, the *excuse* is the excuse.

Far from being disappointed, I take remarkable comfort from this realization. Everyone is here to further their own ends. Somehow adapting *J&J* to the big screen helps all these people build better lives for themselves. This is also a reassuring thought. It gives the movie a sort of a de facto inevitability.

For the first time ever, I believe we're really, truly, actually making a movie.

Holy fucking shit.

I spend the next hour mingling with well wishers, Hollywood types and studio execs. Conversation is easy when people heap compliments on your head. I finally meet Nadia, Lloyd's assistant who planned the event and drove Elaine crazy with twice daily telephone calls to talk about the gift bags and signage. She introduces me to Hamilton Frisk, the president of Chancery and the guy who actually gets things done. I pitch *J&J* as a television show. He laughs but doesn't dismiss it entirely.

Through it all, I keep one eye on Moxie, fascinated by her every movement. She goes from one pose to the next without stopping. Even when she steps away from the backdrop, she continues to model. People jockey to get near her. They're subtle but smothering, giving her just enough room to breathe in but not to exhale. Eager acolytes pose around her like she's a cardboard cutout of herself. Maybe she is.

If this party isn't about me, it's not about Moxie either. She's just another juicy morsel to feed on.

No wonder she's flashing her hoo-ha across forty-eight languages. It's an act of violence and aggression, like cutting your arm to make yourself bleed.

To my utter amazement, I find myself feeling sympathy for the young star. My concern for her well-being extends only as far as my own self-interest. I want her to hold on long enough to do my movie; after that I don't care to what depths of depravity she sinks. I'm like everyone else here—out to get what I can from her and walk away.

I'm still troubled by this notion a half hour later as I order a club soda at the bar. Next to me, a man lifts a martini glass and smiles. "I really liked your book."

With streaked blond hair, tan skin and bright gray eyes, he's as sleek as everyone else in the room, but his untucked shirt gives him a pleasantly disheveled appearance. I smile back. "Thanks."

He shakes his head. "No, that was sincere. I mean, I actually read your book. And I'm prepared to prove it. Ask me anything."

His earnestness is endearing, and I play along. "All right, what's Ada's father's name?"

"Carlyle," he spits out in disgust. "That doesn't count. It's in the blurb on the back. Give me something challenging."

I find it impressive enough that he's read the back copy but think of another question. "What's Ada's assistant's name?"

He pauses a moment to consider. "Trick question," he says with a snap of his fingers. "She doesn't have one."

Amazed, I clap. "You *have* read it."

"I might be the only one here who did," he says. "If Lloyd Chancellor had he might have cast an adult in the role of Ada Clare instead of a teenager."

"Film's a collaborative medium, a blending of visions," I say with complete sincerity. Repeat something enough times and it stops being bullshit. "Lloyd's ideas will work for the big screen."

He considers me silently for a moment, then smiles. "Sticking to the party line. Smart. I could be a reporter for all you know."

Although the thought hadn't occurred to me, it's entirely possible. Or he could be a friend of Lloyd's or a guy from the studio or even a relative of Moxie's. "Are you?" I ask.

"Nah. Reporter requires way too much effort than I'm capable of. I'm an actor. Harold Skimpole," he says, holding out his hand. "But that's just for the credits. I much prefer Harry."

As we shake hands, I examine him for signs of familiarity. I don't think I've seen him in anything, but he has that put-together, famous look.

"Nope, I wasn't in that," he says.

I tilt my head. "In what?"

"In whatever you're thinking I might have been in. I'm still kicking around the back lot waiting for my big break. Mostly, I go to parties and schmooze people. Like you."

This makes me laugh. "You're schmoozing me?"

"Yeah, can't you tell? After complimenting your book, I'm going to tell you how beautiful you are. I'm very calculating in everything I do."

His cynical tone is belied by the glint in his eye, and I find myself fascinated. "So what else do you do while waiting for your big break?"

He shrugs. "I write screenplays with dashing leading men that I'm perfect for. If I had any real energy, I'd write novels like you, but I'm a lazy bastard," he says with obvious self-deprecation. One blond curl slides into his eye, and he casually brushes it aside. "You should think about screenwriting yourself."

The idea is so silly, I laugh. This is the problem with churning out a novel: People think you're a writer. "I don't know about that."

"Absolutely. It's a great scam. See here, how long is your average book?"

I shrug. "Seventy thousand words give or take."

"And half of them are descriptions, right? I mean, you have to describe someone walking across the room. You can't just write, John Doe walked across the room every time he walks across the room."

Some writers embrace repetition, but even they have to mix it up a little. "This is true," I say, as the bartender puts my drink on a napkin that says *Jarndyce and Jarndyce* in bright blue letters under the Sunset logo. I'll have to snag a few of those for my scrapbook.

"That's the beauty of the screenplay," he says enthusiastically. "You can write John Doe walked across the room every single time. And it taps out at, like, fifteen thousand words. That's—what?—a short story for you. Now, some people will go on and on about structure being very important and impossible to master. Don't let them intimidate you. You can pick that stuff up in no time. It's easy. I'm telling you, screenplays are Hollywood's dirty little secret. Minimum effort, maximum reward."

I can't figure out if he's serious. People play down the importance of what they do all the time. I'll never admit paralegaling is vital and necessary to the legal process but sometimes it very much is. And often it's hard work requiring more than half a brain (but I'll never admit that either).

I take a sip of club soda and promise to take screenwriting under advisement.

He doesn't believe me. "Seriously, you've got one of the best agents in the city. You write a screenplay and I absolutely, positively guarantee he could sell it for half a million bucks. Maybe more."

As much as I want to dismiss his claim as hyperbolic nonsense, I can't. I stand to make that much when *J&J* goes through. Inconceivably, the amount I could get for the movie is fifty times more than I got on the advance for the book. That's lifestyle-changing money. Imagine pulling in that kind of cash for what is essentially a short story.

It's mind-boggling.

Harry has my attention now and he knows it. "Here, I'll write down a few titles of books you should read. Or there are courses you can take. UCLA and USC film schools are the obvious ones. Or I could hook you up with some writers if you're not into the classroom experience. A lot of people find one-on-one to be really helpful. You don't have to fight for the attention of the instructor with two dozen other hopefuls who have equally brilliant ideas. Trust me, I know. I got my MFA at USC and it was a constant struggle."

He hands me the napkin, which I glance at thoughtfully. It wouldn't hurt to take a look at one of the books to find out exactly what is required of screenwriting. After all, I already have one of the best agents in the business working for me. And he described it as writing for nonwriters—isn't that me?

"I also added my e-mail address," he says, pointing at the napkin as I tuck it into my purse. Harry looks at his watch and says he should be going.

"The *Wallabee Brothers* premiere. There's supposed to be a fabulous dinner spread and I'm starving."

He says it so seriously, I can't help laughing.

Harry winks. "Hey, I'm just an honest freeloader trying to get by."

After he leaves, the party starts to wind down. I find Elaine by the gift bag table, which is completely empty. With a Gucci wallet, a Tiffany key chain and Stila makeup, the bags were a hot commodity.

"They were gone in the first half hour," Elaine says. "My mom didn't even get one."

"Me neither," I realize.

"Don't worry. I've got you covered. I figured there'd be a run, so I left two in my room."

I thank her for her remarkable foresight and sigh. I'm amazed how relieved I am that this is almost over. Being feted is wonderful and amazing, but now all I want to do is get out of these killer heels and eat something. The butterflies that taunted me all day have finally gone away.

Kevin from Maire invites us to the after-party with Lloyd and Moxie, but neither one of us is up for it. Instead, we return to the Marmont and order a feast from room service, everything from seared monkfish to mini-burgers. She tells me about her party (stealing a copy of the book from someone's gift bag to give to Moxie's people) and I tell her about mine (Moxie's complete vapidity).

At twelve she leaves, and although I expect to be up all night reliving recent glories, I'm out the second my head hits the pillow.

Golden rays wake me again at dawn, and for the second morning in a row I watch the sun spill over Los Angeles. The light falls over the city, first the hills, then the houses, then the skyscrapers, with breathtaking splendor. Lying there, my back against a soft feather pillow, my head filled with memories of the night before, I think L.A. is the most beautiful place on earth. I watch the show, feeling a strange sort of peace, a consuming optimism that paints a future more vibrant than anything I've ever imagined. Life is a series of opportunities just waiting to present themselves; all I have to do is reach out and grab them.

They don't call it the dream factory for nothing.

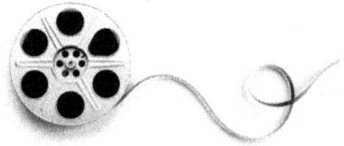

Day 825

MY NATIONAL TELEVISION debut consists of a one-second shot of my hands as they close a copy of *Jarndyce and Jarndyce* after signing it for the *Access Hollywood* cameras. The interview itself had lasted ten minutes, and while I wasn't naïve enough to think they'd actually air the whole thing, my enthusiasm led me to believe they'd use at least part of it.

In fact, *J&J* isn't mentioned at all in the forty-five second segment. In a voiceover, Shaun Robinson introduces the piece by announcing the stars turned out to celebrate Moxie's newest project. It cuts immediately to the starlet talking about the role of a second-year law student who interns at a high-powered firm in Manhattan. "It's a great opportunity for me to transition to older parts." Then it jumps to Lloyd saying he thought of Moxie the second he read the book. "It's a smart role and she's a smart girl. I knew it would be a perfect fit." Next it shows scenes from the party, flashing from one celebrity to another: Kitty Dunleavy, Pammy Hester (the statuesque blond), Bella Masters and this year's British Idol winner. Bella broods sultrily for the camera—as an heiress and notorious sex kitten, it's her only talent—and says she wants to be cast in the film. In her sly announcer voice, Robinson says, "Well, America, you heard it here first," as the segment closes on the tips of my manicured fingers.

Not all the press coverage is like that. *Us* magazine ran a contest to win the gift bag from the party and included an image of the book. The blurb that ran along side included my name in boldface. *People* mentioned me (roman type) in a full-spread piece about party-hopping with Moxie. After Boodle's, she dropped by the *Wallabee Brothers* premiere, then the Fenix for a friend's birthday and the Whiskey for an album release. During the evening, she has two costume changes and by the time she's rocking to Dave's Cousin's Band, she's wearing a miniscule black skirt and six-inch heels. *Life*

& Style, OK, Hello and *Star* also cover the event, including my name and the book somewhere in their item.

The best moment of all is when *Hollywood Reporter* quotes me. I get in two full sentences about the strangeness of the experience. "It's beyond real," I say. "Writers from New York never stand on red carpets while photographers call their name." It was on the tip of my tongue to say paralegals, but I managed to catch myself at the very last second.

The *Hollywood Reporter* article is the extent of my quotations. I'm happy with it (Lloyd had only one sentence) but disappointed that none of my other finely honed sound bites made it to print. My expectations were high, but it's not my fault. Six magazines interviewed me about everything from my dress to my favorite Moxie movie. They seemed interested, but now I know they were only being polite. It would have been terrible rude to simply turn away in boredom when the publicist introduced them to the author of the book.

I wish they had.

The fall to earth, precipitated by the *Access Hollywood* piece but aided by sluggish book sales, is hard and brutal. I thought the party would have far-reaching implications in my life but it's hardly a blip on the radar.

I return home Sunday night, and my life immediately resumes its normal routine. I get up Monday morning at seven, do forty minutes on the elliptical at the gym, make oatmeal for breakfast, watch *Live with Kelly,* check e-mail, talk to Carrie, scavenge for lunch, take a practice LSAT, score it, take another practice LSAT, have frozen pizza for dinner and go to sleep. On Tuesday, I wake up and repeat.

It's like the party never happened.

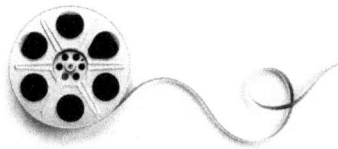

Day 828

WHEN QUENTIN TARANTINO drops out of *The Hanging Judge at Midnight* movie, Carrie e-mails me the clipping under the subject heading of a winking emoticon. She has set her Google alerts to let her know whenever the competing project is mentioned in the press. In recent months, the references have been considerably less frequent, which is a relief to me. I know it's not a contest and yet I can't help but feel like I'm locked in a head-to-head struggle with the other book.

The Hanging Judge at Midnight is a fictionalized tell-all about a notoriously eccentric supreme court judge by a disgruntled former clerk; it came out two weeks after *J&J*. Although the author swore up and down that the story was pure invention, everyone knew Delacourt Hardscrabble was a thinly veiled Delano Scabbard. The judge's famous quirks—raw eggs for breakfast, rendering judgments in haiku, his maniacal temper, a beloved Colt 45 called Corky that goes everywhere with him—were all in evidence as well as a few that never got airtime before like the honey-and-oatmeal mask he applies every night to keep his sixty-eight-year-old skin looking young and fresh.

The novel was scathing, revealing more about the depth of author Jonas Woodsmith's anger at being abused by one of the most prominent men of the twentieth century than about the most prominent man himself. Still, it was an excellent career move for a junior law clerk who barely lasted six months on the job.

The tabloids ate it up, as did the public, who couldn't wait to read salacious tidbits about the judge who had sent thirty-five men to their death in Dallas. The reviews, universally negative save for an inexplicably fawning one in *EW*, did little to slow sales. People were greedy for every last detail.

Into this feeding frenzy somehow slipped *Jarndyce and Jarndyce,* which was cited as further proof that the slaves were turning on their masters. Taken together, our novels were seen as disturbing proof that young people today are no longer willing to serve their time in the trenches. No, we are all impatient, grasping and ungrateful peons eagerly waiting for a chance to bite the hand that feeds us.

The comparison struck me as grossly inaccurate—I had no access to power and could therefore not betray it—but I gladly rode Woodsmith's coattails, especially when they carried me to the magazine section of the Sunday *Times*. My novel was a mere footnote to the larger story on Woodsmith but a mention in the *Times* is a mention in the *Times*.

I was giddy for a week and only came down from the high when *Variety* announced that Universal bought the rights to *The Hanging Judge* for $700,000. It didn't seem fair that a book with such terrible reviews could be worth so much money, but notoriety has its own accounting system.

David Fincher immediately signed on to direct. Eight months later, Ron Howard was at the helm. Since then, a series of rotating names has been suggested for the top position. Not a single part has been cast. I, meanwhile, have Moxie.

If filmmaking is a race, then it's a long hike to the finish line. *The Hanging Judge* just doesn't seem to have the endurance. What a tremendous coup if *Jarndyce and Jarndyce*, the little book that could, got there first. It's dizzying to consider.

But of course I tell Carrie it's something I never think about and ask her to please stop forwarding the articles.

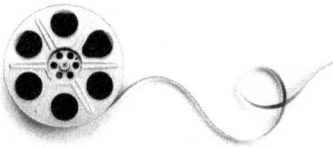

Day 840

AFTER SIX WEEKS of listening to increasingly erratic explanations of why a woman named Esperanza Diaz is answering my phone, Mom calls human resources at Hertzberg, Wright, Silver and Penn and asks to speak to the person in charge. She gets Henry, who completely rats me out. Not only does he admit that I no longer work there, he also explains her that it was my own decision.

Mom freaks. She packs a bag, bakes a ham-and-cheese casserole and shows up on my doorsteps with seven books on how to find a job, including *Careers for Dummies*. Agitated, confused and angry, she sits on my couch and announces she's not leaving until I am gainfully employed.

I try not to take offense.

There are no two words in the English language more reviled by my parents than *I quit*. Carstones never quit. Not because we're stubborn, persistent or focused but because we're terrified of change. "Hang on and be miserable" is the family motto. Someone should translate it to Latin and stick it on a crest with lions.

"It's going to be fine," I say, showing her the half-finished book of practice LSATs. After two and a half weeks of plowing through one test after another, however, I'm not so sure. It's not that I can't figure out the logic problems if I apply myself; it's simply that they're so incredibly boring I don't want to. Standing next to a copier for three hours is more engaging. "I needed the time to study for the LSAT. The firm kept me too busy."

It's truth retrofitted to meet the circumstance but truth all the same.

Mom flips through the book of practice questions and notes my scores. She nods slowly. "Yes, you do need to study. You can't get into Harvard with anything less than a 175."

I'm surprised by her ambition. When I was applying to undergrad, my parents were sensible and frugal. They said we had go to a state school unless we were willing to take out loans to cover half the tuition ourselves. But now that it's graduate school, the expense of which will be shouldered one hundred percent by me, she's all over the pricey private institutions.

Just thinking about it gives me a stomachache. I'm not sure I can handle getting a hundred thousand dollars in debt for something I don't love.

"What you need is test prep," Mom says. "Mrs. Heller's son took a course at the Y and got into Princeton. He had an excellent tutor for the logic section. Let me call and find out his name."

As Mom whips out her phone, I move her suitcase into my bedroom and quickly straighten up. Except for the Dior dress, which is hanging on the closet door, I haven't unpacked from L.A. I shove my luggage and dirty laundry into the closet and sketchily make my bed. The room is still a mess, but it's the neatest it's been in three months.

I'd let her sleep on the couch, but that would constitute parental abuse. The foldout's all springs and metal bars. It was a gift from my grandparents when I started college. Even new, it was a torture device.

Mom is putting down the phone as I reenter the living room. "There, that's all settled. Mrs. Heller's son's instructor is going to give you private lessons Mondays, Wednesday and Thursdays at four-thirty. Here's his address."

The tutor in question lives in Sunnyside, Queens, an hour away from here. There are plenty of prep services in Manhattan, some down the block, but I don't say anything. I just take the slip of paper and thank my mother.

I look at the time—it's a little after five—and wonder when my father will show up. Mom can't handle a crisis of this caliber alone.

As if on cue, the buzzer sounds.

A few minutes later, Dad steps into my apartment and gives me a bone-crushing hug. "We'll get through this together," he says gruffly.

I nod solemnly.

"Part-time work, Carl," my mom says by way of greeting as she walks over to my desk and turns on the computer.

Dad nods. "A morning shift from nine to one."

Mom smiles. "Then afternoon study from two to six."

At first I have no idea what they're talking about, but as soon as Mom starts updating my résumé I put it together. Dad stands at her shoulder, helping with adjectives and verbs. Suddenly my dull paralegal career starts to take on the glamour and adventure of spy work. Now I leverage top-secret documents and coordinate covert meetings. By the time they're done, I've practically overthrown Castro on my own.

When I point out the gross inaccuracies, Dad pats me on the head and says everyone pads their résumé.

Mom begins work on the cover letter, a two-page manifesto on the importance of a good paralegal. Seen through her prism, history is a series of clerical errors that could have been avoided with the right support staff.

The phone rings. I assume it's Carrie calling to say she'll be late for dinner—the smell of ham-and-cheese casserole is already wafting through my tiny kitchen—but it's Lester Dedlock with the news that Tipston and Field have finally signed.

"Arcadia is cutting the set-up-bonus check right now," he says. "You should have it by the end of next week."

I thank him, put down the phone and lean against the wall. Suddenly I have twenty-five thousand dollars. Twenty-five thousand dollars to save or to spend or to waste or to invest. It's my money—not a legacy from my grandparents to be used responsibly with parental oversight—and I can do anything in the world I want with it. My heart rate kicks up. Twenty-five thousand dollars.

In the living room, Mom asks my father the dates of the Holy Roman Empire.

For years, I've been waiting for something to change my life. First I thought it would be the book, then the movie, then the party. But the only thing that will ever change it is me.

While Dad Googles Julius Caesar and Mom looks up how to spell *Byzantine* in Webster's Eleventh, I run into the bedroom, pull my suitcase out, open the top drawer of my dresser and start packing my bag.

I'm moving to L.A.

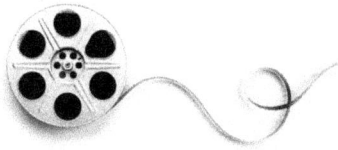

Day 856

ALTHOUGH THE *JARNDYCE and Jarndyce* movie is nothing more than a series of well-executed publicity stunts, people are making box office predictions. Omar545 estimates it will do $8.5 million on opening weekend and $26.2 gross. MoxieWhore is much more optimistic, giving it $12 million opening and $56 worldwide. You_Know_You_Like_It comes in with a dismal $4 and $10 million, respectively. He—or she—counts Moxie as a plus but lists Tom Tipston as a bigger drawback. "Guy totally sucks."

But he doesn't say why.

I sign in as Kitty_Chat_22 and post a message asking what's wrong with Tipston. I check hourly for a response but I never get one. The IMDB chat boards are frustrating like that.

The moment *Variety* announced Moxie's involvement, an entry for *J&J* materialized on the Internet Movie Database. It listed Moxie as Ada Clare Jarndyce, Lloyd Chancellor as executive producer, Hamilton Frisk as producer and six Arcadia execs.

I immediately added myself as the author of the book the movie is based on, then spent a full half hour stressing over whether to post a photo. I checked the listings of other source material writers and the results were split: Jennifer Weiner, yes, Meg Cabot, no. Since I've never liked my author photo, I decided against it.

Topics other than box office are discussed on the site. Twenty-three posts are required to establish the correct age of Ada Clare in the novel. Harmony_LA kicks it off by saying Moxie's too young to play a twenty-three-year-old. Moxter writes, "Duh, she's, like, 25 in the novel and MB could so pull it off." Stylegrrl chimes in with a "U R wrong." Sole_Diva agrees. "MB can't even act her age." Hammer8 tells her to lay off poor Moxie. "MB great actress. Ada 20 in book." LaMaestra_NYC suggests they go with someone older like Heather Henley, the Oscar-nominated star of Ingo Kagan's new film. "Dumb ass," writes I_c_u_dealing, "Henley is 18 too."

And on it goes.

Reading the posts is both painful and exhilarating. It's amazing that people, even teenage people, are talking about my book and upsetting that not a single one can be bothered to actually pick up a copy and read it.

Unable to take it anymore, I create another screen name for myself and post Ada's actual age: 29. I also add that *J&J* is a fabulous book and they should check it out themselves.

I wait days for someone to agree with but nobody ever responds. I'm the end of the string.

Being a Moxie project, the listing is inevitably a battleground for the ongoing Moxie-Millie feud, which began with a bang five years ago when Moxie's boyfriend, teen singing sensation Mark Mumm, guest starred on an episode of Millie Sherwood's tween hit, *Lolly Dolly,* and kissed her while a cannon sounded in the background, per the script. (It was the Easter special.) When Moxie heard about the scene—and that it required *twenty* takes to get it right—she was irate and immediately began calling Millie names in the press. She never actually used the words *big fat ho,* but a gleeful Perez Hilton reported that it was strongly implied.

There's nothing like warring thirteen-year-old girls to up circulation.

Their fans, perennial tweens themselves, instantly took sides. Either you were a Moxie or a Millie. Either you were a sweet, wronged girl with a broken heart or a slut. In recent years, the roles have switched. Millie has earned a squeaky-clean, virginal reputation and Moxie has become the slut. The fans don't care. Once a Moxie, always a Moxie.

There are nine conversations devoted exclusively to the feud. Dontthankme started the most recent one with the subject head Favorite Moxie Characters. "Moxie should play Millie in the movie of Millie's life!" he or she writes. HiLife_07 doesn't take that lying down. "MS could play MB better!!!!!!!!" Dontthankme shoots back with "MS can't even play herself!!!!!!!" Later in the string, someone suggests that the producers of *J&J* should call the evil character Millie Sherwood.

I don't know which character that refers to. They're all evil in their own way.

There are other threads concerned with more mundane matters like when auditions are being held and where the shooting is taking place. These posts, remarkably adorable in their naiveté, are my favorite. Imagine believing substantive information is conveyed over IMDB chat boards, that people with real power spend their days surfing discussions about movies that don't even exist. It's a network of pimply teenyboppers sitting in their preadolescent bedrooms in buried-deep places like Missoula and Fayetteville worshipping their idols.

And yet when samson&delilah posts the day before I leave for L.A. that everyone knows Moxie's not involved anymore, my heart stops.

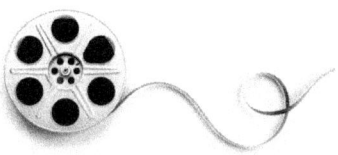

Day 863

I ARRIVE IN L.A. with a used Toyota Corolla, three telephone numbers and a check for $21,250. Each one is a disappointment in its own way. I'd wanted to buy an adorable red Miata—in remarkable condition for a ten-year-old car with ninety thousand miles on it—but my parents literally restrained me. My dad took my left arm while my mom took the right. After a long struggle in which I twisted my shoulder, they bribed me with cousin Carol's cast-off. A doctor in Westport, she just bought herself a BMW M series and was happy to make a donation to the less fortunate.

The numbers are also courtesy of my parents. The first belongs to the daughter of a woman my mother went to high school with and hasn't seen in twenty years. As they speak regularly on the phone, my mother doesn't think it's at all weird for me to call up the daughter of a person I've never met and ask if I can crash for a few days. The second is a distant cousin in the valley named Sloan Meeks. Mom insists he's a power player in the record industry but when I Google the name all that comes up is an auctioneer in Tallahassee. The third is another old army buddy of Dad's—he has one for every occasion. I refuse to make the call, so my dad does it for me. With not a spec of understanding for my deep, deep mortification, he triumphantly hands me his address and tells me I'm expected on October 15th by 5 p.m.

If I don't arrive by then, Dad and his buddy will call out the military. I can't imagine anything more humiliating.

My parents, who don't have their fingers in every single pie, have nothing to do with the check. It's my own fault that I forgot my agents split a fifteen percent commission. It's not hugely significant in the grand scheme of things, but right now, while I'm starting from scratch in a new city, the extra $3,750 would have meant a lot. It costs me almost half that to drive cross country.

Bob Pirelli and his wife, Janet, are waiting on the doorstep when I arrive at 4:46 on the prescribed day. I'm two hours later than I expected to be but of course I got stuck in traffic.

Look at me—here for less than a day and already I'm behaving like a local.

The Pirellis take me inside their split colonial and offer me a startling array of refreshments: coffee, hot chocolate, iced tea, Coke, juice, water, club soda, beer, gin, whiskey. They both talk at the same time as they run through their welcome speech, exhorting me to treat their home like my home.

I thank them, consider whether that means I can put my shoes on the furniture and ask for iced tea.

Mr. Pirelli, who insists I call him Bob, plops down in an overstuffed blue armchair and tells me to do the same. I sit on the edge of the couch. In a flash, his wife is back with a tray of drinks. I take the iced tea gratefully.

"I can't thank you enough for letting me stay," I say, feeling stupid. I would have much rather have paid for a few weeks at a Motel 6 rather than deal with the awkwardness of being a grateful guest. All I want to do is find a quiet room and hide.

Janet waves me off. "It's what we would want someone to do for our children."

"Your father saved my life, you know," Bob says.

"No, I didn't," I say, honestly amazed. My father's army career, as far as I know, was remarkable only in its uneventfulness. He spent two years filing draft records at Fort Dix in New Jersey. When he talks about hazardous duty, he means getting his paperwork-averse colonel to sign a form in triplicate.

Bob sees my surprise and launches into the tale. "We were out one night drinking to the coming nuptials or fatherhood—I can't remember which—of our staff sergeant. After my sixth whiskey shot, I remembered I had to pick my parents up from the train station and shot out of there like a bat out of hell. Your father followed me to the parking lot and wrestled the keys from me." He shakes his head. "Best damn thing anyone ever did for me."

Now that sounds like my father.

Janet nods her head, remembering the solemn occasion. Turning to happier matters, she says, "Tell us about your plans."

Without going into too much detail, I explain about the book and the movie and how I want to try my hand at screenwriting but also want to be in L.A. to keep a closer eye on the movie. "Not that I'm going to be looking constantly over the producer's shoulder," I hasten to add.

"Screenwriting sounds so exciting," Janet says. "Didn't your mom also mention something about your working in a law firm?"

"We'll see," I say vaguely, unwilling to divulge the web of lies I told my parents to get them on board with the move.

Janet asks how one goes about being a screenwriter—"We know nothing of the industry despite living here. Bob sells insurance and I'm a dental hygienist"—and I say I'm going to take some classes first. I tell them a friend's helping me get started. I barely know Harold Skimpole, but it's simpler to call him that than explain that a stranger I've been e-mailing hooked me up with one.

A timer dings and Janet jumps up. "Dinner."

We have lasagna and brussels sprouts with Entenmann's coffee cake for dessert. Conversation during the meal is surprisingly easy. They talk about their three children, and I talk about my parents. Afterward we go into the den and watch television for a few hours. We all go to sleep after *The Good Wife*.

My room is a small pink square in the back of the house on the ground floor. Lace-curtained windows overlook a small lawn, a wood shed with two window boxes overflowing with petunias and a six-foot chain-link fence. I can't see the sunrise or the Hollywood Hills or the lights of the Sunset Strip, but I have that same feeling of optimism.

Even with the sensible car and the creepy cousin in the valley and the missing five grand, I know everything's going to be all right.

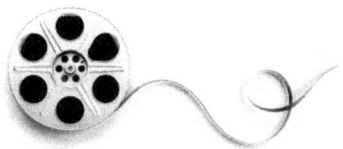

Day 865

PRODUCTION SHUTS DOWN on Moxie's new movie, *One-Way Ticket,* when she's admitted to the Vanderbilt Medical Center for severe abdominal cramps and vomiting. The attending quickly determines it's food poisoning and prescribes liquids to prevent dehydration. She's released after thirty-six hours but is too weak to return to filming for another three days.

Her publicist issues a statement thanking the public for its generous support and identifying the culprit as the samba sashimi deluxe at Samba Sam's Sushi on 12th Avenue near Kirkwood.

The story is fishy in more ways than one—who gets sushi in land-locked Tennessee on a Sunday night—and rumors begin to circulate that she had her stomach pumped. They pick up momentum when Samba Sam insists to Page Six that Moxie didn't touch her sashimi. She ate half a miso soup, drank four glasses of sake, wrote "Millie is a cunt" in her kittenish scrawl with big hearts over the *i*'s on the bathroom wall and left at ten-thirty with her entourage while her assistant stayed behind to settle the bill. Then he lists the names of six other customers who had the samba deluxe that night.

Recognizing the self-interest inherent in the restaurant owner's claim, Cindy Adams ends the item with an ellipses. It's up to the reader decide.

Star isn't so coy, and when a telephone call to the hospital's billing department turns up no cases of food poisoning for October 3rd, it declares on the cover: MOXIE'S TERRIFYING TANGLE WITH DEATH. "Moxie Bernard came perilously close to crossing the line—the little white line, that is—on Sunday night, as doctors scrambled to save the frail, one-hundred-pound star from the consequences of her own alleged cocaine addiction. Says a nurse on duty, 'She's lucky to be alive. It was touch and go for a while there. She's such a pretty girl. I wish she'd take better care of herself.'"

Impatient with the delay, the director of *One-Way Ticket,* Stewart Purcell, complains to the bartender at the Peabody that Moxie is the most unprofessional actor he's ever worked with, and that's including Horace, the one-eyed chimp from *Do No Wrong.* He sends Moxie a memo, cc'd to the head of the studio and leaked to the press, insisting that she cease and desist her party-girl lifestyle for the duration of the film. There are only five more weeks left.

Reporters are on the set Monday morning when the movie resumes shooting, and Moxie, in good spirits but still pale, swears to stay off sushi for the rest of her life. The line gets a laugh from Nancy in the studio, who says, "Me too."

In the Pirelli's mint-green living room, I switch off the television and stare at the blank screen, trying to convince myself that sushi is code for cocaine, that getting her stomach pumped sobered Moxie in more ways than one, that the young actress has repented, seen the light and changed her ways.

But even as I wish for it with all my might, I know it's too much to hope for.

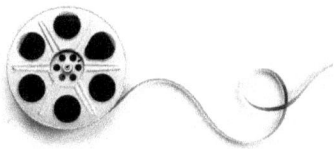

Day 871

WITH ALL THE stress from the move, I had no time to obsess over samson&delilah's *everyone knows* pronouncement. But now that I'm in L.A., in the candy-striped bedroom of Charlene Pirelli, I have all the time in the world.

I finger the numbers on my phone, debating whether to call Nadia in Lloyd Chancellor's office. Our relationship so far as been limited to my gushing over the fabulously amazing party she threw and her insisting it was nothing. I sent her and Lloyd each a box of chocolates as a thank-you but neither ever acknowledged receipt. I know they got them because I tracked the packages to their office. A Chris M signed for them at 1:23 on August 28.

A week later, I picked up the phone to play dumb and ask if my gifts arrived but my nerve fell short of open passive aggression.

Now it's falling short again. I e-mailed Nadia last week about the post, and she has yet to respond. I can't decide if her silence is because: 1) I'm so off her radar she doesn't even know I exist; 2) she's horrified that I read IMDB boards; 3) it's true and she can't bring herself to tell me.

I'm sure it's the first. She's so busy she can't even take a millisecond to thank a pathetically grateful writer for a box of pricey Jacques Torres truffles. And, really, why would she want to spare my feelings? I'm just some random stranger who happens to have her e-mail address.

Still, Lester's speech about not taking things for granted plays in my ears. This is what he meant. Nothing is anything until it is something.

The lack of hard information is killing me.

I dial Chancery Productions. As the phone rings, I list all the reasons why calling is stupid. I'm going to look like a stalker. If Nadia wanted to talk to me, she would have talked to me. I should stick with low-impact communication. I should let her control the dialogue. It would save her the embarrassment of awkward conversation in real time.

I'm about to hang up when a cheery voice chirps hello. I ask for Nadia.

"She's unavailable," she sings. "Can I take a message?"

I freeze. Do I want to leave a message? No, then I can go back to brooding and pretend I never called. And yet I hear myself say, "Yes, please tell her to call Ricki Carstone."

"And to what is this in regard?"

"The *Jarndyce and Jarndyce* movie," I explain, then cringe as the dead silence on the other end grows. "I wrote the book."

I don't know why I add that other than I feel stupid and insignificant, like some IMDB groupie trying to find out when auditions are.

"What's the number please?" she asks.

Silently berating myself for calling, I give her my cell and hang up.

Then I sit on Charlene's ruffled pink bed and wait for Nadia to call back.

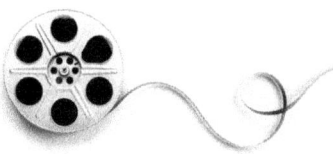

Day 876

I MOVE INTO Bleak Lofts on North Hampshire because the apartment has a large balcony where I can grow Meyer lemon trees and it's smack in the heart of a neighborhood called Los Feliz. The Happy.

I can think of nothing more wonderful than happiness and homemade lemonade.

The space is empty, and the manager hands me the keys as soon as I sign the lease. The place is mine.

By the end of my second week in Los Angeles, I'm promising to have the Pirellis over for dinner as soon as I settle in and carrying my meager belongings into a spacious apartment with an actual room for dining. We don't have those in New York, only multitasking living rooms and alcoves.

Not only is the apartment amazing, the building has a pool. I can swim laps every morning if I want to. Or every night. Or in the middle of the day when I'm feeling stiff and tired from writing.

Welcome to L.A.

As I'm rolling in the third and last load, the door next to mine opens. A tall guy with wavy brown hair, blue eyes and a five-o'clock shadow steps into the hallway and eyes me suspiciously. In ratty jeans, a gray UCLA T-shirt with holes and a torn seam and bare feet, he looks scruffy and out of place.

If anyone should be suspicious, it's me.

"Please say you're the new tenant."

"I'm the new tenant," I respond dutifully.

He nods abruptly. This information, although exactly what he wants to hear, does little to improve his mood. "OK, now say it like you're not blindly appeasing a stranger."

I try for a little conviction. "I'm the new tenant."

He closes his eyes and lets out a long sigh. "Thank God."

"Old tenant not much of a prize?" I ask, smiling at the intensity of his relief. I've had a few dismal neighbors myself. On Charles Street, I lived next to a snake charmer. She played the same six bars of music over and over for months until she was bit. They carried her out on a stretcher, and I never heard from her again.

"The old tenant was great," he says, resting his shoulder against the door frame. "Iraq War vet. Real quiet. Always asked if I needed stamps when he went to the post office. He skipped town three months ago to run a golf course in Scottsdale and left me with a conscienceless building manager who lets his niece throw raves here every Sunday and Monday night. If they were partying on the weekend like normal folks, I might have been cool with it because I'd be out partying myself but Sunday and Monday are emphatically at-home nights. Stealing yourself for the first day back and then recovering from it."

I know exactly where he's coming from. Paralegaling was all stealing yourself and then recovering.

"Well, I can pretty much guarantee that I'll be quieter than a full-blown rave. Even a half-blown one. More like no-blown," I say.

"Bless you, my child."

I laugh and realize he doesn't look that scruffy after all. His appearance is more athletic-male-fixing-a-leaky-pipe. "Actually, all things considered, I'm amazed the apartment's in such good condition. I would never have guessed it was the sight of so much debauchery. The walls are scratch-free, and it doesn't smell like a frat house."

"I was going to the store," he announces, and I feel myself blush. Of course he's going somewhere—store, plumbing, it's all the same. Just because I have all the time in the world to chat with my new neighbor, who now qualifies as one of the four people I know in L.A. (and that's counting the Pirellis as two separate people, which they really aren't), doesn't mean he does too.

"Right, of course," I mutter, fiddling with my keys.

"The store was the plan. I'm out of eggs and waffles. I need both for breakfast tomorrow. I'm big on breakfast. Keeps me going until lunch at two, which is important. But now I'm thinking I'd rather be neighborly and treat you to a welcome-to-Bleak drink. Do you have the time? Or would it be more neighborly if I offered to help you move? I'm prepared to carry small items of furniture. Armchairs but not couches." He smiles with a hint of shame, as if refusing to lug around a stranger's overstuffed sofa is a crime against humanity.

"No, this is it. I'm done," I say, relieved yet again to have divested myself of all my worldly goods. It feels wonderful to carry my life around in my arms. Like pure freedom. Even if I begin the acquisition process all over again tomorrow, I'll do it better this time—a few special pieces, not as many things. "A drink would be great. Let me just drop this stuff." I unlock the door and push my suitcase inside. "All set."

"Cool. I'm Simon Barlow." He holds out his hand.

"Ricki Carstone," I say, taking it. His grip is firm and warm.

As the elevator takes us to the lobby, he tells me about my other new neighbors: Mrs. McEnery on the right, a compulsive baker who will bring me cookies whether I want them or not ("But don't get too excited—they're always oatmeal"), and Roscoe Esterman across the hall, a curator at the Griffith Observatory.

Nothing is within walking distance in L.A., but less than two blocks from Bleak Lofts is a pub called the Growlery. It's long, dark, narrow and seedy. There are tables in a red-tinged pool room in the back, but we stay near the bar in front. The walls are covered with old movie posters from the seventies. The style of decor is familiar but none of the films are. All the usuals are absent—*The Godfather, Star Wars, Chinatown*—replaced by obscure B-features like *God Told Me To* and *Day of the Animals*.

"This is the Growlery," Simon says, sliding into a booth. Most of the stools at the bar are taken, even though it's only four on a Saturday afternoon. The clientele is a mix of journeymen and college students. "When I'm in a bad mood, I come and growl here."

"A place for growling is important," I say. "In New York, I had a breakery."

He nods solemnly. "A breakery. I like it. What'd you break?"

I think of the tantrums I've thrown over the years. "Mostly dishes but sometimes eggs or my parents' heart." I look around—at the lineup of liquor in front of the mirrored wall, at the knocked-around bar, at the grizzled floor—and suddenly feel very happy. I wouldn't have picked an apartment based on its proximity to a local dive, but I'm delighted to have a bit of New York with my lemon trees and swimming pool. "Do you come here often?"

"That's a tricky one," Simon says, "because the subtext is: Am I in a bad mood often? To that I'll say no, not anymore. Things were bad for a while but I've got a proper job now with lots of regularity and normalcy. So no, I don't come to the growlery often. But Growlery with the capital G I'm at at least twice a week. The bartender runs a quiz night on Tuesdays, which is fun. The questions are always arcane and you leave here feeling like a dumb fuck, but it's a good night out and someone has to win the thousand bucks."

"Have you? Ever won, I mean."

He shakes his head. "An honest man like me doesn't stand a chance. One thousand dollars tax-free would set you up pretty nicely around here, and people come from far and wide for a chance to win the pot. They've got their smartphone and iPads at the ready. People used to be surreptitious about it but in the last few months they're as bold as brass. Carly, who runs the quiz night and considers it a matter of honor, keeps threatening to cancel but her old man's making too much money to let her."

Just then a waitress comes by, more to say hello to Simon than to get our order. She sits down in the booth and asks him what's up. He gives a noncommittal shrug, which she takes an invitation to vent about her life. She starts with an audition on Thursday for a toothpaste commercial, which she knows she didn't get. She was the only one of her type there (smoldering Latina with huge breasts); the eight other women were blond ingénues. Before she can launch into yesterday's trespasses, the boss calls her to the bar. She's three feet away before she twirls around and remembers to take our order.

"Wren gets that a lot," Simon explains. "Most of her reel is presenting work. She's hosted a few countdown shows for ESPN. You know, the hundred worst sports injuries. But she can't seem to catch a break with the acting. This commercial agent is new. I hope it works out."

At first I think there's something between him and the waitress. He's too relaxed and aware for them to be only patron and server. But the longer we sit in the pub drinking beer, the more I realize it's simply the way he is. Simon knows names, histories, preferences. He remembers the in-laws visiting from Providence, which you mentioned in passing the last time you saw him.

By the time he walks me back to the apartment and says, "Good night, neighbor," I feel like there's something between us. It's not a lust thing. I know the fleeting stab of desire too well to mistake it for liking. No, this is straight-out friendship, the kind where you both hear the click.

Add a good neighbor to a local dive, swimming pool and Meyer lemons and you might just have the best spot in the whole entire world.

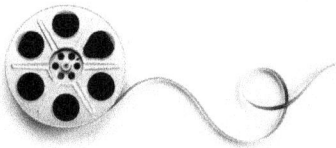

Day 885

HARRY TAKES ME to dinner at the Ivy for the full on Los Angeles experience.

"You might as well know the worst of it now," he says, pressing his hand to the small of my back as he opens the front door. "Nothing will make you feel more insignificant than the sneer on the lips of the maitre d'. It's excellent."

Tonight the part of the sneering maitre d' is being played by an emaciated Asian woman in a Pucci scarf. Although she looks like she hasn't eaten in months, she has enough energy for thorough contempt. She doesn't even acknowledge our presence until our third hello. Then, without even looking at her book, she informs us we don't have a reservation. Harry assures her it was confirmed twice and is even clever enough to drop the name of the person he spoke to. For his effort, he gets a snarl and a brusque "wait"—just wait, no please, no have a drink at the bar. Thirty minutes later she leads us to a table. Interlopers like us don't deserve the famous patio so we're seated inside with the English kitsch. The only thing saving the rustic antiques and worn chintz from complete shabbiness are the beautiful hanging baskets of roses.

Our waiter Gerald is little better. He greets us without making eye contact and rattles off the specials while he searches the room for more interesting customers. He expects us to order dinner immediately and actually sighs when Harry tells him we need some more time.

As soon as he's gone, Harry leans forward. "I'm so glad they're behaving. I was afraid they might have had a spiritual awakening or something and treat us decently."

Having lived in New York for eight years, I'm quite familiar with scorn from browbeaten power-trippers who can't wait to pass the oppression on. I know what it's like to go out on a Saturday night in your best Tory Burch skirt and your cutest top feeling beautiful and perfect and have the supermodel wannabe at the door look right through you. But Harry's savoring of the experience is entirely new. He's the first person I've met who thinks of ignominy like an attraction at Disneyland. It's surprisingly charming.

"Now, as for as the food, which was always secondary anyway, I can recommended the crab cakes," he says. I open my menu but he doesn't touch his. "They're plump and crispy, just the way your mom makes them. The Caesar salad is another favorite. Stay away from the spaghetti and meatballs. The meatballs were raw inside the last time I got it. The prime rib is also good but ask for it with the Cajun spices on the side. Some of the line cooks have a heavy hand."

As he runs through his list, I read the descriptions. I'm torn between crab cakes and spinach linguine with a peppery tomato-basil sauce. I do eenie-meani-mo in my head as the waiter uncorks a bottle of Pinot. Harry grins delightedly at me as Gerald waits for him to try the wine as if he's bored to death.

I have to admit Harry's right: It's like theater.

Our orders are barely brought into the kitchen before Gerald returns with our salads. He lays the plates on the table and disappears.

"This is my favorite part," Harry says as he lifts his fork, "the rapid turnaround. If they're in really top form, they'll bring the entrées while we're finishing our starters. It's very smooth the way they clear your dish while you still have the fork in your mouth."

While we eat, Harry reminisces about the first time he came to the Ivy—ten years ago with his parents. He was so awed by all the celebrities, powerbrokers and paparazzi that he didn't even eat his meal. He took the whole thing home in a doggy bag, another humiliation that he insists we must suffer. ("If we're lucky, Gerald will roll his eyes.")

Harry came out to L.A. to be a movie star.

"Don't get me wrong," he says, sipping the wine, "I love the theater. There's nothing like adulation from a live audience. But acting is dull and repetitive. I hate memorizing lines and learning blocking and all that other stuff you have to do as a performer. I'd much rather lounge in my air-conditioned trailer while assistants plan my lunches and squash games."

Harry's speech strikes the perfect note of irony, balancing between sour grapes and genuine indifference, but I know better than to take his words at face value. A veneer of cynicism is necessary for survival, especially in a place where failure is dished out daily. You can take only so much disappointment before it eviscerates you completely.

To Harry's dismay, the busboys wait until we finish our salads before clearing the plates. "It's a Monday night," he explains apologetically. "Things are probably slow."

But in an instant, our main course is on the table and I'm cutting into a golden crab cake. It smells delicious, but the crust is soggy and the center is cool. This is what we get for lingering too long over our salad.

When Harry asks how it is, I tell him it's yummy. He cuts off a piece of his prime rib. It's dry and overcooked but I gush about that as well because I don't want to seem like a New York food snob. In Manhattan it's virtually impossible to get a bad thirty-dollar crab cake. In fact, it's almost impossible to get a bad thirty-dollar anything. Unless you're in Times Square. But if you're eating there, you deserve what you get.

"Do you go on lots of auditions?" I ask while the busboys hover. I'm eating my crab cake slowly because it's hard to swallow but it has the desired effect of curtailing the rapid service. Harry gives me a nod of approval.

"Not anymore," he says. "They're a total drag and nothing ever comes from them." He shrugs. "True success isn't the result of hard work; it's pure serendipity. I see other actors scurrying around and worrying about their headshots and their craft—and don't get me wrong, I admire their diligence greatly—but that's just not going to work for me. I prefer shortcuts."

I laugh because I know it's not true. Only a hardworking person could say something like that. The truly lazy have to maintain the illusion of their industriousness for themselves and others.

But I don't call him on it. He has the right to whatever image he wants to project. Instead, I ask about his friend John Vholes, a successful screenwriter who teaches classes in the art of screenwriting. His course isn't cheap—it runs $995 for four three-hour classes—but it's considerably less than enrolling in the film program at USC. It's also a better value than Robert McKee's famous Story seminar, an intense four-day session with hundreds of other hopefuls. For an additional $995, I'd get personal attention. For twice that, John would work with me on my screenplay.

I hesitate. Two thousand dollars is a lot of money to an unemployed paralegal.

Harry reads me easily. "Hey, no pressure. You have to do what's right for you. The four-session course is a great intro. It'll give you the principals of storytelling and explain the ins and outs of Hollywood as a business. It's a really good start. So it doesn't get into the nitty-gritty details of the story you're telling. But it gives you a firm basis to figure those all those maddeningly frustrating points on your own. I couldn't afford it. Then again, my book isn't about to be turned into a movie with Moxie Bernard for hundreds of thousands of dollars."

He's right. I know he is. I didn't come all this way to flinch at the last moment. The cost is steep, but it's an investment in my future. If I don't believe in myself, who will?

As soon as our table is cleared of soggy crab cakes and dry beef, Gerald hands us dessert menus. I've barely opened mine before the hostess comes over and takes it away. She actually grabs it from my fingers. I stare amazed as she does the same to Harry. "The next reservation has arrived," she announces in a stage whisper. "I told you we'd need the table back."

She said no such thing, but Harry is too delighted to argue. "This is better than I ever imagined. Usually they let you finish dessert before the next reservation arrives."

Gerald places the check in the middle of the table, smiles amicably and assures us there's no rush. Now that his tip is in sight, he's pulling out all the polite-waiter stops.

Harry smirks and reaches for his wallet. "I'm surprised he bothered. He knows he'll get a straight twen—" He breaks off and pats his pockets. Then he stands up and pats them again. "I don't have my wallet."

My heart flutters. "Think. When did you last have it? In the car? At home? Did you tip the valet? Could it have been stolen?"

He sits down, rests his elbows on the table and closes his eyes. "I had it at the newspaper stand. I bought the *Times.* Then I went home to shower." He straightens up and looks at me. "It must be sitting on my dresser. I can see it there, right next to my watch, which I also forgot. Damn it."

He looks so distressed, I reach across the table and take his hand. "The important thing is it's not stolen or lost."

"Yeah, but I asked you out to dinner and now you have to pay."

"You can get it next time. We'll go to Spago and get abused there."

His bottom lips protrudes, like a sulky little boy's. "They treat you decent at Spago. It's not the same." I laugh, and suddenly Harry sees the humor of the situation. "All right. But we're going to as soon as I can get a reservation."

"Deal."

The tab is in the low three hundreds, thanks to the pricey bottle of wine Harry ordered. Although I genuinely don't mind paying it, part of me—a very small part of me—begrudges the expense. For that amount, we could have had the tasting menu at BondSt in Nolita, where the food would have been spectacular. And we certainly wouldn't have paid a hundred bucks for a pedestrian bottle of Pinot.

Pushing these thoughts aside, I sign the credit card slip and fold the receipt into my wallet. Harry wraps his arm around my shoulder as we walk to the parking lot. A few minutes later, the valet hands him his keys and waits awkwardly for something—a tip, I realize. I look at Harry and then remember. I slip the man two dollars, unsure if the denomination is appropriate.

At my apartment building, Harry walks me to lobby and says good night. I thank him for dinner.

"You're welcome," he says, "but I should be thanking you."

I shrug, wondering what I'm supposed to do next. Even though I paid, this is his date. If it is a date. Maybe it's a business meeting. We did talk about his friend John. Or maybe he's just welcoming me to the neighborhood, like Simon. Our drinks at the Growlery were definitely not a date.

My doubts are laid to rest when he leans down and kisses me. His lips are hot and urgent, and my heart leaps in response. It's been too long since I've felt this way.

He pulls back, lays his forehead against mine for a brief moment and steps away. "I'll call you," he says, pressing the call button for the elevator. It arrives immediately and I get inside, holding the doors open as he leaves the building, walks down the path and climbs into his car. When he drives away, I let them close and float up to my apartment.

I love L.A.

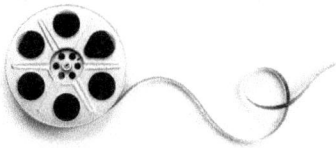

Day 895

MOXIE RAMS HER silver Porsche 911 Turbo into the pink-and-yellow van of Petal Pusher Florist at the corner of Sunset and Larrabee on Wednesday night after having drinks with an unidentified female friend at Le Dome's famed circular bar. Moxie escapes with only minor cuts and bruises while the driver of the van is loaded onto a backboard and taken to the nearest hospital.

As paparazzi swarm, a shaken Moxie extricates herself from the airbag and runs into the Easy View diner next to the Viper Room to escape the attention. She reappears a few minutes later to retrieve her purse from the damaged car, then hides in the diner's bathroom until her mother arrives. The police gather statements outside while the young star pulls herself together.

"She seemed very upset when she ran across the street," reports one bystander. "Her face was red and she was in tears. I think she was in shock. I told the EMTs. I hope she's all right. *The Nancy Drew Files* is my favorite movie."

When Moxie reemerges three hours later to tell her version, she claims the accident was caused by rabid photographers chasing her down Sunset Boulevard. She was only trying to outrun them when she sped through the light at Larrabee.

The story makes the rounds on the 11 o'clock news, but by Thursday morning conflicting reports emerge.

"I didn't see any photographers on her tail," says an eye witness. "I was buckling my little girl into her car seat and all of a sudden this car comes racing out of nowhere. It was the only car for blocks, and I remember thinking how dangerous it was and good thing my daughter wasn't in the street. Then I heard the crash. Poor Willow was so scared, she started crying."

Two dozen other witnesses and eight traffic cameras corroborate this account. Nobody believes the paparazzi story, especially not Julien Zevon, Mr. Petal Pusher himself, who immediately brings a multimillion law suit against Moxie for reckless endangerment. During the second hour of *Good Morning America* he charges the Los Angeles County Sheriff's Department with conspiring to cover up Moxie's drunkenness. "Why did it take three hours for them to give her a Breathalyzer?"

While pundits extrapolate what a .07 blood alcohol level three hours after the fact means, gossip columnists speculate what in her purse was so important she braved swarming photographers to retrieve it.

"Her stash of blow?" asks TMZ, voicing the thought had by Moxie watchers everywhere.

"Why do you think she went into the bathroom. Hello? The toilet. Everyone knows it's the best place to dispose of illegals," adds Carmen Cardosa of HotScoop.com.

While the speculation flies, Moxie's publicist, Jessica Hornet, sticks closely to the paparazzi story, insisting that photographers giving chase on foot are just as terrifying as those in cars. She cites their immediate presence as proof of their culpability. They were at the scene of the accident as soon as it happened, ergo they must have caused the accident.

The logic is dizzying and takes Matt Lauer, a senior correspondent and a dry-erase board five minutes to figure it out.

I watch the story unfold with a growing sense of detachment. At first I'm incensed at the paparazzi. There are enough things that can go wrong with a movie in Hollywood without voracious photographers running your star off the road. In my head, I write letters to the editor, invoking the name of Princess Diana and calling for sweeping changes in the paparazzi laws. Ten years minimum for tailgating.

For once this is something I can control. Public outrage will lead to a political response, which will make Moxie just a little bit safer.

But then the truth comes out, and I realize it's just another act of an out-of-control teenager. They all trash their parents' cars. It's a rite of passage.

In many ways, this is a comforting thought. Seeing Moxie as a run-of-the-mill eighteen-year-old gives her an edge of invulnerability. Every generation has its parties and designer drug, and every year millions of teens emerge to become mature, responsible adults who pay FICA and mow the lawn.

There's nothing new here.

But even as I try to remain calm and reasonable, I can hear Carrie and Ruby listing all those who didn't make it. Marilyn Monroe. Judy Garland. John Belushi. River Phoenix. The list is long and predictable, the story as boring as it is sad.

By the end of the third day, when the police swab the bathroom at the Easy View looking for evidence of cocaine, I know I have to stop thinking about it. Obsessing over Moxie's life, worrying over every choice she makes or doesn't make, is slowly destroying me. Because all I can think of as I imagine her mangled body at the wheel of a silver Porsche 911 Turbo is myself. Rehab I can work with. Death I can't.

I know I can't save Moxie. I can't sit her down in a quiet room and make her understand that the streets of Hollywood are littered with drugged-out rag dolls like her. That's for someone else to do, her mother, maybe, when she sobers up, or her manager.

But I can save myself.

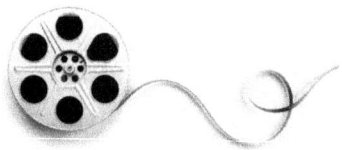

Day 896

IN AN AGE of self-conscious facial hair, John Vholes takes it to the next level with unreconstructed muttonchops. Epic, they start nimbly as sideburns, tread thickly across his cheeks and bloom into wholehearted bushiness along the line of his jaw. His naked chin, like a swath of cleared underbrush in a primeval forest, seems to point the way forward.

I like him instantly.

He greets me at the door to his studio with a glass of milk. "Rule number one," he says, "calcium is essential for strong bones."

I wrap my fingers around the glass and follow him inside.

Like every other home owner in Los Angeles, he has a small guest house in his backyard, a white clapboard building with bright blue shutters, and it's here that he's set up shop. The space is spare but comfortable. A maroon couch runs along the black wall and faces a well-used table buried under several stacks of scripts. There's a laptop computer at one end and a tray of chocolate chip cookies at the other. Off to the left side, adjacent to the French doors, which lead out to a stone patio, is a compact galley kitchen, the kind you frequently see in New York City apartments.

"Sit, sit," he says, indicating to the couch. He brings over the cookie tray and places it on the cushion between us. I eye them hungrily. Per my new habit, I skipped lunch this morning to take a dip in the pool, which was empty. As far as I can tell, I'm the only one in the building who uses it.

John pushes the cookies closer to me. "Please take as many as you want."

I don't see the connection between snack time and screenwriting, but I'm willing to give him the benefit of the doubt, especially since the chocolate chips are so warm and gooey they practically melt in my mouth.

"These are delicious," I say. "Did you make them?"

"Got 'em from a bakery on La Cienega. Rule number one: Never waste time doing something yourself that someone else can do better."

I snag another cookie. "In that case, I'll let you buy all my baked goods from now on."

He smiles, and the lush jungle on his cheeks flutters as if in a breeze. "You can put in your order at the end of the session. So I'm gonna get right into it in unless you want to run through a few getting-to-know-you exercises. Some people find that helps to get their creative juices flowing."

I'm pretty confident that my creative juices, if they exist at all, don't respond to familiarity, so I shake my head. "Nope, let's just do it." I take a pad and pencil out of my bag.

He crosses his legs and leans back against the thick cushions. With his relaxed air and crazy muttonchop beard, he looks like a Victorian Buddha, Chester A. Arthur at the knee of Siddhartha. "Good. Rule number one: Your very first line should be your inciting event, not the second line, not the third and not, God forbid, the fourth. Jump right into the story. Some people will say it's OK to take a few pages to get there. They're wrong. Do it immediately and never look back. It's the only way to grab your reader."

Nodding, I scribble: No. 1 rule—make first line inciting event. Grab reader immediately.

I underline *immediately* four times.

Vholes continues at the same breakneck pace for the next three hours. He explains what an inciting event is and how it effects the entire screenplay. He has dozens of examples, all of which he's memorized, and he goes through the list as if reciting the lyrics to a favorite song. One flows melodiously into the next.

At first, I write down each example but my hand tires quickly and I realize three are sufficient. After a while, he's no longer making his point so much as showing off.

As he talks, I apply rule number one to the screenplay I hope to write. I plan out the first scene: High school senior opens mail box, takes out thin envelope from Harvard and sees he's number five on the wait list.

No, that's already wrong. The first line has to be the incident that kicks off the entire action. So forget the mail box and opening the envelope: Start with the kid's eyes, the shock and disappointment as he realizes he didn't get into Harvard. But all is not lost: number five on the wait list!

The first scene is so solid and clear, I feel some of my anxiety fade. The last few weeks have not been easy. Shaken by samson&delilah's know-it-all tone and Moxie's accident, I've second guessed my decision to move here a million times. I'd sit on my balcony, with the blindingly beautiful California sun shining down, and wonder what I was doing three thousand miles from my career and everyone I know. I should be home, studying for the LSAT and shopping for kitchen cabinets with my sister.

It got so bad, I even bought a new book of practice tests. I promptly sat down in the café, ordered a low-fat latte and applied myself to logic problems, zipping through the section with a breezy ease I've never experienced before. Here, I thought, relieved that the logical part of my brain had finally kicked in, was the omen I was looking for. I'd buy my return ticket first thing in the morning and put this whole mad escapade behind me.

I am enough of a Carstone to regret change.

But as soon as I started grading the test, I realized my easy comprehension wasn't because I was suddenly full of logic but because I'd already taken this exam.

No wonder Mary and her 5:05 out of Saratoga seemed so familiar.

Disappointed that the fates weren't pushing me in a particular direction, I stayed in the café for the rest of the day, drinking coffee and reading magazines. I flipped through twenty and not a single one contained an indication of what I'm supposed to do with the rest of my life.

The universe is never there when you need it.

During the three-hour session, John stops only once, to refill my glass with milk. I tell him it's not necessary, but his commitment to calcium and good bones is resolute. He brings out another tray of cookies, ensuring that my faith is just as strong.

John treats screenwriting very seriously, as an art form worthy of years of hard work and study, and he shares none of Harry's cavalier attitude. He believes there are far easier ways to make a living than writing scripts and cautions me against getting involved if I'm not willing to submit myself entirely to the craft.

I am, I think, as he moves on to the next point. I really, really am.

I'm ready to submit myself entirely to *something*.

John's passion is in every sentence he utters. His talk on characterization is fervent and precise. "Rule number one," he says, "we have to root for your hero. He or she has to be likeable, vulnerable, with clearly identifiable and generally relatable goals. Someone you'd want to be friends with. Make him human. Look around you at the people you know and figure out what makes them real. Break them down to their elements. Rule number one: Humanity is in the details. Identify their quirks and use them. That's how you create a believable character. You're not aiming for Superman here. Nobody likes perfection. Give your hero a judicious amount of faults, just enough to humanize him without pushing him over the edge into a disaster waiting to happen. That makes people uneasy. You want your film to be a hundred percent watchable."

At first I think his constant use of "rule number one" is a verbal tick or a lazy speech pattern he's never bothered to correct, but I soon realize it's a by-product of his conviction. He believes in all his axioms equally. Rule number one: Everything is rule number one.

Far from being annoying, this vehemence, so unexpected in a man who has muttonchops—I mean, seriously, they have to be an ironic comment on goatees and soul patches—is oddly endearing. The more ardently he talks, the more I like him.

We wrap up day one at the end of act one, at which point the inciting event turns into a decided course of action. This is where poor wait-listed Tad Johnson realizes the only way to ensure his admittance into Harvard is to knock off the four people ahead of him in line.

My story is a black comedy, like *War of the Roses* and *Heathers*. It's dark and a little twisted with flashes of humor. I hope Lester will like it and want to represent it.

When I try to bring up my movie idea with John, he quickly interrupts and explains that he can't discuss script specifics during this class. "We're doing intro to screenwriting, which is an overview of the industry. Getting into the details of an original project is the next level, which requires a different pricing structure. It's all been formalized by the guild and has nothing to do with me. I'm sure you understand. The rules are in place to protect both of us."

"Yes, of course," I say, embarrassed to have stepped over the bounds. I hate not knowing proper etiquette.

John nods. "So next week we'll do act two. Cookies OK or would you like to try the brownies?"

"Brownies," I say immediately.

John walks me to the door, promising to pick up a box of chocolate chips cookies for me to take home. Warmed by his generosity, I assure him it's not necessary, but he won't listen. "I'm allowed to spoil my new favorite pupil. You have a lot of talent, Ricki, I can see it, and I want you to think carefully about going all the way. It's not something I recommend to everybody, but I think you could do it."

Life, so recently dreary as I contemplated a spread of Oprah's favorite things in *O* magazine, suddenly seems flooded with possibilities. I might not be a logic genius, but I have other skills that will take me farther than a small windowless cube at Hertzog, Wright, Silver and Penn. John thinks I can be a great screenwriter if I just commit. And I will. I'll do whatever he advises.

This is my future, and I have to grab it with both hands.

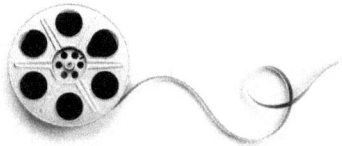

Day 912

ALTHOUGH LESTER CALLS our meeting an official welcome-to-L.A. breakfast, I expect him to spend the entire meal trying to talk me out of the move. As I look for parking, I can hear the lecture about hitching my dreams to impossible stars and setting myself up for failure. "Go back to New York, my dear, where there's a misguided paralegal for every light on Broadway." I imagine him taking a backroom bribe from my parents to play on my insecurities. I wouldn't listen to the Pirellis—an insurance salesman and a dental hygienist—but a Hollywood superagent telling me I'm wasting my time would send me scurrying to the airport.

But Lester is warm and encouraging. "I think it's wonderful," he says after the waitress takes our order. We're sitting in the back garden of a light-filled café on Sunset Boulevard. The menu selection is a brisk and efficient array of fresh-baked goods, fruits and cereals, making me realize this is going to be a short meeting. Lester's calendar is full to brimming; we arranged this gathering a month ago and still he had to squeeze me in at eight A.M.

"You have a very nimble style and tend to write quick, staccato scenes, which I think will translate well to the screenplay format. You're very talented and I can't wait to see what you do next." He pauses as the waitress brings our muffins—blueberry for him, corn for me—to the table. She refills my coffee and brings Lester more hot water for his tea.

Flustered by such effusive compliments from an experienced Hollywood player, I unthinkingly drink from the refreshed cup and burn my mouth. I try not to sputter as the steaming Peruvian blend scalds a trail down my throat. It hurts but I'm too excited to care. For days, I've been working up the nerve to ask him to read my script when it's finished and thought for sure I'd be humiliated with a brusque no, or, worse, a polite yes while inside he curses his bad luck to be stuck with yet another upstart novelist with delusions of grandeur.

"The important thing to remember is a screenplay is tricky," he says. "It takes a lot of work, and you'll probably go through two dozen drafts before it's ready. Don't lose heart. It's typical."

I nod. John had made the same gloomy prediction, and while I'm not surprised to hear Lester confirm it, I couldn't help hoping he'd feel differently. I want to be practical and realistic in my outlook, but it's hard to imagine the twentieth draft when you haven't even started the first. John is still teaching me the basics of screenwriting. This week's lesson was on the third act—the shortest of the three but the most action-packed.

I cut the corn muffin in half and ask Lester if he's heard anything about the movie.

"There'll be nothing to hear until the script's in. The quality of the material is the single biggest factor in whether a movie gets made. The story has to be on the page. If it's not, the project is dead in the water," he explains.

"When do they expect to get it?" I ask, although I'm not convinced the script is as important as Moxie. I go to the movies; I see the trash they churn out. Clearly not everyone is worried about the story being on the page.

But I don't pursue it. Lester is part of the industry—more than that, he helped *build* the industry. He has to believe in the quality of what he does.

He raises the mug to his lips. The steam curls, rises and disappears. "There's no telling. Sometimes it can take up to a year, depending on what other projects the writer has going."

"A year?" I repeat, appalled. "An entire year?" The amount of time seems inconceivably long, an epoch required by a lazy, indulgent idler who can't be bothered to have one complete thought a day. It took me six months to write *J&J*, and that's a whopping seventy thousand words. A script is fifteen. I could churn that out in a week.

Lester smiles sympathetically. "Most likely less. But you're due for a second option payment in March, which is only four months away. That's good. The longer this drags out, the better for you."

"Right," I say, but I don't need him to remind me about the second option payment. I think about the twenty thousand constantly. What little I have left from the movie is dwindling rapidly, and I need something to refill my coffers. It's either that or cut in to my inheritance from my grandparents, which I can't do—under any circumstances. It's for my retirement or when I buy an apartment or to put my kids through college. "And Moxie's still attached?"

"As far as I know."

"I hope she holds on. I'm terrified that by the time the movie's ready to start filming, she'll be in rehab, or, worse, in some fleabag hotel in Puerto Vallarta passed out on the floor."

Instead of putting my fears to rest, Lester reaffirms them. "She's a very troubled young woman. It's sad what's happening to her. But don't worry. It won't come to that. If she becomes a problem, Lloyd will pay to get rid of her. It's done all the time."

I nod and look down at my muffin, oddly dismayed by his comment. I should find his knowledge and confidence reassuring, but it's more depressing than anything else. All these events that are exciting and alarming and require intensive hours of examination are just another day at the office for him. He's lived through every combination and permutation. And that's the scary thing. If Hollywood is the same story over and over again, then I already know how this ends. Badly.

Lester motions for the check. The waitress nods and disappears inside. "If you really want to worry about someone—and I can see that you do—worry about Esther Rogers. She's the new head of Arcadia and she's brought in a whole new team of people. Which means the old regime, with whom Lloyd had his production deal and who knew his father, is out. There's no telling if the new regime is going to be interested in *Jarndyce and Jarndyce*. In the next few months, they'll be reviewing all the projects in development and deciding which they want to scrap. Now, I think we're safe because Rogers likes fun, young movies. She green-lighted *Sanibel Daze* and *Wish You Were Here* for Paramount. But that's the situation you want to keep your eye on."

I nod and promise to devote all my anxiety to worrying about Esther Rogers.

Lester laughs. He thinks I'm kidding. "Good. And I'll call Lloyd in a few weeks to discuss the renewal. In the meantime, good luck with your script. I'm looking forward to reading it." The check comes and he throws a twenty onto the table to cover the tab. "I hate to run but I have another meeting at ten."

Of course he has to dash. His life is an endless meeting with breaks in between to sit in traffic. No doubt he's off to another breakfast. I was just the prebreakfast snack. "Thanks for the muffin. It was delicious."

He smiles. "My pleasure. You are one of my favorite clients, and it's always a pleasure to talk with you. I'll be in touch," he promises with a wave as he strides down the cobblestone path to the parking lot, where his classic red Mustang is parked next to my sensible gray car. I watch him pull out and make a left onto Sunset.

With nothing to do today except worry over regime change at Arcadia, I gesture to the waitress and get another refill on my coffee. The sun is warm, the breeze is gentle, and the Peruvian brew, when not gulped piping hot, has a lovely bitterness to it. It's only a little after nine in the morning. There's still plenty of time to do a full search on Esther Rogers: her movie credits, her career history, etc. I'm happy to follow my agent's orders and obsess over someone new for a little while.

But when I finally get home after an afternoon shopping at the Galleria for a coffee table and folding chairs, I turn on my computer and Google Moxie.

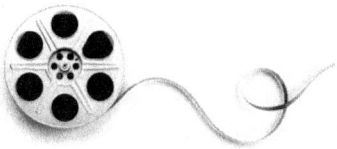

Day 925

SIMON CALLS HIMSELF sixth-generation Hollywood but on closer inspection I discover he means sixth-generation California. Having crossed the Rockies with a pick axe and a mule called Sadie, his several-times-great grandfather arrived in San Francisco in 1849 just in time to find gold. His strike wasn't huge but contained enough glitter to buy property along the Mokelumne River, marry a pretty girl named Joannie and start a family.

Still, Simon sets himself up as an expert and cautions me against getting in too deep with the movie. "Don't invest," he says, sitting on the stone wall in front of the Griffith Observatory, a sweeping dome perched on the south-facing slope of Mount Hollywood. Stretching before us are the L.A. basin and the Pacific Ocean. "Emotionally, financially, psychologically. Just go on with your life like it doesn't exist and you'll be fine."

The purpose of this expedition is to introduce me to my new neighborhood. The observatory is by far the most well-known landmark of Los Feliz, and every morning when I pull out of the driveway I see it poised on the top of the hill like an eagle preparing to take flight.

Or at least that's what I thought the purpose was. Now I'm not so sure.

"But throw yourself into the pit of expectation, into the—and, yes," Simon says deprecatingly, "I know how melodramatic this sounds—the abyss of hope, and you'll destroy yourself. I've seen it happen a million times."

The abyss of hope sounds more like a rousing IMAX adventure than a psychological condition, and I have to bite back a smile. My eyes focused on the skyscrapers of downtown Los Angeles, I tilt my head slightly and assure him there's nothing to worry about. I'm not stumbling into any abyss of hope or otherwise.

But he's far from convinced. "Some movies take a lifetime to not happen. Young men have faded into fathers and grandfathers waiting for their moment."

Although I'm the newcomer here, listening to Simon makes me feel like an experienced professional. He's not an industry insider. He's a copywriter who spends his days composing snappy descriptions of Los Angeles neighborhoods for a rental website. He knows the landscape, not the lay of the land. Just because they shot *Entourage* in your office building doesn't mean you're part of the movie business.

If proximity made one an expert, Bob Pirelli would be editor-in-chief of the *Hollywood Reporter* by now.

When I don't say anything, Simon laughs. It's a surprisingly cynical sound. "I know what you're thinking but you're wrong. I do know of what I speak."

"Sixth-generation Hollywood, right?" I say with a smile.

He returns the gesture. "Former screenwriter. My heart has been broken by the best of them: Paramount, Arcadia, Fox. Rocking Horse Pictures optioned my first screenplay six times over ten years, told me every few months they were minutes away from a green light and cut me lose without a backward glance three weeks before the supposed start of shooting." The breeze kicks up, and he digs his hands into the pockets of his jean jacket. L.A. is shockingly chilly in early December, hardly the warm-year-round paradise I packed for. "So when I say don't invest, I mean don't invest."

"That must have been hard. Did it really go on for ten years?" I ask, appalled at the possibility of waiting a decade to see Moxie play Ada Clare Jarndyce. Although, in ten years she'll finally be old enough for the part.

"Yep, ten years of living in perpetual expectation, of putting off major life decisions because I assumed the money would come through at any moment and give me more options. I lost a lot of time, wasted a lot of energy and wound up exactly where I started. Don't do it, Ricki." His tone is oddly calm for the urgency of his words. "Pretend there is no film and move on with your life."

A gust of wind blows my hair into my eyes, and I pull it back into a loose knot. Stray pieces escape within seconds but not enough to impede my view. I can see Simon clearly, his face scruffy and serious under a Dodger's baseball cap, his blue eyes intense as he looks at me with concern. "What film?" I say.

But it's only for his benefit. Although I'm sympathetic to his plight, I know it won't happen to me. Our situations are nothing alike. The world's hottest star didn't attach herself to his project the day after her movie opened at number one at the box office. *Variety, Hollywood Reporter, People, EW* and *Newsweek* didn't announce its development in a flurry of publicity that extended as far as Jaipur, India. His producer didn't throw him a fabulous Hollywood bash with studio execs, thousand-dollar gift bags and Moxie Bernard.

Most movies don't make it. Everyone knows that. The cards are stacked against it, but sometimes it does happen. A book moves effortlessly from page to screen. There's no rhyme or reason as to why one crosses the finish line and another never gets out of the gate. It's random and arbitrary, and I don't know why my fairy god producer looked down on *J&J* from the heavens and decided it will be one of the lucky ones. All I know is he did, and I'm grateful.

"You said first screenplay. Were there many others?" I ask because I feel guilty for not being more interested. Simon's ten-year ordeal, his lapsed option and heart full of thwarted dreams means he's already failed. There's no redemption from a thirty-five-square-foot cubical in the downtown offices of RentLA.com.

"Six," he says, matter-of-factly. "I spent most of my twenties holed up in a one-room apartment on Crenshaw writing spy thrillers. I was obsessed with Graham Greene and John le Carré. *The Lindell Assignment,* the one Rocking Horse toyed with for ten years, was a total knockoff of *The Secret Agent*, even down to the plot to blow up the Greenwich Observatory. I didn't even have the creative energy to change it to, say, I don't know, this one here. That's what kills me. My most immature attempt—what was essentially my senior project at USC—went the farthest. There were nibbles for the other projects but no bites. Three years ago, when the project fell through once and for all, I got out. I wanted to have some control over what happens to me, rather than endlessly waiting for someone else to decide my future."

I wrap my arms around my legs, huddling for warmth, and look for some sign of bitterness, but there isn't any. He's calm and detached. "Did you think about moving?" I couldn't imagine living here, in the middle of the film industry, in what is basically a company town, after it had spit me out.

His eyebrows dart up in surprise. "Leave L.A.? Never. I love everything about it—the weather, the ocean, the way nature trails butt up against the freeway. I even love traffic. It gives you time to think. I do some of my best writing in the car."

I picture him in his little mint green VW Bug dictating into his iPhone and laugh. "It's a lucky man who loves the bars of his cage," I say with genuine envy. "I can't stand traffic. Forget the soul-destroying effects of perpetual expectation. Try perpetual frustration. My blood pressure must be through the roof by now. Every time I get stuck, I have to fight the urge to get out and walk, even on the 405. I'm always late now wherever I go, and I used to be the most prompt person I know. I hate having a car. The price of gas is killing me, and I resent insurance. I should be allowed to try my luck without it. Life is a gamble, isn't it? Other than being a giant purse, which is tremendously handy, I can't figure out how the car is anything but a scourge on humanity."

"A giant purse?" he asks.

"Yeah, you know, for carrying books, magazines, lipstick, a change of shoes, your laptop. In that way, I'm fully behind the automobile."

"Of course," he says with a smirk, as if he too doesn't drive with half his belongings on the floor of the back seat. It's endemic to the lifestyle. "I tend to think of mine as a giant backpack."

I accept his gender-specific amendment and look at my watch. It's a little after two. "What time's the show?" Our curator neighbor, who I only met briefly this morning when we did the handoff, supplied the planetarium tickets.

"Three. We've got some time. If you want, we can check out the Leonard Nimoy Event Horizon."

I have no idea what that is but it sounds fabulous. "Let's. If my new neighborhood has an event horizon, then I must be introduced to it posthaste," I say, getting to my feet. The weather is still brisk, and I shiver as the cold wind blows through my sweater. Simon wraps his scarf around my neck and leads me inside.

The Event Horizon is a 200-hundred-seat multimedia theater featuring a short film narrated by Leonard Nimoy. We sit down and catch the last eight minutes and then wait five until it starts again. It's impossible to watch without picturing Mr. Spock, and Simon makes me laugh by translating everything into phony Vulcan. As I watch the credits roll a second time, I can't help thinking how much I like Simon. I trust him and want to take what he said about *J&J* to heart.

But it's so much easier to forget his advice than the movie.

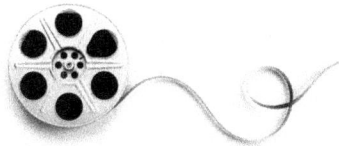

Days 946 through 953

MY PARENTS AND sister descend the day after Christmas and leave New Years morning. It's the most time the Carstone family has spent together since our weeklong trip to Puerto Rico during my sophomore year in high school, and even then we saw each only other at dinner. My parents hung out at the pool at the hotel, and Carrie and I walked the one block to the beach. A champion tanner, Carrie would soak up rays for hours, shifting her towel like a human sundial every time the sun moved a fraction of the inch, while I read trashy novels in the shade. On one particularly good day, I read *The Valley of the Dolls* and *The Betsy*.

While we wait at baggage claim for my father's black suitcase, which is indistinguishable from every other black suitcase in the universe despite the many pink ribbons Mom has given him to tie to the zipper, I wonder if the old system would work now. My apartment has a pool. Although considerably less glamorous than the Embassy Suites San Juan, it has four sleek lounge chairs, multicolored floating noodles and a vending machine that sometimes works. I could set them up there while Carrie and I cruise Robertson for high-end kitchen appliances.

I'd only have to hear about Dad's subpar packing abilities during dinner.

In the car, Mom rattles off a list of things she can't wait to do like Disneyland and Mann's Chinese Theater, and I realize I'm stuck. There's no you-go-your-way-and-I'll-go-my-way-and-we'll-meet-up-for-steaks-at-Ruth's-Chris-at-eight. We're in this together.

Oh, God.

Luckily, my parents insist on staying at the Super 8 on Western. I offer them my bedroom—Carrie and I could share the couch in the living room—but they say they're on vacation and want to be pampered. What kind of luxuries they expect to encounter at a cut-rate budget motel, I have no idea, but I don't say a word. Far be it for me to reason them out of a comfortable distance.

By the time Mom and Dad are settled in their standard king bedroom, daylight is gone and I suggest places for dinner. Their dining habits are safe and predictable. Dad likes red meat and red sauces. With Simon's help, I've pulled together a comprehensive collection of pubs, diners and Italian restaurants. I also have a list of attractions and activities like the Getty Museum, Universal Studios and Santa Barbara. The point is to keep them so busy they don't ask about my job hunt. They'd freak if they knew I was investing money in my writing career.

My efforts to distract my parents work for three days, but during lunch at the Santa Monica pier Mom pulls out that morning's *L.A. Times* and hands it to me. Nine positions are circled in blue pen. "I didn't know which ones you've already applied for, so I sent your résumé and cover letter to each. It never hurts to be too thorough."

Appalled, I picture the Super 8's inadequate business center, a closet of a room with a hanging bulb, a computer and a dot matrix printer. Apparently, that's all you need.

Next to me, her mouth full of New England clam chowder, Carrie giggles.

Biting back a cutting remark about her touchy-feely, clingy boyfriend, I pretend to examine the paper with intense concentration. "Yes," I say after a minute, "I've applied to all of these." Since I'm already lying to my parents by omission, I might as well go all the way and add commission. There's no point in being dishonest *and* uncomfortable.

"Are you sure?" Carrie asks with a big grin, spooning more soup. "I don't remember seeing you at the computer this morning."

She has no idea how vulnerable she is with her loser boyfriend. But I take the high road. "Positive. I did them when you went to the bakery to buy Mom and Dad croissants for breakfast." I turn to my parents. "How were they? I sent her to a wonderful little bakery on Los Feliz. They make killer pastries."

Mom's eyebrows knit. "We didn't get any croissants."

"Oh," I say. "I guess Carrie ate them all."

In her rush to defend herself, my sister swallows wrong and chokes. She says, "I didn't——" several times but can't get out the full sentence.

Dad pats her on the back. "That's all right, sweetie. We all know how you love to eat."

Gasping for breath, Carrie stares daggers at me.

As far as family bonding moments go, it's one of our best.

Carrie sulks for the next day and a half and it's only when Mom is fitting her hands perfectly into the cement impression of Bette Davis's ("Look at that, George. We could be twins.") that she tells me Glenn is moving in with her.

The admission is so stunning, I need a moment to regain my breath. I knew it was coming from the proprietary way he talked about her cabinets and yet I'm totally shocked. I try to imagine what it will be like to be related to him. I picture introducing him to the people in my life. Hi, Simon, do you know my brother-in-law, Glenn?

My stomach ties itself into greasy knots.

I plaster a smile on my face and tell myself it's not about me. "Congratulations. When's moving day?"

"We're thinking February. He hasn't told his landlord yet. But it shouldn't be a problem. The person he got the apartment from broke her lease, too."

I nod and try to think of something positive to say. "You'll save a ton on rent."

"I know. We're thinking of getting an iPad with the extra money."

If they're buying things together, all hope is lost. Co-ownership is the same as marriage. Wren, let me introduce you to my brother-in-law, Glenn.

The topic is so depressing, I immediately change it. "How's Ruby? Her last e-mail was garbled and confused. They're adopting a puppy?"

Carrie smiles as Mom slides off her sandal and puts her left foot into the casting made by Jean Harlow. "They're having a baby."

"A baby and a puppy?" I ask, surprised. I can imagine Lionel easily juggling the two but his wife is a little more scattered. No doubt she'd put the puppy in the cradle and the baby on a leash. "That's a double whammy."

"No, just a baby," she says. "Puppy is Ruby's term for it but she forgets that everyone doesn't know the code."

"In that case, I better give her a call. My response was to suggest obedience training and Wee-Wee Pads."

"Please. I bought her a bag of pig's ears from Costco."

We laugh and Glenn is forgotten. Hopefully he will always be so easy to dismiss.

On their last night, we go to the Pirellis for a New Year's Eve party. There are a dozen other things I'd rather do, like poke myself with needles while "Living on a Prayer" plays over and over again with deadening repetition, but I can't think of a way to extricate myself gracefully without seeming like an ingrate.

Janine envelopes me in a hug as soon as we arrive gushes about how sweet I am to my parents. "I just know she's going to be a huge success, and then we can say we knew her when."

Mom looks surprised at this, as if she's trying to figure out how a successful career as a paralegal can make you famous. She's blocked out the screenwriting idea completely. It's like I moved to L.A. for the weather.

Bob offers us drinks and leads us to the bar, where a young guy in a tuxedo is making piña coladas. "The specialty of the evening," he announces without any irony. "Our theme is the tropics. Janine bought wonderful coconut shrimp with a poi dipping sauce. Be sure to try some. It's delicious. Last year we did old Paris and made crepes. We had a small kitchen fire, which is why we ordered in. As Ricki knows, Janine usually takes great pride in her cooking."

Everyone looks at me. Carrie raises an eyebrow. "She's an excellent cook."

Bob smiles approvingly and for a moment I fear he's going to invite me to move back into the house—he and Janine suffer from a virulent case of empty-nest syndrome—but he just turns to the bar and orders four piña coladas. They come complete with a little umbrella and a plastic monkey hanging off the side of the glass.

"How delightful," Mom says, taking a sip. Unless she's at a wedding and feeling particularly festive, she usually sticks with Diet Coke. Dad's a straight beer guy, Carrie likes mojitos and I lean toward Manhattans with smooth bourbon, but we all gush over the drink like it's the best thing in the world.

Satisfied, Bob wanders off to mingle with his other guests. Slowly and with no preorganized plan of action, we each take another few sips, then discreetly leave our cup in some dark corner of the living room. We meet up again in the center by the coconut shrimp.

It's another great bonding moment.

Far from being the endless nag-fest I expected, this trip has been remarkably easy and stress-free. I've even had fun on occasion. It's like everyone sent the best version of themselves to represent them at a West Coast summit. Mom mentioned dad's luggage only once, while waiting for Space Mountain, and that was admittedly a very long line. She had to say something.

Janine introduces us to everyone in the room so we won't start the New Year off with a bunch of strangers. It's a great idea in theory but it makes for a long, boring evening of small talk. My parents love it. I take Carrie to the backyard to drink our sea breezes in silence. We sit on the plastic lounge chairs, which are as chilly as the air. I wrap my arms around my knees.

"What are you doing?" Carrie asks.

I look up. "Huddling for warmth."

She sighs loudly. It's too dark to see the expression on her face, but I can imagine it. Her mouth is turned down and her eyes are dark with disgust. "No, what are you doing out here? What's the point of this?"

Several answers occur to me, but I know they won't make sense to a Carstone. Taking a gamble on yourself and trying something new aren't valid reasons. "I'm keeping an eye on my investment," I say finally. "I've already gotten better information about the movie from being here than I did in New York."

Carrie nods—not to convey approval but to indicate she heard me. "Tell me more about this Vholes character. Who is he? What do we know about him?"

"He's a successful screenwriter," I say, trying not to be offended by her suspicion. Although Carrie is only three years older than me, she sometimes sees herself as my third parent. I blame my mom for deputizing her as my baby-sitter at the tender age of eleven. Clearly she was too young for the responsibility.

"If he's so successful, why does he have to give classes?"

"He has a skill to pass on," I explain with what I think is considerable patience. "I'm very lucky to be working with him."

Carrie is unimpressed. "What's he done?"

"None of his screenplays have been produced," I admit reluctantly.

I know exactly how she's going to react, and she doesn't disappointment. "And you're lucky to be working with him? I'd say it's the other way around. If a bunch of unproduced screenplays is an indicator of success in this business, what's failure?"

Sighing loudly myself, I launch into a brief explanation of the complicated, convoluted and often Byzantine movie industry. I tell her about the super hot writers hired for *J&J,* who cost half a million dollars and haven't had a produced film in almost a dozen years. I explain how you can make a very good living in this town without getting anything made.

It sounds bizarre, even to me. Like Carrie, I'm used to gauging material success by a positive outcome. A good writer writes a good screenplay that gets made into a great movie. Anything less seems to imply failure, even a good writer writing a good screenplay that gets made into a bad movie.

But Hollywood is its own counterintuitive little universe. Bad writers churn out awful screenplays that get made into terrible movies that do spectacularly well. The system shouldn't work and yet it does. Somehow from this trash heap Oscar Winners and Sundance selections emerge as the new classics.

Just like in a relationship, you need the bad to balance the good.

What this means for *J&J,* I don't know. I hope it'll be one of the good ones that surprise critics and moviegoers alike but I fear, given the choice of Moxie—a choice essentially of star power over substance—that it will be just one more forgettable flick you watch on a plane while waiting for the flight attendant to collect the remains of your rubbery chicken and oversalted mashed potatoes.

But these thoughts have nothing to do with Carrie's question and I force myself to return to my original point, which is I'm lucky to have someone like John showing me the ropes.

Still unconvinced, she shakes her head, like I'm the unknowing dupe of some intricate scam like a pyramid scheme. I resent her condescension and it's all I can do not to say the same thing about Glenn: What are you doing? What's the point of this? Does he really make you happy? Are you sure you can't do better? When did you stop being my sister and become his security blanket?

It's hard when you find out someone isn't the person you thought they were because you have to go on loving them anyway.

The bartender leaves at the stroke of midnight and twenty minutes later the guests follow. Carrie and I watch the mass exodus with confusion and relief.

Mom offers to help Janine clean up but she's summarily dismissed. "I have someone coming in tomorrow to do it," Janine says with a yawn. Twelve-thirty is the latest the Pirellis have been up in three hundred and sixty-four days.

As soon as we get into the car, Dad announces he's starving, and I pull into the nearest In and Out Burger. I'm not hungry but I order french fries and a chocolate shake to start the year off right. We bring the food back to their Super 8 and cluster around the small table to eat. The overcrowding and greasy fast food reminds Mom of our childhood and she starts to tear up. My move to California is harder on her than I thought.

Feeling generous because they're leaving tomorrow, I suggest we play cards like we used to when we were kids. I expect to get universally pooh-poohed but Mom's eyes light up and Dad runs down to reception to buy cards. The gift shop is closed at one A.M. on New Year's Eve but somehow he convinces the night clerk to sell him a deck. He returns to the room triumphant and ready to win. Dad has always had a competitive streak.

We play Oh, Hell until three in the morning, only stopping when Mom nods off in the middle of a hand. Carrie and I go home and open a bottle of Chardonnay. We toast to the new year, her new kitchen, my new career.

In the morning, I drive them to LAX. Against my parents protests that it's too expensive, I park the car in the airport lot and roll Mom's luggage to the check-in line, which moves slowly and takes twenty-five minutes. The man at security is nice and lets me accompany them to the gate. On the way there, I stop at the newsstand to buy everyone a cheesy souvenir of Los Angeles—an Oscar statuette for Mom, a palm tree snow globe for Carrie and a La Cienega T-shirt for Dad.

When their flight is called, Mom's eyes well up again and she gives me a bone-crushing hug as she makes me promise to come home soon. "How's Presidents Day? That's not a big travel weekend."

"I'll think about it," I say.

Dad seconds the invitation and sweetens the deal by offering me miles. Carrie snorts in disgust. "I went to London for a year and nobody flew me home free."

They board the plane a few minutes later and I hang out by the window, watching the cargo crew load the bags. Black suitcase after black suitcase disappears into the luggage compartment. The loudspeaker crackles and the flight attendant announces the last call for flight 178 to New York JFK. A few stragglers line up. As soon as they board, the gate closes and the plane taxis down the runway. It's almost noon and I have a lot to do, but I stand there at the glass, waiting until the plane takes off. Then, feeling oddly bereft, I turn away and walk to the parking lot.

Somehow, I miss them already.

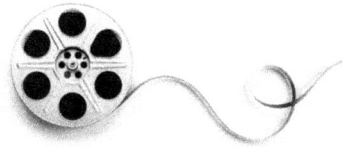

Days 954 through 962

FOR THE NEXT week, I field interview requests from every major law firm in Los Angeles. The first call is a complete shock.

"Ms. Carstone, this is Sari Gavin from Merttleson, Sleazak and Eriks. We have your résumé here and would love to talk to you about a paralegal position. How's Monday at two? Please call to confirm."

I assume it's a one-off but the next day two more calls come in from equally prestigious firms. Torn between horror and amusement, I ring Carrie at work and swear her to secrecy. Mom would open her own headhunting firm if she knew how effective her cover letters are.

At first I delete the voice mails as soon as they come in but as the week progresses, I start to save them. There's something exhilarating about being wanted, even by an industry you don't want, and I replay the messages before I go to sleep each night as a sort of meditation exercise. I close my eyes, breathe deeply and repeat, "This is Humphrey Simmons from Grear Associates calling for Ricki Carstone. We're very impressed with your résumé and are eager to set up an interview. Please call us immediately."

It's an ego trip but I enjoy the ride.

Then the Visa bill arrives with all my Christmas shopping and the expenses from my parents' visit. I don't know why I insisted on treating everyone to Disneyland but there it is in black-and-white: four 1-Day Park Hopper tickets: $420, plus dinner at the Cajun restaurant overlooking the Pirates of the Caribbean ride. We didn't even need the fancy tickets. We barely went into the California Adventure park.

Adding the credit card bill to my other expenses—rent, health insurance, car insurance, gas, groceries—I realize my financial picture is far worse than I imagined. My movie money is almost gone and I can barely account for all of it. The screenwriting classes with John are the single biggest drain but that's not the corner to cut. Those lessons are my future.

Health insurance is much more expendable. As long as I don't do anything risky like learn how to ski or bungee-jump, I should be fine.

But even as I decide to cancel my policy, I imagine the drive to the supermarket, a supposedly safe journey that now seems full of hazardous obstacles like dodging pedestrians and distracted drivers.

Instead, I contemplate life without a car. A bus ticket costs $1.50; a gallon of gas is more than four dollars. Even in New York the M5 will run you two dollars to go up Sixth Avenue.

People in L.A. like to talk as if their city doesn't have a vast network of buses crisscrossing the metropolitan area, but in fact there are hundreds of lines. The transit map is a dense spider web of veins and arteries connecting one end of the city to the other. With a little forethought and planning, you can get anywhere you want. Thousands of people pull it off every day.

The least I can do is give it a try.

My pioneering spirit lasts two days. I manage to get to get to the Beverly Center in forty-eight minutes, taking the 780 to the 14. Free transfers aren't included, so the trip winds up costing twice as much as I expect but I easily fix that with a three-dollar day pass. The return trip takes a half hour longer, not only because there's traffic but because there are so many people on board the bus stops every two blocks. This is why I always take the subway at home: Giving everyone a say in where they get off is far too democratic and time consuming.

I also take the bus to the Ralph's on Hollywood, which is much closer than I realize. My arms laden with three overflowing bags of groceries, I walk home, delighted that Los Feliz feels like a city, not a suburban development. The Happy indeed.

But then I try to get from my apartment to John's, and the limitations of the L.A. MTA are suddenly made clear. I'm prepared to suffer the indignity of long wait times and traffic and six bus changes, but his East Avenue 42nd address doesn't come up on the trip planner. It's like it doesn't exist at all.

I go to Google maps just to make sure it's still there. Yep, it pops up with a little red arrow pointing directly at it. I try entering the street name as it shows up on Google, E Avenue 42, but it makes no difference. I call the information line and am told by two different operators that there isn't an East 42nd Avenue, maybe I mean West 42nd Street. Frustrated, I hang up.

Since car insurance clearly isn't the corner to cut, I consider a more drastic measure: paying only the minimum on my Visa.

No Carstone in the history of consumer credit has ever paid just the minimum. Even as the idea flashes through my head, I can hear my dad expounding on its evils. "On a $5,000 balance," he'd say every year as he handed me and Carrie our new cards, "it would take you a staggering twelve years to pay off the debt, at which point you will have paid a mind-boggling $2,915.66 in interest, 58.3 percent of the original charge." Then we'd each get an Excel spreadsheet with interest-principal breakdowns, which we had to initial and date as proof we read it.

Even knowing this, I find the thought of paying only the minimum very seductive. Credit is a loan, and loans are paid off over time. A credit card isn't just the convenience of not carrying cash or protection against theft, it's a cash advance, money you don't have at the moment but will soon enough.

It's really not that big a deal.

And it's better than cutting into my life savings.

Still, I can't do it.

Two days later, another law firm calls, Harkness, Zoom and Schneider. I'm home but I don't answer the phone. I just listen to the message over and over. "Hi, Ms. Carstone, we think you're an excellent candidate and would make a great addition to our team. Call us at 310-555-8634. We look forward to hearing from you."

I reach for the phone three times in the next twenty-four hours. Finally, I pick it up and start to dial. Life has its own inevitability, its own built-in plot that we either can't escape or don't want to. This is mine.

The phone rings once, twice, then another call beeps in. Happy to avoid the unavoidable for a few minutes more, I click to the other person.

"Ricki, this is Lester," the voice says, brusque and businesslike and music to my ears. "I just wanted to let you know the script is in. Lloyd loves it."

I grip the phone tightly. "Really?"

"They're making a few changes, then submitting it to the studio. I'll call you when I know more. We should hear something about the option renewal by the end of the month. I'll be in touch."

And just like that, my crisis of faith is over.

I hang up, delete the messages from the law firms, pay my full credit card balance and go to sleep.

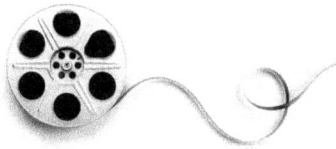

Day 967

MOXIE STUMBLES INTO Raptures at three in the morning. With the help of gal-pal Bella Masters, she commandeers a corner table, evicting several confused mechanics, and orders Jaeger shots and grasshoppers. The strip club doesn't have crème de menthe or crème de cacao or even double cream, so the bartender mixes a pitcher of Long Island ice tea without the Coke. If the girls aren't too drunk to notice the difference, they don't say anything.

According to StripperNation.com, Raptures is a cozy little strip club just off the far south end of the Las Vegas strip, the sort of homey, relaxed spot where you'd want your granddaughter to peel off her clothes to catcalls and drooling men. It's a low-key hangout with a center tipping stage, a bar and a fair-priced VIP lounge ($100, includes three lap dances). The clientele is mostly local—it gets a good after-work crowd—but in-the-know tourists searching for an alternative to the cold impersonality of the mega clubs along the Strip sometimes drop by. Horny bachelors on the prowl for the ultimate Vegas nudie-bar experience should look elsewhere.

Downing her fourth glass of Long Island ice tea, Moxie jumps up, runs to the stage, trips over the legs of a man in a Stetson, regains her balance and climbs onto the stage. Slowly at first but with growing confidence, she starts writhing around the pole, her head thrown back in wild abandon, her hips gyrating provocatively.

The man in the Stetson yells, "Way to go, honey."

It's unclear from reports whether or not he knew Moxie Bernard was Moxie Bernard. He sticks a twenty in her skirt. She winks at him, slides to the floor, rolls around, then stands up again with a wobble.

After two songs, Bella joins her onstage, and the two swing around the pole, their arms around each other as they caress.

The crowd goes wild and calls repeatedly for the girls to take it off.

Moxie opens the top button on her magenta silk top, then the next and the next until the shirt is entirely undone. Underneath, she's spilling out of a black lace demi cup bra.

Bella follows suit, taking off her camisole and throwing it into the crowd. Less curvaceous than Moxie, her bare chest doesn't arouse the same response as her friend's half-bare one.

The music shifts, from hard rock to trip hop, and the girls rub their bodies against each other, then kiss long and deep.

The man in the Stetson is beside himself.

One by one, the Rapture strippers leave the stage. It's almost the end of their shift, and they look at their watches, wondering if they should go home.

The dancing ends when Moxie stumbles to the ground and Bella pokes her in the eye with her big toe.

"Ouch," she says, giggling and covering her eye.

They leave the stage and the bar without paying their tab. Bella forgets her top and ties a napkin around her chest like it's a scarf. The patrons watch them climb into a black limo.

Gawker breaks the story with several eye witness accounts of the show. "They didn't go in for any beaver action, but it was still hot," reports one customer who had a front-row view. "It was wild. I'm gonna tell my grandchildren about it some day."

One day later, the *New York Post* prints an e-mail message from Moxie: "The media has misread and misappropriated the fun fey-gey [sic] boogie I did with Bella Masters, and I'm disgusted by how it was carried out."

Nobody knows what to make of her vaguely incomprehensible statement. Her disgust, clearly not turned inward, seems aimed at a media who—for once—reported an incident without embellishment. They don't add prurient details because the story already has them: two teenage girls, alcohol, hot lip action, a stripper's pole, Las Vegas. The editors of Penthouse Letters couldn't have done better. Even the choice of venue is perfect—an out-of-the-way spot where working stiffs who get off on naked women go to relax after a hard day at work, offering none of the self-conscious irony or the tourism of the glitzy topless emporiums on the Strip.

Moxie sure knows how to pick them.

Her publicist, Jessica Hornet, moves in with the spin immediately, insisting with increasing shrillness that her client was only demonstrating some favorite moves from her cardio strip class at Tighter U Fitness Studio.

"If Moxie got carried away in her enthusiasm to show her friend a new routine, it's only because she believes that cardio is essential to a healthy lifestyle," Jessica explains to George Stephanopoulos on *Good Morning, America* before announcing the launch of a line of fitness videos to be produced by Moxie.

But it's no use. #FeyGeyBoogie is already off and running. In a matter of hours, it trends worldwide. Suddenly, every stupid or embarrassing act is an example. "Stupid Spanx tore along seam and now ass is hanging out. #feygeyboogie." "Doh! Texted wife name of restaurant, instead of girlfriend. #feygeyboogie." "Listen up: Drinking bleach isn't going to help U pass drug test. #feygeyboogie."

The nine days' wonder lasts a full three weeks, twice as long as Queen-gate. Moxie keeps a low profile for the duration while Bella continues to turn up on every red carpet on three continents. She has to. Being famous for nothing requires constant effort.

Every day that passes without a Moxie incident, I relax a little more. It seems entirely possible that this time she realizes she's gone too far, and when she shows up with her mom at the Court Street Baptist church for Sunday morning services in a demure black suit, I'm almost convinced she's completely reformed.

But I know that's just wishful thinking.

Even in her Sunday best, Moxie is dangerously close to the edge, and each breath she takes brings her nearer. It's only a matter of time before she falls into the abyss.

I'm doomed.

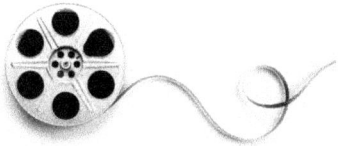

Day 978

WHEN HARRY INVITES me to *In Style*'s Golden Globes after-party, he doesn't tell me we're crashing, so when I find myself in the basement of the Beverly Hilton Hotel, I'm surprised. The red floor-length gown I bought especially for the occasion isn't made for shimmying up elevator shafts.

When I express reluctance, Harry grins at me and asks where's my sense of adventure. "Anyone can go through the front door," he says, with as much enthusiasm as a teenage boy getting his first set of wheels, forgetting, I suppose, that anyone *can't*. That's the whole point of Hollywood. "Trust me, it's entirely worth it. This bash is second only to *Vanity Fair*'s Oscar party. I go every year. I have to see and be seen. How else am I going to become famous?"

His logic is irrefutable, and I slide off my three-inch heels and reach for the ladder. We emerge a few minutes later in a dark corridor. Harry waits until I put on my shoes before opening the door. We're at the back of the ballroom.

"Mission accomplished," he says.

Overwhelmed by the glamour of the event, the flawless faces and the perfect bodies, I make a beeline for the bathroom to see how much damage crashing did. I feel like there's a far–from-endearing black smudge on my cheek, even though Harry swears there isn't.

"I'll get you a drink," he says. "What would you like?"

"Champagne," I say without pausing. Only one thing will do at a party like this. "But stay right there. I'm afraid I won't be able to find you again."

I'm also afraid of being identified as an interloper and thrown out, but I don't mention that.

The bathroom is crowded with regular women and a smattering of celebrities, and as I sit down at the vanity, I have the very surreal experience of watching Meryl Streep wait for the toilet. It's impossible to look away, and I observe her discreetly in the mirror until she disappears into a stall. I hear a faint tinkling sound and a chill runs up my spine.

If only you could sell experiences on eBay.

While Meryl washes her hands, I examine my face for damage. My makeup seems relatively unharmed by our little escapade, but my hair, piled high on my head in ringlets—yes, I paid an obscene amount of money to a woman at Frédéric Fekkai to create the effect—is starting to come down. I stare at myself, exasperated by my normalcy. Why can't I be perfect like everyone around me?

Although not clever enough to bring emergency pins, I spy a basket of products on the ledge and I dig through the collection of hairspray bottles, lip glosses, pantyhose and needles.

"Can I help you?" a soft voice asks.

I freeze, convinced that "can I help you" is only prelude to "find the door because you obviously don't belong here." I glance up guiltily at my accuser, a petite woman in a raspberry-colored ruched dress. "I'm looking for pins," I say hesitantly.

Far from tossing me out, she smiles, puts a briefcase on the counter and opens it with a quick snap. In her bag, she has the entire contents of a Macy's cosmetic counter. "Here," she says, giving me a handful of glittering bobby pins. I know the stones aren't real, but they're so sparkly and beautiful I almost turn them down.

"Thank you," I say, a little breathlessly as I close my fist around them. Whatever she discovers about me, she's not getting them back.

"Is there something else I can help you with?" she asks.

I look at her and then again at the contents of her case, grappling with my conscience. It's wrong to take free stuff at a party you weren't even invited to. I'm not so hard up that I can't afford to buy myself a new tube of Great Lash. But the selection of high-end brands is humbling. The Sisley Phyto-Proteine mascara alone costs more than any bra I own.

"Um, mascara?" I say.

The woman gives me a tube of the Sisley in black. "Have you tried their eyeliner?"

Amazed, I shake my head.

"Here"—she hands me a dark-brown pencil—"you'll love it."

"All right," I say, baffled. I can't imagine who she thinks I am. Although I took some pains getting ready, I couldn't hide my average-girl provenance. My dress is nice but off the rack and my makeup is total amateur hour. I actually sat with a copy of *Glamour* magazine open, copying the illustrations as I tried to trace the ridge of my brow line.

Still, I go with it, taking one of everything she offers, even a little sample of Narciso Rodriguez's new perfume. The makeup stash barely fits in my purse, and I have to throw away some recent receipt to make room for it. Feeling like a superstar for getting away with something—what, exactly, I'm not really sure—I return to the ballroom.

Giddy, I find Harry just where I left him. He's holding two flutes of champagne and surveying the crowd. In his black tuxedo, he seems right at home among the glittering and the elite. Nothing about his golden blond hair, handsome face and impeccable surfer-dude body says gate crasher.

He smiles as soon as he sees me. "That was quick."

I'm not sure if he's being sarcastic or sincere. One loses all sense of time in the presence of free makeup. "At the risk of sounding like a yokel, I have to say this: I heard Meryl Streep pee."

"Not at all," he says, handing me champagne. "That why we're here." He holds the flute in the air. "To Meryl Streep's toilet. May it always flush."

It's the perfect toast, and I raise my glass high. "Hear, hear."

A waiter breezes by with a tray of caviar-topped blinis and I realize that I have to eat something, not just because I skipped lunch to get my hair done but because this might be my only chance to eat Golden Globe after-party food.

"There's a table of hors d'ouevres to the right of the bar," I say. "How do you feel if we make our way toward it?"

"I was about to suggest it myself."

Having never crashed a party before, I never realized how easy it is to feel welcomed in a place you don't belong. But Harry is so confident and comfortable that I find myself relaxing despite my nerves. Standing next to him, I feel the same sense of entitlement he does and snag yet another crostini with fois gras.

It's all just a game, seeing what you can get away with.

An expert player, Harry strikes up conversations with people left and right. Some he actually knows from previous parties; others are complete strangers. His manners are perfect, appreciative but not gushy, and everyone responds. Watching, I'm amazed he's not already rich and famous. Ninety percent of success is networking and making sure you know the right people. Whatever the remaining ten percent is, I'm sure he has it. Harry is unusually well-rounded and informed. He knows something about everything. With the vice president of Imagine Entertainment, he discusses Spain's chances in the World Cup; with a reporter from the *Times,* he talks about the new production of Begonya Plaza's *Theresa's Ecstasy* at the Cherry Lane Theatre in the West Village.

Although I try to stay discreetly in the background, Harry introduces me to everyone he talks to as the author of *Jarndyce and Jarndyce.* Inconceivably, some people recognize the name.

"Moxie Bernard, right?" a producer for Focus Features says.

"Yes," I reply.

She pats me on the shoulder. "Poor you. She seems to be off the rails at the moment. Although to be honest, we'd all like to have your troubles. It's when the coked-out star of the moment won't attach her name to your project that you're in trouble."

One guy, a freelance reporter, actually lights up when he hears my name.

"I loved *Jarndyce*," he says, before launching into a brief plot description for his date. She laughs politely several times but doesn't seem genuinely amused. I try not to hold it against her. "It's all about the insanity of office politics. I work at home, so, sadly, I'm not exposed to that stuff. The scene with the photocopiers made me devastated that I don't work in an office with crazy people. Your life is so much more fun than mine."

As he is a legitimate guest of *In Style,* I'm not so sure about that, but I accept the compliment with a high blush. It's beyond anything to be standing in the same room with Helen Mirren and George Clooney and every hot young thing in Hollywood and find myself a fan.

And I thought listening to Meryl Streep urinate was surreal.

At eleven, the crowd starts to thin as the glamorous go to their after-after-parties. The superglamorous are long since gone, and Harry suggests we take off too. You never want to be the last guest at a party. "And this is the best part," he says, directing me toward the exit with a hand on the small of my back. "We get to leave through the front door."

We're passing the dessert table and I grab one last cream puff. They're not as decadent as the caviar and fois gras but still feel like wonderful, ill-gotten gains. "Yeah, but anyone can leave through the front door. Where's your sense of adventure?"

Harry laughs and instantly changes directions. We're walking back toward the elevator shaft. I stop midstride. "Nope. Just kidding."

He turns us around again. "All right, but only if you're sure...."

I smile and snag a chocolate-covered strawberry. I don't really need it but it's mere inches from my hand. "Positive. I'm the kind of girl who likes to use doors."

"I'll keep that in mind for the Oscars."

The hint of a future date thrills me, but I try to keep my expectations in check. Unfortunately, Harry's schedule keeps him very busy. This is only the second time I've seen him since our Ivy outing and the first one doesn't really count, since it was a coincidental meeting at John Vholes's office. We grabbed dinner afterward but it was at a diner down the street, a far cry from Spago.

Limos line the drive in front of the hotel, and we weave through the madness to get to Harry's car, which is parked across the street and down the block. My feet are killing by the time we get there and as soon as I sit down, I take off my shoes. I wiggle my toes, lean back and sigh. "I had a wonderful evening. Thank you for inviting me."

Harry links his fingers through mine and lifts my hand to his mouth. "The evening's not over yet," he says, kissing my knuckles.

My stomach does a backflip.

Half the point of putting on a beautiful red dress is having someone else take it off, and I don't hesitate a moment in inviting Harry up to my apartment. I make the usual noises about another drink or coffee but as soon as we're in the elevator, I lean forward, press my body against his and kiss him. Neither one of us realizes when the doors open, and it takes an embarrassed, "Excuse me," from the Griffith Observatory curator across the hall for us to notice.

I jump back but Harry holds steady. He leads me from the elevator, then waits for me to indicate the way. We walk slowly toward my door like in a dream. My hands are shaking slightly, so I can't open my door. I try once, twice; the third time's a charm.

Harry says, "Nice apartment" as soon as I shut the door and pulls me into his arms. The kiss is long, deep and mindless. A few seconds later, we're in the bedroom, falling onto the comforter, pushing the pillows to the floor. He moves the strap of my red gown to the side and trails kisses along my shoulder. Every moment from the night whirls together in a kaleidoscope of impressions, and I feel powerful like a sex goddess: irresistible, invincible, famous, successful.

Whispering something against my skin, he brushes the second strap aside and reveals my breasts. Harry moans in delight and I feel another surge of emotion as liberating as it is wild jut through me.

Clearly, I'm in love.

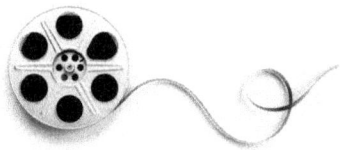

Day 980

JOHN AGREES IT'S time for me to strike out on my own.

"You know all that I know," he says at the end of our last lesson.

I've taken two four-week courses with him: Screenwriting 101 and Intermediary Hollywood. He's taught me everything from the basics of constructing a screenplay (Rule number one: The emotion has to be on the page) to the inner workings of the movie industry (Rule number one: With every film they make, they're asking, Can I get a theme-park ride out of this?). All I have to do now is sit down and write.

That shouldn't be too hard. I have my story, my title, my characters. I just need to string them together with dialogue.

"You'll be great," John adds. "I've worked with a lot of people but you're the most talented by far."

I simper accordingly.

Before the advent of my holiday Visa bill, I considered continuing with John. He offers a tutorial in which he guides you through your screenplay step-by-step. As much as I'd love to have someone hold my hand, I couldn't do it at the expense of my health insurance. I have to make sane, rational decisions, not just because I'm a Carstone but because it feels good. There's something oddly glamorous about making the right choice, a comforting sort of smugness.

It's invigorating after eight years of inertia.

"Don't let the technical details psyche you out," he continues. "You can do this, I know you can. Yes, there are lots of things to keep in mind about how to enter a scene, leave a scene, describe a scene, camera angles, interior shots, exterior shots. We didn't go over any of it but I know you can figure it out. It's pretty easy stuff. And don't for a minute believe the success of your screenplay depends on how well you conform to the rigid format. A lot of people say your success is riding on that, but they're wrong. Rule number one is story. The rest will follow. So trust your instincts. You'll figure out how to construct a montage or a voiceover. And like I said, it's not make or break if you get it wrong. Sure, some readers won't finish the first paragraph if the structure isn't one hundred percent right, but you don't want a doctrinaire like that reading your story anyway."

The more John flatters me, the more my confidence fades. I know nothing about the technical details of a script. For weeks, he's been lecturing me about multidimensional villains and classic reversals, in which a scene ends in the exact opposite place it starts. The words *camera angle* never once passed his lips.

Seeing the panicked expression my face, John rushes to reassure me that all readers aren't so rigid. "Don't worry. Some will overlook a few structural mistakes if they like the story."

Now I know he's only being kind. Readers are the people producers send out scripts to for an initial take, and for weeks John has been pounding into me their importance in the Hollywood system. Rule number one: Coverage runs this town. Any reader worth his salt is just looking for an excuse to consign your work to the dust heap. Don't give him one.

"You've got FinalDraft, right?" John asks.

I nod. I haven't actually bought the $249 software yet but I intend to.

"Then you're fine. It's smart stuff, not as smart as, say, a person who's been in the business for years and years, but the next best thing. It has all the lingo; you just need to figure out when to apply what. For someone like you, it's as easy as cake."

He snaps his fingers to prove his point and looks at me with so much expectation I have to turn away. It's wonderful that he believes in me so strongly, but I know it's unfounded. When I submitted *J&J* to Julie, it was one endless chapter of events and conversations. She broke it up into nineteen separate episodes, which my editor further subdivided until it looked and read something like a novel.

"Really, I can't wait to see what you do," John states, bringing the tray of cookies to the kitchen. "It's going to be fantastic."

Thoughtful, I watch him put the remaining six back in the pastry box and retie the white-and-red string. He sticks them in the fridge. While he refills the Brita, I consider my options. I can write the screenplay on my own and hope for the best, or I could hire the best.

Sighing deeply, I reach for my bag and pull out the checkbook.

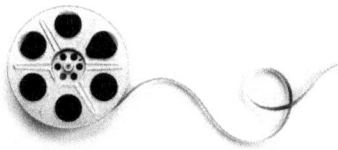

Day 983

AS MUCH AS I want to take Simon out to thank him for his help in feeding and entertaining my family, I can't bring myself to face him. His failure to have his movie made—which I know isn't really his failure and yet is somehow inimitably his—is a constant reminder of how fragile my own success is. In this town, everyone has the same story. Agents and producers and studio execs swear up and down that their film will happen. They hold meetings, revise scripts, hire actors, plan budgets. And then it doesn't happen. Then it's over, gone, not a trace remains, and you're left wondering if you imagined the whole thing.

I've heard the same sorry tale a thousand times since moving here, and with each retelling I have to work harder and harder to insulate myself. It's their story, not mine. Mine is different. Mine has a fabulous Boodle's party, Moxie Bernard and the savviest fairy god producer in Hollywood.

Simon doesn't say it, but I know he expects me to fail like he did. He doesn't wish it and would do anything he could to stop it, but he's marking time until it happens.

He has to be. The only way to cope with your own failure is to wait for someone else's.

We bump into each other in the elevator and he says he was just coming to see me. "It's been a while. I thought we could go down to the Growlery and you could tell me how the visit went."

Deeply mortified, I stare at the buttons and try to think of something to say. This is the problem with avoiding people, it feeds on itself, so that after a while you're avoiding them because you're avoiding them.

The elevator hisses and pings as it travels from floor to floor. The silence is deafening.

"I was just about to suggest the same thing," I say with too much enthusiasm. "My treat. All your choices were a big hit. Mom's still raving about Taylor's."

"That's a relief. When I didn't hear anything, I was imagining a tapeworm or food poisoning or indigestion at the very least."

The elevator arrives at the fourth floor. "No tape worms or food poisoning. Indigestion, yes, but that's just because my dad won't stay away from the things that set off his GERD. I can't blame you for that."

Simon digs out his keys and unlocks the door. "Cool. So fifteen minutes?"

"Sure."

At the bar, I get a lite beer, which is embarrassing but necessary. Since adopting the car lifestyle, I've gained eight pounds. In New York exercise is endemic. You burn hundreds of calories going from your apartment to the subway to your office to the deli on Sixth to the movie theater to your apartment. Here you only go from your car to the front door. Just thinking about it makes my muscles atrophy.

On the plus side, it's remarkably lovely to wear sexy high heels and not have to worry about your feet being mutilated before you even arrive at the party.

"So what's going on?" Simon asks.

Since I have nothing new to report on the movie, I tell him about the screenplay I'm writing. "*How Tad Johnson Got into Harvard.* Overachiever gets wait-listed fifth at Harvard undergrad and decides to whack the four people before him on line."

"It's dark. I like that."

"Yeah, total black comedy. But I know the antagonist still has to be likeable and relatable, so the first death is an accident. He's just checking out the competition and pushes the guy in front of a car when he trips on a pot hole. He's totally freaked and feels awful, but that's where the idea comes from."

"Does he get away with it?"

"That's the million-dollar question. I think yes, scot-free. I see the last shot as the camera pulling away from him as he crosses the quad with his L.L. Bean backpack. But John thinks there should be some comeuppance."

"John?" he asks, taking a sip of his full-calorie Guinness. I watch in envy.

"John Vholes. He's a screenwriter. You might have heard of him."

"Yeah, I've heard of him," he says.

His tone is cool and his smile cynical; both make me uncomfortable. "You don't make that sound like a good thing."

He shrugs.

I narrow my eyes, unnerved by his response, which is completely unexpected. "If you've got something to say, I wish you'd just say it."

"All right." He finishes his beer in one thick gulp, puts the empty glass on the table and gestures to the bartender for another. "John Vholes is a mediocre screenwriter who offers his questionable agenting skills for a sizable fee to newbie screenwriters who don't know yet that they should never pay anyone to read their work."

Heat suffuses my face, but I'm not sure if it's anger or embarrassment. Nobody has ever called me a newbie anything before, and the insult of all it implies—gullible, naïve, trusting, dupe—seeps through me. That's he's wrong doesn't make it any better. It's what he thinks of me that counts.

I take several deep breaths and wonder how to respond. I don't know whose honor I should defend first, my own or John's.

The bartender delivers a second round of drinks, bringing me another Corona Lite even though I didn't ask for one. I push the lime into the bottle before responding in a lively, indifferent tone. I don't want him to know I'm hurt and disappointed. It's none of his business.

"I don't know where you got your information from, but it's completely inaccurate. John Vholes teaches seminars in screenwriting to students of all skill levels, including up to but not excluding experienced, nonnewbie writers. His seminars are informative, educational and practical. I've learned as much from him as I would at USC or UCLA in far less time and a fraction of the cost," I say, my carefree, indifferent tone losing some of its carefree indifference as I warm to my subject. I am far more offended than I originally think. "He's never offered to agent my work for either free or a fee. He's given me advice, guidance and the best pastries this side of Patisserie Claud on West Fourth Street. He's a mentor and a friend, not a scam artist looking for an angle, and I resent your implying that I'm too stupid to know the difference."

I end my speech with a bang, pounding my fist as well as the Corona bottle against the table. The head immediately bubbles up and beers slides over the side of the bottle and onto the table. Not willing to let the spill ruin the effect, I ignore the mess and continue to stare at Simon.

He grabs a few napkins and wipes it up, making me look and feel petulant. "All I'm saying is be careful. There's an entire industry out here set up to take advantage of people like you—writers, actors, musicians looking for a toehold—and it feeds on hope. For a fee, they'll make over your image or rewrite your résumé or invite you to parties where the right people are supposed to be. For a considerably larger fee, they'll get you access to agents, casting directors and studio execs. Everything in L.A. is for sale but success doesn't have a price tag, so however much you spend, you never get anywhere. And, no, I don't think you're stupid. You're inexperienced. And I *know* you're smart enough to recognize the difference."

He balls the wet napkin in his fist and pushes it to the other side of the table against the wall.

I get it. The industry is full of businesses, organizations and people—all legitimate, which is the amazing thing—that exploit the dreams of struggling artists. Just last week, Wren plunked down four hundred bucks to meet with the casting directors of five soaps: *Love & Valor, General Hospital, Days of Our Lives, The Bold and the Beautiful* and *The Young and the Restless*. It's a workshop, not a job interview or audition, and the vast majority of participants don't receive offers as a result of these meetings. Wren knows this, and yet she still hands over her hard-earned money.

But understanding where Simon's coming from doesn't help. His know-it-all attitude, smug to the corners of his smile, puts my back up. He has a way of making me feel like my experiences aren't my own, as if they're mere echoes of things he's already done. His present isn't my future, and I'll thank him to stop acting like it is.

Still, I don't want to seem defensive so I promise, with quiet dignity, to keep his concerns in mind.

He sees right through me. "You're annoyed."

I take a sip of beer and look over his shoulder at a poster for a movie called *The Van* starring Stuart Goetz. "No, I'm not."

"You are," he says, grabbing my hand and squeezing. "You're sitting there calculating how many minutes it'll take you to finish your drink so you can walk out and never see me again. Don't deny it. Your face is very expressive. All right then, I'm sorry. I overstepped my bounds. I wouldn't have done it but—" He breaks off, shakes his head. "Nope, I won't say it. See? I've learned from my mistakes. You've made me a better person. Thank you."

His expression is such a mixture of eagerness and pride, I can't help laughing. His reformation is probably as sincere as it is long-lived, but I give it to him. Holding grudges isn't my strong suit, unless it involves my sister's boyfriend.

With surprising tact—perhaps he did learn a lesson after all—Simon changes the subject entirely, entertaining me with stories from a recent bachelor party camping trip to Kings Canyon with a group of rank amateurs who'd never set up a tent before. "Once the stripper showed up, it got very *Blair Witch* very fast. And by that, I do not mean the shaky camera work," he says.

I finish my beer and the bartender brings me another. Simon's camping disaster culminates with a pair of flat tires outside Sequoia National Park. I follow that with the story of how my college roommates and I spent three days in Yahoo, Mississippi, with a broken timing belt.

Two hours later, I've completely forgotten why I'm annoyed at Simon. He's kind, funny, smart, easygoing and charming enough to cajole a rattlesnake out of its bad temper.

In my tipsy mood, his disheveled hair and five-o'clock shadow start to take on the sexy appeal of a cologne advertisement. Simon's a man's man: woodsy, outdoorsy, self-sufficient, athletic.

At midnight, I push these thoughts aside and suggest we leave.

Somewhat unsteady, I hold on to his arm during the ten-minute walk to Bleak Lofts. When we get there, I decide to take the stairs for the exercise but the elevator is waiting and he pulls me into it. The space is small and confined, and I recall how just hours before we'd been in the exact same situation, although then I was avoiding him and now we're best friends.

When we reach the fourth floor, Simon takes my hand and leads me down the corridor to my apartment. Like a gentleman, he waits until I unlock the front door before going home himself. I tell him he's really too sweet to exist, but he just laughs and points out that home for him is two feet to the right.

I know he has a point, but it still seems like a mighty impressive courtesy, and I kiss him on the cheek, adding a heartfelt "my hero."

Simon laughs. "You are so drunk."

I shake my head and say "nuh-uh," vaguely aware in some part of my brain that the use of such a juvenile, schoolyard response can only mean total inebriation.

He laughs again and brushes his finger against the tip of my nose as if I am indeed a little girl. "Get some sleep."

I nod but don't move. He gently pushes me inside, reminds me to lock my door and goes home. Willfully disobedient, I stand on the threshold for a long while, thinking about Simon.

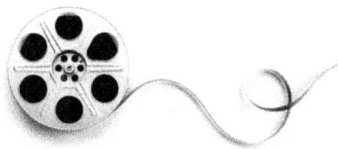

February 1

THE SECOND I hear Lester's voice, I know. It's all there in the pitch of his hello, an entire universe of disappointment couched in a single syllable.

Bad news is never delivered; it's always conveyed.

"The studio passed. They didn't like the script," he says, his voice soft with sympathy. "The project is dead."

The news hits me in the gut, a sucker-punch straight to the stomach. I can't breathe.

When I don't say anything, Lester continues. "I still have high hopes for *Jarndyce,* and I'm eager to take it out again as soon as the option lapses."

My head begins to ache as I force air into my lungs. It makes no difference; I still feel sick.

"The climate isn't the same, of course," he adds. "There's a lot more material like this circulating now, and *The Hanging Judge at Midnight* is going to be a problem. Before it wasn't far enough along to cause a conflict, but people might take the attitude of wait and see, which is not necessarily a bad thing. I just want you to be prepared."

Closing my eyes, I clutch the phone in my both hands. He wants me to be prepared. What a joke. "I don't understand," I say.

"All right. What can I clarify?" he asks, his usual matter-of-factness reasserting itself as he reverts to the superagent he is.

I struggle to think clearly. At the moment, not a single thing in the whole entire world makes sense; it's all a glaring Day-Glo jumble of lost opportunity.

"What about Lloyd?" I ask, after a long silence, meaning, What about the party? What about Moxie? What about the sexy new edition of *J&J*? What about the buzz? What about the IMDB entry? What about Chancery's grand plans? What about all the promises he made?

Which is really all to say, What about me?

Predictably, Lester answers only the question that was asked. "When a studio passes on a project, a producer has the option of taking it elsewhere. That won't happen in this case for two reasons. One, the script is worth a half million dollars so whatever studio takes it on would have to first buy the script from the old studio—this is done for copyright reasons—then invest another half million in a rewrite. It's very unlikely a studio would do that for a project that's already been rejected. Second, Lloyd has a deal with Arcadia, which he needs to protect. All his contacts left with the old regime, so it's as though he's starting from scratch. Trying to set up the project somewhere else would only offend his new bosses. Now, that isn't to say he wouldn't team up with a partner if one approached him. It's simply that he won't expend any energy in the next six weeks looking for someone. Lloyd's done with *Jarndyce and Jarndyce*."

Although I hear every word of Lester's long speech, the only thing that penetrates my stunned brain is the sentence "Lloyd's done with *Jarndyce and Jarndyce*." It repeats in my head like a security announcement in an airport. It has that same note of detached urgency.

I block it out. I have to. It takes up so much room in my mind I can't think. *Lloyd's done with* Jarndyce and Jarndyce. *Lloyd's done with* Jarndyce and Jarndyce.

The truth is, Lloyd's done with me.

I've never felt so abandoned in my entire life.

Taking a deep breath, I close my eyes and sort through the rest of the information. There has to be some scrap of hope I can cling to. "Would the script necessarily need a half-million-dollar rewrite? I thought it was good."

"It has problems. Nobody really likes it," he says.

A hot spurt of anger surges through me as I latch onto a genuine grievance. I might have dug my own grave, but here's a concrete example of Lester handing me the shovel. "But you told me they did. You said they liked the script."

He doesn't bother responding to this. What he said or didn't say doesn't concern him. All he deals with are the facts as they exist in this moment. He doesn't reexamine the past or project into the future. "I know this one's a heartbreaker, but I'm hopeful something else will come along. We haven't submitted to TV yet and pilot season is coming up. It's a huge disappointment but that's the way it sometimes goes. It's an up–and–down business. But don't lose heart," he adds, the sympathy back in his voice for the time being. "You're a wonderful writer, and this is no reflection on the quality of the material."

Somehow I know he's said these exact same words to every client he's ever had. We're all wonderful writers, and it's never a reflection on the quality of the material.

"I'll call you when I hear anything," he says. "Take care, Ricki, and don't hesitate to call if you have any more questions."

And just like that he's gone, without even waiting for me to say good-bye, and I'm alone with the fading shadow of something that used to exist.

No, I've never felt so abandoned in my entire life.

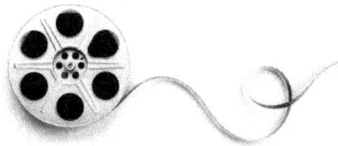

February 2 through February 15

I TAKE TO the couch.

For two weeks, I curl up on my Jennifer Convertible and read trashy novels by Nora Roberts, Rosmunde Pilcher, Jacqueline Susann, Jilly Cooper, Danielle Steel, Harold Robbins, Jackie Collins, Sidney Sheldon, Judith Krantz, Dominick Dunne, Ivana Trump, Stella Cameron, Maeve Binchy, Olivia Goldsmith, Colleen McCullough, Victoria Holt, Susan Howard, Grace Metalious and Susan Isaacs.

As soon as I finish one book, I throw it across the floor and reach for another. *Peyton Place* is followed by *Rage of Angels,* which is followed by *Wanderlust, First Wives Club* and *An Inconvenient Woman,* then *The Pirate, Players* and *Princess Daisy.* Having read them all in my misspent use, I'm vaguely familiar with the stories, and when Audrey Discoll has a miscarriage while Charlie's in Cairo spying on General Rommel, I know it will happen a second before it does. This makes me feel strangely clairvoyant.

For the first time in 984 days, I stop counting the days. Without the numbers, time loses meaning. Day bleeds into night and into day again as I lie there wrapped in a lamb's wool throw from Crate & Barrel, surrounded by everything I need—water, food, books, dental floss. I don't get up except to pee, brush my teeth, sign for deliveries from Amazon and prepare meals.

I survive on a steady diet of microwave popcorn. Amazon has thirty-five different types: Newman's Own with Butter, Newman's Own with Light Butter, Newman's Own Unsalted, Pop Secret Homestyle, Pop Secret Extra Butter, Pop Secret White Cheddar, Pop Secret Yellow Cheddar, Pop Secret Jumbo Pop Butter, India Tree Paloma Dorada, India Tree Paloma de Colores, Jolly Time Blast O' Butter, Orville Redenbacher's Movie Theater Butter, Orville Redenbacher's Tender White, Orville Redenbacher's Kettel Corn, Orville Redenbacher's Pour Over Cheddar, Orville Redenbacher's SmartPop with

Butter, Orville Redenbacher's SmartPop with Movie Theater Butter, Orville Redenbacher's Sweet 'n' Buttery, Orville Redenbacher's Ultimate Butter, Orville Redenbacher's Corn on the Cob, Orville Redenbacher's Butter Light, Orville Redenbacher's Old-Fashioned Butter, Black Jewel Natural, Black Jewel with Butter, Black Jewel Kettle Korn, Act II Movie Theatre Butter Pop 'n Serve, Act II 94% Fat-Free Butter, Act II 94% Fat-Free Kettle Corn, Robert's American Gourmet Zen, Dave's Gourmet Insanity Popcorn, Bearitos Organic No Oil Added, Ass Kickin' Habanero, Pop Weaver Butter, Pop Weaver Extra Butter, Pop Weaver Butter Light and Pop Weaver Kettle Corn.

I try them all.

Redenbacher's SmartPop with Movie Theater Butter is my favorite—it is sufficiently greasy to re-create the actual cinema experience—followed closely by Jolly Time Blast o' Butter. Pop Secret Yellow Cheddar is inedible, and the point of kettle corn escapes me completely.

I order one token Jiffy Pop to make popcorn the old-fashioned way, but I almost burn down the apartment when I forget to watch it. There's a subtle but significant difference between stovetop cooking and microwaving, and it's clearly worth remembering.

Luckily, I manage to stop the aggressive buzz of the smoke alarm before anyone notices. The last thing I want to do is attract attention. I want to be left alone to luxuriate in my misery. Carrie calls 10 times and leaves increasingly apprehensive messages. "I've checked all the area hospitals," she says, "so I know you're fine. Unless you were admitted as a Jane Doe because they found your body in a ditch off the freeway and they have no idea who you are. Oh, God. I should alert the police. If you're not lying in the hospital with amnesia, call me right now."

Mom also leaves concerned messages, but her only worry is the progress of my job hunt. "Ricki, honey, I don't have your new work number. Did you forget to give it to me? I know you must have one by now, since we sent out so many résumés and you're so qualified. There's no rush. Your father and I are away this weekend. Oh, and call your sister. She thinks you're lying dead in a ditch somewhere."

Everyone else leaves me alone.

My literary agent, Julie, sends me an e-card in which a darling little house with a candy cane chimney expels heart-shaped pink smoke and Hello Kitty floats down on a fluffy white cloud. The message reads, "We'll get 'em next time, kiddo!"

I delete it immediately and stop checking e-mail.

I miss an appointment with John but he doesn't call to follow up. Harry cancels our plans for an Oscar marathon at the AMC Century City—pay for one movie, see them all. Although his frequent last-minute rescheduling usually bothers me, this time I'm relieved. I can't deal with explanations or kindly sympathetic murmurs or reflexive upbeat bromides. Things don't happen for a reason and I'm sure it's not all for the best.

There's nothing good about this situation, and I don't want people trying to make me believe there is.

My entire future hinged on *J&J* and now it's over.

I have no future.

Reaching for another novel, I snag *The Valley of the Dolls*. I haven't read it since I was fifteen but something about the story strikes me now as deeply profound. I feel a kinship with Anne Welles, the misguided heroine from a small New England town who winds up addicted to prescription pills, one of the inevitable many who climbs the mountain of success to such heights that the air is too thin to breathe. Writes Susann in the prologue, "Anne Welles had never meant to start the climb."

I never meant to start the climb either.

Level-headed and practical, I didn't set out to take Hollywood by storm. I never planned on writing a novel that would be optioned by Lloyd Chancellor and turned into a movie starring Moxie Bernard. I'm a paralegal. I spend my life being shit on by lawyers. I don't believe in the essential goodness of mankind or happy endings. Life is repetition; it's the same document photocopied a few million times.

I know better than to dream.

But even the most hard-hearted cynic wouldn't be impervious to a glamorous Hollywood party thrown in her honor to celebrate the relaunch of her book with a gushing quote from Moxie Bernard.

I defy anyone not to have her head turned by that.

Tears well up and spill over as memories from the party come flooding back, that sharp shot of optimism I felt while signing books, the inevitability of the future. Of course we're making a movie, I'd thought.

Of course we're not.

That too seems inevitable now.

Of the one percent of books that actually make it to holy filmdom, a vast majority are already best sellers: your Stephenie Meyers, your Stephen Kings, your J.K. Rowlings. It was absurd—a monumental act of absurd conceit—to believe, whatever the provocation, that I'd be one of the select few.

Numbed by the pain, my eyes drooping from fatigue and the rigors of self-reflection, I lay my head against the pillow and extend my legs. My back hurts from being curled in a ball for hours on end, and my entire body cries out for a good, thorough stretching. Ignoring both, I drift off into sleep, my grip loosening as *The Valley of the Dolls* tumbles to the floor.

That night, I dream Anne Welles tells Lyon Burke, the cheating, lying, good-for-nothing love of her life, to take a hike. Then she kicks the Seconal and Nembutal and starts her own successful modeling agency, where she helps other beautiful woman from small towns avoid the pitfalls of fame.

She saves herself.

Just like in the movies.

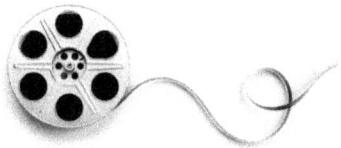

February 16

SIMON BREAKS INTO my apartment carrying a bag full of voodoo dolls.

"It's not breaking and entering if you have a key," he says and holds up the one for my front door. "It's just entering, and you can't get in trouble for that."

Amazed, I stare at him from my nest of books, a bowl of popcorn in my lap and a Liquid Lightening energy drink in my hand ($15 instant rebate from Amazon when you buy forty-nine dollars' worth). Even though I'm fully covered in sweats, I pull the blanket up to my chin, feeling curiously exposed.

"Where'd you get that?" I ask, but I already know the answer. I can't believe the super would hand it over to anyone who asked. Maybe I can sue him for invasion of privacy or wrongful embarrassment. I can just imagine what I look like. I smooth my hand over my frizzy rat's nest but it's no use. My hair is sticking out in every direction.

He clears a path through the Amazon boxes to my dining room table, where he drops the key. "Your sister."

"It's positively criminal for the su——" I break off my tirade at the words sink in. "My sister?"

"She was worried so she asked me to look in on you. Apparently you've been in a deep freeze for two weeks. So she FedExed her spare key. You forgot to get it back," he explains, upending the tote bag onto my table. Eight white dolls with blank faces tumble out. They're folksy and creepy.

"But you don't know my sister," I say.

He digs a case of markers out of his back pocket. "We met on the elevator. She looks exactly like you so I introduced myself. She tracked me down yesterday thought RentLA.com. Very resourceful. I like that. Is she dating someone?"

Annoyed, I push the blanket to the side and stand up. I don't know what I should do first——ball out my sister or put my hair in a ponytail. Vanity wins.

"Yes, she's dating someone, unfortunately," I call out from the bathroom. "But she lives in New York."

"So does my cousin. They'd be great together. Are you sure she and this guy are solid?"

I take a quick detour to my bedroom and change my T-shirt. The one I'm wearing is covered in greasy butter stains. Sadly, the only napkins Amazon sells are the sanitary kind.

My feeble mind can't take thoughts of Glenn at this difficult time, so I ignore his question and return to the more pressing topic. "Listen, I still don't get what you're doing here," I say, coming out of the bedroom feeling marginally more human.

Simon draws the last of my window shades, blocking out all natural light. It's a very strange act. Usually when you're rousted from your den of depression by a cheerful savior, he opens the windows to let in the fresh air. It's a symbolic act.

"I'm here to cajole you out of your blues." He meets my gaze across the dining room table. "I know about movie deal."

Amazingly, it's like a punch to the stomach—again. "How?"

"Your agent is friends with your sister, remember? Julie called Carrie to see how you were doing when you didn't respond to her e-mail. I know it sucks, but you've got to think of these things when you're going into deep freeze. Otherwise annoying neighbors wind up in your living room," he says with a wink.

His cheeriness is more than I can handle. Maybe in a few days I'll be able to field winks but not right now. "I appreciate your stopping by, really, but I'm fine. I'll call Carrie and tell her that right away."

Simon looks around the room, taking it all in: the novels, the Liquid Lightening cans, the packing slips, the congealed popcorn kernels sitting at the bottom of empty plastic bowls. He shakes his head. "No, you are definitely not fine."

The blush starts at my toes and creeps up my body. "Really, I'm—"

"You went with books," he says, squatting to look through the pile. He picks up *Players* by Jilly Cooper, glances at the cover of a man's hand on a woman's butt and smirks. "A good choice. I did DVDs. I watched every episode ever of *The Simpsons*. It was all downhill after the fourth season, but I kept on for another nineteen. It was enjoyable in a masochistic way. But there comes a time when you have to shake off the self-pity and pick up the pins."

I blink. The inspiring, motivational speech I'm all prepared to dismiss doesn't mention pins. "Huh?"

He takes the six colored markers out of their plastic case. "There are times when growling just doesn't cut it and you need something stronger like a voodoo-ery. Or, er, voodoo-torium. Since one doesn't exist, I had to create my own. Herewith, everything you need to distill evil spirits and make yourself feel better."

Simon hands me one creepy white doll and watches me with an air of expectation. I don't know what I'm supposed to do.

"Here"—he holds out an orange marker—"start with Lloyd Chancellor. Draw his hair."

Slowly at first and with growing enthusiasm, I color in his wild curling red hair. Then I add his bright green eyes and sooty lashes. I save his thick lips for last.

Simon looks over my shoulder. "Oh, no, much thicker than that."

I double the width of his lips and hold the doll up for inspection. It looks like a nursery school portrait. It could be Lloyd. It could be Simon. It could even be me.

"Not bad for a first effort. Now for the fun part." He shakes a plastic box of sewing pins and opens it.

I stare at them warily. Poking needles into Lloyd Chancellor hardly seems like the mature way to handle my grief.

"Trust me," he says coaxingly. "It's juvenile but cathartic."

I grab one with an orange ball to match Lloyd's hair and press it against the heart. It goes through the foam in one easy, gliding motion.

"How'd that feel?" he asks.

I take a deep breath and let it out. I'm a terrible human being. "Good."

He shakes the box again. "Ready for another one?"

Nodding eagerly, I stick the pin through the middle of his forehead. It looks like a bindi. I put the next one in his kidney and the fourth in his spleen. Or where I think the spleen should be.

When I reach for a fifth pin, Simon stops me. "Uh-uh. Four's the limit. Just in case."

I stare at him in surprise. "Just in case what?"

He shrugs. "It's not just a bunch of hocus-pocus."

I find his superstitiousness adorable. "All right."

"So who do you want to do next?"

"Nadia. She never returns my calls."

"Excellent."

After Nadia, I make effigies of Tom Tipston and Allan Field, the supposedly superhot scribes who get half a million dollars to write shitty scripts nobody wants to produce. Angriest at them, I insert a needle into their brain with deliberate slowness, pinning them together at the point of their most useless organ. I stick the other seven in all their joints so they can't move.

Simon gives me props for finding a loophole in the four-only rule.

Satisfied, I grin and say thank you. It's remarkable that something so blatantly juvenile can make you feel so much better.

My stomach growls and for the first time in weeks I'm in the mood for something other than popcorn. I try to imagine what's in my fridge. Some sour milk, a few potatoes, maybe a carton of eggs. It's been so long since I've looked inside, I'm not really sure.

While I contemplate a potato omelet, Simon hands me one more doll.

I look at it in its blank face. "What's this for?"

"Esther Rogers, the new CEO of Arcadia who killed *Jarndyce*," he says. "You're not alone. The new regime has been terminating projects right and left. Anything that was set up before they arrived is getting the ax."

"Really?" I ask, imagining a fleet of devastated novelists holing up with Danielle Steele and PopSecret. We should form a support group. As a public service, we could insert a pamphlet about the dangers of gullibility and stupidity with every option payment and set up an 800 number you can dial whenever you feel a hint of optimism seeping into your pessimism.

"It's been all over the trades. They claim they're taking the studio in a fresh, new direction, but it's really just ego," he says. "Everything in this business is ego. Once you get that, things make a lot more sense."

Because I don't know what Esther Rogers looks like, I start with her mouth. I assume it's red like everyone else's.

Simon hands me the brown marker. "For her eyes. Her hair is sort of a dignified salt and pepper. I'm not sure how you want to render it, since we don't have gray."

I make some black polka dots and leave the rest white. It's remarkably unattractive, even for a voodoo doll.

"Excellent. You've nailed her," he says.

After I insert the pins, I look at him expectantly. "What comes after voodoo therapy?"

"Well, I renounced the movie industry and got a job with RentLA.com."

I laugh. "Hmm. That sounds like step twenty-seven. What's step two?"

He thinks for a moment. "You go to the Dresden and get really greasy burgers."

On paper it sounds like a good plan, especially considering how poorly I make omelets, but the thought of stepping into the big wide world where I'm nothing but an unemployed paralegal is too daunting. The second I pass through my front door my demoted status becomes permanent. Here in my apartment reality is deferred. In the smog-ridden outside it's a fixed constant.

"OK, step one and a half," I say.

"We order in from Simply Thai?" he offers.

I nod. That's more my speed. "Can we eat in your apartment?" I ask. The hallway isn't outside, not really. "This place is probably rank. Actually, now that I think about it, so am I. I'm going to hop in the shower first."

Now Simon opens the windows to let in fresh air. He lines the voodoo dolls along the sill like they're pretty potted plants. I like the way they look. "Cool. I'll order. What do you want?"

"Green curry with chicken and spring rolls."

He commits it to memory. "Come by whenever you're ready."

I nod and watch him pack up the markers, overcome with a feeling of gratitude I don't know how to express. I would still be on the couch developing bed sores if it weren't for him. "I, uh, you know, thanks," I say awkwardly.

"Please," he says with an unself-conscious smile. "I'm a voodoo whore. Any excuse to stick pins in a doll."

His remarkable graciousness puts me at ease. "Well, regardless, I appreciate the intervention."

Simon shrugs like it's nothing and tosses the leftover dolls into the tote bag. Then he bends down to pick up the scattered Amazon boxes, and it occurs to me that he might be the best human being I've ever met.

"Absolutely not," I say, grabbing the boxes from him and pushing him toward the door.

He wraps his hand around the knob, jiggles it for a moment, then turns to me. "I'm sorry," he says.

"I know," I say softly. Whatever he might have expected to happen, he hoped it wouldn't. I get that now. He wanted to save me from this. But of course nothing could save me from this, not even a ream of pamphlets.

He nods once and opens the door. The hallway is silent and we both hear my stomach rumble loudly. I laugh with embarrassment, he with pure amusement.

"Maybe I should go order the food," he says.

I smile. "Maybe."

"See you in a bit."

"Yes," I say, closing the door.

It's almost entirely shut when he pushes it open again. "Oh, and call your sister."

Yep, it's official. The best human being I've ever met.

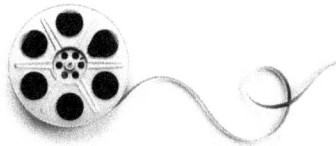

February 17

I QUIT MOXIE cold turkey.

From the moment Lester delivers the fateful news, I lose all interest in her future. Without a personal stake in her career, the drama of her life is ultimately meaningless, and I marvel at the rest of the world for caring. What's in it for them? What are they getting out of it? Where's their payoff?

My Moxie worry is deeply ingrained and it's hard to shake. When she shows up for the first day of shooting of *Where's Willa* with unexplained bruises on her arms and chest, I immediately tense up, imagining her drunkenly tripping off the roof of her house or, worse, the Russian mafia roughing her up.

Then I remember it's not my problem anymore. It's her mother's and her publicist's and her agent's and her manager's and her director's and her costar's and her stylist's and her Pilates instructor's and her dealer's and the dozens of other people who make their living off her.

But not me. I don't care.

I mean, she's a human being so of course I care in that global, detached, children-are-starving-in-Africa way. I hope she pulls herself together and has a long, happy life, if not career.

More than that, however, I can't offer. Our bond, existing almost entirely in my head, is broken.

The hard part of quitting Moxie is finding something to fill the hole she leaves behind. At the height of my mania, I had a full Moxie circuit that consumed a significant part of my waking hours. First I'd visit Moxie-specific sites (MoxieBernard.com, ILuvMox.com, MoxieCentral.com, MoxieWatch.com), then head to general gossip pages (Gawker, E! Online, Page Six, The Superficial). Some days, when big scandals broke, I'd lose whole news cycles to the story. The sun would set outside my window and I'd wonder where the day went.

Now when I sit down at my computer in the morning, all I have is my screenplay. I open FinalDraft, find where I left off and stare at the blinking cursor, waiting for something to break the monotony.

Nothing does.

When I was writing *J&J*, work itself was the distraction. With pesky associates and partners buzzing around, I had to always seem consumed by law-related projects. I kept documents open on my desk to click on swiftly when someone walked by. I wrote most of the book and all of the original e-mails over and through these interruptions.

The days flew.

The movie proved even more diverting. In a state of perpetual expectation, I checked my e-mail constantly, hoping for some new piece of information: that Moxie liked the script, that Lloyd cast Ada Clare's father, that Steven Soderbergh signed on to direct. Every few minutes, I'd refresh my inbox like I'm pulling the lever on a slot machine. Come on big money, I'd think.

Without that thrill of anticipation, life is almost unbearable.

Hello my name is Ricki, and I'm an update junkie.

These days all I can look forward to are e-mails from Carrie with jpegs of refrigerators. If I'm lucky, she'll include a link to the site so I can explore every inch of it. I went so deep into SubZero.com, I even read the years-old press release announcing their acquisition of Wolf. That I found the story of their merger, the marriage, as they put it, of "ice and fire, cold and hot," strangely moving proves the depth to which I've sunk.

I need help.

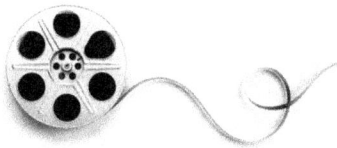

March 2

HARRY STILL BELIEVES unconditionally in the movie. His optimism is sincere, wholehearted and well reasoned. It's not simply a reflexive reaction. He subscribes to darkest before dawn one hundred and ten percent.

"This is Hollywood, the land of the comeback. Nothing is ever over, not Harvey Weinstein's career and not your movie. So the option lapses in two weeks." He shrugs with complete indifference. "Big deal. Everyone's option lapses at least once. It's a badge of honor. Like notches in a bedpost. When *J&J* does get made and you're making the rounds on the morning shows, this is what you'll talk about. Fodder, baby, fodder. Some people would kill to be as unsuccessful as you."

His confidence is infectious. Maybe all is not lost after all.

"In the meantime," he adds, "you still have your screenplay, which, according to John, is pretty great. He says it just needs a little more work."

I smile wryly at the understatement. The "little more work" Harry claims the screenplay needs is an entire revision. Draft one is solid but it has some major flaws. It's supposed to be a black comedy and yet there are long stretches without a laugh. Even though *J&J* is a workplace comedy of manners, I don't know the first thing about being funny. Writing is so much harder when you're not taking dictation from the senior partners.

John still thinks the project has lots of potential and is willing to work on the revise, but that's another course. The screenplay class I signed up for only covers the writing of the first draft. Knowing my situation, he feels terrible about charging me but sees no way around it. It wouldn't be right to give one student, even his favorite, preferential treatment.

I get this in principal, but I don't know what would be so wrong with a little disparity. Nothing else in the world is fair.

Seeing my discouraged expression, Harry throws his arms around me and tumbles me to the couch. We're in the brown-and-beige living room of the little pool-house cottage he rents from an old college friend. The amount he pays each month is so miniscule, Harry dismisses it as a token. For the most part he gets to live here for free. I can't imagine how he managed to arrange such a sweet deal. When I ask him, all he says is most people admire an honest freeloader. He says it seriously, like it's a famous quote from the bible or Shakespeare, but I know he's teasing.

"Hey, if show business were easy, everyone would be doing it," he says, his hair falling forward as he looks down at me. "It's hard but you have to stick it out. Every movie that ever got made has the exact same story as yours. This is Hollywood, the land of the twenty-year overnight sensation. Where do you think the myths come from? Right here. Right where you are. So take your setbacks and create your myth. That's why you're here. It's why any of us are here."

His enthusiasm is irresistible, and I smile, feeling some of my tension drain away. I love Harry's vision of Hollywood. Simon's is too pragmatic. There's no romance in it, no Lana Turner at the soda fountain at Schwab's. For him, Hollywood is a place that breaks writers—Dorothy Parker, Nathanael West, Aldous Huxley, Donald Ogden Stewart, Robert Benchly, and most famously of all, F. Scott Fitzgerald. It's the town that kicked one of the greatest writers of the twentieth century off the adaptation of Clare Luce Booth's *The Woman* because his dialogue wasn't catty enough.

I appreciate the value of his attitude and agree that realism is needed to balance the euphoria, but it's impossible to see things his way and remain in the business. You *have* to renounce and get a job with RentLA.com.

"Which is why," Harry continues, "you're going to call John first thing in the morning and sign up for the revision course. You need to get that script as shiny as possible before you give it to the estimable Lester Dedlock. Then he'll sell it to Paramount for half a mil and you can take me to the Ivy for dinner every night."

The thought of five hundred thousand dollars makes me giddy. I could buy a lot of popcorn. "Oh, is that what I'm going to do with my money?" I ask, laughing.

"I hope so. I've always wanted to be a kept man."

He leans forward and brushes his lips against my forehead, cheeks, nose. By the time he gets to my lips, I'm no longer laughing. The kiss is gentle and sweet.

"Promise me," he whispers in my ear. "Here and now."

I turn my head slightly, trying to remember the topic. "What?"

"Promise me you'll call John tomorrow. I hate to seem relentless, but it's your future. You have to protect it. As much as I want to, I can't do that for you."

I sigh.

Without the second option payment, my finances are in a dismal state. I have barely enough money to cover my shockingly large credit card bill. All those cans of Liquid Lightning add up fast, even with the $15 rebate.

I have no idea where I'll get another thousand to shell out for the script. I couldn't possibly borrow it from my parents. Maybe Carrie? No, she has that new kitchen to worry about. (I can say with one hundred percent confidence, SubZero's aren't cheap.)

But Harry is right. How can I come this close only to turn away at the very end? It's my future on the line. I'm the only one who's going to sacrifice for it.

"Promise me," he says again, pressing kisses along my neck and collarbone. Sweet little shivers run up my spine. "Promise."

Sighing, I close my eyes and promise to call John.

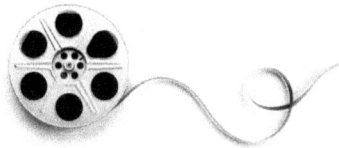

March 5

LOSING YOUR MOVIE deal is like going through the worst breakup in the history of the world. Everything is a reminder—not just a few songs or a favorite restaurant but every goddamn thing on God's green earth.

I can't turn on the television or open a newspaper or walk down the street without an ad for some film hitting me smack in the face. Outside my bedroom window, thirty feet from my pillow, is a billboard for *The Confession*, a romantic comedy about a gossip columnist who tries to reform her ways. Next to the tag line, "No good deed ever goes unpublished," is the prominently displayed words *based on the best-selling novel by Annie Wyath*.

It's like the universe is taunting me.

I keep my blinds drawn but it doesn't make a difference. I know it's out there, perched on its great steel frame like a lumbering beast waiting to attack.

Out of sight is several leagues away from out of mind.

On the way to John's, I pass sixty-two reminders: forty-four billboards, three bookstores, five movie theaters, one video rental store, three ads for Disney, three ads for Universal Studios, two production offices and the Marmont Tower hotel.

By the time I get there, I'm practically suicidal.

I dart into his apartment like I'm seeking cover from enemy fire. I feel besieged.

John is drinking coffee while reading the newspaper at the table; the *Today* show is on quietly in the background. Matt Lauer is interviewing a class of kindergarteners about the compost heap in the school's garden. A little girl with a blond ponytail and freckles across her nose makes a face and says worms are icky. Her fellow students laugh and agree.

In her first film, Moxie plays a tomboy who puts worms in her nemesis's pencil case. The girl discovers them in the middle of a spelling test. The worms escape, hilarity ensues and Moxie wins a Nickelodeon award.

It's all too painful to bear, so I switch off the television.

John looks up. "I like your single-mindedness. No dawdling." He folds the paper and tosses it on the table. "And you're right, we should get straight to it."

I sit across from him and pull out my script. I've read it through a hundred times and still can't figure out what to change. Every scene seems essential to me, even the unfunny ones.

In publishing, it's your editor's job to identify what's not working and suggest ways to fix it. With *J&J*, Elaine added the romantic subplot. Unfortunately, screenwriting doesn't have an equivalent. Producers want a script to be perfect before they buy it and put their own personal stamp on it. This is why I had to sign up for John's revision course.

"Rule number one: no *ing*," John says, getting right down to business. He doesn't even offer me a tray of cookies first. My stomach rumbles sadly. I'd been counting on them as my breakfast for two reasons. One: They're so delicious. Two: For a thousand smackers, I should get something more than just advice. "Don't say, Tad is standing on the corner. Say, Tad *stands* on the corner. A screenplay is all about action. Make it present tense and intense."

I flip over the first page of the script and jot down the saying. Present tense, intense. I love advice that rhymes.

For the next two hours, John and I go through the script, activating sentences. We eliminate almost every single *ing*; only the ones used in dialogue get to stay.

Next we edit all my action descriptions down to three lines. "Rule number one: Blocks of text slow you down. A screenplay has to move. You want the reader's eyes to fly across the page, not get bogged down by text. Text means plodding. Remember, screenplays are visual as well as literal. Each page should be swaths of cool white paper with black words in the center. Like modern art."

We break for lunch—egg salad sandwiches—and John asks how I'm holding up with the *J&J* disappointment. Rather than explain that everything in the world is three degrees removed from the film (egg sandwiches: the remake of *The Egg and I* was produced by Harriet Sneider, who coproduced *Catcher and Rye* with Lloyd Chancellor), I tell him I'm fine. "Working on *How Tad Johnson Got into Harvard* helps."

He nods. "It's always therapeutic to focus on a new project. I like to think of it as having a horse in the race. You can't win if you don't enter."

Yes, I think, that's it exactly. A new horse.

When we get back to work, I feel energized. Some of it is the wonderful relief of having food in my stomach but mostly it's excitement about the possibilities of my screenplay. Fine, *J&J* didn't work out but it's not the only idea in the hopper. (Denise Hopper played Edi Leisel's dad in *The Long Way*, and Leisel costarred with Moxie in *American Grrl*.)

"Now let's talk about the romance. Rule number one: Use and abuse your lovers. The whole point is to keep them apart as long as possible, and if you have to give one of them brain cancer to do it, then you give them brain cancer. You don't have obstacles in your story. Maryanne doesn't have a boyfriend; Tad doesn't have a girlfriend."

"But she's number four on his list," I point out. "Isn't that a pretty big impediment?"

John shakes his head. "It's a start, a good one, but Maryanne still needs a boyfriend, preferably a self-involved preppy asshole who doesn't understand her. And we'll give Tad a beauty queen girlfriend who won't mess up her hair."

"But those are clichés straight from the cliché handbook," I say, appalled. I might not have much experience with writing but I know enough high school English to recognize trite characters when I see them.

"Exactly," John says with satisfaction. "Rule number one: Embrace your clichés. Trust me, you don't want to veer from the formula. The closer your material hews to the familiar, the more they're going to think they love it. And by the time they realize they don't, it'll be too late. It's not about getting the movie made. It's about selling the rights. Get in, get the cash, get out. You do one standard rewrite, per your contract, then you're done. If they want more from you, they have to pay you again. It's a fantastic arrangement courtesy of the Writer's Guild, which you should always remember in your prayers. It's an amazing institution. A little Mafioso in their negotiating but what union isn't."

"That's insane," I say. With novels, you write and rewrite until one of three things happens: Your draft matches your editor's vision, you convince your editor her vision is wrong or your editor realizes you're incapable of fulfilling her vision and lets you off the hook. There's no stopping because she hasn't paid you more money for your time. In the publishing world, your time isn't worth diddly-squat.

John knits his brows in confusion. "What part?"

"How can a writer not be responsible for her own work?"

"Once someone else buys it, it's not her work anymore, is it?" he says reasonably. "Film is a collaborative medium. The more, the merrier. But you can't have your script ruined by a dozen other writers until you've finished writing it yourself. So make a note about the preppy boyfriend and the snobby girlfriend. You can tweak their characters a little—maybe the beauty queen is a brunette instead of a blonde—but don't go crazy. Rule number one: Well known is well liked."

As horrifying as I find John's ideas, they conform to everything I've seen as a movie-goer. The same clichés are repeated over and over ad nauseam. I always thought that was bad moviemaking, but now I understand that it's good moviemaking.

I make a note to think of some interesting traits. Maybe prep boy could be obnoxiously nice rather than the usual obnoxiously mean.

Or is that going crazy?

"Have you thought about adding more action?" John asks. "Everyone loves explosions. Maybe Maryanne is trying to kill Tad while he's trying to kill her. A Mr. and Mrs. Smith Goes to College."

Sighing deeply, I remind myself that I'm paying thousands of dollars for exactly this sort of insider information and jot down the idea.

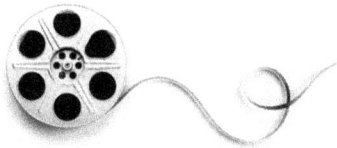

April 3

I REALIZE THINGS are desperate when I have to transfer money from my life savings to my checking account to cover my obscenely high tax bill. Even writing off the entire move as a career expense and putting away several thousand for retirement, I still owe more than four thousand dollars. It's the set-up bonus that really does me in, and the depth of my resentment for Tipston and Field, already bottomless, grows impossibly deeper.

Needless to say, I also have to draw on my inheritance to cover April rent and other random necessities.

Watching my savings drop—from $64,682 to $55,682—for the first time ever is a profoundly uncomfortable experience, and to counterbalance it, I send résumés to the eight law firms that contacted me in January to set up interviews. They all go smoothly and by the end of the week I'm shopping for boxy suits at Marshall's. I buy five from the sale rack to get me from Monday to Friday without repeats. They're all loose in the shoulders, but I don't care enough about the job to spend money on tailoring. Wearing ill-fitting clothes, like I raided my father's closet, feels like an act of aggression. I'm rebelling.

Josiah and Barton is a midsize firm specializing in entertainment law. Their offices are downtown, near the Disney Concert Hall, and on my first morning it takes me almost an hour to get there. By the time I find a parking space and take the elevator to the thirty-second floor, I'm twenty minutes late.

Symphony Brodsky in Human Resources—tall, thin, with a black pageboy cut—scowls at me while she leads me to my desk. She purses her lips and tsk-tsks but never actually says anything critical, which is considerably worse than a tongue-lashing.

I remind myself I'm only in this for the paycheck. I might be paralegaling but I'm no longer a paralegal. I'm a screenwriter picking up some extra money while she waits for a sale.

There's a huge difference between the two.

My desk is in the middle of a large, gray room with high-walled cubicles and bookshelves. Instead of the lively buzz of productivity—phone chatter, keyboard clicking—there's dead silence. I neither hear nor see any sign of life.

The eerie stillness is strange and disconcerting. I've never worked under tomblike conditions before but I'm sure I can adapt.

Symphony points to a chair and directs me to sit down. Intimidated by her austerity, I comply immediately. As soon as I make contact, the springs in the base squeak, and the sound reverberates in the quiet room. Symphony looks down disapprovingly, as if I myself emitted the noise and not the office furniture.

I smile graciously and wait for instructions. I refuse to let her get to me.

"We like to start our new hires off slowly," she says, laying her hand on top of a thousand-page document. "Here is the Whitman case for Bates numbering. You will report to Herb Fennessy, a junior partner. His office is around the corner to the left, down the hall, through the door, to the right, down the stairs and at the end of the corridor."

I have a pen out, but I don't bother writing down the directions. Clearly I'm not meant to.

"He expects all the documents to be numbered and scanned by five o'clock. If you're running behind schedule," she says, looking at her watch, a not-so-subtle dig at my lateness, "inform his secretary and she'll provide another paralegal to help you. This case goes to litigation soon and we cannot afford to lose more time. Bates machines and scanners are in the supply closet. Anything you sign out you are responsible for. Lost or damaged equipment will be deducted from your paycheck. Someone will be down presently to connect you to the server. If you have any questions, please call. Have a nice day." She turns abruptly to walk away.

"One thing," I say, before she can disappear. "Where's the supply closet?"

She sighs impatiently, as I'm making up questions just to torture her, and says, "Left at the exit sign, right at the water fountain, left at the end of the hall, another left at the conference room and down the stairs."

Once again it's complete gibberish, but this time I make her repeat it slowly and wait while I write it down word for word. Now I *am* just torturing her. But she makes it so easy.

"Thank you," I say.

She scowls and walks away without responding.

Yikes. What a witch.

As soon as she's gone, I stand up and look around the room, expecting to see the heads of colleagues pop up. Not a single one does and I feel the surprisingly sharp sting of disappointment. I don't need conversation or friendship or even sympathy from my coworkers, just the extended eye contact of the oppressed.

Finding the supply closet is easy; getting supplies is somewhat more challenging. There's no electronic record of my employment, so Nate the equipment Nazi won't give me a Bates machine or scanner.

When all logical arguments fail, I say, "Do I seriously look like the kind of person who goes from law firm to law firm scamming supplies and selling them on eBay?"

"Well...." he says, trailing off meaningfully.

Deeply offended, I narrow my eyes. "What?"

"It looks like you scammed that suit from someone."

I growl with frustration and do the last thing in the world I want to: call Symphony. She's snappish and annoyed and puts me on hold three separate occasions for a total of ten minutes, but eventually she's forced to concede that it's her oversight that caused the confusion.

Confusion—she can't own it enough to say *problem*.

Back at my desk, I boot up the computer and check my phone for messages. It's been three weeks since I gave Lester my script and I haven't heard a word. I can't imagine what's taking so long. It's ninety-six pages of mostly blank space. He could whip through it while waiting for the valet to get his car.

On the so-bored-I-want-to-slit-my-wrists scale, Bates numbering falls somewhere between photocopying and redacting. It's more interactive than the former but doesn't require as much thought as the latter. It's mostly mindless repetition but it has its own rhythm and with iTunes playing quietly in the background, it's not the worst way in the world to earn thirty dollars an hour.

In complete silence it's agony.

I look at my watch. It's eleven-thirty and still nobody has come by to connect me to the server. I can't go online without a login, which means I can't listen to music or read the *Times* or check my e-mail or do anything other than stamp Bates numbers onto an endless stack of papers.

At two o'clock, I'm only halfway through the document, so I call Herb Fennessy's secretary, Valerie Smith, and leave a brief voice mail explaining the situation. Then I dial the operator and ask who I should speak to about getting a login for the server. She puts me through to Harvey in tech services. He isn't there either.

Drawing on my reserves of heroic stoicism, I pick up the Bates machine and return to work. The day drags at a glacial pace as I wait for Valerie or Harvey to call.

At four fifty-seven, Symphony materializes at my desk. Her face is red and blotchy and I wonder if she's having an allergic reaction to something.

Unfortunately, it seems to be me.

"Herb Fennessy just called to inform me that you've neither finished your scanning nor called his secretary to alert him to the fact that you will not finish your scanning by the agreed-upon time," she says in a huff. "He's appalled by your irresponsibility and lack of forethought. He asked you to do one thing. One simple thing and the fact that you can't makes him seriously doubt your future at this firm. He further believes—"

"Hold on," I say, more puzzled than angry. Yes, my sense of justice is outraged since I did *exactly what I was asked*. It's not my fault Valerie Smith doesn't know how to pick up her messages. But the fact that the withering set down is being delivered by Symphony is baffling. "What does this have to do with you?"

Taken aback by the question, she actually answers it. "Chain of command."

"What?"

"The chain of command," she explains calmly. The red is starting to fade from her cheeks. "Lawyers speak to me and I speak to the paralegals."

"So let me get this right," I say. "Every time a lawyer has a problem with me, he'll tell you about it and you'll take me to task?"

She nods.

"All right," I say, putting the stamp down on top of the pages yet to be numbered. Then I slide my chair back a few inches, stand up and grab my purse.

Symphony is agog. "What are you doing?"

I don't answer. I just shake my head and walk away. My time at Josiah and Barton is done. Hello, unemployment and parental disapproval and dwindling inheritance.

I breeze past reception and into the elevator lobby, feeling curiously free.

I'm a professional. I can deal with preternaturally silent coworkers, territorial supply Nazis, snippy secretaries and irate lawyers. Being shit on by egomaniacal junior partners is in the job description, and I accept it like I do a forty-five-minute lunch break and a crappy HMO insurance plan. But I will not tolerate being shit on by some pinched-faced witch named Symphony. Maybe if she were a Carol or a Judy, I could handle it better. But a tight-assed human resources drone with a drag queen name?

No, absolutely not.

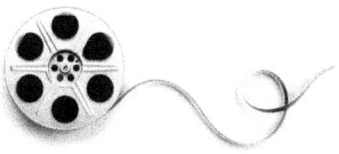

April 20

LESTER ASSURES ME I've got a solid beginning.

"Your premise is fun and original. It definitely has a commercial edge, which is what studios look for," he says. "The dialogue is sharp and effective. You have a real ear for natural speech patterns. But your characters don't come alive."

I tighten my grip on the phone, knowing this is the beginning of the negative part of our conversation. So far it's all been cheery small talk and positive feedback. "They don't?"

"We need to really care about these people to be invested in their future and their happiness," he explains, his voice full of authority. "Your story needs to enthuse reality. It needs to breathe the truth. It needs to be the realest real."

"The realest real?" I repeat, wondering what that means. I have no idea.

"Yes, the realest real."

He says this sincerely and earnestly with no sense of irony. It's like he doesn't realize he's calling from Hollywood, USA, the international capital of the fakest fake and saying *the realest real* like it's an actual thing. The realest real is a concept, an advertising slogan made up by men trying to sell you a talking mouse and a singing mermaid.

Frustrated, I throw myself on the couch and decide I'll never leave it again. Bad things seem to happen when I go out into the world. First Symphony. Now the realest real.

"Don't rely so heavily on coincidence," he adds.

I sit up. Specific information is good. I grab a pen from the dining room table and start taking notes. "All right."

"Coincidences are lazy. Your character interaction should be based on real mechanisms, not false ones. Maryanne should meet Tad in a more natural setting. His mother shouldn't be her gynecologist. That's too easy. He needs to find out about her medical condition some other way."

Nodding, I write it down: coinc bad, real mech, natural, no meet through mom. "That makes sense. Thank you."

"Work on characterization. Make us really love the characters."

"In what way are they unlovable?" I ask, struggling to understand.

But he doesn't give me examples. He pulls back and goes in an entirely different direction. "Think of John Cusak in *Grosse Point Blank.* He's doing something we don't approve of, but we love him anyway. That's the important thing to remember. Or Winona Ryder in *Heathers.* These people touch us. We really believe in them. That's the key component of a screenplay."

"I understand that, but can you give me specific examples of why those characters are the realest real? What traits make a character the realest real?"

"Watch the movies and you'll see," he says mysteriously, like the oracle at Delphi.

Thoroughly defeated and suddenly very tired, I lie back on the couch and put the notepad over my eyes. Maybe if I lie very still, I'll be back in my apartment in New York getting ready for another day at Hertzog, Wright, Penn and Silver. Those people might have been crazy but at least they made sense.

"The action is good," he adds. "Having Maryanne go after Tad is good. Build more of that into your script."

"But that only works because of the mother-gynecologist connection," I point out.

"Be creative. Good storytellers don't rely on coincidence. Wow us. Make it the realest real possible."

And there I hit a wall—at the intersection of realest real and movie magic. There's no Maryanne trying to kill Tad without Mom's misdiagnosis.

Exhausted, I wonder what I'm going to do next. Talk to John, I suppose.

Remembering Simon's cynicism, I ask if Lester knows John Vholes.

He repeats the name softly several times. "He's a screenwriter?"

"Yes," I say.

"A pretty decent one, too, I believe, though I can't say if he's sold anything recently."

As success isn't always an indication of quality, I feel vindicated in my defense of him. Take that, Simon.

I thank Lester for his time.

"My pleasure," he says gracious as always. "I think you've got a great voice and tremendous potential, and I consider it an honor to read your work."

His compliments are mere client upkeep, the knee-jerk minimum schmoozing of any good superagent, but I'm still flattered. Whatever the circumstance, it's always nice to hear the word *honor* in reference to yourself.

I put down the phone and fetch the last can of Liquid Lightening from the fridge to shore up my energy as I sit down to review my notes. I rewrite them neatly in full sentences in an effort to understand them better but it's no use. The more I try to figure out Lester's comments, the less I understand them.

Every point he made runs counter to what I know about the movies. The contrived plot coincidence, a time-honored tradition that dates back to

Dickens and Shakespeare before him, is the backbone of great filmmaking. Where would *Casablanca* be if Ingrid Bergman didn't just happen to walk into Humphrey Bogart's Café Americain?

And his exhortation to be the realest real—where does he see reality in today's films? Not only are premises implausible (flighty homecoming queen with no relevant experience gets into Harvard law), time and space are frequently bent to suit the script. Books are published overnight. High school graduations fall three days after Christmas. Overweight moms shed forty pounds in two weeks.

At the core of every film is a logic hole, sometimes miniscule, sometimes gaping, and at one point or another the viewer will turn to the person next to them and say with disgust, "That would never happen."

But this is the beauty of film, the narrative economy that makes the celluloid universe so much more sleek and beautiful than the real one. Devoid of extraneous details and the time-consuming effort of sorting through them, movies are the good-parts-only version of life. Important moments are scored with the appropriate John Williams theme so you don't miss them.

If only people came with such easy-to-read cues. Maybe then I'd understand what Lester was trying to say.

Determined to remain open-minded, I watch *Grosse Point Blank* and *Heathers*. I get halfway through *GPB* before I have to turn it off in frustration. The man John Cusak is hired to kill is the father of his old high school girlfriend, who he's trying to get back with. *Heathers* is just as bad. No excruciating coincidences but it scores a point five on the realest real chart.

Clearly there's a double standard at work—one for the movies the studios want to make and one for all the rest.

My head pounding, I stop *Heathers* and close my laptop. This is way too much work. Paralegaling was almost easier.

And why do I have to work so hard anyway?

What is the studio really buying? With *J&J* it was just the premise. Obviously with Moxie Bernard lined up to play the title character, Chancery Productions wasn't sticking to my original story. Why can't producers do the same thing with *How Tad Johnson Got into Harvard*? Why can't they buy the core idea and rework it until it fits their demographic vision? They're going to rewrite it anyway. Simon calls it ego, John professionalism. But it doesn't matter. The bottom line is no script goes to production in its original form. So why does my screenplay have to be perfect when so many other aren't?

It's a question without a satisfying answer, one of the infinite things in life that comes down to the arbitrariness of the universe. I might as well ask why the sky is blue.

Confused, exhausted and discouraged, I trudge into my bedroom and pull back the spread. Too tired to brush my teeth, I peel off my jeans before climbing under the covers and laying my head down across from the window, where the poster for yet another film with catastrophic coincidences and little reality shudders, breathes and mocks.

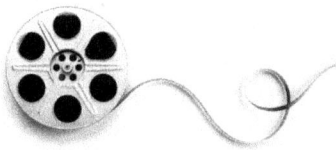

April 21

JOHN SAYS THE solution to my problem is the three Cs: cancer and community college.

"This is par for the course," he says when I show at his door step distraught.

Far from bringing wise counsel, a good night's sleep has only brought panic. All I can think is, if my life is tied up in my script and if my script is shit, then my life is shit.

Finally, a logic equation I understand.

Bring on the LSAT.

John invites me into his apartment and takes full responsibility for my condition. "I should have warned you," he says, offering me a cookie. Thank God, there are cookies. "Agents are always rough on the first go-around, even if they think the draft is decent. Everything can stand to be made better."

The possibility that *Tad Johnson* might not be totally useless is the first positive thought I've had in twenty-four hours. "Really?"

He nods emphatically while chocolate chip crumbs fall into his beard. "Certainly. Some can be perfect monsters about it. You should hear the conversations I have my agent. He doesn't even bother to lead with the positives. You know, a few token things he likes. It's just—bam, this is what sucks."

"Ouch," I say, flinching. My experience with Lester was too similar for comfort.

John shrugs. "Rule number one: It's a business. Nobody's here to hold your hand. As long as they can make money off you, they're interested. The second they can't, they're done. It's the way it works. Everyone's like that."

I take a deep breath and sigh. I'm really not cut out for this.

"Don't worry," he says, "you're still in the money category. If Lester

Dedlock thought your script had no potential, he wouldn't have called you. Six months from now, you would have sent him an e-mail saying, Hey, what's up with that script I sent you, and he would have ignored it completely. So bad news is good news."

Slowly but surely, Hollywood is turning into opposite land. Everything bad is good and everything good is bad. It's a hard concept to wrap your head around. I understand how things sometimes aren't what they seem and the appeal of willful misunderstanding but not the complete reversal of societal norms. "All right."

"As far as your script goes, I think some of his concerns are legitimate and I have ideas about how to address them."

"Really?" I ask, afraid to believe him. I came here this morning determined to leave it up to fate. If John said my script was past help, I'd go back to New York, pass the LSAT, become a lawyer and take the 7:04 out of Norwalk every weekday for the rest of my life. At some point, you have to move on.

But if John thought there was hope, I'd pay him any amount to fix it.

I don't realize until this moment, when it's curtain number two, how terrified I am of returning to my old life.

"Absolutely. Your agent hasn't said anything I haven't heard before. Actually, they all say the same thing. They learn it at agent camp."

"Great. And how much does the second revision cost?" I ask with trepidation. Although still remarkably relieved not to have to return to Connecticut, I'm not immune to the fact of my poverty.

John contemplates me quietly for a full minute. "Oh, what the heck! Because you're my favorite student and I think your story has real potential *and* I know you'll recommend me to others when you get the chance, I'm going to give you a deal. Only one thousand dollars."

I'm grateful for his generosity, but I don't quite see the deal. "The other courses cost one thousand too."

"Yeah, but they were beginning classes. Second revision is advanced. Because the framework of the script has already been establish, the possibilities are limited, which makes it more of a challenge. So I charge fifteen hundred. But I like you and know you won't rat me out to anyone." He winks.

Feeling equal parts grateful and apprehensive, I write him a check for a thousand dollars, quickly calculating how much interest I'm losing with the withdrawal. Compounded over ten years, it's a significant amount but there's no help for it. Spending my inheritance isn't the worst thing in the world; falling short of my potential is.

Besides, as soon as I sell the script, I'll put the money back. My parents will never even know.

John takes the check and hands me another cookie. "Bon appetit," he says.

"Now, as far as your agents notes go, the concern we should address first is character. I told you at the onset that likeability was going to be an issue here."

I don't remember him saying anything so specific or emphatic but I let it go. "All right. How do we fix it?"

"Community college," he says with a hint of triumphant.

The genius is escaping me. "Community college?"

"We take away Tad's safety school and introduce the looming threat of Tukawa County Community College, the worst community college in the entire country. There's no way he could get into Harvard, or any Ivy league, from there, even with his perfect SATs and ten AP credits. Without strong undergrad, he won't get into one of the nation's top law schools, which means he won't get a federal clerkship when he graduates or work his way up to a chief justice of the supreme court. In a flash, he sees his entire future crumbling. This is the one moment on which everything else depends. He must get into Harvard."

As he talks, I feel the old excitement return. This idea isn't so dead. "That's really good."

John takes a small bow. "As for Maryanne, we turn her benign cyst into full-on ovarian cancer. Rule number one: Everyone loves a cancer patient."

"That's it?" I ask, surprised. It seems too simple.

"Absolutely. Nothing makes a character more real than a little suffering. Trust me, Lester will love it. And if he doesn't, you should think about finding another agent. Don't get too caught up in a sense of loyalty. It's all one-sided. Like I said, Lester would dump you in a heartbeat if he thought he couldn't make any more money off you."

"I'm not sure I'm ready for that," I say honestly. The thought of finding new representation is overwhelming. I wouldn't know where to start. Google "Hollywood agent"?

"Don't worry. I'm here to help if it should come to that. I know some people who know some people. But let's not get ahead of ourselves. As I was saying, ovarian cancer is the way to go. She'll have a cute, pixie Audrey do, which we'll later learn is because of the chemo."

"Lester said the coincidences have to go," I say, still mildly resentful, "so how will he find out she's sick?"

"He figures it out when her wig falls off just as he's about to shoot her. He discovers she's dying and he can't bring himself to kill her. He lets her live and keep her slot at Harvard, which he thinks of as his."

"And when he sucks it up and goes to Tukawa, it's a testament of his love," I say excitedly. It's the perfect ending. I can see the last shot: Tad in flannel walking across Tukawa's quad, a large cement square with a lone sapling struggling to survive in the center.

"Well, no. He moves to Boston, takes classes for non-matriculated students and enrolls the following year."

"What?" I ask, recoiling at the eminently sensible suggestion. Nothing like that had ever occurred to me. "Doesn't that invalidate the whole story? Why doesn't he just do that in the first place?"

"It's the surprise twist," John says with a triumphant smile. "Nobody will see it coming."

This logic seems shaky to me, but I don't press it. John is the professional and I'm the rookie who just got bitch-slapped by her agent.

I stay another five hours, working out the intricacies of the new plot and adding as much artifice as necessary to make it the realest real. It's much tougher than I expected and at one point I have such a headache from thinking hard that I want to give up entirely. Suddenly the 7:04 out of Norwalk doesn't seem so bad.

By the time I leave, I'm drained but happy. The script is in a radical new place. It's better, stronger, more real. With so much input from John, it doesn't quite feel like my own anymore but I don't let that bother me. Film is a collaborative medium.

It's about time I understood what that means.

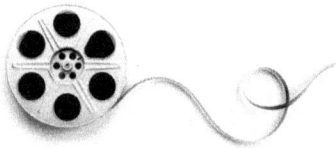

April 30

I BRING HARRY to the Growlery for quiz night because it's a fun evening and there's always a chance we might win the thousand-dollar prize. The competition is still stiff but the owner recently instigated a no-technology rule to level the playing field. Anyone caught using an electronic devise is immediately disqualified.

This is the first week it's in effect and everyone has a new sense of purpose.

Simon and Wren are there when we arrive, and we squeeze into their booth. The bar is so crowded, there's barely enough room to stand, let alone sit comfortably. A pitcher of beer is on the table and I fill our glasses while making the introductions. Simon is as affable as ever, but he eyes Harry warily.

"You're an actor," he says.

Harry laughs easily. "An aspiring personality. I want to be famous for being famous. It seems like a lot less work."

Wren, whose most recent audition for a midseason replacement series went well enough to break her heart, clicks her tongue. "I don't know about that. Don't you need a head start for that? Famous and/or rich parents?"

"No," Harry says, "that's to be Miss Golden Globe. For personality, all you need is one inciting event. I have to be held hostage in a bank for nine hours or save a man from getting run over by a train."

"Or reality TV," Wren throws in.

Harry shakes his head. "Well, no, then you're famous for being an asshole, which is a whole nother thing."

Wren laughs and moves the empty pitcher to the end of the table to get the attention of one of her colleagues.

"So what do you do while you're waiting to be kidnapped?" Simon asks.

"You know, a little bit of nothing," Harry says casually.

"Don't listen to him," I say, used to his modesty. Pretending he's not really into it is Harry's way of dealing with the ups and downs of acting. There are thousands upon thousands like him in the city, striving every day to make it, and he finds it embarrassing to think of himself as one of the struggling multitude. "He works hard."

Simon isn't satisfied. "Doing what?"

Before Harry can answer, Molly stops by to pick up the pitcher. "Can I get you some eats? The jalapeno poppers are especially good tonight."

Wren laughs. "Why? Is Mickie defrosting them differently?"

"New brand. So what will you have?"

After we order chicken wings, mozzarella sticks and nachos, the conversation turns to more general topics as Wren mentions a trip to Vancouver for a bachelorette party. "I can't afford it but she's my best friend so I have to go."

"And treat her to everything she wants," I say, remembering my cousin's. It was only to a transgender Chinese restaurant in the East Village and a Broadway show plus a whole lot of bar hopping but it still set me back a pretty penny.

"Speaking of Canada," Harry says, "the last time I played Trivial Pursuit, it was the Canadian edition—it had a stamp on it that said NOT FOR EXPORT—and most of the questions were Canada specific. Things like which Western Canadian city once had the world's largest paper mill?"

"Vancouver," Wren says with conviction.

Harry makes a surprisingly harsh buzzing sound. "We were looking for Powell River, British Columbia."

"British Columbia. That's Vancouver, which is what I said."

Her faulty logic doesn't impress Harry. "All of Western Canada is in British Columbia, so that's like saying Western Canada's largest paper mill was in Western Canada."

"Which is true," Wren says.

"But not right," Harry contests.

Wren refuses to concede the point and they continue to discuss it for some time to their mutual entertainment. Listening to the nonsense, I'm relieved Harry feels comfortable after that shaky start. I know Simon's pressing him on his job made him uncomfortable. Of late, things have been tight for Harry. When we go out, I pick up the tab because he can't swing it. Deprecating as always, he makes jokes about being a sponge or a kept man, but I see through him. He's trying to deflect the nicks to his pride with humor. It's really very sweet.

Simon's silence is unusual, and I lean over to ask if everything is all right.

"Fine," he says. "So how long have you guys been going out?"

I shrug. "A couple of months."

He nods. "You never mentioned it."

His tone isn't the least bit accusatory but I still feel defensive. Mostly because he has a point. I haven't mentioned it. I'm not sure why other than the moment never seemed right. "It's not serious," I say, wondering for the first time why it's not. Harry's a nice guy; I like him. We have fun together. Yet there's something very fly-by-night about our relationship. We crash parties and sneak into movies. How can that be real?

"Where'd you guys hook up?" he asks.

Harry emerges from the Western Canada debate to relate the story our meeting. "It was at the Hollywood release party for *Jarndyce and Jarndyce.* The very first time I saw her she was standing next to Moxie Bernard having her photo taken and she looked like a genuine, grade-A movie star. Very beautiful. Very glamorous. I was instantly intrigued. Then we got to talking and I discovered she was brilliant too."

I fight the urge to tell him to stop because I know it will sound coy, but his effusiveness is genuine, grade-A mortifying. I can't figure out if it's for my benefit or Simon's.

"The connection was instantaneous, at least on my side. Then she moved out here, which seems too good to be true. Although I like to think I had something to do with that," he says with a wink. "I knew she had talent and would excel at anything she did, so I suggested she try screenwriting. I hooked her up with someone I know and as far as I can tell, it's worked out pretty well."

Simon seizes on that. "You introduced her to Vholes?" Simon asks, his eyes narrowed in suspicion.

I was afraid this would happen. Mine and Simon's easy relationship rests on the tacit agreement that we don't talk about John Vholes. I know he thinks I'm a naïve fool to pay him and he knows I think he's a cynical, sanctimonious, judgmental know-it-all. Not saying the words out loud makes them not real.

"Who's John Vholes?" Wren asks as the loud speaker screeches.

Harry leans forward to explain, but Jody's high-pitch welcome to the first-ever tech-free quiz night preempts him. She runs through the new rules, which alternately earn her cheers and boos. In the middle of her speech, a cell phone rings and true to her word, the player is immediately disqualified.

"Let that be a lesson to you all," she says over the applause.

Wren laughs. "She's been waiting two years to do that."

The room falls silent as Jody reads the first question. "Who was the first quarterback in the NFL to throw 5,000 yards in a season?"

"Easy," Harry says and writes down a name on our answer sheet. "This is going to be cake. I wonder what I'll spend the thousand dollars on first."

"You mean five hundred," I say. "We split the kitty, remember."

He immediately smiles and backtracks—"Well, of course. My half of the thousand"—but his flippant tone makes me look at him twice. Maybe he didn't want to remember.

Molly brings by our assortment of appetizers and the fresh pitcher.

"Sorry it took so long. Things are crazy," she says, putting down a stack of little white plates and extra napkins. "I'll be right back with silverware."

She runs off as Wren takes a mozzarella stick. "I've been dreaming about this all day," she says, her teeth sinking into the melted cheese.

The next question is about Laura Ingalls Wilder and Harry loses some of his confidence. Next to us, Wren scribbles down the number of books Wilder wrote for the Little House series.

As the questions get tougher, the crowd gets rowdier. When Jody takes out her iPod for the name-that-tune portion, someone yells, "Hey, no technology." Everyone laughs when Jody threatens to hum.

Through it all Simon is quiet and thoughtful. He tells Wren the answer when he knows it but for the most part he keeps to himself. Every so often he looks over at me consideringly and I know what he's thinking. Harry's introduction to Vholes is playing in his head, and he has much to say on the topic.

The truce is over.

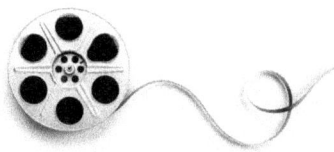

May 5

WHEN I RAISE the window shade Sunday morning, the site that greets my eyes is so horrifying, I scream.

The Hanging Judge at Midnight advertised on my billboard. Rendering judgment in theaters across America on June 6.

It's official. The universe hates me.

Simon insists it's a testament to my strength. "Clearly you're a tough nut to crack, so the universe has to work harder. When my movie went down in flames, there were no billboards outside my window thumbing their nose at me."

"Your option went on for ten years," I remind him.

He leans against the sill and looks at me. Having rushed directly from my window to his door, I'm still in pajamas. He's dressed in worn jeans and a light blue T-shirt; his feet are bare. "So?"

"By that time, you'd probably had all the nose-thumbing you could stand. My option was only eighteen months. I have eight and a half more years of this," I say, quickly doing the math. "That's a hundred and two months. You could start a space program, launch a shuttle and discover life on Mars in that time."

Simon is untroubled by my dismal future. He just laughs and lowers the blinds. "There," he says. "Problem solved."

I roll my eyes at the remarkably simplistic thinking. "Yeah, cause I have no short-term memory and can't for the life of me remember what's behind that. I'm not even sure what that glass thing is. Wait, do we call it a window?"

"Like I said, problem solved. Let's eat breakfast. What do you have?" He wanders down the hall and into my kitchen. I hear him opening cabinets.

Sighing, I scowl at the window one last time and follow the noise. "Cereal and frozen waffles," I say.

But Simon is already on it. He takes a bag of flour from the pantry and puts it next to the canister of sugar. "Pancakes."

"I don't have eggs."

"No worries. I do."

I'm not in the mood, but I go along with the pancake plan. I can't remember the last time I had a real breakfast. "Can we add chocolate chips?"

"I don't know. Do you have chocolate chips?" he says practically.

"In the crisper."

Simon opens the fridge. "Hey, look at that. You do have eggs."

I peer over his shoulder. "Really?"

He takes out the carton. "Hmm. It even seems full."

"Yeah, well," I say with a shrug. I have no idea how long the eggs have been in there, but if Simon doesn't have a problem with them, then neither do I.

Breakfast only takes twenty minutes to make and before I know it we're sitting down to maple-soaked pancakes. "These are fabulous. Thank you."

He shrugs it off. "It's the least I could do on the morning the universe tries to destroy you."

"You mock what you don't understand."

"True enough."

We eat in silent for a few minutes, my mind straying to the billboard and *The Hanging Judge at Midnight* and then, inevitably, to Moxie Bernard, Lloyd Chancellor and all the hopes and dreams I'd pinned on the movie. The life I could have had if only....

It seems so stupid now.

Somehow or other, it always comes back to that—how thoroughly and completely I believed. Like a day-old kitten with no defenses at all.

"Do you know," I say contemplatingly as I take another pancake, "I actually believed that I was David. I thought *J&J* versus *The Judge* was a David and Goliath story and I was the plucky underdog with a slingshot. I had Moxie and they didn't even have a script. I really thought I was going to win."

Simon takes my hand and squeezes. "You're supposed to. A) It's the nature of the business. B) It's the nature of the beast. Human beings have hope. It's a great scourge on humanity but what can you do?"

I laugh dryly. It's so true. Hope *is* a great scourge. "The real narrative, of course, was you can't fight city hall. The top dog always wins. Their movie is coming out in four weeks and mine is dead." I'm drifting into self-pity again but I can't help it. You can no more fight the universe than you can city hall. "All that time spent worrying about Moxie. Will she hold on? Will she OD? Will she catch a cold from not wearing panties and die of consumption? And it was fucking Esther Rogers all along. It kills me." I look at Simon, at his floppy hair and scruffy smile. He so has it together. A real job, a nice apartment, the skill and know-how to make pancakes on a moment's notice. "Do you ever worry that you'll reach the end of your life and find out you've spent the whole time worrying about the wrong things entirely?"

He smiles. "Of all the multitude of things I've come up with to worry about, from being trapped under a pylon in a ferry crash in Norway to the shape of my face is too square, that one never occurred to me."

"That's because you're sane, sane enough to get out of the movie business and not wallow in it like me."

He's silent for a moment. Then he says, "Did I? Or did I just run away?"

Surprised, I turn to him sharply, expecting to see something different in him, some physical manifestation of his mental doubts, but far from growing a second head, he's the same relaxed Simon as always.

I have no idea how to respond. None at all. I don't want him questioning himself or doubting his decisions. More than that, I don't want to be responsible for the reevaluation. He's together, I'm not.

Silently I butter my pancake.

"You should write that," he says a few minutes later. "That bit about David and Goliath and city hall. You should put it in an essay. It's good."

The idea is so crazy, I laugh and relax again. If he's not going to obsess over his comment, then neither am I. "Yeah, like I'd know the first thing about writing an essay. The last one I did was in college. Senior year English lit. Emma Woodhouse: Faultless Despite Her Faults. I'm pretty sure I got a B minus."

"It'll be easier now," he says, as if the nature of the essay has somehow changed. "No research required. Just you at the computer recording your experiences. The party's great material. I wish I could have seen it. And that stuff about worrying about Moxie. You have a unique story. What happened to you, millions of people dream about happening to them. Plucked from obscurity."

"Then immediately deplucked."

"Yeah, but that's your angle. Plucked and deplucked. You went full circle."

"And wound up exactly where I started."

"The perfect ending. That's why people will want to read it."

"So they can gloat in my failure. She had it coming, they'll say." I can just imagine Victoria Wright's triumphant little smile.

"The failure wasn't yours." When I don't respond, he says. "It'll give you something positive to do with all that negative energy swirling inside you."

I squeeze the last of the syrup onto my plate. "Negative energy? That's a little new agey. Maybe you should stick—no pun intended—with the voodoo dolls."

"OK, how about this: Maybe you can sell some books. An article in the *New York Times* has to be good for a few hundred copies."

Appealing to my sense of greed is smart, but it's not possible solutions to my escalating poverty that gets my attention. "Hold on. You think the *New York Times* would run it?"

He spears two more pancakes and drops them onto his plate. "Maybe. Or *USA Today*."

"But you honestly think the *Times* is a possibility?" I ask, stars in my eyes. I'm too much of a New Yorker not to feel a thrill at the prospect of seeing my essay on the pages of the *Times*. The byline alone would be exhilarating enough.

"Absolutely. In the Arts and Leisure or maybe Styles."

I think about all those people who would see it, the millions of readers across the country who have never heard of me. Maybe they'll smile at my self-deprecating humor and think, Tough break.

That wouldn't be so bad.

Then I remember all the people who do know me, the ones who purported to be happy for me when they heard about the movie deal but are really just waiting for me to sink back down to their level.

Still, they're going to find out about it some way. When the movie doesn't start shooting, when Moxie never mentions it again, when they bump into me on line at Food Emporium and I have to explain shame-faced that the studio hated the script. Their knowing is inevitable. It's a fact of life. I might as well announce it myself *and* get a piece in the world's most famous paper.

I mean, failure would almost be OK if it could get you into the *New York Times*.

"All right," I say. "But you have to help me sell it. I don't know anything about peddling an article."

"Fair enough. I'll start asking around to get some names." He cuts the stack of pancakes in half, then in half again before reaching for the syrup. The bottle is empty but he valiantly extracts three drops. "You're lucky, you know. My story isn't interesting enough to write about."

"That's what Harry keeps saying. He thinks all my suffering will make excellent fodder on the talk-show circuit."

It's the first time I've mentioned Harry's name since Tuesday night and I watch Simon out of the corner of my eye for his reaction.

His response is far from what I'm expecting. "He seems nice."

"He is," I say defensively because I don't trust his tone. "He's actually very sweet. Very supportive and encouraging."

"So he's friends with Vholes?"

And there it is! "I wouldn't say friends exactly. More like acquaintances or colleagues. There's nothing wrong with it."

"All right," he says as he lifts the fork to his mouth.

His mild reply puts my back up. "I don't know what you're trying to imply, but I don't appreciate it. Vholes is a professional. I needed help. End of story."

"Of course."

Oh, how smug he sounds.

Annoyed, I stand up and start clearing the table. I take the butter and the juice and the glasses and the serving platter and Simon's plate. "Hey, I'm not done."

"Yes, you are."

He smiles again.

God, it's so condescending.

He slides his chair out. "All right. I've got a lot to do today anyway, starting with but not limited to getting my hands on the e-mail of the editor of Sunday Styles."

I put the lid on the butter dish and stick it in the refrigerator. "That's all right. I don't need your help. I'll just pay Harry for his."

Now he laughs. "Well, if you're sure you can afford it...."

Angry, I slam the fridge closed, causing the two bottles of mustard and one jar of relish to rattle. I want to tell him to go to hell, but I don't say a thing. He walks to the door, opens it and thanks me for breakfast. I maintain a dignified silence as I put the dishes into the sink. Then, just as he's about to shuffle out, I say, "Not Sunday Styles." I keep my back to him, my grip on the hot water faucet. "It's too flashy. Too Candace Bushnell at Barneys. Go with Thursday."

He's silent for a long moment, and I brace for another argument disguised as a pep talk. But he just says all right and leaves.

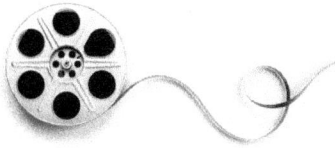

May 7

THE DIRECTOR OF *Where's Willa?* fires Moxie in a spectacular on-set scene witnessed by the cast, crew and a writer from *Vanity Fair* doing a cover story on Moxie. The focus of the piece is the teen star's reformation, her decision to quit drinking and take her craft more seriously now that she's nineteen years old.

Despite her recent commitment to clean living, she shows up on the set at nine in the morning so hung over she can barely open her eyes. She stumbles through one take before Louise Manfra pulls her aside and quietly suggests she go to her trailer sleep it off. "We'll pick this up this afternoon."

Moxie insists she has nothing to sleep off and says they'll pick this up right now. Her feeble voice cracks with the effort of speaking, and a helpful PA brings her a cup of chamomile tea to soothe her vocal cords. Not in the mood for tea, Moxie pushes it away, upsetting the cup and scalding the assistant. The PA struggles manfully not to cry at the painful second-degree burns while Manfra orders Moxie to apologize. She says, "Jeez, I'm sorry," with so much indifference, the director's control snaps and she calls her a spoiled bitch. "Get off my set and don't you *ever* come back," she says. Moxie storms out.

Despite the convincing performances, the firing doesn't take. Manfra doesn't have the ability to sack Moxie or any of the four leading actors in the film. Her contract only gives her power over supporting cast, day players and extras.

Unable to deny an argument witnessed by the entire cast and crew, a spokeswoman for the studio announces that the heated discussion had the beneficial affect of clearing the air. "Moxie and Louise are eager to résumé filming," she says. Nobody believes her, least of all the writer from *Vanity Fair.*

Although my interest in Moxie has disappeared, the rest of the world's hasn't and when I turn on my computer in the morning, there are twenty-two e-mails about the incident. Everyone includes a jokey comment about Moxie being free to do my film now, even people who know the movie deal fell through.

After the first few, I delete all the messages without opening them.

It amazes me how persistent the bond between me and Moxie is. It ceased to exist the moment Arcadia killed the film—if, indeed, it ever really did exist—and yet nobody will acknowledge it. I'm still their go-to girl for Moxie news and updates. They send me almost daily reports of her exploits, the minor mishaps and the major blowups until I feel like a clearinghouse of Moxie information. I'm where all the stories intersect.

I hate it.

Every mention of Moxie is another aching little reminder of what might have been, a tiny pinprick in my soul, and no matter how many times I tell people I don't want to hear about her anymore, they keep sticking me with needles.

I'm so tired of the pain.

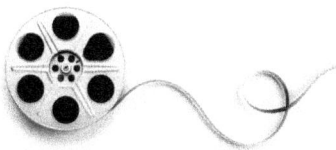

May 9

I START BY calling myself a ward of Chancery Productions because making a movie in Hollywood bears a striking resemblance to the slow, arcane nineteenth-century British judiciary system with which Lloyd's company shares its name. Cases go on for years and by the time they're resolved the original participants are very likely dead.

The comparison is a bit dramatic but that's how I feel, and Simon said the point of the essay to write about my emotions.

It's a remarkably satisfying experience.

Hours pass as I record the long, varied process, the many days (numbered and not) that finally brought me to this place. It takes me a while to get the tone right—I'm afraid of seeming ungrateful—but in the end I think I come across as sad and self-aware.

It's not an awful combination.

Following Simon's advice, I conclude with David and Goliath. Everyone loves an underdog story, I write, but this isn't one. This is a you-can't-fight-city-hall tale, and they never have happy endings.

I read it through several times before e-mailing it to my sister. Then I call to make sure she sees it. It's only eleven fifteen on the East Coast but somehow I wake her up. I blame Glenn for this. He's just the sort of wimpy-ass nine-to-fiver who would go to bed before Jon Stewart.

Carrie's tired and cranky but when I explain what it's about, she agrees immediately to read it. She turns on the light and boots up the computer. In the background I hear Glenn whining. "What're doing? It's the middle of the night."

He sounds so put out, I resolve to come up with a reason to call every night at eleven fifteen. If I started a new book, I could send her chapters daily.

"I'm opening it now," she says. "Do you want to hang on or should I call you back when I'm done?"

"I'll wait," I say, my stomach rumbling as I try to remember the last time I ate. Writing the essay was considerably more engrossing than I expected. Forcing myself to concentrate on the constricting formula of a screenplay is so difficult, I can barely pull myself away from the fridge. Hours drag by as I struggle to break up the frustration with dozens of games of solitaire.

John is worth every penny I pay him if for no other reason than he compels me to focus.

Opening the refrigerator, I dig around for something decent. As always, there isn't much to chose from, and I settle on a moldy chunk of cheddar and some whole-wheat crackers. It's easier to cut off the blueish-blackish bits than to make something from scratch.

While Carrie takes an inordinate amount of time to read two thousand measly words, I sit on the couch and turn on the TV. I keep it on mute so I can hear if she laughs. So far I've counted only two giggles and a minor guffaw, which is disappointing. I thought for sure the piece had a few major guffaws.

When she comes back on the line, the first words out of her mouth are "I don't know what to say."

My heart drops.

"This is so unexpected," she adds.

I wait for her to say unexpected in a good way or a bad way.

"I didn't know you were capable of this."

Her string of ambiguous sentences is doing little for my blood pressure and absolutely nothing for my appetite. I push the plate of crackers to the far side of the coffee table.

"It's perfect, utterly and amazingly perfect," she says. "I wouldn't change a word."

I let out a huge breath. "Really?"

"It's an honest, straightforward account of your experience and you've written it in such a funny and humble way that I don't resent you."

In the act of reaching for the cheese, I halt. "Why would you resent me?"

"Well," she points out, "Hollywood threw you a fabulous party, you got a new edition of your book with an extremely marketable quote from the world's most famous teen and *Variety* ran a story on you and now you're whining that it wasn't enough."

"But I'm not whining."

"I know. That's what I'm saying. You're complaining but it doesn't come across as complaining. Instead it reads like you took one on the chin and kept going. It's really good."

I try to process her comment. Will other people—not-related-to-me people—think I'm whining? Maybe I should put in a sentence about how grateful I am for all Chancery did for me. I know I got more than most people do. "Thank you."

"Seriously, I'm impressed. Who put you up to it?"

It's just like Carrie to follow a compliment with a snide comment. "What do you mean?"

"Making a silk purse out of a sow's ear?" Her tone is mildly scornful. "That's not you. You make sow's ears out of silk purses. I'm surprised you didn't write a story earlier about how much it sucks having your book optioned. Did Julie suggest it?"

"No," I say petulantly, annoyed at how neatly she summed up my personality. She's my sister. She's supposed to think nice things about me. "It was Simon."

"Oh, that's good. We like Simon."

I roll my eyes. She doesn't even know Simon. One conversation in an elevator does not a relationship make. "Is that the royal we?"

"Mom, Dad and me. We think Simon's great. You should go out with him."

It's amazing how your family can manage to be a pain in the butt from three thousand miles away. "First of all," I say, "he hasn't asked me. Secondly, I'm already going out with someone."

"Yeah, we don't like Harry."

"Mom, Dad and you?" I ask, rolling my eyes again. It's just like them to make snap decisions about something they know nothing about. You're supposed to teach your kids not to be judgmental, but my parents went in the opposite direction. We learned the sooner you can sum people up, the better.

"We think he's dodgy," she says.

Her audacity is staggering. Clearly she has no idea how vulnerable she is in the area of boyfriend disapproval. If she's opening the flood gates, I have several leagues to say about Glenn, starting with his air of middle-aged disappointment and ending with the way he grabs her ass.

"Dodgy," I repeat, wondering what she's getting at. Clearly she has something in mind.

"Yes, dodgy."

"And your evidence is?"

"His name, for one."

I rest my head against the couch and close my eyes. "His name?" I repeat flatly.

"Harold Skimpole. Skimpole. Skimping," she explains. "The symbolism is so unsubtle it's almost insulting."

"You're holding his name against him," I say, wondering where she's going with this. It has to be a joke.

"He 'forgot' his wallet when you went to the Ivy. Classic Skimpoling."

She can't really be using that honest mistake against him. "I'm hanging up now."

"And he introduced you to that writer guy who charges you every time you sneeze. You must realize we have a fundamental problem with anyone who sets you up with a siphon."

It's official. I'm never telling her a single thing about my life again. "The phone is inches from the receiver."

"Fine. Go. Great article. I'm really proud of you."

The quick fire change from mean sister to supportive one flusters me. I can't remember the last time Carrie said she was proud of me. "Thank you."

"Call me tomorrow."

Not ready to forgive her, I say maybe and hang up. As annoyed as I am about her ridiculous comments about Harry—classic Skimpoling!—I'm too excited about her reaction to the essay to think about it. I type in Simon's e-mail and send him the article. Although it's insane to expect him to be online at nine o'clock at night, I press refresh ten times in the next hour. When it's obvious that he's not going to respond right away, I finish the cheese, wash it down with some stale Milanos, wash up and go to sleep, leaving the blinds open.

For the first time ever, *The Hanging Judge at Midnight* billboard doesn't bother me at all.

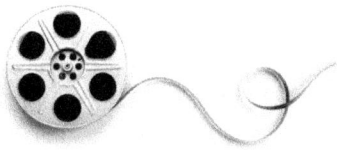

May 10

LESTER STILL THINKS I have a solid beginning but that's all I have.

"The premise is intriguing and original but the story is too dark. Black comedy is the hardest genre to sell because few people manage to do it well. Studios look for movies with mass appeal that will draw the largest possible audience. *Tad Johnson* is too niche," he explains. "I'm afraid they'd never go for it."

As John had said something similar about black comedy, I'm not entirely surprised by his response, but it annoys me that he didn't mention his concern the first time I showed the script to him. If the problem all along was the story's black comedy-ness, why did I spend four weeks and one thousand dollars trying to make it the realest real?

It's not that I believe there's some kind of conspiracy afoot or anything paranoid like that; it's simply that it seems like no matter what I do, Lester won't like it.

Maybe this is the hazing process all screenwriters go through. Maybe you have to realize your script will never be right in order for it to be right. Maybe you have to take a Zen approach and submit to the universe.

Or maybe it's all just a mind fuck.

"What about as an indie film? Couldn't it work as one of those?" I ask practically. If the studios won't go for it, then fine. The dark broody colors of early Soderbergh would dovetail perfectly with Tad's teenage angst, which is what I want anyway.

"Possibly," he concede, "but there's no money in it. Your work has value and should be appreciated accordingly. You wouldn't get anything for an independent script. Have you thought about trying it as a novel? Studios are a lot less critical of books than they are of screenplays. It's easier for them to see the potential and miss the flaws. It's something to think about."

Realizing it's futile, I thank Lester for his feedback and hang up. I have a million arguments in my head for why his reasoning is wrong—there's more to building a career than cashing big paychecks. In the movie business, I am nobody, but one solid independent hit and I could write my own ticket. Everyone has read the success stories about the little script that could. Independent films are the perfect backdoor to Hollywood, a way of paying your dues and creating a name for yourself while dodging the small-minded politics of the studio system.

I'd never be so confident as to assume I deserve to start at the top. The bottom is good enough for me as long as there's room to grow.

But what did I really expect? I've known all along that Lester is only in it for the money. I've had this epiphany once a week for three years. Trying to push it any farther would be like banging my head against a wall.

Frustrated, I boot up my computer, open the *Tad Johnson* file and read through it, struggling to envision the story as a novel.

As hard as I try, it never adds up to anything more than a few hundred lines of dialogue.

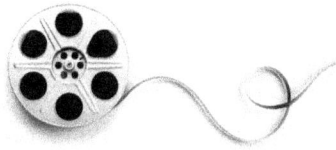

May 13

SIMON DIGS UP two names for the *Times*.

"Richard Edson is a culture writer for Arts and Leisure. He covers mostly television but does some movie stuff as well," he says, placing a Post-it with e-mail addresses next to my computer. "Angela Deering is deputy editor for Thursday Styles. My friend from Columbia thinks you should go with her. A lot of her classmates have had success with the Thursday section. Apparently they're hungry for material."

As I study the Post-it, butterflies flutter in my belly. I don't know what I'm more nervous about: being rejected or being rejected by the *New York Times*. "So Angela," I say.

He nods. "Yep, Angela."

I'm not ready for his easy consent. I figured we could debate the matter for a few hours before making a decision. "Should I do it now?"

"You're welcome to sit here all day obsessing over it if you want," he says, with a quick look at his watch, "but I have to get to work so if you need me to hold your hand while you send it, then, yes, you should do it now."

I pick up the Post-it. It seems like such a simple thing to type in Angela Deering's e-mail and hit send. "She's going to hate it."

"She's going to love it as much as I do."

"She's going to think I'm whining that my movie didn't get made."

Simon sighs. "Seriously, I'm happy to have this discussion for the *fifth* time, but it'll have to wait until after work. I'm already running late."

"You really think it's good?" I ask hesitantly.

He stands up and grabs his messenger bag. "So we'll pick this up at seven. I'll bring the sushi, you bring the crazy."

The thought of sitting on the Post-it for an entire day is unbearable. "OK, OK." I type in the address, sit back and stare at the empty subject line. "What do I write? It needs to be something smart and grabby."

"Hollywood broke my heart," he says, without even thinking about it.

I replay it in my head. "Doesn't that sound needy and desperate?"

"It sounds true. Now go on, type it. Traffic is backing up on the 405 as we speak."

I enter the sentence, then cut and paste the snappy pitch we wrote last night after we discussed for the fourth time whether or not I sounded whiny. It's amazing how Simon's opinion doesn't change. Mine does by the minute. "Should I paste the essay into the letter or attached the Word document?"

"Both and make a note that the article is below and attached. That's how I get most résumés these days."

It only takes me a second to comply and before I know it my cursor is hovering over the SEND button. I can't believe how heavily my heart is pounding. When did this become such a big deal?

"Whenever you're ready," Simon says when I don't move for a full minute.

I close my eyes and click the mouse. When I open them again, the e-mail is gone, sent, skedaddled. There's nothing I can do now.

Simon honors the moment with an extended silence. Then he picks up his messenger bag again and kisses me on the forehead. "They're going to love it. You'll see."

"Thank you," I say, grabbing his hand and squeezing it. "Really, thank you."

With typical Simon-ness, he shrugs it off. "We're still on for dinner, right? Me sushi, you crazy?"

I think of an entire day spent waiting for a response from Angela Deering. "With an extra helping of insane."

The second Simon leaves, I refresh. Nothing. I dart into the bathroom to brush my teeth. When I come out, I click it again. Still nothing.

At eleven, Harry calls to see if I want to go take in the Magritte exhibit at the Los Angeles County Museum of Art. "It's closing next week," he says.

As a former volunteer docent at the Museum of Contemporary art—he did it for three hours—Harry has an ID card that gets him and a guest into any museum in the city, and, apparently, the country, for free. It's also good for ten percent off at gift shops and museum restaurants.

"I'd love to but I can't," I say, feeling none of the regret I try to imbue into my words. There's no way I'm leaving my computer until I hear back from Angela Deering. An article pitch is like crack to an update junkie.

"Why? What are you up to?"

For some reason I don't want to tell him about the essay. I e-mailed him a copy days ago for feedback and never heard a thing. Now I'm too embarrassed to ask. He must have thought it was a special kind of awful to bury it so deep. "Nothing really. Just some work I need to catch up on."

"You sure you can't do it later?" he asks cajolingly.

I refresh the page and get an e-mail from my sister with granite samples.

I can't believe a kitchen can take this long to design. "Nope, it has to be done now. I'll call you later. Have fun."

At four o'clock I get a response. My heart beating ferociously, I click on the message. Angela is succinct. "Interesting. Let me see."

I immediately call Carrie with the good news. "The *New York Times* thinks I'm interesting!"

She congratulates me and asks what I thought of ash versus slate, two colors so similar they might as well be the same. "Please say you liked ash. Glenn is pushing for slate but I think it's too dark."

"Ash. Definitely."

"Thanks."

"My pleasure," I say, thinking of the domestic discord I just fomented. "I'm always here for you."

Angela's next message, a half hour later, is just as concise. "We like. Please call."

My hand shaking, I dial her number. She picks up on the first ring and sounds happy to hear from me. "We really love your piece but one thing. How do I know you're Ricki Carstone?"

"I…uh…what?"

"I need to confirm that I'm talking to Ricki Carstone and not someone who wants to sabotage her career."

So many thoughts go through my head, I'm staggered, but one is more persistent than the others. Career sabotage. "You think the article will ruin my career?" I ask, horrified. All I was worried about was people liking it. That I would be shooting myself in the foot never occurred to me.

"Not at all. It's delightful."

"But you just said——"

"We always have to be careful about people using the paper to settle scores. As you're obviously Ricki, I wouldn't worry about it. The piece is charming and funny. We're excited to run it. We've scheduled it for May 25."

I repeat the date softly, trying to do the math in my head.

"That's a week from Sunday," she says.

Sunday styles? Holy shit. "That sounds great."

I click on new message, type the date into the subject line and send it to Carrie. I don't know why I bother. She's probably not online at 7 p.m.

"Good. Do you have any photos from the party we can use?" she asks.

Oh, my God. The *New York Times* is going to run my photo. "No, not really. I mean, I have a few snapshots, but they're nothing special. Filmmagic.com has some good ones and Getty. I could send you the links."

"No, that's all right. Our photo editor will do it. I think that's it. Congratulations on a wonderful piece. I know our readers will love it."

"Thank you," I say, struggling to seem calm and collected when all I want to do is jump up and down.

"Oh, there was one other thing. A minor detail. When I called Chancery Productions to confirm the story, they said the movie wasn't dead."

I'm so surprised the phone almost slips from my hand. "What?"

"They said they still hoped to make the movie. To be honest, it sounded like the standard party line to me, you know, like a face saver, but you might want to think about softening the language a bit."

"Right," I say, deciding that her explanation made sense. A face saver or the assistant misunderstood the question. "I'll do that."

"Great. I'll be in touch. Congratulations again."

As soon as she hangs up, I call Carrie and screech in her ear for ten minutes. I'm only capable of half sentences and obscenities. She manages to calm me down and forces me to replay the conversation word for word.

"Hold on. What does it mean the movie's not dead?"

I shake my head. "It's just producer speak. It doesn't mean anything."

An hour later, I have the same conversation with Simon. We're at the Growlery, where I insist on taking him to celebrate his genius. "It means nothing, right?" I can't help looking for confirmation.

"Less than nothing," he says. "It's the sort of bullshit you say when the *New York Times* calls. Now let's have another round. My genius doesn't feel celebrated enough."

Wren brings another pitcher of margaritas and Simon makes her sit down while I retell my triumphant story, starting at the moment when he suggests I write the essay. Wren asks to read the piece but Simon tells her to wait for the *Times* like everyone else.

We stay for hours, forgoing our fancy dinner plans for bar nibbles. We try the jalapeno poppers, which I think are better, per earlier press reports, but Simon insists it's only the taste of victory that makes them so delicious. I have no argument for that. Everything tastes sweeter tonight, even the air.

And when I put my head down at eleven thirty, giddy and drunk and excited for the future, the pillow seems softer and fluffier. Within seconds I'm asleep and it's the deepest, most peaceful sleep I've ever had.

It's wonderful to be a *New York Times* writer.

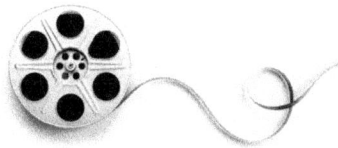

Day 1,092

THE CHAIN OF events goes like this: *The New York Times* calls Chancery Production, Chancery Productions calls Lester Dedlock and Lester Dedlock calls me to say running the article would kill my movie.

What movie?

"Lloyd is still trying to make *Jarndyce and Jarndyce*. He's lining up independent financing," Lester explains.

The words sound so simple when he says them, and yet when I try to arrange them into a coherent sentence in my head, I come up blank. He has to repeat it three times before I finally get it. *J&J* isn't dead. "But you said that wouldn't happen. You said he has to cultivate relationships with the new regime and wouldn't waste another second on *J&J*. That's what you said."

I know I sound accusatory; I don't care. When the movie died, every breath of hope was squeezed out of me, hundreds of pounds of pressure crushing every cherished dream from my lungs until I was as flat as a board. It hurt in every way possible—mentally, physically, emotionally—but I got over it and moved on.

I don't want to learn now it was for nothing.

Lester skirts the issue, staying in the present. "Lloyd is very close to securing the financing, which is why you have to pull the article."

With each new statement he makes, my confusion grows. I close my eyes and take a deep breath. I'm not stupid. I can figure this out. Let's start at the beginning.

"What does the article have to do with the financing?" I ask.

"Your article compares your book unfavorably with *The Hanging Judge at Midnight*," he says.

"No, it doesn't," I say. "If anything, my article compares *The Hanging Judge* unfavorably with mine."

"You say *The Judge* is a national best seller and about to hit movie theaters in two weeks. You say *J&J* barely made a splash and its film deal died on the vine. The *Judge* is the champion and *J&J* the runner-up. That's unfavorable. You can't run an article that's unfavorable. You and your book deserve better."

Well, yeah, if you compare them in the most superficial way, then *The Hanging Judge* wins out, but my article makes it clear that there are estimations of success that don't involve crude dollar signs. Mine was the better book; every reviewer said so. "I appreciate your concern but I'm not worried, and if I were, I think it would be worth the risk," I say, hoping this will be the end of it. I appreciate Lester's advice but his sense of the enormity of the event—Sunday Styles, the section everyone talks about on Monday morning—is skewed by his West Coast-ness. The only daily he reads is *Variety*.

"Ordinarily I'd agree but it's not that simple," he says. "Think about it: Why would anyone want to make, let alone finance, the loser book? Everyone wants to back a champion."

I blink several times and replay his comment carefully in my head to make sure I heard him right. Did he really just say loser book? Am I back in high school? Are producers really such facile creatures that they operate on the principals of the playground? Is some bully going to beat me up now?

Baffled by Lester's logic, I throw myself on the couch and close my eyes. I can't believe this is happening to me. Getting published in the *New York Times* is supposed to be unalloyed joy; now it's just one more thing torturing me.

"They don't have the option," I say. "They let it lapse. If they want to make the movie, why don't they have the option?"

"Chancery doesn't have any money. Their discretionary fund is courtesy of Arcadia and can only be used for Arcadia projects, which this no longer is. When they tie down their financing, they'll reoption it. By all indications that could happen very soon." Realizing the delicacy of the situation, he imbues his voice with sympathy. "I know how hard this decision is. The article is beautifully written and you should be very proud of it. But it doesn't stand up against the movie. I'm seventy percent certain *J&J* will be under option again by the end of the month. That's ten thousand dollars. I know the article is a sure thing and the movie is a gamble, but don't you have to bet on yourself? Trust me, I understand the appeal of the article, but the movie will help your career much more in the long run."

But he doesn't understand at all. He has no idea what's going on inside me. Already hope has infected my body, pumping its way through my bloodstream like poison until it reaches my heart. I think of Lloyd toiling behind the scenes to make my movie happen, not giving up, not abandoning me, not choosing the goodwill of his new bosses over *J&J*, and I feel myself slowly reinflating.

I don't want this. I know the depth of this hole and how hard it is to climb out of. I'd rather cut off a limb than find myself back in the claws of hope.

It hurts too much.

And there is it encapsulated: I don't want to get hurt again. Like any woman who's had a bad breakup, I don't want to rush into another relationship.

I am every Lifetime movie ever made.

I don't say any of this to Lester because I know he doesn't care. My emotional needs aren't his problem. He's here for the fifteen percent and only the fifteen percent. That's why he didn't tell me about the independent financing—because until there's money for the option, the project doesn't exist. It's a gleam in Lloyd Chancellor's eye, and in the meantime it's his job to make sure I don't do anything to screw it up.

Promising to think about it, I hang up and immediately call Simon. Suddenly I'm ridiculously thankful that he's been through it all before. If only my present were truly his past.

I give him a brief rundown of the morning's events and wait anxiously for his opinion. I have no idea what he's going to say. Lester's loser-book take seems ridiculously absurd to me but this is opposite land, where things runs counterintuitive. Maybe he's right.

"Call Lloyd," he says.

This is not what I'm expecting. "Huh?"

"Call Lloyd. If you're going to pull the article for him, he should at least tell you why."

I think of the man I stood next to at the party, the detached professional in the sharkskin suit, and feel a tremor of alarm. It doesn't seem right that someone like me call him up on the phone and presume to talk to him. "You really think I should?"

"I think you need more information. I don't agree with Lester's reasoning. He could be right but he could be wrong. He calls *J&J* the loser book; I call it the underdog. The second you run the article, it becomes the comeback story, and everyone loves a comeback story, especially Hollywood."

He's so calm and rational, I feel some of my anxiety subsiding. If he could see the negative energy swirling inside me now, he'd be knocked over by the gale-force winds. "OK."

"Call Lloyd," he says again.

"Right."

"Then call me back."

"Will do."

He's silent for a moment, then: "Ricki, I'm sorry about this."

Simon thinks this is all his fault, but it's not. It's Lester's. If I'd known there was anything on the line, I wouldn't have written the story in the first place. "Don't be silly. Do you know what a thrill it is for me to know I wrote a *Times*-quality piece? It's pretty amazing."

"Glass-half-full—I like it."

"And they're still trying to make my movie. That's a good thing, right?" I add.

He manages an upbeat yes, but I can tell what he's really thinking: that sometimes it's better to get off the roller coaster than suffer another round of ups and downs.

It's hard to argue with the logic.

The thought of calling Lloyd directly terrifies me, and I pick up the phone six times before I actually dial his number. I don't know why I'm so nervous. He's just a guy who runs a production company, and only a moderately successful one at that. I mean, it's not like he's Scott Rudin.

I chant this in my head while I dial the number.

A woman with a clipped British accent answers, and I fumble through an explanation of who I am. She puts me on hold. Nadia immediately picks up and says Lloyd was hoping to speak with me today. "He's on the other line but should be off in a minute. Do you mind waiting?"

Her niceness is so unprecedented I realize for the first time how much trouble I have caused with my little article, and I smile, imagining the tizzy the call from the *Times* must have set off yesterday. If I can humble just one supercilious assistant who won't give me the time of day, then maybe this awful debacle is worth it.

Lloyd keeps me waiting ten minutes. "Hello, Ricki," he says warmly, "it's been a while since we've talked. How are you?"

Common courtesy is the last thing I expect. "In a bit of a turmoil," I say honestly. "This article for the *Times* has me confused and upset."

"Understandable," he says. "It's a great article, by the way. Very clever and neatly written."

His comment takes me aback and I realize then and there that Lester forwarded him a copy without my permission. Something about this discovery makes me extremely uncomfortable. Suddenly I feel like the target of a vast conspiracy. Why are they working so hard to put me down? Am I that dangerous? Am I really going to do so much harm? Or is it simply the exercise of power for the sake of power? A little flexing of the dictatorial muscle? Kill the little nobody writer's story just because you can.

Maybe they're not even making my movie at all. They don't want it, but they don't want anyone else to want it either.

"As much as I admire it, though, I don't think this is the right time for it," Lloyd adds quickly.

"Why not?" I ask suspiciously, silently daring him to repeat Lester's speech about loser books so I can hang up with a bang. If they're going to make me give up the best thing in my life simply to gratify their egos, they're going to have to do work harder than that.

"You set up *Jarndyce and Jarndyce* as the other *Hanging Judge at Midnight*," he says. "This is a serious problem for me because the hardest part of my job for the last three years has been convincing people that *Jarndyce and Jarndyce* isn't the same book as *The Hanging Judge at Midnight*. So I really can't have the author of *Jarndyce and Jarndyce* announce in the *New York Times* that she wrote the other *Hanging Judge at Midnight*. It would ruin everything for me."

As far as arguments go, it's much better than the one about losers books and it gives me pause. For the first time since this disaster started, I imagine the call to Angela Deering. She'll hate me. The photo department has been chasing down pictures of me with Moxie Bernard for nothing.

The New York Times will never run anything of mine again.

Who am I kidding? This is all I have. One fucking movie that doesn't exist, that might exist again.

When I don't say anything, Lloyd continues. "I know you have doubts but trust me, I will get this movie made. I'm a bulldog. I'm stubborn and persistent and I have a vision. I will not give up. And you're not giving up anything either. You'll see at the premiere."

His confidence is so powerful, it's like a living thing, and I can feel the strong bands of its arms wrapping themselves around me. Right here, right now, I believe in the movie as firmly as I believe in my mother. It is something that has nurtured me for thirty years and could nurture me for another thirty.

"This is a particularly delicate time for me," he adds, "since we're about to lock down the financing. I'm one week away from twenty-four million dollars to make the movie, and I can't risk my finance guys seeing the article and saying, What's going on with this? It's too important. Trust me, I've been working on this film for three years. I've got as much invested as you."

I don't know how it's possible for him to have as much invested as me but something about his argument rings alarmingly true. He *has* been working on *J&J* for three years. Despite the obstacles, he's remained true to his vision. It's no more his fault that Arcadia fired Miriam Heeger than it is mine, and yet he believes so strongly in *J&J* he'd rather risk alienating the new regime than give it up.

That has to be worth something.

More confused than ever, I thank him for his time and promise to let him know what I decide. He says it's been great talking to me and insists that I call with any questions. "Remember, we're in this together."

I hang up, lie down on the couch and cover my eyes with my fists. I know what's going to happen. In six months from now, in nine months, in a year, I'll have nothing: no option, no movie, no Sunday Styles. I'll be back to where I started, with no reason to hope nor any ability to cope. I'll take to the couch and never get up again.

But there's nothing I can do about it. Seeing the future bearing down on me at a hundred miles an hour, I can't swerve to miss it. The only reason I wrote the essay was I had nothing to lose.

Now I do.

Tears welling ridiculously in my eyes, I pick up the phone and call the *New York Times*.

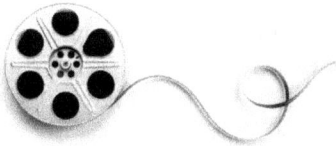

Day 1,094

HARRY THINKS I did the right thing and takes me to lunch to celebrate the regeneration of my movie career. We go to the set of Will Smith's new film, an action adventure being shot entirely on location in Los Angeles. Its budget, in the low two hundreds, mysteriously covers luxuries like excellent craft services.

"Not so mysterious," Harry says as he checks the rearview mirror and straightens the car. He's an excellent parallel parker, a skill that continues to elude me fifteen years after my road test. That I've spent the last decade in Manhattan hasn't helped the cause. "Gordon Cavanaugh is finicky and precise, as a director and a diner, so he insists on the best. Instead of using one of the usual companies, he hires the executive chef at La Cachette to provide all the meals. When I'm hugely famous, he'll be the only director I'll work for."

We turn right on Grand, which is clogged with trailers, klieg lights and electrical wires and cordoned off by traffic cones. Dozens of people scurry back and forth as they rush to set up the shot while dozens of others wait impatiently on the sidelines. The Disney Concert Hall, glistening silver in the sunlight, watches the hum of activity with an air of superior boredom, perfectly indifferent to its fate as a prop about to be blown up by the conductor of the Los Angeles Philharmonic, who is also a spy for Russia. *To Mother, with Love* is a Cold War spoof, a sixties throwback, an ironic pastiche and an earnest effort.

At least that's how Harry describes it when he runs through a brief plot synopsis. According to him, the most important part of craft services reappropriation, as he calls is, is familiarity with the film's details. Knowing that Johnny Depp's character is based on Esa-Pekka Salonen, the philharmonic's Finnish music director, is the difference between a free gourmet lunch and forceful ejection from the set.

Halfway down the block, a young guy with a baseball cap and a clipboard stops us to ask our names. I stare at him blankly, wondering why Harry didn't prep me for this, while my companion rattles off two names I've never heard before. The guy instantly sheds his superior look, nods obsequiously and begs us to have a nice day.

As soon as we're out of earshot, I ask who Cheryl Mohaney and Keith Wharton are.

"Studio execs. IMDB lists the key people involved," he says, turning in the direction of the craft services tent. We're at least ten feet away but the wonderful flavors are already wafting toward me. The smell of Belgian waffles teases my nose.

"Can I start with dessert?" I ask.

"It's your party, you can do whatever you want," he says indulgently. "But I seriously recommend that you try the *bourdin*. Best sausage you'll ever have in your life."

Although it's one o'clock, the height of the lunchtime rush in midtown Manhattan, the tent is empty except for a few stragglers reading the paper and sipping coffee.

"They must be setting up a scene with the extras. Otherwise this place would be teaming with extras looking to supplement their meager salaries with food for a week. Sometimes it's like a college dining hall. I've actually seen people take out Tupperware," he says as he hands me a tray.

His tone is scornful, without a hint of irony, as if the behavior of hundreds of hungry extras taking their official lunch break is somehow worse than ours. In Harry's philosophical outlook, it is more egregious to take a mile when you're given a yard than to steal the entire ruler.

The hypocrisy of it makes me uncomfortable but before I can think it through my eyes meet the salad spread and everything else leaves my mind as I take in the four types of lettuce, the beautiful avocado slices, tomatoes as red as candy apples and luscious goat cheese croutons. I'm in heaven.

Harry suggests we start with the first course and pace ourselves. "Think of it as an all-you-can-eat buffet," he advises. "Do a round of small portions so you can taste everything, then go back for your favorites. And don't forget to leave room for dessert."

Following his advise, I limit myself to only five goat cheese croutons and half an avocado. I chose a balsamic vinaigrette dressing that's tangy and sweet.

With our choice of locations, I pick a table in the far corner to stay under radar but Harry assures me it's not necessary. "Once you get past the power-hungry flunky with the clipboard, you're in. Nobody cares. I've been reappropriating craft services for years and have never been caught. I've even gotten a few parts this way but I didn't take them. They were much too small. I'm not in it for two lines in aisle five at a Wal-Mart."

I'm not surprised Harry could talk himself into a role—he has a natural charm that wins people over—but I'm amazed he could talk himself out of one. Two lines in aisle five at a Wal-Mart seems like a great place to start.

"So tell me more about the movie," he says. "Is Moxie still on board?"

I haven't thought of Moxie in days. It didn't even occur to me to ask Lester if she's still involved. "No, I don't think so. Someone would have mentioned it, right?"

"Do you know who they're thinking of to replace her?"

Another question I didn't think to ask. "No, all I know is Lloyd's one week away from twenty-four million dollars. Although that was two days ago so he's five days away from it now," I say.

Harry twists open a bottle of Coke and pours it into a cup of ice. "*Five days away from twenty-four million dollars* is the most beautiful phrase in the English language, surpassed only by *four days away from twenty-four million.*"

"Yes, yes it is," I say softly. "I wonder who his investors are."

"Producers are very tight-lipped about their financiers because they don't want other people to tap them, but you'll find out in the contract. When do you expect to get the paperwork?"

I shrug and bite into a goat cheese crouton. It's as delicious as it looks. "I have no idea. Everything's still up in the air. Things seem like they're in a good place right now but who knows what will happen. It could still fall through," I say, as much as a reminder to myself as to him. This time around I want to keep my expectations in check. But it's hard. All I can think is Lloyd Chancellor didn't abandon me. On the contrary, he's as invested as I am in the dream of *J&J*. He'll make it happen. He's a bulldog.

"Don't be so tense. You're already passed the fall-through stage and are now on your way to the big-money stage. I told you this is how it would be, didn't I?" he says, with an assured smile. "I said everyone's option lapses at least once. This business is as predictable as L.A. weather."

I look at him—his confident grin, his bright eyes, his self-assurance—and I feel the last remaining knot in my stomach unwind. Simon's attitude has been so different. When I told him about the pending money, he'd smiled at me sadly and said, "Honey, he's a producer. He's always one week away from twenty-four million dollars." His tone was gentle and soft and made me feel like an idiot child who doesn't know how to cross the street.

It's a feeling I can't quite shake. Sometimes I suspect I'm just a pawn in a game so huge I can't even see the board.

But then I talk to Harry and everything inside me calms down. He's always so certain. He never doubts himself or the circumstances. From his perspective my pulling the article was a no-brainer. With so much possibility looming, it was the only reasonable choice.

Harry makes me believe that it's OK to believe.

"Well, now that that's back on track, what's going on with your script?" he asks.

I sigh loudly. "Nothing. Lester thinks I should turn it into a novel. Black comedies don't sell to the studios and there's point in pitching an independent because there's no money in that."

"But it's not all about the money."

"That's what I said."

"It's true."

"I know. It's about building a career, investing in your future, creating a name for yourself. I mean, sure, I'd love to make some dough. It kills me to take from my savings each month. But it's bigger than that."

"You're lucky you have a little something put away to get you through a rough patch. Most people don't."

"My grandparents left me some money. I'm supposed to buy an apartment or something with it, not pay my rent."

"It must be a nice chunk if you can swing an apartment."

He sounds so impressed, I have to laugh. "Please, in New York City fifty thousand is barely the down payment on a studio."

"I'm not sure Lester's the right agent for you," he says breaking off a piece of bread and buttering it.

Surprised, I put down my fork and look at him. "But last year you said he's the best in the business."

"*One* of the best. And he is. He's a legend. However, that doesn't mean he's the best one for you. He's too mainstream, too big. You need someone who's willing to take risks," he says.

As much sense as his argument makes, I find the thought of getting a new agent completely terrifying. Maybe if I believed more in my screenplay, I'd have some confidence about my chances but as it stands now, I can't imagine a stranger taking me on without the potential compensation of *J&J*. "I don't know. Lester strikes me as fair."

"Was it fair not to tell you that Chancery is still trying to make your book?" he asks with disgust. "Was it fair to let you write that crazy article, which caused you so much grief?"

He leaves the questions hanging and I repeat them in my head now as I have for days. No, it wasn't fair of him not to tell me, especially when he made such a convincing argument for why it would never happen. Would knowing have changed anything? I think of my darkened living room, the scattered books, the hundreds of pounds of popcorn. Yes, it would have changed everything.

Harry sees me wavering. "Look, why don't I show your script to a few people to get their opinion. It's not a commitment or anything. Just, you know, another perspective. If everyone agrees with Lester, then you'll have the peace of mind of knowing his take was right. And if everyone doesn't, then you'll know you have options. It's win-win."

I consider it for only a moment, looking for the obvious down side and not finding it. "All right, sure. I'll e-mail you the most recent draft as soon as I get home."

"Cool, and I'll pull together a list of names immediately. I think you're going to be surprised how many people love it. You better be prepared to show them something else. Are you working on a new idea?"

Biting into the last of my crouton, I sigh. Suddenly screenwriting seems very similar to novel writing. People always want you to have more. But I think of the amount of work I put into *J&J* versus *Tad Johnson* and there's no comparison. I could write twelve *Tad Johnson*s in the same amount of time. "Nothing in particular."

"That's all right. Don't put pressure on yourself. A new idea will come to you." Harry finishes his salad and gestures to the buffet table. "Ready for round two?"

"Absolutely."

I make a beeline for the soup tureens while Harry heads straight for the cured meats. All three options—lobster bisque, French onion and split pea—look delicious and I take a bowl of each. I'm not sure how I'm doing in the pace-yourself department but I'm excelling in Gorging Yourself 101.

Just as we're about to make a hot-plate sweep, a mob of extras enters the tent in torn clothes and bloody cheeks. They're victims of the bomb explosion, and as hungry as Harry predicted they'd be. Within minutes, the goat cheese croutons and most of the pâté is gone. I haven't even tried the latter.

Harry sees the panic in my eyes. "Don't worry. As soon as they're gone, they'll bring out more."

Sure enough, the caters restock the tables ten minutes after the extras leave to reassume their positions on the hoods of cars and under lamp posts. Not willing to take chances, I fill up two plates at once, making sure I get one of everything. Harry laughs at my preemptive strike but compliments me on how neatly I've separated my steak au poivre from lamb au jus. I tell him it's a gift.

The afternoon passes quickly as actors and crew members breeze through the tent. Some stay, but most pick up their food and go. At one point, we spot the hot young actress playing the love interest over by the coffee bar but her name eludes us both. I think it's Cynthia something. Harry says it sounds like Sienna.

Will Smith never comes through.

At four, we take our trays up for the last time and thoughtfully select an assortment of cookies and cakes to take on the road. We wrap them in napkins and stick them in our pockets, which is very different, Harry assures me, than using Tupperware, which implies intent. Our actions are spontaneous.

Hardly in the mood to disagree, I follow him out of the tent and down the street. I stay a few steps behind because I don't have the energy to catch up. I'm stuffed beyond Christmas and Thanksgiving combined and can't imagine ever eating again. Even my pinky finger feels distended, and when I bend to get into the car, I wonder for a moment if I'm going to through up.

Still, I can't think of a better way to celebrate the rebirth of my movie career than this.

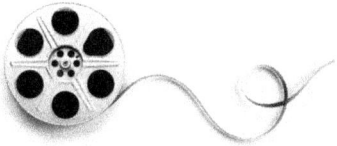

Day 1,105

LESTER IS RIGHT. By the end of the month, *Jarndyce and Jarndyce* is back under option with Chancery Productions. But it's not the same as last time.

"They're offering you a dollar," he says right off the bat. "A dollar for eight weeks. If, at the end of that time, they have their financing in place, you'll get ten thousand dollars for a one-year option. That's an improvement over last time, when you got ten thousand dollars for an eighteen-month option. When the money drops, you'll get a $35,000 bonus, which is ten more than last time. They're still offering you two point five percent of the budget, only this time the floor is $300,000 and the ceiling is $550,000. That's a fifty thousand dollar bump on both ends. There's no renewal clause because Lloyd doesn't think he'll need it. They'll be in production by the end of the twelve months."

As Lester runs through the numbers, I jot them down on a pad so I'll have all the details straight when I e-mail people with the good news. I can already see the subject line: Back in business.

It's not until I start mentally composing the message—realizing not only the intense relief I feel but the validation—that I understand how much of my identify is tied up in the option. Suddenly I am someone again.

"They're offering you full reversion of rights, which is another improvement over last time," he continues.

Full reversion is a coup. Arcadia refused to budge on that issue, stubbornly insisting that even if they don't make the movie, they have the right to keep the rights. They would rather *J&J* spent eternity buried in a dark little filing cabinet in a smelly dank basement than give it back to me after an interval. The only hope for *J&J* would be if some curious producer happened to stumble across it, see the potential and revive interest. This is called turnaround, and it is, as far as I can tell, a fable writers tell each other to give comfort on dark and stormy nights.

"What happens if they don't have their financing?" I ask. Reversion doesn't mean a thing if they never buy the rights in the first place.

"The option will lapse," he says succinctly. "But in the meantime, we retain the right to shop *Jarndyce and Jarndyce* to other producers. If someone makes an offer, we take it to Lloyd, who will either pick up the one-year option or release you from your obligation. They're being very fair in this provision. They could close us off to other negotiations, in which case I'd advise you to turn down the deal. As it is, I think it's a decent offer and advise you to accept."

"All right," I say without hesitation. I've been prepared for this moment for three weeks and every day it didn't happen, I became a little bit more convinced Lloyd Chancellor had been fucking with me with his one-week-away-from-twenty-four-million dollar claim. I began to believe Simon was right.

But here, finally, is proof that he's sincere. He's in as deep as I am and will do everything in his power to get the movie made.

The relief I feel is stunning.

"Good, I'll draw up a deal memo right away and e-mail it to Lloyd."

The mention of paperwork sobers me immediately. "Last time it took nine months to negotiate the contract," I remind him. "What if that happens again?"

"It's not possible. The situation is entirely different. For one, the contract won't be nearly as complicated. It's basically a one-page memo repeating what we just discussed. It should take three days at the most. But we don't need the contract. The eight weeks begin tomorrow morning."

"Really?" I ask, running to the bedroom to look at a calendar. I count eight weeks and circle the date: July 22 (day 1,161). I make cheerful little stars around the number. At long last, I have something solid and finite to pin my hopes to. The miasmic, interminable, neither-here-nor-there Hollywood system is finally being held to a real number. Either we commit to making a movie on July 22 or we give it up for good. Either I get ten thousand dollars or closure.

It seems like a fair deal to me.

"Yes. The clock starts ticking now," he says.

"That's fabulous."

"Good. So I'll contact Lloyd right now. Please don't hesitate to call with questions," he says.

Lester hangs up and I stare contemplatingly at the Hello Kitty calendar, at the stars sparkling around the magical date, which seems so far away. Suddenly July feels like another century and I will have to pass through eons to get there. It's frustrating but this is what my life has become.

Moviemaking is all wishing and waiting.

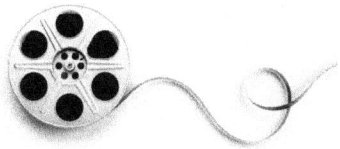

Day 1,157

SIMON OFFERS ME a job in his office.

"You don't have to know HTML, although if you do, I can get you another three dollars an hour," he says during a commercial break for *The Wet Season,* a Lifetime TV original movie written by Kevin Drake, a guy he went to film school with. We're pretending to watch the show, but really we're just tearing it apart. Poor Kevin's idea of drama is convoluted plotting, familiar dialogue you've heard a million times before and endless shrieking. So far we've counted eight blood-curdling screams and we're only thirty-eight minutes in. "Mainly we're looking for a proofreader. It's only twenty hours a week but if you work out, I can probably push that up to thirty. It's pretty straightforward. We just need you to read for sense, style and grammar. The content editors are good, so the copy won't need a lot of work. The previous freelancer recently became full time, which is a always a possibility if you're into that. What do you think?"

It's been seven weeks and three days since I accepted Chancery's offer and I still haven't seen a contract. I e-mail Lester every Monday morning for an update, but he always says it's with Lloyd's lawyers and not to worry. The memo is a mere formality.

Still, I find the lack of action unbearable. The eight-week option feels so ephemeral that the only thing I have to hold on to is the promise of a signed document, incontrovertible proof that it really does exist. Without it, I sometimes suspect I dreamed up the whole thing and then rush to reread Lester's e-mails to make sure it's not all in my head. If it is a delusion, then at the very least it's a collective one.

I shift a pillow and pull my feet onto the couch. "I don't know," I say in response to the job offer.

"Come on, it'll be fun." His tone is wheedling and cajoling. "You get the cube next to mine, and I'll tell you everyone's dirty little secrets. Like who's sleeping with who. Plus, Lucy in marketing keeps a jar of Hershey's Kisses on her desk, so you can have all the free chocolate you want. How's that for a sweet deal?"

As tempting as he makes it sound and as much as I could use the income, I can't bring myself to agree. The thought of office work—any at all, not just the paralegal kind—makes me cringe. I can't stand the idea of being at someone's beck and call. I'm all out of "yes, sirs" and "no, sirs" and polite smiles that nobody notices. Josiah and Barton seems to have burned them out of me, leaving a charred husk.

It will probably take years to undo the Symphony Brodsky damage.

"It sounds great," I say, trying to soften the rejection. I know he just wants to help. "But the timing's off. I've got some stuff going on."

He looks at me cynically, suspecting evasion. "What stuff?"

I shrug. "You know, things." On the TV screen, the image of a woman in a padded cell flashes. "Hey, it's back on."

"Like fake option things?" he asks.

Simon calls my eight-week deal with Chancery a fake option. He thinks Lloyd did it to keep me in line because I've proven myself to be dangerous. "It's classic appeasement," he said deflatingly when I announced my big news. "They're afraid of what you'll do next. Now really terrify them and publish the article. It's not too late."

I shake my head, trying to erase his words, which replay in my mind all the time. They're the reason I e-mail Lester weekly and obsess compulsively about the contract. The longer it takes to sort out, the more I second guess my decision.

Do I think about running the article?

All the time.

"No, I have other things too." The protest sounds hallow and overly defensive to my own ears so I make something up. "I'm working on a new project. Writing. And," I add with some temerity, "it's *not* a fake option, so please stop saying that."

Simon doesn't listen. He's too much of a know-it-all to consider the possibility that this time he's wrong. "If it were real, you would have signed the contract by now. But you haven't because Chancery doesn't want to waste its money paying lawyers to read it. In a week the option's going to fade away like it never existed in the first place and you know why? Because it never existed in the first place. It's a figment, an illusion created to make sure you don't change you mind about the article."

He isn't saying anything I haven't said to myself a dozen times during the last few weeks, but it doesn't help matters for me to hear it. Once the doubt creeps in, it's all over for me. I lose the ability to eat, sleep, function. I sit on my couch and stare across the room at the voodoo dolls lined up on the windowsill. I can't even swing the passive productivity of reading.

For this reason, I simply shrug and say OK. To argue would be to expose myself to more logic.

I turn back to the television, where Heather Locklear is being fitted for a straitjacket. Her cheeks are unnaturally puffy but I can't tell if that's from too much Botox or the steroids the doctors have her character on.

Simon sighs loudly and puts a hand on my shoulder. He doesn't knows how hard I have to work to not listen to him, but he's sympathetic anyway. "Look, I'm sorry. It's just that I get so angry when I think of them taking advantage of you. Lester should know better."

I nod but keep my eyes on the screen. Lester is also a touchy subject. I haven't told him yet that I'm meeting with another agent tomorrow. I know he wouldn't approve. Whatever he says about Lester, he respects his experience and trusts his judgment. If he thinks *Tad Johnson* needs another twenty-seven revisions, then *Tad Johnson* needs another twenty-seven revisions.

Plus, he'd just get on his high horse if he knew Harry had anything to do with it.

Simon is silent as he watches Heather chew through the ropes around her wrists. When she finally escapes and climbs over the asylum wall, he says, "What other things?"

I stare at him, confused.

"You said you had other things. What are they?"

It's just like him to be relentless. "I'm sorry but I don't want your stupid job," I say sulkily.

"I'm over the stupid job," he says with a smile, making it clear that indeed he is. No doubt he has someone else in line to offer it to. Maybe Wren. "Now I'm just curious."

Despite my resolution to come up with a new screenplay idea, all I've done for the past seven weeks is go to the park. I went the first day hoping the fresh air would inspire me and returned every day after to soak of the peace and quiet and sunshine. I bring my notebook with me but never open it. There's little inspiration in owners chasing their dogs and nannies playing with their charges.

"I'm working on a new novel," I say after a moment. If I'm going to lie, I might as well make myself sound good.

Simon nods approvingly. "What's it about?"

"A girl and her dog. It's really too soon to tell."

This sounds like the height of evasiveness to me, but he accepts it. "Good," he says, turning his head toward the television. Heather is now swimming across the English Channel in a bikini. "How is that possible? Wasn't she just in Georgia?"

"It's supposed to represent the geographical disconnectness of her mind," I say, making it up on the fly. "She has no boundaries, literal or metaphorical. Watch, at the end we'll find out the entire story took place in her head and that's she's still sitting in the same rocking chair where the sheriff shot at her."

"Old Kev was never a creative genius but he had enough sense not fall back on that tired cliché."

But Simon overestimates old Kev, and in the end we learn it's a thousand times worse than we imagined. The rocking chair itself is pure fantasy. Poor Heather never even got out of the ravine her abusive husband threw her in after bashing her on the skull with a cast-iron frying pan.

Oh, yeah, I think as the credits roll, that's the realest real possible.

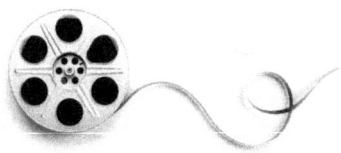

Day 1,158

I MEET HOWARD Tulkinghorn at the Griddle Café on Sunset Boulevard next to the Director's Guild. The space is simple and small, with maroon booths and a cool glossy red counter. I don't see a lone male sitting by himself among the crowd of young hipsters, so I take a stool at the counter and order black coffee. He arrives ten minutes later in a disorganized rush of folders and envelopes. When we shake hands, a notebook slides out of his grasp onto the linoleum floor.

We both lean down to pick it up.

"Please, let me," he says. "I know I look like an old man but I'm pretty spry for my age."

According to his website, Tulk, as he prefers to be called, is seventy-eight and has been in the business for fifty-six years. He started as a recent NYU grad in the mailroom of William Morris and worked his way up until he struck out on his own in 1986. His long list of clients include twelve Emmy winners, five Golden Globe winners and one and a half Oscar winners. At this point in his career, he takes on very few new clients and only read *Tad Johnson* as a favor to Harry.

"All set, then," he says, straightening his shoulders as he stands. Tulk is short and round, with thick bifocals, a Colonel Sanders goatee and bushy gray eyebrows. He speaks with a faint Brooklyn accent. "Ready to eat? I'm starving."

There's a thirty-five minute wait for a table, so we settle in at the counter. The waitress refills my coffee as she hands us the menus.

"Everything's huge here," he says. "The pancakes are as big as your head, so watch out if you're on a diet. People rave about the apple cobbler French toast but I stick with the eggs. The ham and cheese omelet is an exquisite balance of ham and cheese. Sometimes you get too much of one element and the whole dish is off. What do you want?"

I've barely had time to look over the menu, which has too many different types of pancakes to choose from: Oreo, banana, raspberry-lemon, pumpkin, streusel, chocolate. Overwhelmed, I order plain old scrambled eggs and bacon.

Tulk launches right into why he liked my script. "It's dark. I like dark. So many movies these days end on a false high note. Studio execs like to force happiness down our throats whether it fits the story or not. But that's what I love about your script. It's gritty and edgy. That edge is what makes it real. It's the kind of story you could see leading the evening news. I can hear the teaser during a *CSI* commercial on a Monday night: Suburban teen goes on shooting spree to get into college. Film at eleven. It's great indie material. The studios would never go for it. They'd worry about the kind of message it sends. Is it endorsing cutthroat competition in high school? But it's perfect for an independent director looking to make his mark with something fresh and original. You've got it, kid. You've certainly got it. Now you give it to me and I'll take it to the next level."

The last thing I expected from this meeting is an aggressive pitch. I assumed he took the meeting as a favor to Harry, but it seems as though Harry's the one who did him a favor.

"You really think you can sell it?" I ask, hoping to hear more praise. His attitude is so different from my agent's. Everything he likes about it Lester despises.

"Absolutely. I can think of six people off the top of my head to send it to."

The waitress brings our food, and I see immediately what he means about the portions being huge. It looks like an entire carton of eggs was scrambled for my dish. "I can't tell you what a relief that is to hear. The last agent I submitted it to didn't like it at all. He thought it had too many coincidences and wasn't lifelike."

"What is life but coincidence? Picture this: 1998, I'm in a little bookstore in a tiny town in Bhutan and who should walk in but my old neighbor from Astoria. That's real. But that's the nature of the business. One man's gold is another man's dross. Everyone has a story of how they turned down *Titanic*. It's like that apartment on Fifth Avenue that your aunt Marge sold for thirty thousand dollars in the 1978. Woulda, coulda, shoulda." He shrugs and pours some syrup on his omelet, smothering the exquisite balance of ham and cheese in maple flavor.

I take a bite of my eggs and reach for the salt. "We have one of those stories in my family, only it was a duplex on Fifty-second."

"It's a human universal. How are the eggs?"

"Delicious," I say, although they're actually a little rubbery. But the bacon is perfect, crispy and greasy and melting in my mouth in a scrumptious pool of fat.

"Now, keep in mind, it's the independents, so there's not a lot of money in it, and in fact it might even cost you a small something. But you're just starting out and need to build a foundation. That's my byword: build. You're building a foundation. You're building a résumé. You're building a career. Nobody starts at the top. You have to build the staircase to get you to the next level. And that's where I come in. I'm here to nurture you career, to take it through all the steps, not just the ones that pay out the big bucks. We'll get to the blockbusters eventually but for now we start on the bottom rung and build the ladder. See how I work in my byword? I really believe there's only one way to do it. And it's worked for me for fifty-six years. Even when I was sorting envelopes in the mailroom at William Morris, I knew what my philosophy would be, and I've remained true to it. That's the real secret to my success, and to yours."

Every word he says is exactly what I want to hear. Some of it I said myself to Harry during an anti-Lester rant.

"That sounds great," I observe, relieved to discover that my outlook isn't as skewed as Lester led me to believe. Obviously he has the right to run his business the way he sees fit, but just because it works for him doesn't mean it works for me. Right now, he's all about making *J&J* happen, which I respect and appreciate. I've put too much on the line for the film to simply fall through. But I am more than my one novel; I'm an entire oeuvre as yet unwritten. Lester isn't willing to invest in that. He has his own priorities that are far different from mine.

It's no big deal. As Harry said, it happens every day.

"I was hoping you'd say that. As soon as we finish here, I'll make some calls. I should have some news for you by the end of the month."

The waitress comes by to refill my coffee but I pass. I'm buzzing already.

"Now, as you know, I don't get paid unless you get paid. That's the gentleman's code of honor as well as the AAR's ethics policy. However, sometimes these independent films are more like partnerships. I'll introduce you to a director who's looking for material and you and he might decide to coproduce the project together. In those cases, an investment from you might help the process along. Again, I don't get any money from that arrangement. But I'm happy to pass up a small free now in expectation of a greater one later. That's part of the building process. Of course, I'm not saying we'll go that route, but it is a possibility. It's something I want you to think about. No decisions are being made today or tomorrow. We'll go slowly."

"All right," I say calmly, as if it's a possibility. But of course it's not. It's one thing to chip away at my inheritance to cover the annoying but necessary expense of daily life. But to bet it all on the unlikely outcome of a single long shot—no, siree. Carstones aren't made that way. Carrie gambled her savings on real estate—prime Manhattan real estate. Those are the kinds of odds we in my family take.

But I don't mention this to Tulk. It's only our first meeting, and I want him to like me. Besides, there's no point in making a big deal about something that will most likely never happen.

"Good. Now that that's settled, tell me what else you're working on. I love when my clients are prolific."

I have no more to tell him than I did Simon, but I'm even more reluctant now to spill my unprolific guts, so I tell him about the girl and her dog. I expand on it on the fly, including a mischievous monkey and an evil Buddhist monk.

I expect Tulk to call me on the nonsensical plot, but he loves my animated adventure and wonders if he should pitch Pixar.

Part of me recognizes his enthusiasm for what it is—a Hollywood schmooze job—but the rest of me embraces it blindly. He wouldn't make the effort if he didn't think I had a future.

Sundance, here I come.

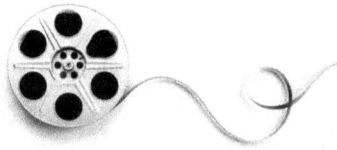

Day 1,161

I WAKE ON the morning the eight-week option expires full of anticipation like it's Christmas or my birthday. Nobody has told me what to expect next, but I have several ideas, namely that Lloyd calls with the signed contracts in hand or pitches a four-week extension to the tune of a fifteen-thousand-dollar option.

To keep busy, I turn on the television and watch *Good Morning, America,* then *Live with Kelly.* I boil an egg for breakfast and limit myself to refreshing my e-mail only during commercial breaks.

Despite these practical efforts, the morning drags.

While I wait, I mentally compose the e-mail response accepting the extension offer, a gracious missive with a hint of impatience. I mean, seriously, how long is this going to take?

At noon, I make myself a grilled cheese sandwich and sit on the couch, compulsively pressing the refresh button every five minutes. I can no longer force myself to wait until commercials.

My confidence begins to fade.

By two, I've come up with several unlikely but still entirely plausible explanations for the lack of communication. Lloyd is in a meeting with the money guys right now signing the contract. Lloyd is stuck in traffic on the 110 and can't get reception on his cell phone. Lloyd is in the hospital having his appendix removed. Lloyd's plane crashed in the San Bernardino Mountains.

I turn to CNN to see if there's any breaking news but it's all election coverage. The ticker on the bottom lists HMO reform and Moxie's entry into rehab. I couldn't care less about either and flip back to *Love & Valor.* It's been a decade since I've caught a full episode of the soap but it's remarkably easy to catch up. Ten years later and Jinx, Marcos and Marita are in the exact same place. They haven't budged an inch: the same squabbles, the same betrayals, the same sweeping romantic gestures like flutes of champagne and single red roses.

Life is so depressing.

When it's over, I put on Ellen DeGeneres. Her guest is an arachnologist who has just placed a tarantula on the host's arm. The camera zooms in as Ellen jokes about the creepy, creeping crawler reminding her of an old boyfriend. "No wonder I'm gay." The audience laughs; I stare, fascinated. Then she announces that every member of the studio audience will get a remote-controlled Mexican red-knee tarantula with realistic furry texture and everyone cheers enthusiastically.

I glare enviously at the happy studio audience.

My life sucks.

Of course I have the power to make it better. Every day I think about starting the new screenplay I discussed with Tulk. Some ideas have already come to me. The mischievous monkey is really a prince transformed by the evil monk who wants to rule his country. The girl has the power to undo the spell but she just has to believe in herself in order for her magic to work.

It's Disney meets Miyazaki.

But despite my intentions, I never get myself to work. It's like a kind of paralysis: I can think the action but I can't make my muscles respond. Each day, I watch the clock wind down, constantly recalibrating how much time I have left. Noon: If I start now, I can finish the first act. Three: If I start now, I can finish the first scene. Five-thirty: If I start now, I can finish the first page.

And yet nothing happens.

It doesn't seem like such a pressing matter as long as the option is a go. As unproductive as I personally may be, little elves are out there in the world assiduously settling my future. Sometimes it feels like I myself am hard at work, too.

As the day progresses, my fantasy scenarios desert me one by one, and by the end of *Access Hollywood,* I'm forced to admit that Lloyd isn't trapped in an elevator or hammering out the final details of a twenty-four-million-dollar contract. Lester isn't desperately trying to get in touch with me. He's not seconds away from ringing my doorbell in an anxious flurry and frantically apologizing for his land line, cell phone, Internet and telegraph machine being down all at once.

The eight-week option ends, not with a whimper but with a sigh. It might as well never existed.

I hate Simon for being right.

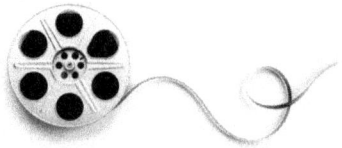

Day 1,174

MOM SENDS THE Pirellis to spy on me. Two weeks after the fake option lapses, Janine and Bob invite me to dinner at Morton's. The famous steakhouse is far too extravagant a place to take a slight acquaintance, but the Pirellis won't listen to reason. It's their favorite restaurant in the city, and they can't wait to share it with me.

That alone sets off alarms, but when they insist on coming up to see my apartment, I realize something funny is definitely going on.

"It's not at its best right now," I say, unlocking the door. During the elevator ride up, I tried desperately to remember if I cleared my plate from lunch. "I wasn't expecting company."

"Don't apologize, dear. We know what it's like for you busy single gals. My daughter, Charlene, is exactly the same way."

I turn on the light and quickly survey the damage. It's not as extensive as I thought. I rush over to the couch, fold the fleece blanket and throw it over the arm of the sofa. "Please sit down. What can I get you? I'm afraid I don't have much to offer. Some red wine, beer, vodka." I open the fridge and see a week-old carton of orange juice. "I can do screwdrivers."

"The red wine will be lovely," Janine says.

Bob sits down. "I'll take a beer."

As I dig glasses out of the cabinet, Janine wanders around the living room. She picks up photos, looks through my magazine stack and peers out the terrace window. "You have a lovely place," she says, examining the Lloyd voodoo doll with interest. "Very warm and homey, a nice size in a good neighborhood. If you don't mind my asking, how much is the rent?"

The directness of the question takes me aback, and I pause in uncorking the wine for a brief moment, then regain my balance. "Surprisingly reasonable," I say, mimicking the answer I gave Mom eight months ago. It's sufficiently vague and has the side benefit of being true: My Bleak apartment is remarkably affordable for its size and location, although it's still more than I can afford.

But that's none of Janine's business. Or my mom's.

I hand them their drinks, then pull together a sad plate of hors d'oeuvres from the meager offerings in my kitchen. Bob dives into the Triscuits with cheddar while Janine sorts through the mail on the dining room table. She doesn't bother to be subtle about it, holding each piece up and flipping it over. Luckily, it's all credit card offers, Planned Parenthood solicitations and coupons from local businesses. There's nothing revealing in the pack.

Still, it's disconcerting to watch her poke through my stuff with shameless abandon.

Bob asks me about my neighbors and noise pollution while Janine disappears into the bedroom. I don't know what she's looking for but I know she won't find it in there. The only important document I keep in there is my passport in my underwear drawer. All financial documents are in a folder in the hall closet. She'd have to be pretty bold to start going through my coats right in front of me.

"The construction seems sturdy," Bob says, pounding on the wall, "solid. Brick. I bet not much gets through. When was the building built?"

I don't have a clue but Bob wants facts so I say 1954 because the flat stucco lines of the apartments look midcentury to me.

The answer works for him as well and he nods solemnly. An awkward silence follows as he taps the baseboards with his foot. It's unusual for the two of us to be alone together without Janine.

"What kind of building does Charlene live in?" I ask, pouring myself a glass of wine. I have no idea how much longer we're going to be here. I guess it depends on what Janine finds under my bed.

"Pre-pre-pre-war," he says in the vernacular of New York real estate. "It was built in 1834. When you go into the basement, you can see the original stone walls laid by masons almost two centuries ago. Talk about solid construction."

Janine reemerges after a brief stop in the bathroom. I hear her rattle the bottles in the medicine cabinet: Tylenol, Advil, multivitamins. Since I rarely remember to take the One-a-Days, the container is almost full, and I can see Janine marking that off on her checklist to report back to Mom, who bought me the tablets in the first place. She's worried that neither Carrie nor I get enough calcium. Osteoporosis runs in the family.

By the time we leave for Mortons, the evening already feels endless and I focus on the thought of a rare, eighteen-ounce porterhouse steak to get me through the car ride, a gentle inquisition of what I've been up to since they saw me on New Year's Eve. Vague answers don't satisfy them and the pair grow increasingly determined as the night wears on.

At the restaurant, they ply me with excellent wine and mouth-watering beef, hoping the mind-numbing effects of both will lull me into honesty. But cream spinach is not a truth serum, and I cling doggedly to my story that I work as a temp for a variety of law firms. When pressed, I give up a few names, the same ones I gave my mother two weeks earlier after she called every major law firm in Los Angeles to find out where I work. Thinking on the fly, I explained the reason I'm not on the books is I'm a freelance temp at different places. The freedom is nice and the pay is better.

She seemed to accept the story.

But as Bob talks about his first job as a talent booker's assistant—the realization that the music industry wasn't the right place for him, however reluctant he was to tell his parents (hint, hint)—I realize Mom didn't accept anything at all. She was simply biding her time until she thought of another plan of attack.

Poor Janine and Bob.

Determined to put me into a complete food coma, they order three desserts: New York cheesecake, upside-down apple pie and the self-proclaimed legendary hot chocolate cake. Having licked the bone of my steak clean, I can't possibly eat another bite.

The Pirellis insist with such force that I'm almost prepared to tell them everything just to get them to relent. The only thing stopping me is the thought of Mom calling at five the next morning and screeching in a tone that could curdle milk, "What do you *mean* you've spent Grandma's money?"

The memory of Mom's milk-curdling anger is all I need to fortify myself and I take a tiny taste of the cheesecake. It's sweet and rich and at any other time no doubt delicious; tonight it sticks in my throat. The apple pie goes down marginally better, and the chocolate cake is an effort from beginning to end. The Pirellis alternate between watching in delight as I struggle and bombarding me with questions. Bob asks about various people at the law firms I claim to work at, then sits back and waits for my response. I can't tell if he's made up the names or actually knows the people, but, gambling, I go with the former. As an insurance salesman in Encino, he probably doesn't mingle much with L.A.'s powerhouse legal force.

When I can no longer stand it, I hijack the conversation and launch into a twenty-minute diatribe against the inhumane practices of the American meat industry. I rail against antibiotics and tiny pens and the way cows are strung up by their hooves, cut in the throat and left to hang until they bleed to death. I know it seems hypocritical after devouring an entire porterhouse, but I suddenly feel an unexpected kinship with veal.

The Pirellis are so taken aback they listen quietly. In a somber mood, Bob signs the credit card slip and tucks it into his wallet. We are all silent during the walk to the car, and I feel awful about my ungracious behavior. These people have been kind to me. They took me in when I had nowhere to go and treated me like family. I had no right to ruin a perfectly lovely dinner, however inquisitional.

The guilt I feel is terrible.

But then Mom wakes me up the next morning hounding me about the animal-rights cult I've fallen in with, and I get over it.

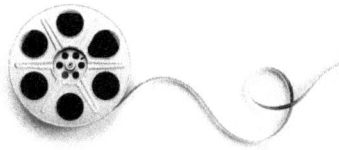

Day 1,199

LESTER CALLS IN the middle of *Love & Valor* to tell me Lloyd has Millie Sherwood, Moxie's arch nemesis, lined up to star. I'm so engrossed in Marita and Avery's wedding ceremony, I don't bother to answer the phone, only picking up belatedly as Lester is signing off.

"Millie wants to meet with the director personally before she commits fully," Lester explains after my breathy hello. "If she's satisfied, she'll write a letter attaching herself, at which point the backers will come on board officially and you'll get a proper option contract and payment."

Although I always love hearing about hot young starlets who want to make my movie, the news of a director is also interesting. This is the first time anyone has mentioned one.

Lester explains that his name is Blake Alden and the last thing he directed was a comedy with Selena Gomez. "He's also a screenwriter and has lots of ideas for the script," he says, "which is why Millie wants to meet with him before she signs on."

While he talks, I pull up Blake Alden's entry on IMDB and peruse his credits. His history is pretty decent. Aside from recent directorial blunders—a series of teeny-bopper features for which he was obviously unsuited—he's had a solid writing career. He even won an Oscar for a psychological thriller with Al Pacino.

"When's the meeting?" I ask.

"In a few weeks," he says, as frustratingly vague as always. After all this time, he still doesn't understand my need for facts and figures. He has no idea what my calendar looks like, with its days numbered like the ticking clock in an increasingly dire hostage situation.

Or maybe he does get me and doesn't care. In thirty years, I can't be the first pain-in-the-ass client he's ever had. Maybe we'll all alike in our constant need for hard facts.

I thank him for the update and immediately turn my attention back to the television, where Marita's daughter is walking down the aisle with a basket of flowers. Thanks to a well-timed commercial, I haven't missed much.

As exciting as the Millie news is, I wait until the show is over before I start Googling her.

Sadly, there isn't much to find.

Millie Sherwood lives a relatively quiet life with her mom in Malibu in a modest house on a three-acre estate near the ocean. Her wild exploits include building houses for Habitat for Humanity, cofounding a charity called Kids Helping Kids to introduce youngsters to philanthropy and visiting sick children in hospitals. Most recently she created a perfume called Heart Song; on her website she describes the process of working with French experts at the famous Gallimard perfumery in Provence. "I knew I wanted a simple fragrance with hints of musk and earthy wood tones, but working under the guidance of a professional nose taught me the intricate complexities of even the most simple-seeming scent."

Currently she's in the studio recording her new album, *Allusions to Summer,* to be released in September. The planned world tour will take her from Patagonia to Perth. She's very excited to meet her many international fans.

Her next movie is a romantic comedy called *Upward and Homeward,* about a type-A college student who learns there's more to life than perfect grades when she finds herself homeless over the Christmas holidays. Logan Lerman plays her slacker frat-boy love interest. The film hits theaters next week.

It looks pretty bad but I decide to reserve judgment until the critics actually pan it. Not that it matters what I or Manohla Dargis thinks. Millie's target audience is tween girls, who'll buy anything with her name on it, including *Lolly Dolly* videos by the truckloads. Based on preorders at Target and Walmart, her perfume is expected to break sales records.

In the two hours I spend researching Millie, I can't find a single black mark against her. She subscribes to a healthy lifestyle; advises girls against premarital sex; recommends plenty of fruits and vegetables to keep your energy up; goes to church on Sunday; is kind to animals; and publicizes causes she believes in.

Her image is squeaky-clean.

Worst of all, it seems to be sincere.

There's not a single hint from even the most salacious gossip site that it's all an act and that inside the placid twenty-year-old is an uncontrollable wild child struggling to break free.

She's the anti-Moxie.

I know this is good. A sane, reliable tween-queen movie star won't keep me up nights worrying about when she's going to enter rehab or crash her car into a tree. There won't be any stripping sagas or fey-gay boogies. My days won't be consumed with the minutia of her exploits. Millie doesn't create press. She could stand at a gas pump in stained sweats and no makeup eating pork rinds and still the tabloids wouldn't care.

No doubt the lack of hysterical paparazzi peeping over your backyard fence makes for a comfortable life but what about me? How's my movie going to generate buzz if its star isn't out there doing something shocking every other day? When will *J&J* be mentioned if Millie keeps her underwear on and her knees together? What hope do we have of becoming a sensation with such a staid, responsible adult at the helm? Lloyd might as well have cast Minnie Mouse for all the excitement it will generate.

Still, I try not be disappointed. The important thing is *J&J* is moving forward. Despite the lapsed fake option, the elves are hard at work, keeping to a schedule of hope and promise. Today Millie, tomorrow the costar, next Thursday the twenty-four million dollars. It will happen eventually.

I simply need to believe.

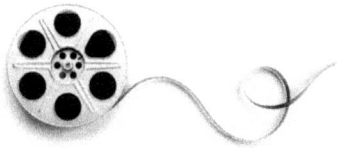

Day 1,228

UPWARD AND HOMEWARD bombs. It opens on fifteen hundred screens and makes four point six million dollars during its first weekend. The following weekend's gross drops more than fifty percent, coming in at an embarrassing two point two million. From there, the numbers get dismal: $900,000 on 1,100 screens, then $400,000 on six hundred.

It is an unqualified failure.

This strikes me as potentially positive because it means Chancery Productions could get Millie to sign on to *J&J* at a drastically reduced rate. Everyone loves a bargain.

But my thinking it all wrong.

"She's lost fifty percent of her value," Lester explains after I harass him sufficiently into calling me back. It's been six weeks since I've heard anything. My repeated requests to find out how the meeting between Millie and the director went have been met with stony silence. Lester doesn't think this is the sort of information he has to provide. When there's something meaningful to tell me he'll tell me. In the meantime, I should sit quietly and mind my own business.

I'm so tired of this. Suddenly my life has become one endless attempt to extract information from unwilling sources. Every day I beat my head against another wall. Just once I'd like him to tell me something without my haranguing him into it.

I suppose this is what my mother feels like all the time.

In my frustration, I write several long, involved e-mails to Lloyd begging him to tell me what's going on. I spend hours obsessing over the wording, striving for that perfect mix of demanding and self-deprecating: Tell me but don't mind telling me because I'm adorable and funny. In every letter, I find myself explaining how hard it is not to regret pulling the *New York Times* article. It might not be fair, it might not even be his fault, but it's impossible for me not to resent him. The only reason I pulled it was he said he was one week away from twenty-four million dollars.

One week.

That was nineteen weeks ago.

I think constantly about calling Angela Deering up and giving her the OK to publish it. There are still things to peg it to, like the DVD release of *The Hanging Judge,* which is slated for Valentine's Day. I watch the date approach and wonder if I'll have the guts to do it.

I know I won't. I don't even have the guts to send my e-mails to Lloyd Chancellor. I stick them in a folder buried deep in my hard drive, so I won't have to look at them whenever I boot up my computer.

I am a moral coward.

But no. The only reason I wrote that article was I had nothing left to lose. Now there are things at stake. Playing it safe isn't moral cowardice. It's smart business sense.

"What does losing fifty percent of her value mean?" I ask Lester.

"That she's not big enough to carry a movie anymore. Her built-in audience can't be relied on to support her films. And that's just the effect on the American market. Oversees, she's a nonentity. The foreign returns were terrible. Somewhere in the low three million. A backer counts on foreign box office to get a significant return on his investment. Millie Sherwood can't be relied on for that," he says.

"So what happens now?"

"They rewrite the script, punching up the male lead so they can cast that role bigger than Millie to anchor the film. The investors are demanding it."

Another thing I'm tired of: these investors, whoever they are. More and more, they seem like Mafioso toughs trying to break into the movie business for the glamour of it. They belong in a Woody Allen film. "Who's rewriting the script?" I ask, exhausted. It's only one in the afternoon, but it feels like the dark of the morning. I want the oblivion of sleep.

"Tipston and Field."

"What? But I thought they were done. No more rewrites without another payment."

"They're doing it in exchange for an executive producer credit. It's a very nice deal for guys like them."

I sigh, surprised yet again—and yet somehow surprised that I could be surprised—at what a backward place Hollywood is. It's the only spot in the world where two talentless hacks can get paid half a million dollars to write a script nobody likes, then get a cushy screen credit to ruin it further.

Where's my exec-prod credit for seraphic patience and Herculean self-control? Acts of self-abnegation are never rewarded.

Life so isn't fair.

"When will the new script be in?" I ask.

Of course Lester doesn't know. "They said early November, but they're not getting paid and have other projects, so it will probably take longer. Think mid-December."

I make a mental note of the first date and decide I'll start e-mailing Lester on the fifteenth. The only time he bugs Lloyd is when I bug him. It's a round robin of annoyance.

"All right," I say, trying to come up with more questions while I've got him on the line. There must be other things I want to know. When can I see the script? Which male character do they consider the lead? But I know it's not worth the bother. The details don't interest Lester; nothing does except the payday.

Another call comes in and he rushes off the phone to get it. I hang up, lean back against the couch and close my eyes. I was supposed to start my new screenplay today come hell or high water but suddenly that seems like a terrible idea. I need some time to get over this fresh blow.

If I don't give myself a break, who else will?

I log onto Fandango and check the local theaters until I find what I'm looking for. Then I get dressed, brush my hair, grab my keys and head to the galleria for the two o'clock showing of *Upward and Homeward*.

It's pure masochism, but I can't help myself.

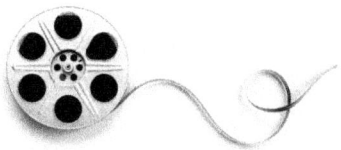

Day 1,298

WHILE SIMON DIGS his mail key out of his front pocket, I press my back against the tile wall and peer at him from behind the green fronds of the lobby's fern. The leafy plant hasn't been dusted in months, and my nose immediately begins to tingle in response. Somehow I manage to hold back the sneeze while he sorts through his mail, puts away the key and waits for the elevator.

As soon as the door closes on his furrowed brow, I let out a huge achoo, dig a worn tissue out of my bag and resolve to call the super to complain about the poor plant maintenance. What does rent cover if not basic cleanliness?

Blowing my nose, I extricate myself from my hiding place and get my own mail, pausing to look through a West Elm catalog to make extra sure I don't bump into him in the hallway upstairs.

Simon is remarkably hard to dodge. Whenever I turn around, there he is, like a shadow or a Secret Service agent.

It doesn't make sense that our schedules are perfectly synched, especially as I don't have a schedule. I come and go whenever I please. Frustratingly, whenever I please seems to be whenever Simon pleases as well.

If he were a woman, I'd swear our periods were following the same cycle.

The coast is clear when I get to the fourth floor, and I'm pitifully relieved to have avoided another conversation about my life. Simon always wants to know what I'm up to. How's the new book going? What's up with the movie? Where's the Tad Johnson screenplay at? Am I sure I don't want a job?

Or he won't say a word and just looks at me with that expression of concerned understanding.

It's unbearable.

And what does he really understand anyway? Nothing. *The Lindell Assignment* was his screenplay. He didn't have to twiddle his thumbs for two months while two slacker-hacks dragged their feet through another rewrite.

As soon as I stick my key into the lock, Simon opens his door and he steps into the hall. He's wearing dark brown sunglasses to ward of the remarkably bright December sun and instantly takes them off when he sees me. He smiles. "Hey, your timing is perfect. Drop your mail, change out of your running clothes and meet me back here in five minutes. We're going to see Pinkie."

Far from being perfect, my timing sucks. If I'd spent one minute less drooling over wenge-wood furniture at West Elm, I would have missed him completely.

Annoyed, I force a bright smile. "Pinkie?"

"Yeah, it's her birthday," he says, sliding off his sunglasses.

I think of all the people I've met at the bar. Any one of them could be called Pinkie. "I don't know her."

"That's all right."

"I don't want to crash a celebration."

"I promise you she won't mind. So go get dressed. It's a mind-boggling gorgeous December afternoon—I swear the temperature just hit 87—and time's a-wastin'."

Now I smile for real. "Did you just say a-wastin'?"

"Yes, I a-did. And I meant it sincerely. No irony at all."

Leaning against the door frame, I contemplate his wide grin and the endearing crinkles around his eyes. In moment like this, Simon is remarkably attractive. His blue eyes sparkle with humor and his hair falls appealing into his eyes.

"I can't," I say, with a semblance of regret. "I have too much to do today."

He puts his hands in his pockets. "Like what?"

With no lie prepped and ready, I take a moment to think of something believable. Work is always good. Either the new novel or a fresh draft of *Tad Johnson*. Not smart. I don't want to introduce a topic vulnerable to the third degree. Maybe I have to clean? Many people vacuum and dust and scrub the bathroom tiles on Saturday afternoons. Or I could have lunch with a friend.

But then why would I say I had too much to do when I had previous plans?

My pause gives me away, and before I can even voice an excuse, Simon is waving it aside. "It can't be that important if you can't remember it. Now you run along and change and I'll wait right here. Go on, it's a holiday of sorts. You can't spend it inside." When I fail to jump to his bidding, he grins again. "Don't make me say *a-wastin'* again. Because I'll do it if I have to."

Knowing I've been outclassed, I give in graciously. "All right, but I'm a-hopping into the shower, so you're going to have to wait here for fifteen minutes."

"Fair enough."

The drive to Pinkie's party takes a half hour, and I spend the time DJ-ing Simon's iPod. We have a lot of the same music, and everything I pick makes him say, "Hey, this is my favorite."

We pull into a large parking lot flanked on the right by a grove of trees. Before us is a long walk and a white pavilion with classical columns. It's a strange place for a birthday party, but I follow Simon, who is humming the last song played in the car.

The sign at the visitors center welcomes me to the Huntington, entrance fee $15. Before I can even balk at the expense, Simon is paying for both of us with his credit card. I protest but he waves my concerns aside. "You don't even know Pinkie," he says. "Why should you pay?"

The Huntington, it turns out, is the once-private estate of a collector who turned his home into a research and education center with three galleries, one library and a series of botanical garden featuring more than 14,000 species of plants. Highlights from the library include the Ellesmere manuscript of *The Canterbury Tales* and a Gutenberg bible.

Simon grabs the brochure out of my hands before I get to the description of the galleries. "We're here to see art, not read about it," he says.

"I thought we were here for Pinkie's birthday. Is she having a picnic?" I look around at the pristine lawns and the elegant buildings. "Are you allowed to picnic here? It seems like a stay-off-the-grass kind of place."

"I'm not clear on the ordinances regarding picnics, but I do know they don't allow weddings. A friend tried to get married in the Japanese Garden, and they referred her to the Arboretum. A pretty spot but not nearly the same," he says, opening the door to an elaborate white building that looks like an Italian villa: the Huntington Gallery itself. The building is cool and has that art-museum smell, a combination of paint, wood and age. I breathe in deeply. "Anyway, Pinkie's plans are much more low-key. She's just going to hang out."

We turn the corner and enter an ornate room with high ceilings and creaking floors. Simon leads me to a portrait by Sir Thomas Lawrence of a rosy-cheeked girl in a gossamer white dress cinched at the waist with a pink sash. One hand is tucked behind her back, the other bent at the elbow and raised slightly before her. The long pink silk ribbons from her bonnet blow in the wind as swirling storm clouds gather behind her. She's standing at the top of a cliff, her shoulders straight against the blue-gray sky and hills in the distance.

Although she looks old enough to go to balls and picnics, the descriptive text places Sarah Barrett Moulton—called Pinkie by her grandmother—at eleven years old.

"She's beautiful," I say, feeling the weight of the sky. The heavy darkness of the storm clouds is oppressive but the wind is curiously light. "I love how she's stares right out at you, like she's not afraid to meet your gaze. Clearly, she isn't a shy girl. I wonder if she kept that or became more demur as she aged."

"She died a few months after the portrait was finished of tuberculosis," Simon says softly.

The fact, almost two hundred years in the past, makes me sad. "That's a shame."

"Her father was a wealthy plantation owner in Jamaica. He sent her to England for school. Her younger brother Edward grew up to be the father of Elizabeth Barrett Browning, so she came from what's commonly called good stock. Lawrence painted it when he was only twenty-five, right after his admittance to the Royal Academy in London," he says, his tone matter-of-fact but his eye intensely focused on the portrait. "She's often paired with

Gainsborough's Blue Boy in popular imagination but the two paintings had nothing to do with each other until the curators here hung them across from each other in the twenties."

Surprised, I turn around and see the familiar portrait of a young boy swathed in elaborate blue silk with too many ruffles and bows. His gaze is as frank as the girl's but he somehow seems false and dishonest. I turn back. "I much prefer Pinkie."

"So did my mom. It was her favorite painting in the world. She saw it the first time when she was eleven years old. It was on a school trip. One look and she was a goner. She bought a postcard and kept it in a picture frame next to her bed and as soon as she was old enough she started coming back once a year on Pinkie's birthday. She used to drag the entire family but after a while my brother and father decided it was silly and stopped coming. When he was fourteen, Judah said the picture never changed so why did he have to keep looking at it."

He says this wryly, as if his brother's attitude doesn't bother him, but obviously it does.

"Was your mom disappointed?" I ask.

He shrugs. "Yeah, but she understood. My mom was really good with the understanding. She got things."

"And you kept coming."

"Every year since I was four."

He's silent and thoughtful as he stares at the portrait, and I realize Pinkie is only a small part of the reason he's here. He really comes to remember his mom. Even though he hasn't said the words, I know she's dead. There's a way you talk about people when they're absent and a way you talk about them when they're gone.

"How?" I ask after a long stretch of silence. I curl my fingers against my palm because the urge to reach out and take his hand is almost irresistible. I don't know why I feel the pull so strongly or why I can't let myself give into it.

Although the question is vague, he knows exactly what I'm asking and doesn't make me explain. But that's Simon. Like his mom, he gets things. "Breast cancer. She caught it early but it was the very resistant kind. Nothing worked and it spread to her lymph nodes. But she survived for five years. Five good years. It's a gift, getting the opportunity to know how much someone means to you and having the time to show them."

Without thinking, I give in to the impulse and grab his hand. It's warm and strong in my own. He squeezes thankfully, and I stare ahead.

We stand like that for a long time, neither one of us moving or speaking, until a tour group comes through and forms a semicircle around us. The guide relates the sad tale of Sarah Barrett Moulton and speculates that the reason her cheeks are so pink is she was already suffering from tuberculosis.

Simon tugs on my hand and I follow him outside into the bright sunlight where no tour groups are waiting to swarm. He leads me into another colonnaded building and we browse through John Singer Sargents, Edward

Hoppers and John Singleton Copleys. We stop in front of a Mary Cassat painting of a mother lying in bed with her arms around her young daughter who seems eager and anxious to explore the world.

The painting makes me sad in a wholly different way than the Lawrence.

After a brief tour of the gardens, Simon announces he's starving and knows the perfect place to go. The Huntington café, in a classic white building in the middle of the rose garden, looks wonderful, but he assures me the food is pricey and average. "I have something much better in mind," he says.

The drive to the beach is surprisingly quick. We hit traffic on the Santa Monica Freeway, but it breaks up as soon as we pass the 405. Simon finds a free parking spot, an excellent omen, and takes me to a tiny hole-in-the-wall on Union Jack Street that serves nothing but tacos. There are two vinyl booths and a counter along the window with weathered stools, but he gets our order to go. He takes an extra stack of napkins—"These babies can get messy"—and walks to the beach. It takes him a while to find the absolute best spot, even though all spots on the beach look exactly the same, and eventually he plunks down with a satisfied sigh. "Are you ready for the best taco you've ever had?"

My stomach grumbles as I sit next to him, facing the ocean, and slip off my shoes. The sand is still warm from the beautiful day. "Yes, yes, yes. I'm so hungry I could eat a whole taco stand."

Simon tilts his head. "Hmm. I'm not sure that was the right answer. These tacos are meant to be savored, not wolfed down like pig slop at feeding time."

Unamused, I give him my killer stare. Another hunger pang gurgles through my body. I hold out a hand.

He relents. "Fine. But I'm starting you off with the tuna because it's not as good as the tilapia. The tilapia must be enjoyed slowly like a fine wine."

The ahi in the taco is lightly seared and seasoned with lime, cilantro and a spice I don't recognize. A hint of guacamole rounds out the flavor. "Yum," I say, after I swallow my first bite.

The sun, which is just starting to sink toward the horizon, is still high, and it's lovely and warm on my face. I close my eyes, feel the gentle breeze, smell the salty air and take another bite of the taco. It's wonderful.

When Simon deems sufficient time has passed, he gives me the second: beer-battered tilapia with a cabbage slaw and tartar cream. Either the breading or the sauce has a bit of kick, and the spice reverberates in my mouth. It's so good all I can do is grunt with happiness.

Simon nods smugly.

When he finishes his taco, he leans back onto the sand and closes his eyes. I sit next to him with my arms wrapped around my knees until he reaches over and pulls me toward him. I rest my head on his chest.

I listen to the seagulls and the surf and kids playing by the lifeguard stand, feeling an overwhelming sense of peace. For the first time in forever the movie is only a memory—a vague, unimportant, distant memory. I am fully engaged in the present.

This could very possibly be the most perfect moment I've ever had.

Simon runs his fingers gently through my hair. "Hey, what's this?" he asks softly.

I tilt my eyes toward him but don't move my head. I'm too comfortable. "What?"

"I don't know. It looks like a leaf from the fern tree in the lobby of our building."

Horrified, I jackknife into sitting position and run my hand through my head before he finds another. Then I remember the shower I took before leaving.

I look down at him. Simon's grin is as wide as the coastline. "The surface of the mailboxes is highly reflective," he says, pulling me toward him again. I resist for a moment, then submit. I cross my arms on his chest and rest my chin there. "I could see you the whole time."

"I dropped my keys behind the plant," I say, giving him my most penetrating gaze.

"You were avoiding me. You have been for a long while."

Embarrassed, I look away. It's always bad to be caught in the act, but his straightforward accusation makes it worse. Suddenly I feel like a coward. "I didn't know you knew."

"Actually, I didn't know until I saw you hiding behind the fern. I just assumed you were busy. But once I figured it out, I made it my mission to thwart you. I kept my eye in the peephole for ten minutes today waiting to ambush you," he says.

He's so delighted with himself, so pleased with his devious plan, that I can't feel annoyed. My hackles make a half-hearted attempt to rise and immediately subside when they see the look in his eyes. It wasn't thwarting for the sake of thwarting. He did it because it had been more than a month and he missed me.

It's a huge revelation, but it doesn't unnerve me or set my heart to racing. I still feel an incredible sense of peace, and even though I know it will ruin everything, I bend my head slowly to his and kiss him. Like my hand in the gallery when it reached out to grab his, my lips have a mind of their own. They work of their own volition.

And so beautifully too.

His touch is gentle and sweet. He wraps his arms around my chest and pulls me closer but keeps the pressure light as he presses his lips against mine. The heat rises and my blood pressure soars but the incredible calm stays.

Eventually the sun disappears and the air turns chill and we go back to his apartment, where he carries me into the bedroom and places me in the center of his bed and takes off my shirt and kisses my neck and I unbutton his pants and run my hands over the warm flesh of his stomach and sigh his name as he makes me feel like heaven.

And it doesn't ruin a thing.

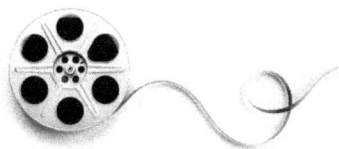

Day 1,300

I'M IN SO deep, I don't think of Harry until Monday. I wake up with Simon, make him toaster waffles while he showers, kiss him good-bye and then return to my apartment, where I sit on the couch, watching perky morning chat shows and feeling awfully smug.

It's only when Tulk calls at one to tell me about a business opportunity—and that's just how he phrases it: a business opportunity—that I remember Harry. The guy I sleep with who clearly doesn't mean that much to me.

Overnight, I've become a slut.

The thought disturbs me but not as much as it should. The stirrings of conscience and waves of guilt I expect to feel don't come.

Oh, God. I'm a heartless slut.

Tulk explains he has a producer interested in *Tad Johnson* and I understand every single word. Not even thoughts of my own depravity can distract me from the conversation. I'm clearly too far gone for help. Poor Harry. Involved all these months with a moral vacuum and he doesn't have a clue.

Hopefully Simon doesn't either.

Does he?

He can't. He didn't bring up Harry once during the entire weekend.

But maybe he thinks I already broke up with him, which would explain why I felt comfortable enough to kiss him on the beach.

Or maybe he thinks I'm a heartless slut.

On the line, Tulk pauses, clearly waiting for me to respond, and I struggle to recall what he said last. I close my eyes. Nope. I have no idea.

"I'm sorry, what?" I say.

"How's a lunch meeting tomorrow to discuss the details? Say the El Coyote one?"

"That sounds great," I say, excited to hear more about the offer. It's an indie producer, so I know better than to get excited about the money. It's the opportunity I'm after, a chance to make a name in the industry so I can coast on it for the rest of my career.

After I hang up with Tulk, I hold the phone in my hand and think about calling Harry. I have to tell him right away. The longer I let it slide, the longer I'm a two-timing hussy. That's not fair to either Harry or Simon.

Firmly resolved, I dial his cell phone. He answers on the first ring. "Hey, superstar screenwriter whose about to be produced. Didn't I tell you this would happen?"

Although this is hardly the greeting I'm prepared for, it's pretty nice. His faith in me has always been his greatest appeal. No matter what happens, he's a source of unflagging support. "Tulk told you?"

"It might have come up while we were talking about other things. So how does it feel? Top-of-the-world-like or floating-on-a-cloud?"

"Very earthbound at the moment. I'm trying to be prudent and practical," I say. "Tulk called it a business opportunity, which sounds a little scary to me."

Harry laughs. "Fine, you be prudent. I'll be imprudent enough for the both of us. As soon as I get back into town, I'm taking you to Spago to celebrate."

I lean against the arm of the couch, wondering if I knew if he was going to be out of town. His schedule's been so busy lately, I haven't seen him in the past two weeks, which is another reason he might have slipped my mind in the Simon giddiness. Out of sight is out of mind.

Great, now I'm a shallow, heartless slut.

The self-revelations just keep coming.

"Where are you?" I ask.

"Visiting my sister in Chicago. My parents are here. We're doing the traditional Skimpole family post-Thanksgiving/pre-Christmas bash. So far we've hit the historic-skyscrapers tour, the river tour, the museum tour and now we're about to do the zoo tour. All this touring is punctuated by intense bouts of shopping on Michigan Avenue. So far I've scored a new couch and a flashy suit from Armani. I'll wear it when we go to Spago. You'll be amazed how handsome I look."

The mention of Spago reminds me of why I called and the fact that I can't break up with him now, today, this moment. I have to wait for him to come back—and in the meantime two-time Simon.

I should tell him about Harry.

I should not tell him about Harry.

"When are you back?" I ask.

"Can't wait to see me, huh? Next week. I'm visiting a friend in St. Louis while I'm so near. Why don't I— Uh-oh, the zoo tour is about to start. The guide is waving a zebra-striped umbrella in a desperate bid for attention. I'll talk to you later."

While Harry oohs and ahhs over three-toed sloths, I sit on the couch and wonder what to do next. Clearly it's my intentions that count. I *intended* to break up with Harry. That he's out of town and unbreakupable is not my fault. Simon would understand that.

Still, I can't convince myself there's any reason to tell Simon at all.

As soon as *Love & Valor* starts at three, I put the matter out of my head and focus on some real problems: what Jinx will do when she finds out her husband, Giovanni, is the mafia crime boss she's hunting, how Kylie will escape from the collapsed salt mine and whether Piers and Arizona will finally consummate their love.

The hour is over far too soon, with few epiphanies and little closure, and I slide effortlessly into an episode of *Dr. Phil* about mom's who can't say no. I watch fascinated as overindulged ten-year-olds bully their parents into buying them everything they want. It seems so simple when they do it, and I realize, observing the secretly filmed footage, that I didn't throw enough tantrums as a child. No wonder my parents didn't buy me a car when I was sixteen.

While the credits roll, I check my e-mail to see if Lester responded yet to my question about the revised screenplay. It's been two weeks since I sent the first message. If he doesn't get back to me soon, I'm considering drastic measures: phoning. Nothing says answer my e-mail as much as an unwanted telephone call.

Luckily, there's an update in my in-box informing me that the writers turned in the script a week ago. "It's better but not as good as Lloyd would like. But it's the best he's going to get from them without paying them more money. He has a meeting next week with the investors to show them the new script. He thinks it's strong enough to get their backing."

This is such good news that I don't even flinch when I read Carrie's e-mail threatening to come for a visit with Glenn. "He's never been to the West Coast. I thought we might start in SF and drive down on hwy 1. Could be very special."

By "very special" I'm terrified she means engagement-worthy, and I shut down the computer without responding. I don't want to think about it.

At six-thirty, Simon surprises me with sushi from my favorite Japanese restaurant. He's amazingly perfect and thoughtful and perfect.

I set the table while he complains about the new receptionist in the office, Colleen, an incompetent woman who doesn't know how to use a computer or understand the concept of a network. "She can't even transfer a phone call. And I'm talking about a simple phone that has a button that says TRANSFER, not one of those out-of-date devices with an F1 function key. She's driving me crazy. Every day she asks the same question about Word. And she refuses to get anyone's name right. She calls Kristin Christine, even thought she's been corrected a zillion times."

"How'd she get the job?" I ask, digging out clear, blue ramekins to use for soy sauce.

"Get this. She worked the desk at Celia's health club, so Cee assumed she had skills and hired her away. All she had to do was scan IDs. But Cee is big on guerilla hiring tactics. She doesn't trust people who are looking for new jobs. She thinks they're discontents. In two years, she's never gone through an agency or ran an ad in the paper. It works sometimes but mostly we wind up with inept dimwits who don't know how to sharpen a pencil. You have no idea how many hours I've spent giving tutorials on Word mail merge."

"You have my full sympathy. I know from personal experience how frustrating that is," I say, recalling the dozens of times at HWSP when I had to give the other paralegals lessons in Bates numbering and Lexus searches, things that should be part of a person's basic skill set.

He laughs and reaches for the napkins. "Are you kidding? I love it. I've been waiting my whole life to complain about my coworkers. It's so middle-America normal." He pulls two pairs of chopsticks out of the take-out bag. "What'd you do today?"

I have a few sets of nice chopsticks but I can't remember where I put them and disposable are so much easier. "I learned that saying no is the most loving thing you can do for your child."

"And where did you pick up this useful bit of parenting advice? The park?"

"Dr. Phil," I say, contemplating the contents of my cabinet. "Wine?"

"Sure."

I take out the wineglasses and retrieve a bottle of chilled Chardonnay from the refrigerator.

"Anything else?"

"I also learned that contrary to popular belief, crime does pay."

"Now I know that's not *Dr. Phil.*"

"*Love & Valor.*"

Simon transfers the sushi from its aluminum container to a serving tray. The presentation is lovely but I resent having to wash another plate. Even with a dishwasher, a novelty I'd never have in New York, doing the dishes is a pain in the butt.

"Any lessons that don't involve TV?" he asks.

I pour the wine, give the table a thorough once-over and sit down. "Yeah, if you don't tell your sister she's dating an asshole in the very beginning she might make him stay in your apartment for several days. That was a huge lesson."

He sits down across from me and lifts the wineglass. "I like your sister."

"Me too."

"It's a shame about the asshole."

I shrug. "What can you do?"

"So any writing today?" he asks. "You haven't told me how the new book's going."

And there, just like that, I'm reminded why I've been ducking him for a month. My giddy mood dims for the first time in forty-eight hours. Not even the discovery that I'm a shallow, heartless slut had been capable of doing that.

"It's good," I say evasively, reluctant to lie further but incapable of not lying a little bit. I'm already in to the depth of one still-have-a-boyfriend omission. In an effort to limit the damage, however, I change the subject immediately. "The new script is in. The producers are happy with it and think they can get the backing now."

Simon takes a piece of salmon sushi and dips it into soy sauce. "Wasn't the rewrite because the investors wanted to cast the male lead big?"

I start with toro because it's my favorite. "Yeah."

"Then they're not going to back the film until the part is cast," he says logically.

"Lester thinks the script is strong enough without it being cast."

"Lester's either grossly optimistic or deliberately misleading you. Take your pick," he explains calmly, his didactic tone having the usual affect on my temper. He's such an obnoxious know-it-all.

My giddiness dims another few notches.

Simon sees my expression and reacts with perfectly thoughtful thoughtfulness. He puts down the chopsticks, takes my hand and squeezes gently. "I'm sorry. I don't mean to be negative. It's just that I don't want to see you get hurt. You expect so much. I can see it on your face. Be prepared for the investors to want more—not that they're necessarily going to but in case they do. Just be prepared. You can't have all your eggs in one basket. That's why I'm excited about the new book. It's something separate and apart from *Jarndyce*. Having a life outside of it is the only way to remain sane."

Everything he says makes sense. I know it's dangerous to have nothing else in the hopper. But that's why I wrote the screenplay in the first place. I know the importance of diversifying. "I also had some exciting news about *Tad Johnson* today," I say eagerly.

He releases my hand and smiles, then snags a piece of eel. "That's fabulous. I didn't know Lester was taking it out already. I thought he wanted you to do another rewrite."

I look down at my plate and reorganize the slices of ginger to avoid his gaze. It's a little too penetrating for my peace of mind. "It's not with Lester. I found a new agent for it."

"Oh?" he asks casually. But his eyebrow raises a few inches.

"Yeah, his name's Howard Tulkinghorn. But he makes me call him Tulk."

Simon thinks for a moment, trying to place the name. He comes up short. "I'm not familiar. How'd you hear about him?"

The last thing I want to do is bring up Harry. "Around. A friend of Wren's might have mentioned him," I say vaguely. It's not quite a lie when you use caveats like *might have*. "He's really great. You should check him out. HowardTulkinghorn.com. He's got a ton of Emmy winners on his roster."

"Cool."

Silence follows his succinct remark as we both reach for another piece of sushi. I go for salmon; he goes for mackerel. I finish my wine and pour a second glass. Simon is only halfway through his.

"So the news?" he asks.

For a moment I'm baffled, but then I realize I never told him what's up. How could I have possibly forgotten? It's huge. "Details still to come—I'm having lunch with Tulk tomorrow to find out more—but an independent film producer made an offer on the script. He loves it and can't wait to go into production."

His response is hardly what I'm expecting. He doesn't jump up and hug me or even smile and say congrats. "What's the producer's name?"

"I don't know. That's one of the details I'll learn tomorrow."

"What else has he done?"

I sigh. I should have known he'd be like this. He's always so cautious. Except when it comes to sex. He didn't think twice about that. "Again, I'll find out tomorrow. Geesh, the important thing is, he wants to make my movie. Isn't that wonderful? I'm going to be a plucky independent."

"Yeah, it's great," he says with a smile so forced it might as well be a scowl.

"Why isn't it great?" I ask impatiently.

"It is great. I just said it is."

"No, you're lying." I wrap my chopsticks around another piece of toro but I can't get any traction. Every time I try to lift it, the sushi falls to the plate. Frustrated, I throw down the chopsticks. "Do you really think I can't tell when I'm being appeased like a little child?"

"Then stop behaving like a little child," he says, his temper snapping for the first time. His eyes sharpen to a deep blue. "Every time someone gives you a sliver of positive news, you go all in. Why can't you hold something back?" He sighs, puts down his own chopsticks and takes a deep sip of wine. I watch him struggle to calm down. "Look, independent films are a long road too. Just because someone wants to make your movie doesn't mean they will. Ninety-nine percent of projects never take off. Ninety-nine percent. Those are odds I'd want only with earthquakes and tornados. So all I'm saying is be cautious. Just please be cautious."

By the end of his speech, his tone is soft and pleading and I find myself softening too. His intentions are good. He only wants the best for me, and it's not his fault he's been hurt so many times by Hollywood that he can't see anything but his own pain. All he wants is to save me from heartache.

How can I hold that against him?

It would be better, of course, if he realized I'm a grown woman who can take care of herself. I'm not the turnip-truck greenhorn he seems to think I am. But that will come in time. He doesn't know me well enough yet.

But if we're ever going to make it that long, we clearly need to stay away from any movie talk. I love fish-tacos-on-the-beach Simon and looking-at-Pinkie Simon and surprise-me-with-sushi Simon but I can't stand this man who knows everything and is just waiting for me to fail. Hollywood-insider Simon is intolerable.

As disappointed as I am that any topic is off-limits, I'm relieved to have discovered the toxic downside to Simon so early on. Now I don't have to wait for the other shoe to drop.

So, for the sake of our relationship and its fragile future, I refill his wineglass and ask him if he knows the three important questions every parent should pose before giving in to a child's demand.

Somehow, he manages to guess two out of three.

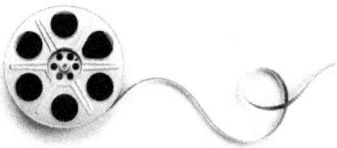

Day 1,301

THE FIRST THING Tulk says after we order lunch is: "We're not going to decide anything today."

It's a pretty dramatic statement for the circumstances but I nod. "All right."

"Today, we talk. Tomorrow, maybe the day after, maybe next week, we can make up our minds. But this is a big decision and I won't let you make it over guacamole and bean dip," he says, with perfect indifference to the fact that we ordered a veggie quesadilla and a fiesta salad.

He was going for imagery. I get that.

"Solution Pictures is new and small and they're looking at *Tad Johnson* as one of their kick-off projects. They've got a few things in the works but Joshua Smallweed, the founder of Solution, thinks your script could be the one that takes them all the way to the Oscars. You know with indies, the big question is distribution, right?" he asks.

I nod. The better your film does at Sundance and Cannes and Venice, the better chance it has of being picked up by a distributor. Many films that are made never get a chance to find an audience. It's a sad thought but not that different from book publishing or even screenwriting. Very few works ever see the light.

"Josh's credentials are solid. He worked with Katzenberg at Dreamworks for five years and Grazer at Imagine for three. He set up Solution about a year ago because he was tired of the Hollywood system of making watered-down movies with mass appeal. He believes it's possible to make quality movies with mass appeal. And he'd like to start with *How Tad Johnson Got into Harvard*."

The waitress brings our platters and refills Tulk's coffee cup. I've never seen anyone eat lettuce and java at the same time before, but he seems immune to the strangeness as he pours blue cheese dressing over the grilled chicken.

"Hmm," Tulk says, breathing in deeply. "Doesn't that smell good? The food here is wonderful. Just wait until dessert. Flan that will make you believe in God."

Although I asked for the quesadilla without bell peppers, it comes stuffed with them, and I pick out a few green strips before I realize it's too much work. I dig in. The cheese is melted perfectly.

"The really exciting thing about Josh's offer is he wants to bring you on board as a producer," Tulk says.

As soon as he says the word, I realize the money situation is worse than I thought. Lloyd gave Tipston and Field production credits because he didn't have money to pay them. But that's all right, I remind myself, blocking out the dwindling balance of my nest egg, I'm here to build a career. A production credit is an investment in my future.

"He thinks you have really great ideas and a strong vision. He wants your input on everything from set design to casting. How does that sound?"

"Amazing," I say with total sincerity. The last time my opinion was sought on a professional matter, the office manager at HWSP asked if she should photocopy that year's holiday schedule onto white paper or beige.

"Josh's keeping the budget small. He thinks he can do it on three hundred thou. He's drawn up a tight, thirty-one-day production schedule, which will keep costs down. He's got Abel Fiero playing Tad. You know who he is, right? He's the star of *Fifties Dreaming*. Very popular with the eighteen-to-twenty-four-year-olds. He's willing to do the film for nothing to prove his acting chops."

I'm not surprised Abel Fiero wants to show the world he can act. On *Fifties Dreaming,* a laugh track sitcom that lampoons midcentury morality and culture, he spends the entire half hour winking at the camera and delivering lines with a gee-whiz enthusiasm. It's painful to watch.

"The tricky part, as with any film, is pulling together the financing. Joshua has enough to cover development but is only just starting to work on production. All he needs is a little seed money to start with. He thinks fifty thousand should do it. Nothing propinks like propinquity, right?" Tulk says. He's so busy talking, he's barely touched his salad.

Although I think it's a rhetorical question, it quickly becomes clear he's waiting for a response. "I'm not sure. What does *propink* mean?"

"I've just dated myself, haven't I, sugar pie?" he says with a self-conscious smile. "It means money makes money. If Joshua can show potential investors that he already has investors, then it'll be easier to get investors. Does that make sense?"

It's an age-old concept, repeated many times at the law firm, and I nod emphatically.

He smiles and takes a sip of his coffee, which must be cold by now. "Good. So what do you think?"

I keep my concern about Abel Fiero winking his way through the movie to myself and tell him I think it sounds wonderful. I can't wait to get started.

"Don't rush into anything," he says cautiously. "Fifty thousand dollars is a lot of money."

I'm about to agree—to say, Yes, fifty thousand dollars is a lot of money—when it hits me that he means fifty thousand dollars is a lot of *my* money. The idea is so insane, so incredibly detached from anything real or possible, all I can do laugh hysterically until tears fall from my eyes. Tulk waits as I struggle for breath and clutch my stomach. I can't remember ever being so amused in my entire life.

This has to be a joke. I'm being punk'd. Where's the camera?

It takes me five minutes to regain control, another three to calm down. By the time I'm able to breathe normally, Tulk has finished his salad. The waitress is refilling his coffee cup.

"I'm sorry," I say, still a little breathless. "It's just that it's such a crazy idea. Don't you think it's crazy?"

Tulk smiles but doesn't seem amused. "Why is it crazy?"

"Because...because..." I sputter. Sometimes something's so obvious, you can't even begin to articulate it. I close my eyes and slow down. Why is it crazy? Because the fifty thousand dollars is everything I own and everything I am. It's my comfort and my security and my peace of mind when things get rocky. It makes all things possible.

I haven't spent my whole life hoarding my grandparents' legacy just to throw it away on the first reckless gamble to come my way.

I try to explain this to Tulk, thinking it's logical and self-evident, but he surprises me by sticking just as staunchly to his point. "*Tad Johnson* isn't a reckless gamble; it's a sound investment. I shouldn't have to tell you that. You've got a producer and a star lined up and a home run of a script. When they talk about limiting liability, this is exactly what they mean. You came out here to be a filmmaker, right?"

As much as I want to cover my ears and block him out, I sit there quietly and nod.

"Well, this is your chance. Think about it."

But the thing is, I don't want to think about it. It's far too scary. My first reaction is the right reaction. This is all a big joke. Sooner or later the men with the cameras will jump out and yell, Gotcha!

"Don't look so serious," he says. "Whatever you decide, this is still exciting news. The deal they're offering is very fair. You'd be a full partner and get ten percent of the gross. That's gross, not net, which is what we want. No film actually nets money but gross is whatever it pulls in. A modest indie like, say, *The Station Agent,* made five million. So in that case you're looking at five hundred thou. How do you like them clams? As for credit, like I said, you're in for executive producer, which means you'd get to accept the Oscar." He winks. "You might want to prepare a speech beforehand. I hate when they go up there and stammer."

I shake my head, terrified of the logic. Everything makes sense when he says it.

"Remember, we're not coming to any decisions right now. We're just looking at our options."

He can say that all he wants but it's clear where he really stands. His mind is made up. "But you think I should do it."

Tulk immediately shakes his head. "No, I think you should do it if you think you should do it."

I lay my head down on the table. "Tulk, that's pure double talk."

"Listen, my job is to give you the benefit of my experience. That's all. I've been around a while and seen some things and then I come here for the flan and tell you about them. I can tell you that the deal is fair. I can tell you that people invest their money and the equivalent in films all the time. Hilary Swank got paid a measly three thou to do *Boys Don't Cry*. How'd that work out for her? Ed Burns maxed out his credit card to make *The Brothers McMullen*. Another not-so-terrible outcome, wouldn't you say? Should I go on? I've got a million of these. The point is, you have to have faith in yourself and your project. If you have that, you have everything. If you don't, then maybe you shouldn't be here." He wipes his hands on his napkin, throws it on the table and looks around for our waitress. "Now, are you ready for flan?"

I smile wanly and nod yes, but the truth I couldn't possibly eat another thing because my stomach still hurts.

And the pain isn't from laughter but fear.

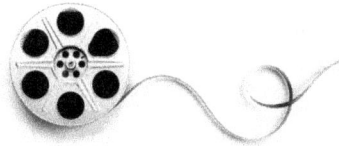

Days 1,302 through 1,309

FOLLOWING TULK'S ADVICE, I decide not to decide. I leave it in the hands of fate: If the investors come through with the money for *J&J*, I'll do it. If they don't, I won't.

It seems reasonable enough and I wait with bated breath to hear about the outcome of the meeting.

The days pass with interminable slowness, each one feeling more like a week than the mere twenty-four-hour period it is. Filling the time becomes a new challenge, and I realize how easy it is to go out of your mind watching the clock. I try to start the new script, but I'm too jittery and impatient to focus. Instead, I spend the hours in front of the television, jumping from *Law & Order* to *Love & Valor* to *Judge Judy* to *Dr. Phil* back to *Law & Order*.

One morning I catch a marathon of *The Real Housewives of Orange County* and in a matter of seconds, I'm hooked.

The day of the meeting finally arrives and I check my watch every ten minutes and think, They could be meeting now. Or, they could be done meeting now. Or, Lloyd could have the money now.

Lester doesn't call, which isn't a surprise, so I give him a day and call myself. He tells me it's way too soon to hear anything. He promises to call as soon as he gets word.

This is unacceptable, so I dash off an e-mail to Nadia in Lloyd's office. I keep it brief, only asking if she heard anything about how the meeting went and making fun of myself for not being able to wait patiently for the information to trickle down to me.

Nadia answers immediately, which I realize is a bad sign. Whenever there's something worthwhile to pass on, she ignores me completely.

Sure enough, she confirms my worst suspicions: The meeting has been postponed four weeks.

Deflated, I turn off the television and stare at the blank screen, wondering how the hell I'm going to get through the next four weeks. The last one almost killed me.

Maybe I should go away, hop on the first flight to a faraway place like Billings, Montana, or Sioux Falls, South Dakota, and spend the three weeks trying to get back to L.A. I could take Greyhound or hitchhike. After a while I might even lose track of the days. Maybe somewhere near Laramie, I'll find an adorable clapboard house among the purple hills and fall in love with the simple beauty of a wide-open sky. I'll get a job keeping books for an ornery rancher and go to barn dances on Friday nights.

I picture myself in overalls and a bandana with hay in my hair and know it won't work. Clapboard houses are for weekends in the country with your boyfriend or children. Real life happens only during the week. No movie has ever been green-lighted on a Sunday afternoon.

Three o'clock rolls around but I don't turn on *Love & Valor,* even though I'm dying to know if Jinx shoots Giovanni in the sting operation before she realizes who he is. This is serious. I have to come up with a plan. I can't just do nothing.

I consider my options.

I can do nothing until the investor meeting convenes in January. This would require calling Tulk and seeing if Joshua Smallweed is cool with waiting at least four weeks for an answer. The advantages to this are: Smallweed might find other backers in the interim and not need my money anymore; I get to avoid making a decision. The disadvantages are obvious: Smallweed could get impatient or lose interest; the investor meeting might get postponed again. Based on the epic slowness with which all decisions regarding *J&J* are made, there's no reason to assume the meeting will take place before Easter, or even at all. I could be marking time for the rest of my life.

Or I could make the decision myself.

It's a terrifying thought and the pain in my stomach instantly returns.

Still, there's no way around it. The postponement is the universe telling me I need to be accountable for my own life. I can't keep abdicating responsibility.

More than a little freaked out (and nauseous), I sit at my computer and start Googling. I begin with Joshua Smallweed. His credentials check out—that is, he worked on Imagine and Dreamworks films—but are less impressive than Tulk made them sound. Aside from *The King in the Parlor,* for which he is listed as associate producer, all his credits are minor assistant-tos or post-production-advisors. His bio on Solution's website lists movies for which IMDB doesn't credit him. I don't know what that means.

I can't find any press announcing the formation of his production company except on his site but that doesn't seem strange to me. A hundred such companies must form every day in college dorm rooms and theater workshop basements. There's even another Solution Pictures, in the UK. The three principals are West

End actors trying to breakout of jukebox musicals. I understand completely how they feel.

Next I look up Ed Burns and confirm that he sank his own money into his first movie. From there it's easy to find other examples of filmmakers who scrounged money from anyone they could—parents, uncles, high school teachers—to pull together enough to finish their project. It's an age-old story. Just like Tulk said.

Mel Gibson personally funded *The Passion of Christ*. Different scale, same thing.

The pain in my stomach intensifies. I don't want to do this.

I spend the rest of the day and most of the night maniacally Googling anything that seems the least bit relevant. I check out Hilary Swank. She did indeed make $3,000 for *Boys Don't Cry*. It's not the same as putting up your own money but there are similarities. It's about sacrificing for the future, suffering now in the hope of a better tomorrow.

By three A.M., I'm convinced I have to do this. I can't believe in myself less than Hilary Swank. I saw all her episodes on *90210,* in which she played a single mom and Steve's girlfriend. She was so awful, Tori Spelling looked like a Shakespearean genius in comparison.

But she knew better. In some deep, dark recess of her soul, she believed she had Academy Award performances inside her. She believed it so strongly that she gave up money and comfort to get it. She chose the hard road because she wanted it badly enough.

How could I do anything less?

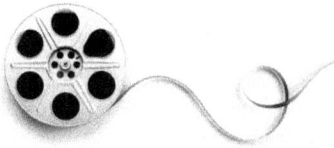

Days 1,310 through 1,318

I WAKE WITH second thoughts and spend the entire day, then week, making and unmaking my mind. Christmas passes in a haze of vacillation. Yes, I'll invest the money. No, I won't invest the money.

Several times I find myself on the brink of asking Simon but I always stop myself because I know exactly what he'll say. Be cautious. Be prepared. Don't get hurt. Don't take risks. The discussion would probably culminate in huge argument in which he tells me I'm crazy to even think of investing my money in a film.

I know I'm crazy. I just need him to tell that me crazy's OK.

I also can't talk about it with my family. Sometimes I think Carrie would understand. When she bought her apartment on Fourteenth Street, she didn't just buy a place to put her stuff, she bought a piece of the future, a belief that the world will turn out the way she expects. She's betting that Al Qaeda won't wipe out the financial district or that global warming won't submerge Manhattan under twelve feet of water. She took a risk, too.

But I know she won't see it that way, and when she calls to give me the details of her visit with Glenn, I realize I don't want to talk to her about anything. The road trip from San Francisco to Los Angeles has morphed into a week in L.A. with day trips to Santa Barbara and Ojai. Glenn isn't into the road-trip experience. He's about the destination, not the journey.

She explains this matter-of-factly, as if he's not the kind of person she used to make fun of. Carrie thrives on long, leisurely drives. She loves stopping to savor the view, then spending the rest of the afternoon watching the sun move across the sky.

The more she goes on about the things Glenn wants to do, the more cut off from her I feel, and I make an excuse to get off the phone as quickly as possible. I love my sister but I'm not so keen on Glenn's girlfriend. That sneaky rat has even convinced her to eschew the bright red cabinets she loves for tasteful ashwood ones to ensure the resale value of the apartment. I can just see him counting his half of the proceeds.

I have no idea how I'm going to get through an entire week with evil groping octopus hands. Poor Simon is going to have to spend every waking hour with us. Good thing he likes my sister.

Lester is the obvious person to talk to, but he doesn't know that I'm working with another agent and I'm not sure how the information would go down. I probably should have told him before I gave the script to Tulk to sell but it felt so unlikely that he'd find any takers that I didn't seem worth the awkwardness that would ensue. Whatever did or didn't happen with *Tad Johnson,* we'd still have to work together on *J&J.*

Now that *Tad Johnson* is going somewhere, I regret my cowardice. I'd love to get his input on the matter.

Not that I can't predict what he'd say, too. Lester's only interest in the big payday. Never once has he shown interest in growing my career or building my reputation. The very idea of investing money rather than making it is repellent to him. In the *Vanity Fair* article, he said the mere thought gave him hives.

No, the only person I can talk about the offer with is Harry.

He wants to take me out for that celebratory dinner at Spago, but I insist on lunch at a diner on Sunset. Dinner is too much like a date. Lunch is friends on the go catching up during a meal. It's entirely harmless.

I fully intend to break up with him but I'm not sure if I should do it before or after I get his take on the Solution's deal. I don't want his feelings about the split to inform his opinion. What if he's so devastated he can't think clearly? Or if he's so angry he gives me bad advise out of spite?

But it seems too calculating to bide my time until I get what I want.

That's what manipulative people do.

Harry spends most of the meal talking about his trip to Chicago—the shopping was spectacular and he can't wait to show me his new flat-screen TV—and I listen, relieved that I don't have to decide anything just yet.

It's not until the check arrives that he asks about me. "And just in case you think I've forgotten about it, let me assure you now that I'm dying to know what happened with Solution Pictures and have only gone on about myself to tactfully give you a chance to bring it up on your own."

As soon as he mentions Solution, I realize I'm going to be calculating.

Sighing deeply, I lean my head against the pink Naugahyde of the booth. "They want me to come on board as a producer and invest fifty thousand dollars for the privilege."

"Yikes," he says.

I look at him out of the corner of my eye. "It's crazy, right?"

"I didn't say that. Tell me more about the deal. Who's behind it?"

I tell him what I know about Joshua Smallweed and Solution Pictures. We talk about Abel Fiero and the thirty-one-day shooting schedule. As I run through the details, I can hear the doubt in my voice and the desperation to overcome it. I make the argument for as if I'm trying to convince myself it's a good idea.

It's terrifying.

The bottom line: I'm not brave enough for this. I should take that as my final answer and move on.

Harry listens quietly, nodding solemnly and only interrupting once to have me clarify a point. When I'm done, he leans back and stares at me. "The question is," he says finally, "do you believe in the script?"

"Yes," I say.

"Do you believe in yourself?"

That's the million dollar question. How do you know if you believe in yourself? Just because you like what you do doesn't mean anyone else will. A work's value is in the eye of the beholder. There is no universal good.

I hesitate too long.

"Come on, Ricki," Harry says. "Do you believe in yourself?"

"Yes."

But the lone syllable comes out more like a question than an answer, and he rejects it on the spot. "You get one more chance. Do you believe in yourself?"

"Yes," I say, my tone emphatic.

Harry is silent for a long while. "Well, I think you have your answer."

I was afraid of that.

I rest my head against my palm and close my eyes, suddenly nauseous. I might as well get used to it, since the sick feeling isn't going to go away any time soon. "You don't think I'm crazy?" I ask.

"I think you're a lot of things. Smart, talented, the author of a brilliant script, destined for greatness. But crazy? No, that's not on the list."

He says it so simply, so sincerely, it's impossible not to believe him, and after we pay the check and leave the restaurant, I find it's also impossible to break up with him. My intentions remain the same, and when he suggests we go back to his place, I make up an excuse to avoid being alone with him. I know it's not right or fair to lead him on, but it seems far worse to break up when he's been so sweet and supportive. I'll wait a day or two, then try again.

Before we say good-bye, he gives me the name of a lawyer and tells me not to sign anything without having someone look at it first. "In this business, you can't be too careful."

His concern is so sweet, I kiss him on the cheek, then wiggle out of his grasp before he can do more. The traffic on Sunset is fierce, and the ride home takes three times as long as it should. By the time I pull into the Bleak Lofts parking lot, I'm angry and annoyed at every other driver on the road and the few pedestrians I saw who don't know how to cross the street and the guy at the gas station who took twice as long as necessary to pay the cashier and with Simon, especially Simon, who doesn't believe in me one-tenth as much as Harry does.

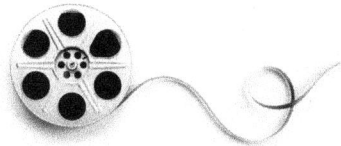

Day 1,326

SOLUTION PICTURES' OFFICE is tiny and spare, more like a one-room studio in Manhattan than the center of a burgeoning moviemaking empire. On the back wall is a huge calendar covered with names and dates. Beside it are headshots of actors, with their résumés posted underneath. Abel Fiero's cocky grin is dead center.

The floor is a speckled linoleum that's seen better days, but it's clean and unscuffed. In fact, the whole office is remarkably tidy for such a small space. There isn't a stray sheet of paper to be seen. Manila folders are neatly piled on the top of a black filing cabinet, and promotional brochures are stacked on the small side table in the waiting area. Above two reception chairs is a sign that says, "Solution Pictures: The Cure for the Common Movie."

Tulk is already there when I arrive. "Come in, Ricki. Don't be shy," he says, leading me into the room. There are three desks. One for Joshua Smallweed, one for his assistant and one for the receptionist, Loretta, who only works Monday, Wednesday and Fridays.

"The rest of the time we let the machine pick up," she says as she holds out a coffee cup that reads WORLD'S BEST PRODUCER on it.

I'm too nervous to drink anything but I accept it gratefully. At least now I have something to clutch in a death grip.

Joshua steps forward and extends his hand in greeting. He's a tall man, well over six feet, rail-thin, with shaggy black hair falling to his shoulders and a salt-and-pepper beard. He's older than I thought he'd be. From his limited credits, I assumed he was late twenties early or early thirties but clearly this is a man in his forties.

His firm handshake is oddly comforting, and I feel some of my anxiety, made worse by the dingy office, ebb. Surely the sparse workspace is a good thing. Why waste capital on creating a showplace when you barely have enough to pay the actors? There are better things to spend your money on and it's good that Solution recognizes it.

Still, I wish it didn't look so fly-by-night. Without the heaviness of clutter weighing it down, it feels like a CIA front, the type of place that can be dismantled and reassembled in another part of town within twenty minutes.

Joshua tells me to take a seat and hands me one of Solution Picture's brochures. While Tulk drags over a chair from the reception area, I skim the pamphlet, which has much of the same information as the website, mostly earnest pronouncements on the importance of good filmmaking. Joshua Smallweed still believes in the magic of the movies.

"You'll have to excuse Amity Jarek, my story editor," Joshua says. "She has a meeting this morning with a potential funder that she couldn't reschedule. She's sorry to miss you, as she's a big fan. She's the one who insisted I read *How Tad Johnson Got into Harvard*. She gave it great coverage. But I think she was inclined to love it, considering how much she enjoyed *Jarndyce and Jarndyce*. It's a great book, by the way. We've all read it here and think it will make a great movie. We can't wait to see it."

I close the brochure, put it on my lap and wrap my hands around the coffee mug, savoring the warmth. All of a sudden I'm shivering. I know it's just nerves, but I can't make it stop. "Thank you."

Tulk places the chair next to mine and crosses his legs. "Shall we get started?"

"If you don't mind, I'd like to skip over all the gushing that's customary in meetings like this and cut to the heart of the matter," Joshua says, leaning a hip against his desk. From my sitting position, he seems even taller. "Here at Solution, we don't like to think of ourselves as Hollywood. We like to pretend we're based on a small Midwestern city like, say, Duluth, with old-fashioned values and real people. At Solution, we often say people are our greatest asset. That means you are our greatest asset. Growing your career means growing our business, and we want to develop a relationship with you to our mutual benefit. We don't want to take what we can get from you and throw you away. That's what we like to call studio think. We're the anti-studio. We keep the process streamlined and efficient. We like to think of ourselves as aerodynamic. Here at Solution Pictures, we can fly."

"That's a great slogan," Tulk says. "Have you thought about using it in your brochure?"

Joshua smiles. "It's being silk-screened onto T-shirts as we speak."

Tulk nods approvingly. "Dark blue on white?"

"Light blue on navy. They're mostly larges but Amity made me get a few baby tees." Joshua looks at me. "I'll send you one as soon as they come in.

"Thanks," I say, clutching the coffee mug tighter as I imagine the $50,000 T-shirt. God, what am I doing here?

With the pleasantries out of the way and Solution's mission well and clearly stated, Joshua gets down to the details of our deal, reminding me with great force exactly what I'm doing here. He hands me a contract, a copy of which Tulk has already marked up.

For the most part, Tulk is happy with how the negotiations are going. As he's said many times, it's a fair offer and Solution has given in on several important points, but there are a few outstanding issues. If they aren't cleared up to Tulk's satisfaction, or if I don't feel comfortable with Joshua for whatever reason, we walk out of here and don't look back.

The freedom to say no is the only reason I'm not hyperventilating.

Tulk's biggest concern is the turnaround clause. He doesn't think it's fair that Solution refuses to allow the reversion of rights when I'm not only the screenwriter but an investor. Joshua makes several arguments about why it's company policy to never allow reversion but in the end he gives in. Tulk doesn't gloat but merely moves on to the next item.

After the endlessness of the *J&J* contract, after cooling my heels for nine months while Lester and Lloyd went back and forth with Arcadia's lawyers, it's a special pleasure to watch the straightforward process of two people hammering out a deal. Tulk proposes, Joshua counters, Tulk amends, Joshua concedes.

It's a thing of beauty.

It takes all morning but eventually we have an agreement. Tulk has managed to get my percentage of the gross up to fifteen percent. Joshua argued that so much is unheard of but Tulk kept pounding home the $50,000 investment. Great risk deserves great reward.

"We're serious about the producer position," Joshua says as his receptionist updates the contract. "We think you have a lot to contribute to the process. If you're willing to deal with the close quarters, we'd love to squeeze another desk in and get you into the office on a regular basis. We can't offer you much compensation other than pizza for lunch every Friday and tons of free screenings but it's part of the relationship we'd like to build with you."

I'm too consumed by the prospect of investing $50,000 to consider his offer, but I promise to think about it. I'm sure in the end I'll say yes. The best way to keep an eye on your money is to stay in close proximity to it.

"Fair enough. If nothing else, you have to come back again to meet Amity. As I said, she was very disappointed she couldn't be here."

The receptionist finishes the contract, prints it out and runs off copies. She hands one to me, Tulk and Joshua. We each read silently. For someone who's used to reading documents, the language is pretty straightforward. My book contract was more involved, not to mention the movie contract, which went on for seventy-two pages about theme-park-ride and slot-machine rights. The Solution deal is much simpler since they've let me keep all those rights. Any Tad Johnson action figures or Happy Meals come through me.

It's lovely to be working with the anti-studio.

Still, I don't feel comfortable signing. This is all happening too fast. I need to give it to Harry's lawyer if for no other reason than to put off the moment of inevitability.

"It looks good to me," Tulk says, making my heart drop. The least he could do is have one more objection. "But if you want to have a lawyer look it over, I won't be offended."

I take out my phone and dial Archibald Seaville. His secretary puts me right through. After I explain the situation, he asks how long the document is. I check.

"Thirty-seven pages," I say.

He's silent for a moment. "That won't take me long. E-mail it to my office and I'll look at it tomorrow."

His answer is entirely reasonable and yet I can't accept it. The pressure in my chest won't accept anything less than immediately gratification. Either I do this now or not at all. "Are you sure you can't look at it sooner?"

"Well, I did have an appointment just cancel on me. I suppose I could squeeze it in. How about you e-mail me the document and I'll see what I can do? If it's straightforward, I'll have feedback in ninety minutes, two hours tops."

Relieved—and yet oddly distressed—I give the e-mail address to Loretta. Then I sit down and watch the second hand travel around the clock for a full minute. Suddenly I feel like I'm keeping a deathbed vigil.

"This is perfect," announces Joshua. "We can grab a bite and discuss my notes for *Tad Johnson*," he says. "It'll be our first working lunch, the first of many, I hope."

We go to a modest French bistro and I nibble at my salad nicoise as Joshua talks about other projects he's developing. He orders a bottle of wine to celebrate our partnership but the Chardonnay doesn't go down any more smoothly than the tuna. I'm too nervous for this.

While he signs the credit card slip, he talks about the changes he'd like me to make in the screenplay. Realizing my attention is divided, he promises to type them up as soon as possible and send them my way.

I thank him.

By the time we get back to the office, Seaville has finished reading the contract and explains his concerns with me. Most of them have to do with my getting my money back if the movie falls through. I put him on speakerphone and listen to him negotiate with Joshua. The head of Solution pictures puts up a good fight but in the end he gives in to all the lawyer's demands.

A half hour later, he's putting the contract in front of me.

Suddenly I can't breathe.

Tulk pulls me aside and says gently, "We don't have to do this. We can still walk out of here and never look back. We don't owe them anything."

He's right and knowing he's right gives me the courage to reach for a pen. Yes, I can walk out of here and never look back. But that's the cowardly Carstone way to behave. For once, I want to be brave.

"Nope, I can do this," I say, more for my own benefit than for his.

But it has to happen now, right now. If we put this off, I'll never do it at all. My courage is a fleeting thing.

I sign the contract and watch silently as Joshua adds his name. Now there's nothing for me to do but write the check for $50,000. I pick up the pen again and open my checkbook. My hand freezes in the middle of all those zeros but I find the strength to continue. Taking a deep, steadying breath, I hand it over to Joshua.

He accepts it with a smile. "I'm torn between cashing this check and hanging it on the wall. Because it's not the money that means anything to me, it's the faith you have in us—and by us, I mean Joshua Smallweed and Ricki Carstone. We're going to go far." He stands up and holds out his hand, which I take.

Strangely, I don't feel sick at all.

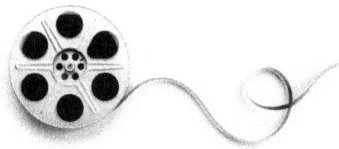

Day 1,330

GLENN ARRIVES ON a flotilla of complaints. He didn't get an aisle seat; his cushion was too thin; the peanuts had a strange curry flavor; he couldn't see the movie screen because of the large head in front of him; the flight attendant didn't give him enough water; the baggage carousel was very slow; there were too many people in the arrivals hall.

From the second he gets into the car at LAX to the moment I pull into the parking lot of Bleak, he goes on and on about the inferiority of air travel. It's like he's never been on a plane before.

Carrie handles it with such good humor, I'm not sure she notices it. Maybe he's been this way since they got out of the cab in JFK, in which case she's probably so immune to his whining, she can't hear it.

Or maybe I sparked it by asking how the trip was. Engaging in the most basic form of common courtesy is a rookie mistake I won't be making again.

As soon as we enter the apartment, Carrie announces she's taking a shower and disappears into the bathroom, leaving me alone with Glenn.

"This is a great apartment," he says, looking out the window toward the courtyard and the billboard advertising a movie with Jack Nicholson.

"Thanks. Can I get you anything? Water? Lemonade? Coke?"

"No apple juice?"

I look in the crisper. "Apples."

"Water's fine," he says in such a resigned way I feel like another disappointment he has to suffer like a slow luggage carousel or a thin cushion.

While I'm filling the water glass, I hear Carrie turn on the shower. "I have some cookies if you want. Milanos? Or roasted peanuts. I promise, no curry flavor."

Glenn sits on the couch and bounces twice as if to test the springs. "I'm all right, thanks."

I put his water on the coffee table and return to the relative safety of the kitchen. Everything is where it should be—no dishes in the sink, no mail on the counter—and I wish I hadn't cleaned for them this morning so I'd have something to do right now. But there's no help for it. I have to talk to him. "You and Carrie will take my room. I'll sleep out here on the convertible."

"That's not necessary," he says.

On the face of it, it sounds like a nice, well-mannered, Long Island boy thing to say, but it's completely devoid of sincerity. It's entirely necessary.

"So you're going to Santa Barbara tomorrow?" I ask.

"We're gonna check out a few wineries."

I'm not really hungry, but I dig an apple out of the fridge to give me something to do. It's so awkward chatting with Glenn. I can't tell if he knows I don't like him or if he's just a difficult person to talk to.

"We're going to do the *Sideways* tour," he adds. "I printed out the map. We've got reservations for lunch at Los Olivos Café. That's where Miles, Jack, Maya and Stephanie have dinner."

"Sounds like fun," I say, although it seems pretty lame to follow in the footsteps of a decade-old movie that's wasn't even that good.

"It should be."

Silence again.

I realize it's my turn. "And Disney the day after?"

"I've never been. I hear they have a system so you don't have to wait on the really long lines."

"Yeah, the fast-pass service. You get a time stamp that tells you when you can go on the ride, so you don't have to wait."

"That's cool. I hate waiting on lines at amusement parks."

"Interesting. Waiting for rides is my favorite part, except for waiting for food. Now that I really love, especially when I'm hungry."

Glenn looks at me funny but doesn't call me on the sarcasm, possibly because he doesn't recognize it. His tendency toward literalness is why he doesn't get me or Ruby. He thinks we're stupid instead of clever.

While Glenn is trying to come up with something to say, Carrie comes out of the bathroom with wet hair and bare feet. "Wow, I feel so much better. It's amazing how the smell of plane diesel fuel really clings to you." She throws herself onto the couch.

I offer her something to drink.

"Nope, I'm fine. Fully hydrated from the plane. And no food either. I don't want to ruin my appetite for dinner. What time's the reservation?"

Tonight we're going to a Japanese spot Simon picked out. It's replica of a palace situated high on a hill, with excellent views of the city and sumptuous red couches. I think Carrie will like it. The food's pretty good too.

"Eight-thirty."

Glenn yawns pointedly. "Yikes, that's late. I hope I can make it with the jet lag and all."

"If you want to stay behind and crash, feel free," I offer, knowing it won't be that easy to get rid of him but figuring it's worth a shot.

He shakes his head. He's in, no matter how much he has to suffer.

Carrie leans back against the cushion and reaches for the remote. "Do you mind if we stay here and chill until dinner?"

I shrug. It's all the same to me.

"Put the game on," Glenn says, sliding closer to Carrie until he's pretty much sitting on top of her. Then he takes one of his octopus hands and put it on her knee. It stays there for a moment before creeping up her thigh to her crotch, where it remains.

It's going to be a long week.

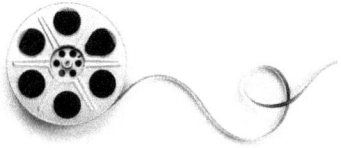

Day 1,335

EVERY DAY I log in to my account to check the status of the check. Because $50,000 is a lot of money and Southfork Savings is based in New York, it takes a painfully long time for the funds to clear. Each day the money sits in my account is another opportunity for me to back out. It would be so easy to cancel the check.

But I hold it together long enough to finally see that my balance is $78.42.

This tiny amount of cash—barely enough for dinner and a movie—somehow sounds worse than zero.

To keep my mind off abject poverty (no, not poverty—faith, investment, the future), I take out the screenplay with comments from Joshua Smallweed. Despite his admiration for my talent and love for the script, he's made copious notes that fill three single-spaced, typed pages. His feedback is more precise than Lester's and certainly more useful. He doesn't just tell me what's wrong with the script but how he thinks I can fix it.

I'm not one hundred percent sure his solutions will work but at least it's a beginning.

Working diligently through the day, I only check my e-mail every hour and a half. The meeting with the investors took place two days ago and now I'm giving Lester time to volunteer information before I have to start hounding him for it. It's a new approach, one that I optimistically believed yesterday would work; today I'm not so sure. I can't conceive that there's nothing to tell me. That there's no information in itself conveys a tremendous amount of information.

I don't know why I'm still fighting this battle. It's been three years, and Lester never once offered up a single thing willingly. Why don't just I give in?

Despite the novelty surrendering presents, I e-mail Lester at four o'clock to ask what's the word on the meeting. Now the ball's in his court. I'll wait until Monday, then try again.

In the meantime, *Tad Johnson* gives me something to focus on. Here at last is a production team that values me. They don't think I'm a fly to be swatted or a creditor to be dodged or even a writer who must be humored with fake options. The difference between respect and sufferance is so huge the Grand Canyon could slip between.

I stop at six when Simon knocks.

"Has the dynamic duo returned yet?" he asks softly.

I open the door. "It's safe. They only left the Getty about ten minutes ago."

"In that case," he says, bending his head toward mine, "I can say hello properly." The kiss is anything but proper and by the time he pulls back, I'm clutching his shoulders for balance. It's amazing how easily he can make my knees tremble. "I know how you feel about public displays."

Feeling a little more steady, I take a step back and let the door close. "I'm down with public displays. It's public obscenity I take issue with."

"Maybe he doesn't realize they're not alone. He could be missing the chromosome that identifies when other people are in the room."

"If only," I say, walking to the kitchen. Suddenly I'm in the mood for a glass of wine. Just thinking about Glenn drives me to drink. "I'd be so much better with it if it were a genetic defect and not him trying to keep my sister on a short leash. It's total ownership. He just knows if he gives her one breath of space she'd run the other way." I put the Cabernet Sauvignon on the counter and sigh. "Right. I promised no more complaining, so it stops right here. How was your day?"

Simon sits on the couch. "Good. Colleen quit today."

I put the glasses on the coffee table and sit down. "Colleen?"

"Incompetent who can't transfer calls. Celia doesn't have the guts to fire anyone, so she tortures them until they quit. Colleen broke the record for holding out. Forty-one days, six hours and forty-two seconds."

"The previous record?"

"Twenty-four days, one hour and eleven seconds. Although it's somewhat controversial because the guy who keeps book insists she came in that day just to clear out her stuff and she officially quit the night before."

"You guys bet on this stuff?"

"Absolutely."

"That's a little harsh, isn't it? I mean, someone's out of a job."

"Amazingly, they all tend to be mean people who are remarkably difficult to feel bad for."

"Convenient."

"Absolutely."

After the stress of the day—it's over and done: I can't get my fifty large back no matter how much I want to, which I don't (mostly)—it's wonderful to unwind with Simon. He's been pretty amazing all weeklong, dealing so patiently with Glenn I'd swear they're best friends and giving me a safe place to hide when Carrie and her octopus get to be too much. You always learn the truth about people in times of crises and now I know Simon is a saint.

Simon takes a sip of wine and asks about my day. "Did you hear anything from Tulk about *Tad Johnson?*"

Having decide not to discuss any movie business with him, I've spent the last month dodging questions about my screenplay. Part of being a saint is keeping up with his girlfriend's career. Most of the time I feel awful about lying but I don't know what else to do.

"No word today," I say.

He wraps his arms around my shoulder and pulls me against his side. Then he runs a hand through my hair. "I hope you're not too disappointed that the offer hasn't come through."

Ashamed by the concern in his voice, I bury my face in the glass. "It's the way it goes sometimes."

He presses his lips against my forehead but doesn't say a thing. I'm relieved. I don't know how much longer I can keep this up. At some point he's going to find out the truth.

I should just tell him now.

But nothing has changed. Not until *Tad Johnson* is actually made—or at least starts shooting—will he stop thinking of me as a naïve fool who believes in miracles. He'll lecture on long shots, warn me about investing emotionally and constantly remind me of his own dismal experience. I can't handle that, especially not on the day my entire life savings disappeared from my bank account.

I'll tell him in a couple of weeks, when the shooting schedule is firmed up and casting is complete.

Besides, it's almost seven and the dynamic duo are about to return any minute. There's no time to get into a heavy discussion about the future of my career even if I wanted to.

Oh, well.

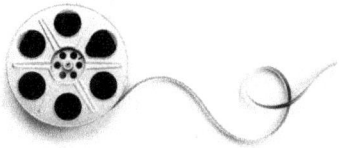

Day 1,337

ON THEIR LAST full day, Carrie and Glenn want to relax and hang out in my neighborhood. We hit my favorite greasy spoon for lunch, then walk over to the Griffith Observatory, where Glenn turns into a total astronomy geek and spends hours lecturing us on the movement of the solar system. He even contradicts a few details in the Hall of Sky exhibition copy.

At five, I leave them at the apartment and drive to Ralph's to pick up some food for dinner. I figure since it's their last night here, I might as well make something special. My repertoire is pretty limited but I've printed out a recipe for beef stroganoff that seems simple. I'll make a Caesar salad to go with it and caramelized brussels sprouts. For dessert I pick up cannolis from Simon's favorite bakery.

Eager to start cooking, I unlock the front door and step into the apartment. Carrie is sitting at the dining table with every single piece of paper in the apartment scattered around her: bank statements, credit card bills, food receipts. All the drawers in the kitchen are open and the couch cushions have been overturned. It looks like the apartment has been ransacked by thieves.

Glenn comes out of the bedroom. "No luck. All I found in her underwear drawer was underwear and her passport. It's a pretty terrible photo too. Look."

The groceries almost slide from my arms. "What are doing?"

Surprised, Carrie looks up. Far from appearing guilty, she seems angry. "Funny. I was just about to ask you the same thing."

I put the bags down on the couch and stride over to the table. "I can't believe you'd do this."

She laughs without humor, somehow affronted as if she's the one who walked in on her sister snooping around her apartment. "You can't believe I'd do this? *I* can't believe you'd do *this*." She holds up a stack of papers and I instantly recognize it as the Solution Pictures contract. "I mean, seriously, Ricki, have you lost your mind completely? You gave them your entire life savings.

Everything you have. Are you crazy? Have you fucking lost it entirely?" Her voices raise as she stands up and walks toward me. "And we were worried that you didn't have health insurance or weren't replacing your oil every three thousand miles. Not that you were handing over your *entire life savings* to a bunch of wannabe movie producers. How fucking stupid can you get?"

The anger I feel is so cold, my heart is frozen. It stands in my chest surrounded by icicles and doesn't move. The only beating is in my head, a loud pounding like a horse's hooves across an open field. Despite that, I'm remarkably calm. I take in the entire scene—the ransacked apartment, my sister's outrage, Glenn holding my passport open to the photo—and feel strangely detached from it all. I grab the contract from Carrie's hands and start gathering up the other papers on the table.

"So that's why you're here?" I ask, ignoring a fresh paper cut on my thumb. "To spy on me? To report back to Mom and Dad?"

"No, I'm here because I'm worried about you," she says softly, her tone now the embodiment of sisterly concern. "We all are. You're so secretive. You never tell us anything. You keep saying everything's fine but you don't have a job or any detectable source of income. You lie to Mom about working at a law firm and avoid answering questions. We thought if I came out here and spent some quality time with you I might be able to figure out what's going on."

And—bam!—just like that, my anger goes from cold to hot. "Oh, my God, you're so full of shit. If you were so concerned about me, why did you bring...that"—I can't think of a word fulsome enough to describe Glenn—"*thing* with you to paw over my underwear? This trip hasn't been about quality time with me, a one-on-one with the Carstone girls. You've spent every minute with your needy, cloying boyfriend who can't seem to breathe if he's not fondling you obscenely. Oh, and when he's not doing that, when, say, you're in the bathroom and indisposed, he's fucking complaining all the time. So don't you *dare* say you came out here because you wanted to be with me. I'm not fucking stupid."

Carrie curls her hands into fists but struggles to appear calm. Her voice is as smooth as silk when she speaks. "You're angry with me, and I understand that. But don't take it out on Glenn. I'm your problem, not him."

Her tone, her stance, her words are so fucking superior. I can just hear her telling me to listen with my ears, not with my mouth, like some fucking kindergarten teacher. "No, Glenn isn't my problem. I don't have to spend the rest of my life with a lame-ass clingy octopus in my lame-ass ashwood kitchen because I'm too scared to risk not finding someone better. So you're right. Glenn's your problem. And you're welcome to it."

I swing around and march toward the door, which I slam shut with a satisfying bang. Then I pound on Simon's door, muttering, "Please be home. Please be home."

He opens it a second later. "Hey," he says with a grin, "I was just about to—"

I brush passed him and into his apartment. "She's fucking unbelievable. To come into a person's apartment and go through their stuff and read their private documents and then have the gall—the utter, *utter* gall—to claim she's concerned about you. And to bring that whining, fondling machine with you and pretend like this visit wasn't about taking long, romantic walks through the *Sideways* vineyards. And all that, 'We're worried about you, Ricki.' 'You never tell us anything, Ricki.' 'We know you're lying, Ricki.' God, it's so fucking unbelievable."

Simon watches me pace back and forth in his living room until my tirade runs out. Then he grabs me by the shoulders and looks into my eyes. I'm so angry I can barely see him.

"Take a deep breath, count to ten and tell me what's going on. You had a fight with your sister and found her snooping."

"He had his hands in my underwear drawer."

He leads me to the couch and gets me a class of water. "That's not fair. I haven't even seen your underwear drawer."

I smile wanly and feel myself calming down. "My parents were worried about me not having a job, so they asked Carrie to come out and spy on me."

"Yikes, that's pretty harsh."

I knew he would get it. "Isn't it? And the thing that kills me is she had the *gall* to pretend this visit was about spending time with me. In seven days she didn't ask me a single question about my life and then fourteen hours before she leaves for the airport, she ransacks my apartment to find out what's going on. It's the hypocrisy that gets to me."

Simon sits on the arm of the couch, takes my hand and squeezes. "Come on, now, be fair. You'd be mad regardless."

"Well, yeah. When I came into the apartment and found her holding that contract I was gripped by an ice-cold rage I've never felt before. And she had the audacity to get angry at me."

"What contract?"

"Solution Pictures."

The second the words are out of my mouth, I realize what I've done. Fucking hell.

Surprised, he shifts his position to get a better look at me. "Solution came through for *Tad Johnson*?

I nod.

"But that's great news," he says, with a wide grin, "and the answer to your parents' concerns. You do have a job. I don't understand why she was angry."

I can lie or I can tell the truth. Instead, I evade. "I don't know," I say, lowering my eyes because I can't bear to see the delight on his face. "She's crazy."

"When did the Solution deal happen?"

I lift my eyes. "What?"

"The Solution deal. When did it come together? If you've got the contract, it must be pretty far along."

"I don't remember when it happened. Recently."

Simon tilts his head down and looks at his lap, where he holds my hand in his. "Why didn't you tell me?"

And just like that, I collide with the moment of truth. No more lies, no more evasions, just unvarnished honesty. I hate Carrie. "I didn't want to argue about it," I say.

"Why would we argue?"

I sigh. Somehow this is harder and easier than I thought—harder because I know his calm is deceptive and easier because I'm almost too exhausted by my knockdown with Carrie to care. "Because they didn't so much as buy the script as ask me to invest in it."

His grip on my hand loosens, then releases, but he doesn't say anything. I wait and wait, but he remains unquestionably mute. The clock on the wall ticks, birds land on his balcony and his across-the-hall neighbor comes home singing loudly to her iPod.

After five minutes, I can't take it anymore. Maybe if he hadn't let go of my hand, I wouldn't read such dire things into his silence but he had, so I do. "Aren't you going to say something?"

"No."

The syllable is short but stunning. "Why not?"

"You obviously don't want my opinion on the matter." He stands up and disappears into the kitchen. "So if you're no longer cooking, what do you want to do for dinner? Order in?"

The last thing I expect from him is little-boy sulkiness. He seems too mature not to fight it out like a man. I stand up and follow him. He's flipping through a binder clip of menus. "Look, it was a really tough decision for me and I knew how you'd feel if I told you I was thinking about putting fifty thousand dollars into a project and I just didn't—"

The menus fall to the floor in a heap. "I'm sorry. How much?"

His tone is mild, but that's just because the amount hasn't sunk in. Unable to meet his gaze, I drop to my knees and pick up the menus. "Fifty thousand dollars."

"Holy shit. Are you out of your mind?"

I feel a perverse sense of satisfaction at his reaction. "See? I knew you'd think I was crazy. You have no faith in me. Harry said I was—"

"Hold on. You talked about this with Harry?"

I nod and suddenly realize there are worst things than lying about the Solution contract. It's not so much what he says as the way he says it: a mixture of shock and disappointment.

"The Harry you were seeing a couple of months ago?" When I nod again, he leaves the kitchen. I rush to my feet, leaving the menus on the floor. In the living room, Simon is pacing. "The one who hooked you up with that Vholes guy, who's been bleeding you dry?"

As soon as he brings John into it, my shame over Harry deserts me. I know I was wrong, but at least I admit it. Simon won't give an inch over Vholes and I'm sick of it. Why are relationships always the same argument over and over again? "John Vholes didn't bleed me dry," I say for the hundredth time. "He gave me lessons."

Simon doesn't care. "So you're still seeing Harry?"

"Yes," I say automatically, then immediately backtrack when I hear the implication. "No, I'm not *seeing* him. I see him." The look he gives me is so intensely furious it could make a statue tremble. "We hang out as friends. We're not dating."

But Simon isn't listening to me anymore. He's wearing a hole in his carpet and mumbling under his breath how this was all a terrible mistake. Then he stops, turns and looks at me. "Obviously I'm wasting my time here."

The words make my heart stop and I open my mouth to argue but nothing comes out. My thoughts are jumbled. All I can think is no, no, no. This isn't happening. Not over some stupid guy who doesn't matter.

"You don't trust me," Simon says wearily, "and I can't do this with someone who doesn't trust me."

I feel the tears forming as I stare at him, amazed at how wrong he has it. Somehow he's turned the whole thing on its head. "No, you don't trust me," I say, swallowing hard to push back the lump in my throat. "You don't trust me. You never have."

He shakes his head sadly. No one in my life has ever looked as stricken as he. "If you actually believe that, then we really have been wasting our time."

The tears threaten to overwhelm me. I don't know when I've ever felt this despondent in my life, like any hope for the future has been washed away. All I have is the present, this one terrible moment to live in for eternity.

Because I don't want him to see me cry, to know that on a basic level he's broken something vitally important inside me, I run out of his apartment, down the stairs and onto the street. I sit on the grass, pull up my legs and sob until my eyes are like sandpaper. I take several heaping gulps of air, shiver from the chilly breeze and straighten my back. I can't sit on the curb for the rest of my life.

I don't have my bag with me but my keys are in my back pocket as well as my credit card from the grocery store, which I didn't bother putting back in my wallet. I could go to the movies or the Growlery or the galleria. But what I really want is a shoulder to cry on. I feel so terribly alone.

I drive to Harry's. I don't care what evil things Simon thinks in his suspicious little mind. Harry is a friend. That he was never more than that makes me sad but there's nothing I can do about it. Some people you love; some people you don't.

By the time I reach Harry's block, I feel more in control. Parking is difficult, and it takes me ten minutes to find a spot. As I walk up the drive, I realize I should probably call first. It's a Saturday night. What if he's not home? What if he has a date? But I don't have my phone with me so I let it go. If he's not home, I'll leave. If he has a date, I'll also leave.

I ring the doorbell and wait impatiently. After a moment, the doorknob turns and there he is. I'm so relieved, my knees go week. "Thank God you're here. I've had the worst day," I say, stepping past him into the room, "and just needed someone to talk to...." I trail off as I see who else is in the room: John Vholes, Howard Tulkinghorn and Joshua Smallweed. All of them are gathered around the table with four empty bottles of champagne and half-drunk wineglasses. I look at Harry, confused. He turns away.

For a moment there is shock, a pervasive amazement that fills the room as they stare at me as dumbstruckly as I stare at them. Then Tulk holds his glass high. "Ricki, darling, we were just drinking to you. To the prettiest sucker in all of suckerdom."

They drink.

The second I see them together, I understand. The scales fall from my eyes and in an instant I grasp the entire picture. From the moment Harry met me at Boodle's, he had this scene planned. All I had to do was go along like a dumb fuck.

Which I am.

I don't even feel anger. The realization of my stupidity is so overwhelming, it leaves room for nothing else but self-condemnation. This is what I deserve for being gullible and overconfident and smug and desperate and hopeful and eager and naïve. They played me like a fiddle, as the saying goes.

John raises his glass. "Hear, hear. You were a pleasure to work with," he says, slurring his words slightly. He's drunk. They all are. Sober men wouldn't rub my face in it like this. They couldn't. Something inherently humane would stop them.

"An absolute pleasure," Joshua adds. "And your script was quite good. I might even make it one day." He immediately starts giggling. "No, I won't. Who am I kidding?"

Turning away from them, I look at Harry, who's standing by the door. He refuses to meet my eyes, and I discover I was wrong. There is anger inside me after all.

As I walk toward him, a million things cluster inside my head, insults and indictments and righteous accusations, but I know it's all a waste of time. Harry is soulless. What I took for artlessness and innocence is really an enduring emptiness, a bleak amorality that cares about nothing but its own comfort.

It's so obvious now. Of course it is.

With nothing to say, I raise my hand, pull it back and slap him across the cheek so hard red welts immediately appear. His eyes glitter brightly with something resembling tears but I can't tell if it's from pain or shame, and I don't care.

Lesson one in the school of hard knocks mastered. Ricki Carstone won't be making this mistake again.

Without turning around, without looking at any one of them again, I walk to the door, open it and step into the cool night air feeling a hundred years old. I keep it together until I get to the car but as soon as I close the door, the grief hits me like a wall of bricks and the tears start to fall. They fall hard and fast and with so much force it feels like a summer squall has taken possession of my body. I try to regain control but it's useless so I simply sink into it. There's nothing else I can do.

Every dream I've ever had has died.

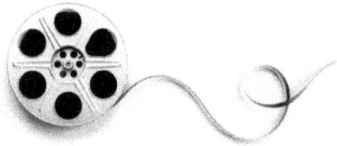

Day 1,338

I WAKE UP in the Wagon Wheel diner with my head on the table and a small puddle of drool on the cocktails-of-the-world place mat. Across the aisle, twin boys in matching Old Navy T-shirts are staring at me. Before I can even blink groggily at them, the one on the right hurls a french fry and hits me in the eye. I throw it back. Their mom, previously absorbed by the morning newspaper, catches me in the act and immediately reprimands me for provoking her two angelic children.

It's obvious from their full plate of fries and my empty table who the provocateur is, but I don't bother to defend myself. I understand how it works now. Life is injustice.

I wave down the waitress, the same one who was on shift the previous night, and ask for my check. She drops it on the table and says, "They're never worth it, sugar," making me think that weeping women stumbling in at one A.M. and ordering coffee and onion rings isn't such a rare thing around here.

My joints are stiff, and I stretch before standing up. The mischievous boys giggle at my old-lady movements and their mom throws me a dirty look. I stare blandly back, then leave.

By the time I pull into the parking lot at Bleak, it's after ten. Carrie and Glenn's flight will be taking off in twenty-five minutes, so it's safe to go home. As I wait for the elevator, I list all the things I want in descending order: shower, hot coffee, oblivion.

Now that my houseguests are gone, I should be able to attain all three.

I just hope someone had the sense to put the food in the fridge. I don't want to come home to the smell of rotting beef—as if that's the only thing in my life that stinks.

Everything is in place when I open the door. Not only have the groceries been put away, all my papers have been returned to their files. It even looks like someone vacuumed.

Relieved, I let the door shut behind me and walk to the kitchen to get started on my second most cherished desire. I measure the coffee, add water, plug in the machine and turn to see Carrie sitting on the sofa,

I jump in surprise.

"Hey," she says. In the same clothes as yesterday, she looks so tired I think I might have gotten more sleep in the window booth at the Wagon Wheel.

Not that her exhaustion's my fault.

"Hey," I say in response, looking around for Glenn. Maybe he's pawing through the stuff in my bedroom again. If he is, he's certainly doing it more quietly than last time.

The coffee percolates as we consider each other silently. I don't say anything because I have nothing to say. My life has collapsed, imploding violently like a played-out coal mine, but I'm still not sorry for what I said. It was mean and cruel and yet not nearly as terrible as spying on your sister. She'll never know what it's like to come home and find the one person you trust above all others in the act of betraying you. It's supposed to be us versus our parents. It's been that way since we were little girls.

I pick up a dish towel, grasp it in my hands and wait.

Just as the coffee's finishing, she says, "The red was discontinued."

It's the last thing I expect her to say. "What?"

"The red cabinets from Ikea. They were discontinued. It wasn't Glenn's fault."

"All right," I say calmly, although she doesn't need to explain herself to me. Her life is her life, just like my life is mine.

"He even tracked down a place in the city that also did the red. It would have cost $35,000 for the whole kitchen."

I take the pot off the coils and fill up a mug, which I offer to Carrie. She accepts and I pour another cup for myself.

We sip our coffee and pretend we're not waiting for the other one to apologize first. I know she expects me to bend a little after her explanation but I don't. Even if he's not responsible for the bland ashwoodness of her life, Glenn has plenty to answer for.

After ten minutes, Carrie begins to cry. I'm tired enough of my own tears to feel impatient with someone else's, but I bite back the mean reply that jumps to my lips.

"God, you're so hard," she says, standing up. "You never give anything."

I don't know what I have to give her except absolution and she has to ask for that first.

She walks to the window and stares out at the cars passing below. "Look, I'm sorry," she says, her back toward me. "I know it was wrong to poke through your stuff. I felt terrible doing it. Part of me was even hoping to get caught so I wouldn't fee so dirty about it. But it's just that you scare us." Her tone turns accusatory as she looks at me. So much for her remorse. "We don't know what you're thinking anymore and you've moved so far away and without any notice and you never come home, not even for Christmas. What are we supposed to do? You don't tell us anything."

Even as I find myself getting angry all over again—how *dare* she purport to be concerned when she brought *him* with her—I acknowledge the truth of the statement. I don't tell them anything anymore because I know they wouldn't approve.

And look where it got me. If I had confided in someone who loved me, I probably wouldn't have been swindled out of my entire inheritance.

But even knowing how foolish it is to keep my own counsel, I still can't bring myself to tell her what happened. I'm too ashamed. Having gotten what I deserve, I can't stand the thought of her pitying me. It would be so much worse than I-told-you-so.

"I'm sorry too," I say. "I shouldn't have said what I did about Glenn. That was entirely out of line. And he's really not that bad."

"Thank you."

With the fragile détente in place, she turns to face the traffic again and I drink my coffee. Even though we've made a rough sort of peace, we're awkward with each other. This has never happened before. It's always been the Carstone girls against the world, not the Carstone girls against each other.

But I don't know how to fix it.

The phone rings and I let the machine get it. I expect it to be Glenn giving a minute-by-minute account of his boarding process, but it's Lester with a movie update.

"Hi, Ricki. I know you're wondering how the meeting with the investors went on Wednesday. According to Lloyd, they're still interested but won't put money in the film until the male lead is cast. Lloyd is going out with the script. It's a tough situation to be in because the script has some problems. He's showing it along with the notes from the director detailing what changes he plans to make but he won't make those changes until he gets paid. So that's where we are. I'll let you know if the situation changes. Hope you're well."

As he talks, I feel the knot inside me unwind and I start laughing, mildly at first, as if I'm not really amused, and then with full-on, breathless glee as the absurdity of the situation hits me.

I can just see Lloyd with his inflated lips explaining with increasing desperation to yet another young hottie that this is the script they would have if only the fucking greedy director would get off his lazy ass and rewrite it. And Blake Alden—I see him sitting on a towering heap of dross, counting brass tacks as if they were pieces of eight, his belt tightening with every hunger pang.

Self-destructive selfishness makes no sense but of course it makes beautiful sense. This is Hollywood, opposite land, where acting in your own best interest sets you back thirty paces. Every widget manufactured in this town is a collaboration and yet there is a no collective good. It's still the gold rush mentality, with everyone staking their claim and guarding it jealously with a Winchester rifle.

The standoff could go on forever. There's no resolution in sight, no way out of this seemingly endless string of catch-22s. Already I've lost my life savings and my self-respect. The only thing left is my dream of a happy ending: a movie premiere at the Ziegfeld Theater with all my friends and family cheering as my name comes across the screen in ten-foot-high letters.

I could go on believing in that. It would take very little effort to suppose it's only a matter of time until Lloyd casts the film and we get the money and the movie gets made and does so well it spawns not just two sequels but a television series and a spin-off.

Hope perches in the soul.

But there's nothing more destructive to the soul than a dream deferred, and I can no longer wait for it to dry up or explode. This has to end now.

Here's where I get off the mountain.

I run into the bedroom and pull two duffle bags from under the bed. I toss one to Carrie.

"Start packing," I say. I open up the top drawer in my dresser and throw everything inside.

Carrie stares at me, baffled. "What are you doing?"

The second drawer is all underwear. I take ten pairs and leave the rest. "Driving you home."

"That's crazy," she says. "I'll catch the next flight. I only stayed because I couldn't leave without talking to you."

"No, you were right to be worried." I grab my passport and close the drawer, then empty the entire contents of my jewelry box into the bag. "I've lost everything, so much more than you can possibly know. This place has ruined me. It's time to leave."

She steps into the room, walks to my closet and takes a pair of jeans off the hanger, carefully folding them.

"No," I say, pulling three shirts off their hangers at once, "dump and go. Dump and go. I want to be out of here in ten minutes."

"What about Simon?"

I pause for only a fraction of a second, but it's enough to clog up my throat. No, I can't think of Simon now. The one thing keeping me upright is not acknowledging just how much I lost. The money I can recoup. The self-respect I can regain. But there's no getting Simon back.

When I don't answer her question, she says, "He's worried about you. He even went out to look for you last night when you didn't come home."

I know she thinks she's trying to help, but she's only making it worse. I can never, ever see Simon again. Love might mean never saying you're sorry but there's no clause about being a fucking gullible dumb fuck. Some things you screw up so badly, there's no redeeming them.

This is one of them.

Carrie drops the subject and finishes stuffing clothing into the bag. I do a brief drive-by in the living room, packing up my laptop and gathering my files. I take the worthless *Tad Johnson* script and burn it.

My sister comes running out of the bedroom when the smoke alarm goes off.

"Don't worry," I say, climbing on a chair to remove the battery. "It's just a little flame, easily extinguished, not a conflagration."

Five minutes later, we have everything. Carrie runs ahead to bring the car around and I linger by the door, my hand on the light switch, taking one last look. All the value I have in the world is in this room and yet it is valueless.

Standing there, I think of the last time I did this—moving from one coast to another, divesting myself of all my material goods, so confident I knew what I was doing. This time I'm following through for real, starting over, leaving scorched earth behind.

No, not scorched earth. Not yet.

I drop my bag, walk over to the phone, dial Angela Deering at the *Times,* wait three rings for her to pick up and tell her to run the story.

Now I'm free.

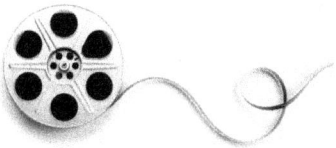

February 13

GLENN CRASHES WITH friends for a month to give me some time alone with my sister. It's such a sweeping act of kindness, I'm forced to concede he's really a nice guy. Carrie, in her turn, admits that the touching is a little much, especially when she's trying to eat ribs, which really can't be done with one hand, and that she has talked to Glenn about it several times. He keeps promising to do better but so far has made no progress. Despite his nice-guyness and all, I still think he needs professional help.

Carrie insists that telling our parents is part of my recovery, and prepared for the worse, I confess all to them in one rapid-fire speech full of remorse and repentance. Amazingly, they take it in stride.

"We're just happy to have you home again, safe and sound," Mom says.

Dad agrees, adding, "It's only money."

He says it with such gushing relief I realize Carrie wasn't looking for incriminating papers but heroin vials and dirty needles.

My parents offer to give me some money to help me get back on my feet but I refuse to take a handout, and in the end we settle on a loan with proper interest and a repayment schedule. Dad complements me on my negotiating skills even as he overrules my insistence that we go as high as the prime rate.

Over the course of many quiet nights at home eating boxed macaroni and cheese and defrosted veggie burgers, I tell Carrie everything. She listens with remarkable patience, never interrupting no matter how much she wants to. She's an amazing listener, and I wonder why I didn't know this about my own sister.

I explain how easy it was for Harry to play me, the one long ego stroke our entire relationship was. Some gushing praise and a few inspiring speeches and I was putty in his hands. I wanted someone to believe in me so badly because I couldn't believe in myself that I never once stopped to consider his motives. And he warned me from the onset: "I'm calculating in everything I do," he said the very first time we met.

Fool that I am, I didn't listen. I soaked up his compliments like a flower starved for rain and shut out the one person who actually believed in me. Simon's faith was as sincere as it was quiet.

Every time I mention Simon, Carrie tells me to call him. She doesn't understand why we can't just kiss and make up. All I have to do, she says, is apologize and he'll forgive me.

But I know it's not that simple. I replay that last conversation in my head and see the disappointment in his face, the sorrow in his eyes when he realized I'd confided in Harry, and know that what I did is beyond forgiveness. He's right—I never trusted him. I put the distrust on him and made myself a victim but all along it was the other way around.

As much as it hurts, I know it's for the best. Any apology would have to include an explanation about Harry, a detailed narrative of my stupidity and newfound poverty, and that I couldn't bear. Opening myself up for more ridicule—I know I deserve it but I can't stomach the thought. Far better to never see Simon again than have him know what a truly stupid, naïve, idiot newbie I am.

At Carrie's urging, I give the Solutions contract to one of my former Hertzberg colleagues to see if I have any recourse. My prospects are dim.

"The hard part will be proving they never intended to make the film in the first place," she says. "All the protections in place apply only if the film doesn't go into preproduction, but their lawyer is insisting that they're still developing the film. You might win if it goes to trial but it'll cost you at least twice what you lost, and that's being optimistic."

When Carrie hears this, she rails for thirty minutes about our inadequate court system, then gives the contract to Lionel for a second opinion. Expecting nothing, I'm neither surprised nor disappointed. It's also what I deserve for being gullible, stupid and willful.

Stiff-upper-lipped, I turn my attention to the future.

With no idea what to do with the rest of my life, I scan the help-wanteds every day. Even though I'm qualified for very little, I feel like anything is possible. I e-mail my résumé to the local hardware store looking for a bookkeeper and to the Fresh Air Fund, which needs a executive director. Neither calls.

Surprisingly, the New York Public Library asks me in for an interview for a research associate position at the main branch, a turn-of-the-century beaux arts building on Fifth Avenue. It's supposed to be a preliminary, half-hour chat with a human resources guy, but several key people are in the building so I wind up talking to most of the research department. Their questions are pretty straightforward, having to do with organization and problem solving, and my years as a paralegal, which is all organization and problem solving, serve me well.

Forty-eight hours later they offer me the job.

Delighted, I spend my first day feeling overwhelmed by the size and the grandeur of the distinguished old institution. More than two million New Yorkers have library cards. The number is staggering, and during my first week, it feels like half of them call the research hotline with questions about obscure facts. At first I'm intimidated by the seemingly endless rows of books, but by Friday I find it comforting and heartening to think there's so much information in the world. It, like the want ads, makes me feel like anything is possible.

The next step is finding an apartment, and Carrie and I are so focused on the real estate section, we're both shocked to see my article in Sunday Styles. But there it is, as bold as day, a photo of me and Moxie in rough newspaper-print ink running alongside it. There's a black blotch on my left arm that looks like the world's worst tattoo.

I don't care.

Carrie insists on reading the article aloud, and, listening, I expect to feel anger or regret or sadness but all I can scrape together is relief—relief that is has nothing to do with me anymore. It's almost like *Jarndyce and Jarndyce* happened to another person.

At work on Monday, nobody connects me with the article. People talk about it during the morning meeting but they don't have a clue the author is sitting right there sipping a soy latte. Although it doesn't speak well of their investigative skills, the anonymity is just what I need. I've said my piece on the subject and have nothing left to add.

Relieved Hollywood is well and truly behind me, I unlock the door to Carrie's apartment and put a pot of water on the stove to boil for pasta. I'm taking a jar of red sauce out of the fridge when I hear a knock on the door.

I pause. Knocks on the door are unusual. People always buzz downstairs first.

I put the jar on the counter, turn down the boiling water and open the door.

And there is Simon. He has the *New York Times* in his left hand and a huge grin on his face.

Staggered, I stand there, my hand falling to my side as I try to think of something to say. But I've got nothing. My mind is blank. Joy doesn't leave room for anything but its own munificence.

Unchecked, Simon keeps his eyes fixed on me as he leans forward and brushes his lips against mine, tentatively at first, then with increasingly abandon as I wrap my arms around his neck and pull him closer. He drops the *Times* to the floor when he presses my back against the door, the force of his kiss making my knees weak as I steady myself against his body.

Faintly, I hear the sound of a door opening and Mrs. Skouras's outraged gasp as she takes in the indecent scene on her threshold. She immediately slams it again.

If Simon notices at all, he gives no indication, only lifting his lips to trail searing kisses along my neck. Dizzy, I throw back my head, dimly aware that we should take this inside, where the couch is softer than the metal frame of the entrance.

But I can't bring myself to break contact. The feel of Simon's muscles bunching under my fingers is something I thought I'd never experience again. I know we have to talk. There's so much he has to know, so much I have to explain. But right now it's enough that he's here. He got it—not the message because the article wasn't a message but the symbolism. What it meant: the break, the freedom, the future.

Simon runs his hands down my back and under my shirt. He moans softly as he makes contact with my warm skin.

I don't know what comes next, how his West Coast–ness will mesh with my East Coast life, but I know we'll figure it out. He didn't come three thousand miles to kiss me on my sister's doorstep, turn around and go home.

No, this flash of desire, seemingly ephemeral and certainly intangible, is more solid and vital than any lavish promise made by Lloyd Chancellor or Harold Skimpole or Howard Tulkinghorn. Like the city itself, they prey on hope, peddling shining kingdoms to which they themselves don't have the keys. It's all chimera and the misguided conviction that if you believe in something hard enough it will come true.

Faith doesn't equal reality—Brigadoon isn't a thought waiting to exist—and in the end there's nothing behind you except a green screen on which to project your desires.

And yet here is Simon running his hands down the length of my back.

Of all the dreams to ever come out of Hollywood, he's the only one that's real.

ABOUT THE AUTHOR

Lynn Messina grew up on Long Island and studied English at Washington University in St. Louis. She has worked at the Museum of Television & Radio (now the Paley Center for Media), *TV Guide, In Style, Rolling Stone, Fitness, ForbesLife, Self, Bloomberg Markets* and a host of wonderful magazines that have long since disappeared. She mourns the death of print journalism in New York City, where she lives with her husband and sons. She is author of seven novels, including the best-selling *Fashionistas,* which has been translated into 15 languages and is in development as a feature film.

www.ingramcontent.com/pod-product-compliance
Lightning Source LLC
Chambersburg PA
CBHW072231170626
46813CB00003B/1171